Frozen Origins

Path of the Ranger, Book 11

Pedro Urvi

COMMUNITY:
Mail: pedrourvi@hotmail.com
Facebook: https://www.facebook.com/PedroUrviAuthor/
My Website: http://pedrourvi.com
Twitter: https://twitter.com/PedroUrvi

Translation by:
Christy Cox

Edited by:
Mallory Brandon Bingham

DEDICATION

To my good friend Guiller.

Thank you for all your support since day one.

Content

Map

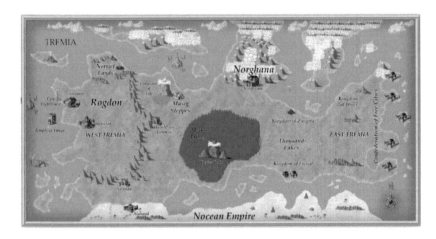

Chapter 1

The tavern was crowded that evening. The bartender was shouting at one of the customers who was leaning on the counter, arguing about the price of the drink and waving his arms, enraged. The customer was thin and tall, whereas the bartender was a huge man with an unfriendly face. The argument was tilting toward the largest of the two, who had brought out a cudgel he was threatening the unhappy customer with.

The Tavern of the Honest Market did not exactly honor its name. It was a meeting point for thieves, pirates, corrupt traders, gamblers, and all kinds of disreputable characters from the slums of Copenghen. This was the largest city on the west coast of Norghana and one of the most important to occupants and traders in the whole realm.

The shouts, fights, and settling of accounts were common here. The owner was a sinister trader and smuggler who never showed his face in the tavern. He had half a dozen hired, armed thugs of ill reputation who kept watch inside the premises. They maintained order and silenced any altercation. And they specialized in doing it the hard way.

The door of the leisure establishment opened and two figures wrapped in hooded cloaks walked in, leaving the door open behind them. The customers stopped what they were doing for a moment to check out the two arrivals. The card and dice games froze instantly, as did the toasts with beer jugs amid guffaws, the arguments at the tables and the counter, the tasting of the painfully dry chicken and steaks tough as shoe soles—everything was suspended while they watched the two strangers who had just walked in.

"Shut that door!" one of the thugs said, annoyed.

The activity was renewed at once in the tavern, the spell broken by the man's shout.

"It's better to keep it open," one of the two figures said in a female voice.

8

"I said to shut the door. What happens in here stays in here," the man replied, reaching for a cudgel with spikes that was hanging from his waist. He was huge, with blond hair and beard which were very unkempt and dirty. His clothes stank of old sweat and could be smelled from several paces away.

"In a few moments there's going to be a small stampede," the second hooded figure said. It was a male voice, his tone one of warning.

"What's going to happen is that I'm going to crack your skull open!" the robust thug said threateningly, signaling to another of his buddies to step closer.

The female figure pushed her hood back, revealing her face.

"I wouldn't advise you to try," Ingrid warned the thug.

"Well, if it isn't a Nordic cutie!" the thug said with a guffaw that sounded sordid and lewd at the same time.

"She *is* cute!" said the other thug, who was as big and ugly as his partner. This one had chestnut hair and beard, and he also stank. Cleanliness was obviously foreign to the thugs. The same could be said for the premises, from what could be seen and smelled.

"Keep your distance," Ingrid warned, reaching out to stop the thug's advance.

"What's the matter with this butterfly, is she lost?" the blond thug asked the other.

"It looks that way. We'd better give her some love so she doesn't feel so out of place," the brown-haired one replied.

"That would be a very bad idea," the other figure said in a warning tone.

"And who's that? Your boyfriend?"

The figure pushed back his hood and revealed his face.

"In fact, that's exactly what I am: her boyfriend," Viggo said with a triumphant smile.

Ingrid rolled her eyes but did not correct him.

"I don't believe it. You're too little a thing to be this snow-covered-mountains beauty's boyfriend," the blond thug said.

Viggo nodded. "You're not wrong. Life is full of meaningless inconsistencies, like you being a thug with the soul of a poet."

"I'm no bloody poet!" the thug said angrily, and he showed Viggo the cudgel, brandishing it threateningly.

"And surely you don't know what inconsistency means. No

problem, me neither. I simply picked it up from my friend Egil, a wise know-it-all I spend too much time with."

"I do know what it means!" the thug replied, annoyed, and he was lost in thought for a moment, his gaze lost.

"You sure you know? You don't look too sure ..."

"It means ... that ..."

"That it's a coincidence?" said the brown-haired thug.

"Almost, but not ..." Viggo said, shaking his head and looking extremely disappointed.

"Doesn't matter what it means!" the blond one cried angrily, unable to come up with the meaning of the word.

Ingrid heaved a deep sigh and shook her head.

"Are you done messing around?" she asked Viggo with a reproachful look.

Viggo smiled at Ingrid, all charm.

"Yes, my precious."

Ingrid blushed, half in rage, half from Viggo's compliment.

"How could I have offended the Ice Gods to be punished in such an insufferable manner?" she muttered under her breath.

"I don't like you. You look like troublemakers," the blond one said, pointing his cudgel at them.

"We do? But we're so sweet," Viggo assured him, his expression suggesting he had never so much as broken a plate in his life.

"You're in the wrong establishment. Get out," the other thug told them.

"Not at all. This is precisely the place we should be," Viggo said.

"We won't repeat it! Get out!" the thug insisted.

Ingrid stared at the thug threatening them with his cudgel.

"We're here on official business. I'm sure you don't want to interfere with a mission ordered by King Thoran."

The two thugs looked at one another. He had caught their attention.

"You're not part of the City Guard," the brown-haired thug said, taking in their clothes.

"We're Rangers on an official mission," Ingrid said with authority.

"Rangers can't come into this tavern," the blond thug said.

"And why not?" Ingrid asked.

"Because we don't like filthy Rangers," the other one said,

reaching for his club as well, this one fixed with a big, solid, wooden head.

Viggo laughed out loud. He pinched his nose with two fingers and then pointed at the two thugs.

"Filthy?" Ingrid said, offended, ignoring Viggo's comic gesture.

"Yes. Filthy. You spend all day in the mountains and woods and then come into town to poke your nose into matters that don't concern you."

"If we poke our noses in, it might be because they're illegal matters," Ingrid replied defiantly.

"There's nothing illegal here, and you two can't come in," the thug replied.

"You can't refuse us entry. We're Rangers and we can go anywhere we need in the realm," Ingrid said.

"Not here,"

"Are you going to make me take you down?" Ingrid said, narrowing her eyes.

"Try it, blondie, and I'll crush that pretty little head of yours."

"Oops… you shouldn't have called her blondie…" Viggo said, shaking his head. "She's going to get angry…"

"Blonde and cute," the thug said sordidly.

Ingrid took a step forward and delivered a right punch straight to his nose. There was a crack and the thug stepped back.

"My nose! She broke my nose!" he cried, feeling it. "I'm going to kill you!"

"Come on, don't be such a drama queen, you haven't lost that much—you weren't exactly handsome to begin with…" Viggo said nonchalantly.

The thug tried to hit Ingrid on the head with his cudgel. His partner followed suit and attacked Viggo. Ingrid gauged the giant's attack which, although brutal in power, was clumsy in execution. She stepped aside. The cudgel came down toward the floor and missed completely. Before he could raise it again to try another blow, Ingrid kicked him hard in the crotch. The thug bent over in agony and fell to his knees on the floor, looking sick.

Viggo deflected the other thug's club with a defensive move using the two knives he'd pulled out with incredible speed. When the thug tried to hit him again, Viggo lunged at him fast and hit the man's Adam's apple with his right fist. The thug began to choke, unable to breathe. He put his hands to his throat. Viggo continued the attack and hit him in the temple with the butt of his knife in a circular move. The thug was totally stunned—he lost his balance and fell to his knees, still struggling for air.

Ingrid delivered a tremendous knee blow to the head of thug on his knees before her, and he fell to the floor, unconscious.

"I told you she was going to be angry…" Viggo told him.

"Will you please deal with that one?" Ingrid said, waving at the thug kneeling beside Viggo.

"This one? But he's harmless…"

"We're not here to play."

"Fine… you never let me enjoy myself," Viggo hit the man on the temple; he fell to one side and lay there unconscious.

The rest of the tavern's thugs and customers had witnessed the fight, and suddenly there was a flurry of movement. Knives, clubs, short axes, and hooks began to appear in their owners' hands.

"This is starting to look like fun," Viggo told Ingrid with one of his smiles which meant he was ready to have a good time.

"Everyone stand still!" Ingrid shouted with authority.

Everybody stared at her for an instant. From under her shirt, Ingrid took out her Ranger medallion and held it up for everyone to see.

"We're Rangers! We're here on a mission for the king!" she said.

"There's nothing here for you," the bartender said.

"We'll be the judge of that," Viggo replied.

The thugs glanced at the bartender, waiting for an order to intervene. Several ugly-looking customers who were already wielding weapons were eying them with hatred. They didn't seem fond of Rangers.

"We're the Royal Eagles! We're here on a mission searching for Dark Rangers!" Ingrid said.

"And what's it to me? You might be Thoran himself for all I care!" one of the armed customers said, laughing.

"We're going to render that pretty face of yours unrecognizable!" another cried.

"Bloody Rangers!"

Viggo got closer to Ingrid.

"Sweetheart, they don't seem to have much love for us in this tavern," he said under his breath.

"Yeah, I've noticed. And these here are the best of the slums of this and several other cities."

They took a step forward. Half the customers were standing with weapons in their hands. The other half were watching silently with surly looks.

"Those who wish to leave and are not Dark Rangers may do so," Ingrid said, indicating the open door behind her.

"Those who want a fight, here we are," Viggo said, opening his arms and showing his knives in invitation.

There was a moment of silence, of doubt. Then suddenly a third of the people in the tavern stampeded out the door. Another third headed to the back of the tavern, and the last third lunged at Ingrid and Viggo.

"This is going to be so much fun!" Viggo said as he deflected the club of one of the thugs and delivered a hard kick to his knee, which broke with a horrible sound.

"Don't kill them, we have to question them," Ingrid told him as, with a knife in one hand and her short axe in the other, she fended off two especially cruel-looking attackers.

Those who were escaping through the open door went out expecting to find more Rangers, but they were wrong. The front of the tavern and the street that led to it were deserted. There wasn't a soul in sight. The first six started to run and heard several "clicks" under their feet. A moment later several ice traps burst, freezing the runners' lower limbs; they fell to the ground amid curses and cries of rage.

Those who came out after them avoided the now-frozen runners and tried to escape up the street, since the docks were at the other end and they would end up in the water. As they were running, they heard more "clicks," and this time large nets shot up from the ground—like fishing nets, but smeared with a sweet, sticky substance. They were caught in the nets and fell to the ground. The more they tried to escape the nets, the more tangled they became and the more smeared they were with the sticky substance.

The last group left the tavern; seeing everybody lying in the street, they turned to run down the street toward the docks, sprinting as though hungry wolves were after them. When they were about to reach the docks, the one running in the lead tripped on a black-painted rope tied from one side of the street to the other. He fell on his face while the others tried to jump over it. They ran a little farther and then encountered another rope which hit them at eye level, making several of them fall backwards. The few who were still on their feet tried to flee while the others were trying to get back up, but they met two Rangers armed with bows waiting for them at the end of the street, the sea at their backs.

"Stop right there if you don't want to have an arrow through you!" Gerd warned them.

In spite of the warning, several tried to dodge them at a run. Two arrows reached the first two; they were Earth Arrows, and they burst, blinding and stunning those who were trying to escape.

"Don't you even try …" Nilsa said, aiming beside Gerd.

Four more did not heed the advice and tried to escape—two back to the tavern and two toward the water. Gerd dealt with the two who were trying to reach the water. Nilsa dealt with the other thugs with two accurate shots.

Inside the tavern, Viggo was bringing down thugs and bandits skillfully. He moved with impressive speed, precision, and balance, dodging and counterattacking with impressive skill. His opponents fell to the ground unconscious or in terrible pain quicker than the blink of an eye.

He was massively enjoying the fight.

Ingrid did not have Viggo's speed or skill in hand-to-hand combat, but she defended herself like a lioness. Her blows were hard and precise. Every time she hit, a rival fell like a log to the ground. She had to be careful not to injure them seriously, which made it harder to defeat them, but none of the hoodlums had the necessary skill to beat her—they were nothing but sewer rats with sharp teeth and claws. Even though a knife almost cut into her thigh forcing her to focus. Ingrid delivered a kick to her attacker's chest, sending him backwards to the ground where he tripped on another comrade who was already down. Before he could get back up, Viggo left him senseless with a knee to the face.

"I'm loving this date. We've got to do this more often," Viggo said to Ingrid as she knocked down a gaunt man with two knives using a circular blow to the head with the flat of her axe.

She looked back at him.

"Will you please take this seriously?"

"I am taking it very seriously. I'm only saying I love it and that we should do it more often."

"This isn't a date," Ingrid told him as she blocked a knife with hers and delivered another kick to the attacker's supporting leg, making him lose balance. She finished him with a crossed left punch with her knife hand.

"Of course it's a date! A perfect one," Viggo said, sliding to one side and hitting the back of the neck of another bandit who fell, unconscious before he hit the floor.

Ingrid snorted. "Only you would call this a perfect date," she said, bringing down the last of the attackers with a left punch.

"Deep down you know you love it," Viggo said as he looked around the hall to see whether there was anyone left standing he had failed to notice. "Some are escaping through the back door," he told Ingrid, indicating the far end of the hall.

Ingrid nodded. She checked the hall: over a dozen men lay unconscious or injured on the floor around them. She brought out fifteen scarves to gag them and an equal number of tying ropes from her Ranger's belt. They were the kind used to tie up prisoners—strong and hard to cut. The Rangers treated them with a special compound to make cutting or tearing them against hard surfaces more difficult.

"Here," she said and threw half at Viggo, who caught them in midair with his right hand without letting go of his knife. He did not drop one.

"Don't you want me to go after them?"

"No, let's tie up all these ones."

"Tying up unconscious morons is boring."

"We've fulfilled our part of the mission."

"Yeah, but I prefer a little more action."

"If you don't do what I say I'll tie and gag *you*."

Viggo smiled, "Yes, my precious," he said and smiled lovingly at her.

Ingrid snorted, shook her head, and focused on the task at hand.

Chapter 2

The group inside the tavern reached the stone wall at the far end. There were no windows and it was dark. Still, the six men seemed to know where they were heading. They did not trip or knock anything down. They reached a large solid oak-wood table; there was an old, frayed blanket under it serving as a rug. After they moved the table aside, they freed the rug. One of the men pulled it out of the way, revealing a trapdoor. He pulled it open and a dark square hole appeared before them, big enough for one person to go down.

They did not think twice, one by one letting themselves down through the hole, entering a dark cellar without any light. The humidity and the filth were overwhelming, making it hard to breathe. They felt around until they found another stone wall which they followed to the end. They felt the low ceiling and found another trapdoor the size of a regular door. A ramp by the wall allowed them access to it. The trapdoor was used to unload supplies into the cellar of the tavern for storing.

The fugitives pushed the trapdoor open and managed to get outside. The night breeze made them feel better; they were in a clearing behind the tavern which was broken up by a path. Three century-old oaks at about thirty paces were all they could see. Everything looked clear—they were going to get away. It had been a close call, but they had escaped. They were about to run off when they heard a voice.

"Nobody move!"

The six men looked around but did not see anyone.

"Who's there?" one of the men asked.

"Royal Eagles! You're under arrest!" the voice said. It was none other than Egil shouting powerfully from behind one of the thick oaks by the path.

The six men drew their weapons. Three of them wielded Rangers' knives and axes. The other three had short swords and daggers like those used by experienced mercenaries and outlaws.

"We're not turning ourselves in!" the one who had to be the leader cried. He was tall and thin, had a blond goatee and hair gathered in a ponytail, and looked strong and nimble—the kind who fought well and managed better than most in complicated situations. He must have been in his thirties.

"You'd better! You're surrounded!" Egil warned them.

The six men looked around again but saw nobody.

"There's nobody else but you here! Show yourself!"

Egil came out from behind the tree with a short bow in his hands.

"He won't be able to deal with all of us! Go get him!" the leader ordered his comrades.

Three of them ran at Egil, who did not move. He was watching them with a calm expression. Raising his short bow, he aimed at the one running in the middle.

"Bad choice…"

"Finish him!"

Egil released with all the skill he was able to muster with a bow, which was not much. To his surprise, he hit the one he had aimed at square in the chest. The Air Arrow burst on impact and a discharge spread through the outlaw, who fell to the ground amid uncontrollable convulsions.

The other two kept running toward Egil, brandishing their weapons. He would have no time to nock again. He hid behind the oak.

"That's not going to save you!" the leader said as he reached the tree.

"Beware!" the leader warned them. He was wary as he observed the fight, two of his men beside him. The other three had Ranger knives and axes, betraying them as being or having been Rangers, which was the reason they were wanted—they had to be Dark Rangers.

The attacker reached the oak and was about to go around it when he heard a deep, loud growl. He tried to stop in his tracks, but before he could a snow panther fell on top of him from a thick branch. With a shriek of fear, he fell backwards and lost his sword. He tried to stab the panther with the knife he still had in his left hand when he found that an invisible force was holding his arm and he could not move it.

"Help! Help me!" he yelled.

Ona held his neck in her jaws and growled. The man stopped screaming and struggling, remaining still as a statue lying on the ground.

"By the Icy Heavens!" the one coming behind him cried. He looked at the panther and hesitated, wondering whether to attack or not.

"Kill the panther!" the leader shouted.

The attacker took a step forward and seemed ready to attack, but an arrow coming from the higher part of the oak hit his heart. The tip broke with a hollow sound. A discharge ran through his body, and he fell to the ground, convulsing.

Egil appeared again by the oak, short bow in his hands. He stepped over to the man on the ground that Ona had in a death bite.

"Don't move if you wish to get out of here alive," Egil warned.

"I...I won't...move..." the man replied, his face white as snow. Ona was pressing against his neck with her deadly jaws.

"As for you remaining three, you'd better surrender if you wish to stay alive."

The one who had received the discharge tried to get up. A second Air Arrow caught him in the chest and rendered him unconscious amid uncontrollable convulsions.

"We're not going to surrender! Tell the Sniper to come down from the tree and fight like a Ranger!" the leader said.

Egil turned to the oak.

"Come down, Lasgol, you're wanted," Egil called.

Lasgol dropped down to the ground with the ease of a monkey. He had called upon his skills for these kinds of situations. He now stood beside Egil; he was carrying a composite bow in his hand with another Air Arrow nocked in it.

"It's three against two," the leader said.

"Yeah, and you're most likely as good as the two of us," Egil had to admit.

"We are. We're weathered Rangers,"

"You must be a Specialist, if I'm not mistaken ..." Egil said, watching him closely.

"You have good vision. I am."

"Specialty?" Egil asked casually, as if they were chatting among friends, except that everyone wielded weapons and were ready to attack one another.

"Forest Survivor," the other said proudly.

"Pity that you're out of your environment," Egil said with a shrug.

"Yes, it is. Otherwise we wouldn't be having this conversation."

"It's a pity you turned to the Dark Rangers," Lasgol reproached in frustration. "I can't understand what drove you to it."

"Some of us became tired of receiving stupid orders and going on dangerous missions, risking our lives for nothing," the one on the leader's right said. He was a strong veteran in his early forties and had light brown, almost blond hair and beard.

"Orders are to be followed and missions completed, no matter how difficult and risky they may be," Lasgol replied.

"Yeah, yeah, spare us the speech, we know *The Path of the Ranger* perfectly well. It's been drilled into us to exhaustion," the other Ranger said. He was about thirty-five, painfully thin and so blond he was almost albino.

"No matter how demanding the Path is, we can't stray from it. We are the defenders of the Realm, of the Norghanian people."

"Yeah, yeah, from enemies internal and external, we know it by heart," the leader said. "You should ask yourself why we serve brainless monarchs without any scruples. Why we accept that everything they order us to do is right when they're only seeking their own gain and wellbeing, not that of the realm, and least of all of their people. You're simply puppets they manipulate and use to obtain riches and power they don't share with anybody else."

"We don't choose who sits on the throne—we defend it and, with it, the Realm and the people," Lasgol said.

"You're just another one of their puppets, blindly accepting whatever you're ordered to do. When Thoran leads you into a war he can't win, driven by greed and the thirst for power, you tell me. Thousands of good Norghanians will die, your friends among them. Perhaps then you'll wonder whether serving the king blindly was the right path to follow."

Lasgol wanted to retort but could not. The words had affected him—he could perfectly imagine Thoran and his brother leading them to a war only to obtain more power and gold.

"You have a point, but that's not reason enough to betray the kingdom and, most of all, the people you defend," Egil told them.

"That's your opinion. We believe we have reasons aplenty."

Egil shrugged.

"We'll have to agree to disagree."

"Exactly."

"Since you won't get past us, you'd better surrender peacefully," Egil recommended calmly.

"We'll see about that!" the leader replied. "Get them!" he cried.

The three Dark Rangers came at them surprisingly fast. They were skilled and clearly knew what they were doing. Egil and Lasgol raised their bows and aimed. The three Dark Ones started zigzagging to offer less of a target. They did this swiftly, sliding at the same time in what was obviously a practiced move.

Egil released and missed.

"Hitting my target twice in a row was too much to hope for," he told Lasgol, dropping his bow and drawing his knife and short axe since he would not have time to nock again.

Lasgol did not lose his focus and, following the zigzagging motion of the one farther to the right, aimed and released. The Dark One moved exactly where Lasgol had expected him to and received an arrow in his chest. A discharge left him shaking on the spot.

"We've got them!" the leader shouted, about to reach them.

Lasgol dropped his bow and drew his knife and axe. He took a defensive stance, knife and axe crossed before his face, one leg ahead and slightly flexed and the other firmly planted behind. Egil did the same and prepared to defend himself from the attack of the two Dark opponents who were already upon them.

At that moment, a figure dropped down from one of the higher branches of the oak onto the two Dark Rangers. She hit them hard— they both received a blow to the chest and were thrown backwards. The figure rolled to one side and stood up with two dark knives in her hands. She hit the head of the Dark One who was still convulsing from Lasgol's arrow and rendered him unconscious.

"And this is our Assassin of Nature," Egil said with a wave of introduction.

"Hellfire!" the leader cried, getting to his feet with difficulty.

"You'd better surrender, or we'll let her deal with you," Egil threatened. "Oh, and it's my duty to let you know that she's extremely good."

"No way! I'm not surrendering!" the leader yelled, and he stood up to Astrid who was watching them, ready to attack. "Let's grab her!" he told his partner.

"She's an Assassin of Nature ..." he replied fearfully.

"We're two warriors! She's only one!"

"Even so… fighting an Assassin is madness," he said and dropped his weapons. "I surrender," he added, falling to his knees with his hands behind his head.

"That's a very sensible attitude and one we appreciate," Egil said.

"Well, I'm not giving up!" the leader said and attacked Astrid.

Egil looked disappointed. "So be it then."

Astrid waited for her opponent to be at an arm's distance before, dodging his first axe attack, she cut him in the arm. The Specialist grunted and delivered a slash with his knife, seeking Astrid's neck, but she threw her head back and the blade passed right in front of her eyes.

"They're poisoned," she said, showing him her knives.

"Hellfire!"

"We can stop here or keep fighting … but you risk dying," she said with a shrug.

Lasgol was watching the fight and wanted to intervene, to help Astrid, but he did not—he knew she really did not need any help. Besides, it was a duel and stepping in would be disrespectful. A Norghanian always managed his or her own fights, Astrid more than anyone else. Instead of risking angering her while the Dark One decided whether to surrender or keep fighting, Lasgol grabbed his bow and stepped back enough to be able to shoot. He nocked an arrow and aimed. If things got ugly for Astrid, he would intervene, although he seriously doubted that would be the case.

"What kind of poison?" the Specialist asked, looking at the cut in his sleeve.

"Take it easy, it's not lethal. It'll knock you out soon though."

"Well, that's a mistake," he replied and lunged, two slashes seeking Astrid's face. With the agility and speed of a panther, the Assassin crouched and slid to one side. The other Specialist turned to attack from above with his axe. Astrid cut him in the thigh and hurled herself to the left, rolling over her head. The Specialist's axe hit the ground hard.

Lasgol now had a clear shot. Astrid was out of reach. He could release and end the fight, and he was about to do so but decided against it—she would not approve. Each one of them had to deal with their own responsibilities; they were no longer kids and needed to act like adults. He would let her decide how to proceed. Astrid glanced at him as if she knew what he was thinking and gestured for him to lower his bow.

"My…arms are heavy…" the Specialist said, even as he tried to keep fighting.

"And soon your legs will be too," she told him.

"Limb-numbing poison…."

"Exactly. A new mix of my own creation I'm experimenting with. It's an area of study I'm quite interested in. If it's any consolation, you're the first one to try it, so you'll be my first test subject."

"Well, aren't I lucky…" he muttered under his breath, full of sarcasm and rage.

"You should be feeling its final effect already."

The Specialist looked down at his wounds. He turned to Astrid as if deciding whether or not to attack but he never made a move; his limbs failed him and he fell on his knees with his arms hanging at his sides, unable to raise them.

"Drop your weapons," Lasgol said, aiming at his chest.

The Specialist finally gave up and did as Lasgol told him.

"Good poison…" he told Astrid, who was watching him with an analytical gaze.

"I see it works well and faster than I had expected."

"I hope it doesn't kill me…"

"Me too," she replied, but she did not guarantee it would not.

"Violet Lotus flower?" Egil asked her, curious about the poison.

"That's right. But I added an enhancer: Black Beech root."

"Wow, that's interesting, I'll have to experiment with that," Egil said with a smile. "We must exchange knowledge and notes about the experiments we do in this exciting area of investigation."

"Yeah, really exciting," Lasgol said, slight irony in his voice. He did not find poisons so interesting.

The Specialist collapsed to one side and lay there on the ground. His partner watched on his knees with his hands behind his head. The third one who was still conscious remained still; he did not even breathe—he was petrified with Ona's jaws around his neck.

Ona, Camu, let him go, Lasgol told them.

Camu at once stopped putting pressure on the Dark Ranger's arm.

Ona let go of the man's neck and the Dark One gasped for air, filling his lungs. He looked absolutely terrified.

Ona, good. Well done.

The snow panther chirped gratefully.

Watch that one. I don't think he'll move at all, but don't let him out of your sight, just in case.

Watch. Right. Ona bite if try to escape.

But don't kill him. He's so terrified, I doubt he's a danger now.

Ona growled once.

Okay. Bite not kill.

That's right, bite not kill, Lasgol said again to make sure they understood what they needed to do. He did not want the man to accidentally die. Fear could drive the Dark Ranger to some foolish idea, such as getting up and making a run for it. That would make everyone react rashly.

"Everybody stay where you are and don't try to escape," he told the Dark Rangers, pointing his bow at them. He used a dry tone to make it clear he and his friends would not hesitate to kill them, although what he really wanted was to stop them from doing something that would get them killed, now that they were beaten with no way out.

"I'm not going to be able to…escape for a while…" the Specialist said from the ground.

"For a good while," Astrid noted, stepping up to the Dark Ones. She removed all their weapons and brought them to Egil.

"Tie them well, please," he told her, handing her the ropes and gags.

"It'd be a pleasure," she replied as she set to it.

Suddenly they heard the hoot of an owl, but with a different cadence, one they knew well.

"It's Ingrid," Lasgol said, recognizing it.

The first hoot was followed by another, very similar but longer.

"And that's Nilsa," Egil said, recognizing the familiar sound.

"Great, that means the plan worked out," Lasgol said, very pleased.

"It would appear so. They're not asking for help, so there must not be any wounded among our friends," Astrid said, looking up at the sky.

"Thank goodness," Lasgol said with a snort of relief.

"Fantastic, then," Egil said, looking pleased. "I love it when plans succeed."

"Yours almost always do," Astrid told him.

"This one was slightly particular," Lasgol said, with a look that meant the operation had not been exactly easy.

"Indeed," Astrid smiled. She had all the Dark Rangers tied and gagged and was petting Ona while Camu, in his invisible state, gave her small affectionate nudges which she loved.

"So what do we do now?" Lasgol asked his friend.

Egil took a deep breath.

"Now we finish the first mission of the Royal Eagles and make King Thoran proud."

Chapter 3

Egil asked his companions to take all the prisoners back into the tavern so they might have a quiet, revealing conversation with them. First, they cleared the tables and chairs inside so as to make ample space. Gerd outdid himself, and between his strength, Astrid's, and Viggo's speed, they had the premises cleared in no time.

Then they brought in all the prisoners who were not there already. This took them slightly longer, since they had to drag or carry them between two people. Viggo was not pleased and protested all the way as usual. To everybody's surprise, Ingrid said nothing and simply told him to keep moving since they did not have all day. Nilsa and Gerd exchanged a smile—this new, strange relationship between Ingrid and Viggo was going to provide them with serious entertainment.

They placed all the prisoners, well bound and gagged, in the center of the room. Those recovering from the traps and arrows did not move much or protest: some from fear, others because the effects had not yet worn off. A few who had recovered quickly were struggling to get free, but unsuccessfully. There was the occasional prisoner who tried to scream under their gags, but when Viggo butted them with his knife they would shut up.

"What a mess," Nilsa whispered to Gerd, leaning into the giant to reach his ear so that the prisoners would not hear.

"You don't say! How are we going to know which of these are Dark Rangers and which aren't?" he whispered back, scratching his head.

Nilsa shrugged. "No idea."

"Have you searched them yet?" Egil asked them.

"Yeah, none of them have the Dark coins or any letter or document sealed with the Boar or the Bear," said Lasgol, who had been busy searching them. He had put all the prisoners' belongings on the counter. There were small weapons of all kinds, marked cards, crooked dice, currency from Norghana and at least three other kingdoms, rope, needles, hooks, and numerous small tools. There were things that Lasgol could not even identify—he had never seen them before. One object that left him wondering was a glass eye that looked authentic. A piece of art. He thought of Ulf and figured it would look good in him, but then he second-guessed himself and shook his head; Ulf would never wear a glass eye. The last thing that old, retired soldier wanted was to look handsome. No, on the contrary, what he wanted was to instill fear, and the lack of one eye served him quite well.

"I'm not surprised we haven't found any trace of the Boar and the Bear. They've learned to get rid of any object that can give them away. They'll only use the symbols when they really need them," Egil commented as he studied the prisoners, trying to determine who was a Dark Ranger and who was not.

"It would've been easier for all of us if they carried the coins on them," Ingrid said in an unhappy tone. "Now the innocent will pay for the traitors."

"Pay? Their idea of payment is hardly payment..." Viggo waved the matter aside. "We've only caused them a slight inconvenience for being in the wrong place with the wrong company. I'm referring to the actually innocent, if there are any in this stinking lot we've caught."

"Well, we are causing them some inconvenience after all," Lasgol said, gesturing to the prisoners. It was much more than a simple inconvenience, and it would be even worse before the night was over, but Lasgol did not want the prisoners to be even more restless. Some of them appeared more than just nervous. What he did not know was whether it was because they were innocent or, on the contrary, because they had been caught and were about to be discovered.

"If they were in this condemned place they can't be very innocent, I'm sure of that," Viggo said, winking.

"Your reasoning makes sense. I don't see much clean wheat here to separate from the chaff, and that's not even mentioning the fact that I don't see a face that looks even remotely innocent," Astrid added. "I wouldn't trust any of them. I have a feeling they're all guilty of some crime or another."

Lasgol was aware that the customers of this joint of ill-repute were criminals, mercenaries, and outlaws of different ilk, so those they had tied up were either all Dark Ones or at least wanted by the city guard, otherwise they would not have stampeded out as they had, and there were also the thugs who had stood up to them who without a doubt deserved to be caught.

"Yeah, a few rotten fish do seem to have fallen into our nets during this fishing operation..." Lasgol went on, wondering how Egil was going to find out which among the group were really Dark Rangers. It was not an easy task. He was sure his friend would have given it thought, but since he had not shared more information than they actually needed for the first part of the plan, this second part was an enigma. Egil's mind had to be working out the solution to the mess that had fallen into their hands.

Egil started walking around the prisoners, lost in thought. Nilsa and Gerd were standing to one side of the circle they had formed in the middle of the establishment. In front of them were Ingrid and Viggo. Lasgol was at the door with Ona and Camu camouflaged beside them. Astrid was watching the trapdoor at the far end of the hall. Nobody could come in or go out, and the prisoners could not get loose and escape. Everything was well organized and executed, just as Egil liked.

There was a moment of silence. The group watched the prisoners but kept an eye on Egil, waiting to see what he had planned.

"Nice group of Dark Rangers we have here…" Egil said casually all of a sudden, almost as if he were speaking to himself, although he did it loud enough for everyone to hear.

"Of those who still remain," Gerd said, crossing his arms over his massive chest. "Right? There can't be many more left in the whole realm. We've hunted them all down."

"That's right, my dear friend," Egil replied, nodding as he continued to pace.

"We've finished with five already… no, six groups," Nilsa said, counting with her fingers. "This one has to be one of the last."

"I have to admit they're well organized," Astrid commented. "Small groups that operate independently from the others they barely know. The orders come along with the seal or coin of the Boar and the Bear. It makes it extremely hard for us to find them and catch them."

"Which is our duty and the reason why we're here," Ingrid said, glaring at the prisoners while she rested her hands on the weapons at her waist.

Lasgol sighed. They were really there because the first mission the king had entrusted the Royal Eagles with was none other than finding and catching all the Dark Rangers left scattered throughout the realm. A mission which was turning out to be a lot harder than they had anticipated. Now that the leaders of the organization had fallen, the remaining groups were operating independently with the head of each group giving the orders. Now it was not Gatik or Eyra who passed the orders down, making it impossible to follow the chain of command. Lasgol had thought that, without leadership, the last survivors would have dispersed and vanished. Unfortunately, that had not been the case. They went on operating secretly, waiting for someone to take charge of the organization; that was something Lasgol and his friends needed to prevent by any means. The Dark Rangers had to disappear. The thing was, it was turning out to be very difficult to find them.

"I think we should cut their throats and end this here and now," Viggo said in a lazy tone, stretching as though he had just woken up. "It's starting to be a pain to seek them out, catch them, and deliver them to the King. It would be a lot more efficient to kill them all and, end of story, go on to the next mission."

Ingrid gave him one of her looks of disgust. But she said nothing. He smiled and made an impish face. Lasgol knew Viggo was not really serious. He did not want to kill them all; he was trying to intimidate the prisoners, and judging by the faces of some, he had succeeded. Viggo continued with his usual amoral and rebellious style which, on occasions like this, was quite useful.

"Before killing them all, let's see if any of them feel like talking and saving their necks," Astrid proposed, following Viggo's game. "We might find a smart one who wants to save his life."

Lasgol noticed that several of the prisoners were nodding, making an effort to be noticed with their movements—Astrid's comment seemed to have had an effect. Maybe now they could glean some information.

"Let's see what this one has to say," said Ingrid, striding over to a man who was shaking his arms and legs as if he were having a seizure. She took the gag out of his mouth so he could speak.

"I... I want to... talk..." he muttered.

"Very well, speak then. What do you know?" Ingrid asked him, staring into his eyes sternly.

"I know nothing, I swear! I have nothing to do with this!"

"Well, that's disappointing..." Viggo said, bringing out one of his knives. "If you know nothing you're no good to us." And he passed his thumb across his own throat in a threatening gesture.

"Please! I'm innocent! I'm not one of the Dark Rangers you're looking for!" he cried, looking terrified.

"And how do you know who we're looking for?" Ingrid asked, raising an eyebrow suspiciously.

"I… I've heard… about you … the Royal Eagles who hunt down the Dark Rangers. That's you, right? It is you, isn't it?" he said, looking at Ingrid and then at the others, eyes wide with terror.

"Royal Eagles, and yes, that's us," Ingrid confirmed.

"Well, I have nothing to do with the Dark Rangers! I was just playing cards! I come here often! They know me!" he said defensively, trying to persuade them he was not a Dark One.

"Sure, and we're going to believe you because you say so," Viggo replied with a wave that meant he was not fooled by the man's speech.

"It's the truth! I'm innocent!" the man was desperately shouting, growing red in his effort to be convincing.

"This is the first time we've heard *that*, isn't it, friends?" Viggo said in the tone of someone tired of hearing the same lies from those they captured.

"Oh yes, it isn't even the first time today," Astrid said, following Viggo, which made the prisoners more nervous about their fate.

Nilsa whispered something in Gerd's ear.

"I can't see how we're going to know who's telling the truth and who's not …"

"If only we had the Herb of Truth Potion …"

"Yeah, if only. But we don't." Nilsa replied, wrinkling her nose.

"Let's see what our friend comes up with," Gerd said, jabbing his thumb at Egil, who continued pacing around the prisoners with a thoughtful look.

Lasgol stroked Ona's head and ears. The panther chirped gratefully.

Stay alert in case one of them manages to get free and surprises us.

I watch. Jump if one get free, Camu transmitted at once.

Camu, I wonder if you realize that, as far as jumping goes, Ona is much better than you. It's enough that you warn us. Ona will jump on them if needed.

I jump very well, he transmitted, along with a feeling of slight offense at the implication that he was not as agile as Ona.

You jump well, yes, but Ona is better. She's a big cat, a great hunter—it's her specialty to jump on the prey to bring it down, Lasgol explained so he would feel better.

I dragon, I more fierce.

Lasgol put his hand to his face and shook his head.

Don't start up again about being a dragon… I've told you a thousand times that you're not a dragon.

I dragon, you see.

Lasgol did not want to continue the argument—it was not the time, and as stubborn as Camu was, he knew he would get nowhere. It was going to take Lasgol a long time to persuade Camu he was not a dragon. He snorted and, opening the door a crack, checked outside. Everything looked quiet. He shot a questioning look at Astrid, who was at the far end of the hall on the other side of the tavern. She nodded back, signaling that everything was peaceful where she was too.

"Let's start to unravel this mess," Egil said all of a sudden, stopping his pacing. "Gerd and Nilsa, would you be kind enough to take those who have fought with Ranger weapons and those who attacked us at the back to Astrid at the far end of this distinguished establishment?"

"Those are all Dark Ones?" Gerd asked, widening his eyes.

"Irrefutable, my dear friend," Egil nodded, a big smile on his face.

Nilsa giggled. "He's taken a liking to that expression."

"Yeah, but he only uses it with me," Gerd protested. "It's nothing bad, is it?"

"No way! You two have a blast working together," Nilsa replied as she dragged one of the Dark Ones by the ankles.

Gerd was not very convinced with Nilsa's reply as he dragged two other Dark Ones by the ankles while they tried to get free unsuccessfully.

"Anyone makes a move and I'll cut their throat," Astrid threatened, showing them her black Assassin knives. They all stopped resisting at once.

Nilsa and Gerd ruthlessly dragged all the prisoners Egil indicated to where Astrid was waiting. When they were done, they stood looking at Egil, waiting for his next order.

"Take the gag off the one I hit with my bow please," he said. "I wish to have a word with him."

Astrid hastened to un-gag the prisoner.

"You were unlucky enough to have been hit by me with my bow. I must be improving," Egil smiled and stood before him, watching him carefully. "Or perhaps the Goddess of Fate has smiled upon me. Whatever the case, I'd like you to answer me a simple question, if you'd be so kind …"

"I won't say a word, you swine!" the Dark One said, spitting on Egil's boots.

"How rude. This one hasn't been a Ranger. He's nothing but a common criminal," Egil said with disgust.

"We already knew they hired thugs, deserters, and other scum without scruples and paid with gold," said Ingrid, who kept her eye on the group of prisoners.

"To increase their numbers and be able to carry out more ambitious operations. They didn't have enough people using only Rangers to do what they wanted," Egil reasoned.

"Yeah, like daring to attack our Master Specialists on their way to the capital," Ingrid said.

"That was a very risky move and I was surprised, I hadn't thought they'd have enough Dark Rangers to make the attempt. See? I also make mistakes," Egil said.

"Rarely," Lasgol corrected him with a wink.

"Seeing that we also err, that we aren't infallible, keeps us humble, in our place, respectful," Egil commented.

The prisoner started insulting Egil and the rest of the group rudely.

"Shut your big mouth," Astrid said, putting her knife to his throat.

"I… won't… tell you anything…" he clenched his jaw.

"You're much better like *this*," Astrid said, pulling his dirty hair back with one hand while she held her knife to his neck with the other.

"You can gag him again. He's useless," Egil said, waving his hand.

"The Specialist you defeated," he told Astrid, "let's try him."

Astrid gagged the man again and went over to the Dark Specialist. She took off his gag.

"How's the poison?" she asked.

"Bad… the effects aren't going away and my head hurts a lot," he replied.

"Oops, that was an unintended side effect," Astrid shrugged and smiled ironically. Egil stood before the Specialist.

"I need to know who the leader of this group is," he said amiably. "If you tell me, we'll finish this interrogation."

"Hmmm... let me think. Why should I tell you? You're going to deliver us to the King and he'll hang us. I don't see any gain in telling you anything."

"He's sort of right you know," Viggo said sarcastically.

Egil did not flinch at his friend's comment.

"Fine. I can offer you a deal—if you tell us who the leader is, you won't hang. That much I can promise."

"I won't hang?" he asked doubtfully.

"The Royal Eagles are allowed certain liberties."

"You can't go as far as pardoning a death sentence. We all know that, if we're captured, Thoran will hang us for betraying the realm."

"Let's say we can commute your death sentence."

"Commute?" the man said blankly.

"We can change it for something else," Egil explained.

"Will you let me go?"

Egil wrinkled his nose and shook his head.

"I said commute, not give you your freedom. You'll have to pay, serve a sentence, but it won't be death. Mistakes must always be paid for, one way or another. That's a law of man and of nature which is unalterable."

"What sentence then?" the man asked.

"Life sentence at the mines."

There was a moment of silence while the Dark One thought about it.

"No deal. I'd rather die than serve forced labor in a bloody mine in endless darkness until I die."

"Are you sure? Forced labor is hard, but it's not death ..."

"To me it's worse than death. I won't end my days in the bottom of a mine. I became a Ranger to live free in the mountains and forests. I can't end in a dark pit working under the whip."

Egil said, regretfully, "All right, if that's your decision ... we'll deliver you and you'll hang."

The Specialist swallowed. "It's my decision."

Egil turned to the main group and looked over the prisoners.

"I need the bartender," he said suddenly.

Lasgol's eyes widened, surprised by the request.

"The bartender?" Gerd asked blankly.

"He's the key here."

"The key? The bartender?" Gerd said, not understanding.

"Yeah, I need him, where is he?" Egil said, looking around.

"He's not among the prisoners," Ingrid said.

"He'll be hiding," Egil jabbed his finger at the space behind the counter.

Viggo jumped over the counter before Egil had even finished pointing.

"There are a couple of back rooms here," Viggo said after quickly inspecting the area.

"He must be hiding somewhere in there," said Egil.

"I'll deal with it," Viggo said and vanished.

The rest remained waiting, puzzled by Egil's request.

Chapter 4

There was a moment of silent waiting, broken by the abrupt sound of an object crashing against the walls and floor. A scream followed, and then more sounds, this time of blows. Then silence again.

Viggo suddenly appeared from behind the counter.

"I've got him," he said triumphantly—

"Don't hit me again!" the bartender shouted as Viggo dragged him in by the ear as if he were a child, seemingly oblivious to the fact that the bartender was a very large man.

They reached the counter. Viggo was straight as a rod, a stark comparison to the bartender, who was hunched, his hands to his ears.

"Jump over it," Viggo ordered him.

"You can go through there," the bartender pointed his finger at the far end of the counter, a section of which could be lifted for passage.

"I want to see you jump over the counter," Viggo insisted as he twisted the burly man's ear.

"Okay! I'll jump over it! Stop twisting!" Rather than jump over it, the bartender climbed up as best he could, belly first, and rolled over to the other side like a sack of potatoes. He dropped down on the filthy wooden floor with a dull thud that made several boards shake.

Viggo did jump over it, nimbly, and landed on his feet beside his prisoner.

"That's what happens when you throw things at my head," he scolded the man who was lying on the floor, face down, covering his ears.

"Thanks, Viggo. Always so efficient," Egil congratulated him.

"And spectacular," he added, shaking the dirt off his shoulders. "Nothing better than a good entrance to catch the audience's attention."

Egil smiled. He looked down at the bartender. "I wish to ask you something. It's a simple question that will help us solve the complex situation we find ourselves faced with here. Your cooperation is needed, and I hope you'll give it to us."

"I don't know anything! I'm simply the bartender!" he protested without even raising his head.

"Of course… of course… absolutely…" Egil agreed in a friendly tone.

"I've got nothing to do with any of them! Not one of them!"

"I understand… obviously…" Egil kept a soft inflexion in his voice, almost affectionate.

"I've done nothing wrong! I swear!"

"I'm sure that all you do is manage this charming and charismatic place and that you're not at all involved in the ugly business that has brought us here in such a discourteous manner, and for which I ask your forgiveness, on my behalf and that of my comrades," he said with a smile. "Still, there's a question I want you to answer."

The bartender turned on the floor to look at Egil.

"One? Only one?"

"That's right, only one," Egil said nodding.

"Well… if it's only one… and as long as it's clear that I have nothing to do with all this…" the man muttered.

"Of course. And I'm pleased to hear that. The question is this: who among all the illustrious customers of this famed tavern pays you to hold discrete meetings in the back rooms?"

The bartender's eyes widened and he shut his mouth. No reply.

"Answer or I'll yank your ear off," Viggo threatened him in a lugubrious tone.

"I… don't…" the man muttered and covered his ears with his hands.

"Or would you rather I cut them off?" Viggo showed him his knife threateningly.

"No! Don't cut my ear off!"

"It's not as if you'd lose much, you're not what I'd call handsome," Astrid said from the far end, wrinkling her nose.

"Okay… I'll tell you… but then you must protect me from them!"

"We can guarantee you protection and safekeeping," Egil assured him. "Speak without fear. Nobody will harm you."

"It's…" the bartender was looking to the group gathered in the center of the hall and pointed his finger, "Sigurd Musteson."

The prisoners were all looking at one another, unsure of who the bartender was pointing at. Then they started to hop away from the center until only one man was left alone in the middle. He was tall and strong, with blue eyes, long blond hair, and a flat nose. A three finger-long scar on his forehead marked him and gave him a menacing look.

"I believe we've found the leader," Egil said, pleased. "Gerd, Nilsa, will you please bring him over so I can speak to him?"

They both nodded and grabbed the prisoner, dragging him to where Egil waited a few paces away from the other prisoners.

"The gag."

Nilsa took it off.

"I haven't done anything and I don't belong to the Dark Rangers," Sigurd said as soon as he could speak. "I've no idea why that scum singled me out," he threw a lethal glare at the bartender on the floor.

"I guessed you'd say that. I'm going to offer you the same deal I spoke of before. I want to know who here belongs to your group and also where the last group is that we still have to catch."

"I know nothing. You're speaking to the wrong person," Sigurd said, and he sounded determined.

"I don't think so. The deal is forced labor in exchange for information. Otherwise, you'll hang," Egil offered, spreading his hands in a gesture that meant it was all he could offer.

"You could offer me all the gold in Thoran's coffers. Even so, I'd still say the same thing. You've got the wrong person. I was here drinking and looking for work. I don't belong to the Dark Rangers."

"Funny place to look for a job," Ingrid commented, shaking her head. "Doesn't seem like a good place to find one."

"Certain jobs can only be found in dubious places like this one."

"You mean dirty jobs," Ingrid said.

"Yes, very dirty. Someone has to do them. I do exactly that," Sigurd admitted with a shrug.

"It makes complete sense that you and your comrades would do that kind of job now, given the circumstances," Egil reasoned. "But this doesn't eliminate you as a leader of a group of Dark Rangers."

"The fact that you say I am doesn't make me one,"

Egil nodded. That's true. Then, am I to understand that you don't want the deal I'm offering you?"

"I don't want it because I'm not who you think I am or have the

36

information you seek."

"You see… I think you do. Something tells me so."

"You can believe what you wish, I'm not going to admit it," Sigurd said defiantly. "You won't get anything from me."

"Well, that remains to be seen. Let's not get ahead of ourselves. The future isn't written, it writes itself with each of our decisions," Egil told him with a somewhat malicious look.

Sigurd stared at him blankly.

"Shall I give him the special treatment to make him comply?" Viggo asked, cracking his knuckles threateningly.

"It won't be necessary," Egil said. "Please take him to one of the back rooms of the tavern. I think I'll have a private talk with him. "I'll be back presently," Egil passed by Lasgol and winked at him before leaving the tavern quickly.

Gerd snorted and shook his head.

"What's up?" Nilsa whispered to him.

"I think I know what Egil's gone to fetch."

"Oh… something bad?" the redhead asked, becoming quite nervous.

"Yeah, bad enough."

This, fun. Camu transmitted to Lasgol.

Ona growled twice—she did not think it was any fun.

Why do you think it's fun? Lasgol asked.

Much tension, fun.

Yes, there's plenty of that, I agree, but that doesn't make it fun. I'd say it's the opposite—nothing fun about a tense situation.

Fun. Like game. Guess who be bad, I guess too.

Well… if you look at it that way…

I tell the bad.

You think Egil is right?

Egil very smart. He right.

So he is, and he's probably right, let's see what happens.

See what happens. Fun.

Lasgol did not find the situation amusing at all, but since everything was a game for Camu and here it was a matter of unmasking the Dark leader and his group, his friend thought it was. He could not blame him for it. From Camu's point of view it made sense to interpret it as a game in which the culprit was unmasked at the end. Lasgol was just hoping they would find the culprit and be able to get out of there.

Ingrid and Viggo took Sigurd away while the others watched the rest of the prisoners.

"You'll see, you're going to have a whale of a time," Viggo told him as they dragged him to the back room.

"You're not scaring me, so you can save your comments," Sigurd said defiantly, certain they would not be able to make him talk.

"If you have any decency left, take Egil's deal and pay for your crimes in the mines," Ingrid advised him. "Otherwise you'll regret it when you hang from a noose and it'll be too late."

"You'll be the ones to regret it when you find out you were wrong about me. I repeat, I don't belong to the Dark Rangers."

"As you wish, I see you have no honor left," Ingrid said reproachfully as they dragged him into the room.

"I'll go fetch a candle so we can see a little better," Viggo told Ingrid.

"Fine. I'll watch him. To think that once you were a Ranger …" she told Sigurd, shaking her head.

Sigurd was about to say something but kept silent.

A moment later Viggo came back with a candle from the bar, and after him came Egil with a black satchel. They walked into the small, dirty room.

"Put him on the bed, please."

Ingrid and Viggo grabbed his arms and legs and hoisted him onto the bed.

"What are you going to do?" Ingrid asked.

"I'm going to introduce him to my two little friends."

Ingrid understood and made a face.

"I'll stay to help him," Viggo told her. "If you want, you can save yourself this unpleasant scene."

"No way. If you stay and stomach it, so can I," Ingrid snapped.

"It's unnecessary and it will upset you. We all know you're the leader of the Panthers, you don't need to prove it over and over," Viggo said kindly.

"It's my nature," she replied, folding her arms over her chest.

Sigurd was staring at them trying to guess whether they were trying to trick him or if something terrible really was going to happen to him.

"I'm simply trying to spare you from a bad time. I can stomach these things. You, on the other hand …" Viggo said, trying not to upset Ingrid by telling her she did not have the stomach for certain things.

"If you can stomach it, so can I."

Viggo sighed and shrugged.

"I tried. Egil, he's all yours."

Egil nodded and opened the satchel.

"Sigurd, I'm going to introduce you to two friends of mine. I'm sure you'll get along splendidly. Stay very still, it's for your own safety… Viggo, if you'll be so kind, gag him again."

A long time passed, and in the main hall of the tavern Gerd glanced furtively toward the room where the questioning was taking place.

"I don't hear a thing," he whispered to Nilsa.

"That's not necessarily bad, is it?" the redhead asked as she balanced from one foot to the other.

"I'm not so sure it's good…" the giant said, glancing at Lasgol, who understood his restlessness and gestured for him to calm down. Egil knew what he was doing. It was a dangerous game, but if anyone could pull it off, it was Egil. Lasgol believed in Egil; he fully trusted his friend. Perhaps too much, because accidents could happen, but he had no choice but to trust.

The prisoners, bound and closely watched, were not posing any trouble for the time being. Astrid had delivered a couple of blows to the head of a few of the men with the back of her knives, inspiring the prisoners in her care to quiet rapidly. Nilsa and Gerd had not needed to be so harsh, but even so, Lasgol was alert to any attempt on the prisoners' part to get rid of their bonds.

Egil appeared a while later. After him came Sigurd, who was whiter than the snow of the northern peaks. His face showed terror and suffering so great that everyone knew something bad had happened to him. He walked on his own two feet, and his hands were free. Ingrid and Viggo were watching him though. They came out from behind the counter and stood before the group of prisoners in the main hall.

"Which ones?" Egil asked.

Sigurd snorted deeply and pointed his finger at four of the men.

"Thank you very much for your cooperation," Viggo said, his voice dripping with irony.

The four accused men tried to get rid of their bonds to escape, but Gerd and Nilsa grabbed them and dragged them over to Astrid by the feet. The brunette welcomed the prisoners with a blow to the head each so they would stay still.

"You stay quiet or you'll end up with a terrible headache," she told them.

"I believe we can consider our mission completed for the night," Egil announced to his comrades.

"We have them all?" Lasgol asked.

"All the ones in this group, yes," Egil confirmed. "They're the ones with Astrid. You can let the rest go," he said, indicating the other prisoners gathered in the middle of the hall. "They're not Dark Ones."

"Are you sure?" Gerd asked.

"Sure. Sigurd has been most cooperative and confirmed it."

Nilsa, Lasgol, and Gerd released the prisoners' bonds with their knives, but the men did not move. They did not try to leave. They were terrified. Besides, Ona was at the door, and she did not seem ready to let anyone out.

"I'm sorry for the inconvenience," Egil apologized. "But we couldn't help it. Seeing that you're prominent citizens of this great city, the honor of having unmasked these Dark Rangers and served the king must compensate amply for the inconvenience suffered."

The prisoners stared at Egil, not knowing what to say or do. One or two were about to protest but on second thought kept quiet. They were all glancing furtively at the door; they wanted to get out of there and forget they had ever been involved in the current situation.

"Lasgol, would you mind telling Ona to let these good citizens through so they can go back to their homes, please?"

Lasgol nodded and used his skill with Ona.

Ona, come to me and let them go.

The good panther came obediently to Lasgol's side, freeing the door.

Camu, you too.

Okay, he messaged back.

The now free prisoners ran out the door and vanished into the darkness of the streets of the harbor city as if Ona were after them instead of sitting very formally beside Lasgol. The bartender was the last to leave. He looked at Egil and asked him,

"Can I go too?"

Egil nodded. "Go, and let this be a lesson."

The bartender ran out after the others without looking back.

"Very well, we have what we came for," Egil said, looking at the prisoners Astrid, Viggo, and Ingrid were watching. "Sigurd, if you'll kindly take your place with them," Egil said.

The leader joined the little group with his eyes on the floor to avoid his comrades' looks.

"Now I understand why the bartender was the key," Gerd said to Egil. "He knew who the leader of this group was," he reasoned, nodding heavily.

"Irrefutable, my dear friend," Egil smiled at him.

"Did you use Ginger and Fred?" he asked, concerned.

"That's right."

"Sigurd… isn't going to die poisoned, is he?" Gerd said, looking at the leader, who did not appear to be very well.

"Easy, big guy, he's perfectly all right—physically that is, emotionally, not so much."

"You've given him the fright of his life …"

"You might say so, yes. But don't be sorry for him. He's a rotten apple, and he doesn't want to pay the price for all the evil he's done. He'll end up hanging."

"You're right. He doesn't deserve my concern for him."

Lasgol came over to them, along with Ona and Camu.

"So, what do we do now?"

"Now we call the City Guard so they can lock up these undesirable characters who've followed the Dark Path. Then we get going."

"Get going? Where?" Lasgol asked him, curious to know what was next.

"To capture the last group of Dark Rangers left," Egil said, beaming.

"You know where they are?"

Egil nodded triumphantly. "Sigurd has been kind enough to tell me. It seems that every leader of a Dark group knows another leader."

"Only one?"

"That's right, only one. It's a brilliant way to keep the whole structure and hierarchy of the organization secret and avoid risks."

"If one group falls it can only point to another one, not the whole organization," Gerd said, understanding the reasons and logic of it.

"Irrefutable, my dear friend."

"Great then, it's time to go hunting him and his group," Viggo said with one of his mischievous grins.

"It's going to be slightly complicated…" Egil said in a mysterious tone.

"Since when has that stopped us?" Viggo asked him, raising one eyebrow.

"Never," Egil smiled.

Chapter 5

A few days later, the group found itself in the middle of the realm, heading to the County of Landesson. Astrid, Egil, and Lasgol rode ahead, behind them came Ingrid and Nilsa, and bringing up the rear rode Gerd and Viggo, with Ona and Camu right behind them. The landscape was pleasant—green pastures covered in snow on both sides of the road. Autumn was departing among snowfalls and increasingly icy and harsh weather. Winter was about to arrive, one they hoped would not be too harsh.

The Snow Panthers' first mission in their new role as Royal Eagles—capturing the remaining groups of Dark Rangers—had turned out to be more complex than expected. The fact that the Dark Ones had been so scattered and well organized to avoid being found had meant a lot of work and long journeys in inclement weather. It was nothing they were not used to and they had born it well, but they were tired and looking forward to finishing their first mission before the weather really turned ugly.

Lasgol squinted up to the sky.

"There's a storm brewing," he told Egil, stroking Trotter's neck, who became very nervous whenever he heard the word "storm." The good Norghanian pony did not like storms, but Camu and Ona, on the other hand, did not seem to mind them in the least; especially Camu, who was immune to them.

Egil looked up at the grey sky and dark clouds that seemed to want to reach them.

"It'll catch up with us before nightfall," he said.

"Better find shelter now and be safe. The last storm we came across was quite bad."

"True, we'd better make camp now and approach the target during the day."

"What's the target, exactly?" Astrid asked him, narrowing her eyes.

"We're after the remaining leader of the Dark Rangers."

"How do you know it's the last one?" the brunette asked.

"I'm not completely sure, but according to my research and

calculations, everything indicates this is the last one."

"I gather he won't be alone, right?"

"You gather correctly, my keen Assassin of Nature."

"I thought as much…"

"We'll have to deal with serious trouble, won't we?" Lasgol asked.

"I wouldn't say serious exactly… I'd say rather that we're coming to a situation that poses some difficulties we must overcome."

"Difficulties? That doesn't sound good. What exactly?"

"You'll know as soon as we get there," Egil grinned.

Lasgol sighed. "When you don't tell me the whole story I know we're going to encounter trouble."

"Trust me, my friend, everything will work out," Egil assured him, patting Lasgol's shoulder to help him relax.

"Oh, I trust you all right…" he replied and glanced back to see Ingrid and Nilsa further back, deep in their own conversation.

"I don't understand why you don't want to tell me," Nilsa was saying reproachfully to Ingrid.

"Because it's none of your business," Ingrid replied with her usual cold self-assurance.

"What do you mean it's none of my business? Of course it's my business," Nilsa frowned.

"Don't see how it can be. It's a private matter and so it will stay."

"It's not private since it affects us all," Nilsa insisted.

"It only concerns me and the knucklehead. It doesn't concern or affect the rest of you," Ingrid replied, steering her horse to correct his direction.

"What concerns you two concerns all the Panthers," Nilsa corrected, bringing her horse closer to Ingrid's.

"Don't be clingy and nosy, those aren't desirable qualities," Ingrid snapped with disappointment.

"It's my job to look after you and the Panthers,"

"You? Look after me?" Ingrid said, opening her eyes wide. "I doubt that very much

"Well, maybe not after you so much, but after the others, yes, and that includes your knucklehead boyfriend."

"I've told you a thousand times he's not my boyfriend," Ingrid said angrily.

"He says he is."

"I don't care what he says. There's nothing between us."

"That's exactly what I want to make sure of. His version of the facts is quite incriminating…"

"His version of the facts is, as usual, incorrect and exaggerated. Don't you know him by now ?"

"I know him perfectly well and I usually don't pay any attention to him, but he's been saying something that's left me puzzled. He says you kissed him."

"Me?" Ingrid cried, outraged.

"You didn't kiss him? He says you did and that it was passionate…" Nilsa said in a tone between insinuating and dreamy.

"No way!" Ingrid retorted, furious. She looked back to see how far they were from Viggo and Gerd and brought her voice down so they would not be overheard. "Shhh," she told Nilsa and pointed back.

"Was it passionate or not?" Nilsa asked, dying to know.

"It was nothing!" Ingrid muttered, trying to keep her voice down. She looked ahead again and steered her horse as she fought back a blush.

Nilsa did not miss it. "If that's not how it happened, then tell me what did. Your version of the facts."

"Nothing happened and that's that," Ingrid snapped, annoyed.

"Something happened. Egil confirmed there was kissing. It might have been accidental, or the knucklehead might have gotten carried away, but there *was* kissing," Nilsa insisted, determined to clear up the matter.

Ingrid grunted under her breath.

"I've got nothing to say about the matter and I won't say anything else!" she barked angrily.

Nilsa snorted, annoyed.

"Fine, whatever you want, but I think it's a shame you're not telling me. I'm your best friend! You should tell me, and I might even be able to give you some advice."

Ingrid turned in the saddle. "What kind of advice?"

"You know… about men…"

Ingrid huffed, enraged. "And what, pray tell, do you know about men? If I'm not mistaken, you haven't had any long-standing relation to learn from and give advice on. In order to teach you must first learn."

Nilsa did not like her friend's reply at all, especially not her tone.

She wrinkled her nose and her freckles seemed to light up.

"Well, you had one relationship that ended badly and another that's starting out even worse, so you're not in a position to reject any advice. Even if it's from someone without practical experience. I think I could be of help."

They both glared at each other, sparks of anger in their eyes— Ingrid's an icy blue and Nilsa's bright brown. A large hole in the ground made their horses move apart, separating their riders. But by the time they came together again after the pothole, the spat between the two friends was over.

"Let's not argue. I'll tell you about it as soon as I finish digesting it," Ingrid said. "If I ever manage to."

"Fine. I'll be patient and try to help you if I can."

The look they exchanged was a lot warmer. Nilsa smiled at Ingrid and her friend winked back at her.

"What do you think about talking improved archery techniques?" Ingrid suggested. "That's something I don't mind talking about."

Nilsa chuckled. "That I believe."

Viggo, further back, had been trying to listen to their conversation. He was craning his neck and stroking his horse's neck, leaning forward to try and hear.

"They're talking about me," he told Gerd beside him.

"How do you know?"

"Because they're whispering and laughing."

"And that's why you're sure it's about you?"

"Who else would they be talking about?"

"They could be talking about a thousand things," Gerd said with a look that said he found Viggo's assumption preposterous.

"I'm sure they're talking about me."

"Yeah, because they're laughing… at you," Gerd said, making a joke and laughing out loud.

"You're as much of a fool as you are large," Viggo replied, annoyed at his friend's joke.

"That was funny, you made it very easy."

"Your sense of humor is as intelligent as the creatures behind us."

Gerd turned to see Camu and Ona. Camu was visible because there was nobody around.

"Camu is very intelligent," Gerd said, winking at the creature.

Camu, seeing the gesture, tried to imitate him but shut both his eyes instead of only one.

"Yeah, very intelligent, just look at him," Viggo mocked.

"If you don't behave he'll make you vanish. And I hope it's only the head, it's really funny when he does that."

"Yeah, and I always split myself with laughter," Viggo said, bad-tempered.

"You might not, but we do," the giant said, slapping his shoulder hard—so hard that Viggo's horse startled and started forward, Viggo struggling to hold him back.

"You're such a brute!" Viggo protested at the top of his lungs.

"Sorry, I didn't mean to," Gerd shrugged, going red and trying to hide it. "Sometimes I can't control my own strength. Well, I don't realize how strong I am …"

"Or how little you have in your head. And they call me knucklehead, scatterbrain, blockhead, and other niceties," Viggo protested.

"Well, you've certainly earned those endearments," Gerd said. "You're not exactly the nicest of people."

"I'll give you that," Viggo admitted, puffing up his chest. "Those of us who are special have that trait."

"Oh yeah, you're special, and aplenty," Gerd laughed, and his guffaw reached Ingrid and Nilsa, who looked back to see what it was all about.

"Nothing to see here, young ladies, proceed…" Viggo said, waving his hands so they would go on.

"They both eyed Viggo with distrust—they knew he was up to something, but they ignored him and went on.

All of a sudden, they heard the sound of thunder tearing the thick clouds in the distance and they all looked up at the sky. The storm was upon them, and the icy winds filled with freezing rain announced its arrival. A huge lightning bolt struck the forest floor behind them, signaling the heavy storm that was about to break upon them.

"It's already upon us!" Lasgol warned Egil.

"We'd better find shelter." Egil pulled up his hood and fastened his cloak, huddling in it.

"I see a mountainous hillside to the east," Astrid said, pointing with her finger through the nearby trees.

"I can see it," Lasgol confirmed. "Let's see if we can find shelter before the storm engulfs us."

She nodded and left the road, heading to the hillside. The rest of the Panthers followed them, assuming they were searching for somewhere to take cover. They kept glancing up at the sky as it got darker and threatened to fall upon them and freeze them, like a furious god seeking to punish any human he encountered.

They reached the mountain side and found a rocky ledge they could huddle under for cover.

"This looks like a good place to wait out the storm," Astrid said.

"Let me explore a little more, I might find a better place," Lasgol said.

"Fine, we'll wait here." Astrid replied.

Lasgol went on with Ona and Camu at his side.

You don't feel the cold, do you?

No cold, Camu's reply reached him.

Ona chirped twice.

Lucky you, he smiled and went on, stepping carefully on the snow. He went around a rocky outcrop, and in the middle of the granite wall that towered above him he saw the entrance to a cave.

We're lucky, he transmitted cheerfully to his friends.

I see if empty, Camu volunteered.

Wait... but it was too late. Camu was already vanishing into the cave, camouflaged.

Lasgol snorted and waited with Ona, who was restless because of the reckless action of her brother.

Empty, the message came and they both relaxed.

They went back to their friends with the news. The storm was beginning to bear down heavily, with icy winds and cutting rain. Thunder and lightning filled a dangerous black sky, the rabid gusts of the winter storm becoming dangerous in the blink of an eye.

Lasgol told the others of their find and shortly after they were all inside the cave. Astrid and Ingrid handled the horses, leading them into the back of the enclosure but facing the large opening so they could see the way out and not get nervous. The girls rubbed them down so they would not be cold and get sick, although Norghanian horses and ponies did well in the cold and storms that plagued the region.

Gerd found some wood that was still dry and Nilsa fetched some relatively dry ferns. They lit a campfire which Egil got going quite easily; he was good with flint and steel and he liked to practice. They soon had a small fire going, which would keep them warm and enable them to spend a pleasant night in their shelter. They both went for more timber and brush to feed the fire during the night. The storm was bearing down heavily, so they had some difficulty finding dry timber.

"Thank goodness we've found this cave, otherwise it would mean being cold and damp out there," Nilsa said when she returned with the last dry branches and bushes in her arms, gesturing outside where the storm was unloading icy rain and wind.

"It doesn't look like a pleasant storm…" Lasgol confirmed, putting his hand out in the open and withdrawing it at once when he felt the bite of the icy water and winter cold the storm was bringing. "I like it when it's only snow, but these icy winter storms, not so much."

"That's because you're a weakling, weirdo," Viggo teased him. He had sat down by the fire and was sharpening his three pairs of knives which he had perfectly lined up in a row on a fine cloth.

"Yeah, as if you were an expert on surviving the frozen woods of the north," Ingrid said as she studied the inside of the cave with a small torch she had just put together.

Viggo watched her going deeper into the cave.

"I must admit it's not my area of expertise. I'm good at action—killing to be precise, surviving in frozen mountains, not so much. The truth is that it's most uncomfortable: the icy cold, the freezing dampness that gets into your bones, and all that cutting wind doesn't exactly thrill me. No, I prefer milder missions."

"Well, you're a Norghanian Ranger. I believe you've mistaken your calling," Egil said with a grin. "Although with the knowledge you've acquired you could go south to the Nocean Empire where it's comfortingly hot and seek out a noble of high birth to lend your services to as an Assassin. It's a profession in high demand among the nobility," he said, now smiling broadly.

"It's *too* hot. That's almost as bad as this. In fact, if you have to cross a desert, I'm convinced it's far worse than this," he said, pointing outside where the storm was growing in intensity, the cold and rain becoming more visible. "You can hide from winter storms and snow, seek shelter, but where do you hide from the scorching sun in an endless desert? And without water to top it off. No, the Nocean Empire is out of the question, not my kind of destination.

What does appeal to me, though, is the Kingdom of Rogdon. The weather there is quite a bit warmer than here, it only rains, and they barely have snow. It's green, with nice prairies and forests. I think I like that better."

"True, the weather there is rainy but warm, and your training adapts well to its forests and mountains. Good choice," said Egil as he rummaged in his bags for something to feed Ginger and Fred.

"There's no danger inside," said Ingrid, who had checked the deepest recesses of the cave. Luckily it was not a deep cave, so she had not needed to go far.

"Camu already checked," Lasgol told her.

"Wonderful. The last thing we need is to stay in a bear cave by accident and run into it," Viggo commented. "Something like that would fit the kind of accidents we stumble into and which, as you all know, we owe to the weirdo. Well, and to the know-it-all who lately has been getting us into more trouble than the weirdo, which is a feat in itself," Viggo protested bitterly.

"Why on earth are you always complaining so much?" Gerd chided him as he put more wood into the fire to keep it going. "You're always claiming you want more action, that you're bored, that your muscles stiffen from lack of use, and a whole bunch of other stuff. You should be glad we have so many accidents, otherwise you'd have already died of boredom with flabby, useless muscles."

Nilsa burst out laughing and choked on the water she was drinking from the water skin.

"What ... a great ... answer!" she said through coughing.

Viggo very funny, Camu messaged to Lasgol.

Lasgol turned to look at his two companions, Camu and Ona, who were lying behind him, resting placidly. Since they were beginning to be considerably big, they now always remained behind the group so as not to interfere with whatever they were doing. Having a full-grown panther and a reptile the size of a lion in the midst of the group made any task difficult. He had explained this to both of the creatures and they had accepted it, although he doubted that they were really aware of their own sizes.

Yes, with Viggo we never lack amusement, Lasgol transmitted back.

I funny too, Camu said.

Yeah, you're a non-stop party.

Ona chirped twice and tilted her head.

Agree.

No way 'agree.' I meant it ironically. Let's see when you begin to understand irony and sarcasm.

Irony not like.

Yeah, because you never get it. You have to start figuring it out.

I understand much.

Sure and you're very well-behaved.

I well-behaved.

Lasgol rolled his eyes and dropped the subject. It was a lost battle. Better to argue another day. He would probably not persuade stubborn Camu of anything, but at least he would try. He stretched back to reach them with his hand and stroked Ona, who chirped with a sound very similar to a kitten's. Since Lasgol was only petting Ona, Camu bowed his head and crawled forward so Lasgol would stroke him as well. Lasgol noticed but made him suffer for a moment, ignoring him. Camu said nothing, but his eyes showed he also wanted to be petted. Lasgol smiled and began to stroke his head. Camu might be stubborn and he was growing in size, but he still behaved much like a baby. Or at least that's what Egil said. His friend studied Camu all the time, writing down in his notebook everything related to Camu's physical, mental, or magical development—the three areas were fascinating to him.

They all sat around the fire to have dinner. They carried Ranger rations made up of salted meat, cured cheese, brown bread, and dried fruits and nuts. It was no banquet, but it nurtured the body and soul, as the Path taught.

"Couldn't we skip this last group and consider our mission accomplished?" Gerd asked. He had finished his ration first; it had not lasted long—he'd gulped, more than eaten, his food.

"No, we can't," Egil replied and gave him part of his ration, since he had more than enough and was aware that the giant needed more food. "If we don't capture this group, we won't have done our duty and we'd always know that. Bad decisions always haunt you in the future. Better to realize and not make them to begin with. Believe me, you'd rue not having captured them."

"I know we have to do our duty, that it's a matter of duty and honor… but you saw what the captain of the guard said when we delivered the last group. They're all going to be executed."

Egil shook his head.

"Don't believe everything they tell you, dear friend."

"No?"

"Thoran wants everyone to think that he is indeed going to hang every Dark Ranger, to the last man. He wants to send a clear message to any possible new conspirator that if you go against the King, you'll lose your life in the attempt."

"Then?" Gerd said blankly.

"He's not going to kill them all," Viggo explained.

"He isn't? Why not?" Now it was Nilsa asking with a puzzled look on her face. She had also thought that all the captured Rangers would be judged for high treason and would end up hanging from a tree or decapitated.

"Because, although it's true that he needs to send a message of having an iron hand," Egil went on, "our King is no fool, and he knows that he can benefit from not killing them. A few of them, the Specialists for instance, he might use for private matters, his and his brother's. Matters he doesn't want to come to the light. Most he will send to the mines and make others believe he's executed them."

"Ohhh, I see," said Gerd. "That's why you offer to pardon their lives and send them to the mines, because you know that's what Thoran's going to do."

"Irrefutable, my dear friend, irrefutable."

"You're a rascal, Egil," Nilsa said with a smile.

Egil smiled but said nothing.

"How about resting a little?" Ingrid suggested. "It would be good to be well rested before facing the last Dark Rangers."

Gerd agreed, stretching his full length. "Perfect."

"I'll take the first watch," Lasgol offered.

"I'll do the second," Astrid said with a wink. Lasgol smiled at her. They would be able to spend a private moment in between watches, as private as possible while being surrounded by their comrades of course.

"Very well, the rest of us will grab the traveling blankets from the horses and huddle by the fire," said Ingrid. "The night's going to be cold with the storm above us."

"I know who I'm going to huddle with…" Viggo said in a playful tone, looking at Ingrid.

"Yes, with Gerd," she said at once in a commanding tone, pointing at the giant.

Nilsa giggled and the rest smiled.

"Oh come on..." Viggo protested. But he followed the order and, after grabbing his blanket, lay down beside Gerd, who was chuckling under his breath.

A while later they were all sleeping. The storm was raging outside, a mixture of freezing blizzards, thunder, lightning, and icy rain. The strength of the wind was impressive, and every now and then it burst into the cave. Lasgol had sat down between Camu and Ona, who radiated warmth as they napped without a care, untroubled by the storm. He watched his comrades. The Snow Panthers were sleeping, huddled by the fire. He felt a pleasant warmth climbing up his body. He wondered what new adventures and dangers were waiting for them in this new stage of their lives.

Chapter 6

With the coming of dawn, the storm started losing strength and it began to snow. Snow was something the Panthers were very much used to and it barely bothered them. In fact, they were grateful it was snowing because in general it was a sign that the worst was over. They left the cave that had sheltered them from the blizzard and, well rested and in good cheer, they continued their journey west.

Ona and Camu, without a doubt, enjoyed the snow the most, and they stayed at the rear of the group, jumping in the snow or trying to catch snowflakes in their mouths. One of Camu's and Ona's favorite activities was to jump into a mound of snow and try to get buried in it. No matter how much Lasgol told them to stop doing it, explaining that they could get hurt hitting a hidden rock, they paid no heed to him. They both seemed to enjoy precisely the possibility of being wrong and falling head first onto a rock.

"How far is it?" Viggo asked toward the front of the party, where Astrid, Lasgol, and Egil smiled at his comment. It was common for Viggo to ask how much farther they still had to go just to mess with them, something he was very good at.

They all turned at once. "Shut up, numbskull!" The reply was followed by ill-disguised laughter.

"You're the worst traveling companions anyone could hope for!" Viggo complained, looking offended and upset. His comrades knew he was pretending, but they kept up the pretense anyway.

"Where would you find better companions than these?" Gerd asked. "There aren't any better to be found in all of Tremia, and you know it. The thing is you're a whiner and a toothache."

"Or companions who'd simply put up with you?" Nilsa added. "I'd bet my hair that you couldn't find a group that would put up with you for more than a week."

Ingrid let out a guffaw. "Yeah, who's going to put up with you with that twisted personality of yours?"

"Just like I said, the worst companions," Viggo went on, shaking the snow off his shoulders in a gesture that as much as said he did not care what they thought.

"We're close," Egil told him, and with that the teasing stopped and they all became a little tense.

At sundown Egil halted.

"We're here," he announced, checking one of his Ranger maps and the snow-covered surroundings. It was still snowing and the sky was overcast, but Egil was skilled at finding their destination even when the weather was bad or visibility scarce.

"Dismount," Ingrid said like an order.

They all did so quickly and scanned the surroundings. They were behind what looked like a snow-covered hill.

"Let's climb the hill and we'll see our target," Egil said.

"Good idea. Gerd, you stay with the horses," Ingrid told him.

"Yes, ma'am, I'll look after them," Gerd said seriously, and they all handed him their horses' reins. He then led the animals to a nearby pinewood, where he tethered them to the trees.

The others began climbing the hill, but before they reached the top, Egil signaled them to get down to the ground to avoid being seen. They crawled up to the top and found themselves looking down on the target.

"That's a bloody fortress!" Viggo said to Egil as he stared at the building eight hundred paces away over an embankment. A river ran before the fortified structure, and to get in through the portcullis first you had to cross a stone bridge over the river.

"You're not going to tell me that the Dark Rangers are hidden inside that fortress, right?" Nilsa said, looking troubled. "It's not that I don't like complicated missions, but taking on a fortress seems a little extreme to me."

"I'm afraid, dear friends, that you're right," Egil said sorrowfully. "This really isn't a fortress per se, it's a square keep built on the rock to defend this valley and it's abandoned. It seems that about twenty Dark Rangers live here now. That's the information I got from Sigurd."

"It has no wall to protect it. It's a great rocky tower with a roof. They'll have archers posted at the top under the snow-covered roof," Astrid said as she watched the keep with narrowed eyes.

"It still looks like a fortress to me, and that complicates things," Nilsa snorted. "If they're Dark Ones they'll be prepared and will be good fighters. Besides, we won't take them by surprise like we did at the tavern. They'll see us coming the moment we go any closer. They must be able to see the whole valley from the top."

"True. Put your heads down so they don't catch us spying," Ingrid told them. "Everyone calm down, we've accomplished more difficult tasks than taking a protected post. This won't be any more difficult than other things we've faced where we ultimately came out victorious. We'll manage as we always do. I know we will."

"What optimism, leadership, and determination my girl has, she's a real chief," Viggo said in a moved tone. And for once he was not joking. He felt that way, and it showed in his voice.

"I'm not your girl, I'm your leader, which is something very different, so behave like an adult. You're acting like a fifteen-year-old," Ingrid scolded, glaring at him.

"And what a character she has. I fall in love with her every day," Viggo smiled with a foolish, lovelorn gaze.

"Later we'll have a long talk, you and I," Ingrid said and showed him her fist threateningly. "Now focus on the mission and forget all that nonsense, smartass."

"Yes, my precious, whatever you say."

Ingrid snorted but said nothing more.

Lasgol used his *Hawk's Eye* skill to study the snow-covered keep. A green flash ran though his head, and with his improved vision he examined the structure and the guards protecting it.

"The keep seems to be in pretty bad condition," he told his comrades lying on the ground beside him. "They've repaired the east and the north walls, but the south and west ones are partly crumbled or propped up so as not to collapse completely. Astrid is right, the top section under the roof is made of wood. It's shaped like a long balcony that goes around the whole keep, and they have watchmen and archers posted there. The roof covers them."

"That makes a surprise attack that much more difficult," Ingrid said.

"Bringing down the archers from a safe distance isn't going to be easy if they're protected by that balcony," Nilsa reasoned.

"We could try at night," Astrid suggested. "We might be able to get in through one of the crumbled sections of the keep before we're discovered."

"Or we might lay siege to them..." Lasgol joined in the suggestions. "Although the weather doesn't help. With all this snow the Fire Arrows are no good, and we wouldn't be able to attack the roof or lay siege properly."

"Let the know-it-all think up a plan. I bet he was already scheming as we were traveling," Viggo interrupted, looking questioningly at Egil.

"Let me think about it a little. The options you've mentioned are interesting, but they all pose big enough problems," he commented as he analyzed the situation with eyes half shut. "For the moment, start preparing Elemental Arrows, as many as you can. And long-range too."

"Fine," Ingrid said and signaled Nilsa to follow her. The others backed down, leaving Egil alone to watch the keep in the middle of the valley, wondering how best to take it without having any casualties.

They began to prepare the Arrows. Ingrid and Nilsa were the experts, so they got started. Since they could not let them get wet, they had to put up a Ranger's tent and work inside, placing the components they kept in their belts on a blanket to be able to manipulate them. Elemental Arrows could not be made in the open. You needed a workshop to do it. What they could transport though were the Elemental Arrow tips, already made, and finish completing the loading and assembly process whenever they were needed. This is what Nilsa and Ingrid were doing now, both intensely focused because it was difficult work.

On the other hand, Viggo and Astrid started preparing their Assassin weapons and poisons. Astrid, in particular, had a good variety of toxic substances with different functions. Viggo preferred direct combat and he was not so interested in poisons, although he carried the usual ones the Ranger Assassins used.

Attack keep? Camu asked Lasgol, who was also checking his weapons and equipment beside Trotter.

Yes, it looks as if we'll have to take the keep. It isn't going to be easy.

Ona growled restlessly.

Keep difficult?

Yes, difficult enough. It's not just the keep, it's that it's very well protected and by Rangers, which makes it doubly difficult.

I understand. We can.

Lasgol smiled. *I knew you'd say that.*

We good.

I know that, but you have to learn that no matter how good we are, every

57

situation presents difficulties we must solve. We can't lunge headlong against them. It would end badly. Really badly.

Wounded?

Or dead.

Ona moaned and shook her head, clearly unhappy.

Dead bad.

Yeah, and that's why we have to think before we act. We can't launch an attack as if we were invincible, because we're not.

We not?

Camu's doubt left Lasgol puzzled. It made him think twice. Ever since he had had Camu, they had managed to solve any situation, no matter how adverse, and come out victorious… or at least they had survived and the Panthers had never suffered any losses. Because of this, Camu seemed to believe that they were almost invincible. Just thinking about it made him shudder. He had to make it clear they were not invincible, that they might die at any moment if they got distracted or made a mistake.

We're not invincible. How many times have I been wounded?

A few…

Exactly. If I were invincible, I wouldn't have been wounded. And going from being wounded to being dead is only a step further. You can't think that we're not going to die, because we can, at any moment.

Ona moaned again mournfully—she was not liking this talk at all.

Any moment?

Yes. You must face situations taking into account that we might die. It can happen to any of us in the middle of a mission, no matter how insignificant or dangerous it might appear at the beginning. Accidents can always happen, unexpected situations that take us by surprise and bring us to a sudden end …

Not want to die, Camu transmitted with a feeling of deep sorrow and tenderness.

Lasgol sighed. Poor Camu. There still were many things he did not understand. Death was one of them. He really was a child in a body that was growing faster than his mind. Because he was so mischievous and daring, Lasgol had actually forgotten that he was only a pup, of whatever kind he was. And no, he was no dragon cub. Of that Lasgol was sure.

Egil took a long time to come back down, and by the time he did, they were all ready to begin the assault on the keep. It had its difficulties, they could all see that, but they trusted Egil to think up a plan that would bring them victory without losing anyone. This was easier said than done, but they all trusted Egil would come up with something. What started to worry them was when their friend said nothing. He kept silent and seemed to be lost in thought, standing before the group that watched him expectantly.

"What have you come up with?" Viggo broke the silence. "Which of our strategies do you find more convincing?"

Egil looked up and opened his eyes wide.

"Really, all of them," he admitted.

"What d'you mean 'all of them'?" Viggo asked, raising his eyebrows.

"They're all plausible theories, and I believe the key to taking that keep is to use them all. Yes, I think that's the approach that gives us the greatest probability of success and, therefore, the one we ought to adopt."

"All of them?" Ingrid asked blankly. "How are we going to use them all?"

"In conjunction," Egil smiled as if what he was proposing were as easy as child's play.

"That means all the strategies at once?" Nilsa asked. She had taken her gloves off and was frantically biting her nails from nerves.

"Exactly," Egil confirmed, nodding.

"All at the same time? Sounds somewhat crazy, doesn't it?" Gerd asked, scratching the top of his head which he had covered with his hood to protect himself from the falling snow.

"Sometimes the craziest plans turn out to be the most sensible and lead to the final victory," Egil said.

"We're going to need to clarify this plan of yours," Lasgol said, trying to rationalize what his friend was proposing and not fully succeeding, "because right now it sounds pretty confusing to the rest of us."

"Yeah, sure, of course," Egil said, smiling broadly and nodding repeatedly. "Let's see, we'll begin with a small siege …"

"We're starting badly," Viggo interrupted him at once. "How are we going to lay siege to a keep without an army or siege weapons?" he protested, waving his arms.

"There are always ways. We don't need a whole army, but an ingenious group with extraordinary skills. That's us," Egil replied with a roguish grin.

"Sure, we're ingenious…" Viggo protested, "and don't get me started on skills…"

"Go on, Egil, don't pay any attention to this melon-head," Nilsa intervened, watching him with great interest.

"The siege will require shooting the watchmen from a distance," Egil explained, looking at Ingrid and Nilsa—he expected them to carry this part out.

Ingrid nodded, confirming this with the self-assurance and pride of someone who knows they're very good at their job and has the necessary ability to perform the job required.

"You carry longbows, right?" Egil asked them.

"Yes, one each. I told Nilsa we should bring them just in case. And what do you know, we're going to use them. Besides, I have with me Punisher, Swift, and Spot-On."

"I carry the composite and the short bow, they're the typical Ranger bows. I must warn you that I'm no good with the long one Ingrid lent me," she admitted and blushed, ashamed.

"I thought I'd seen them on your horses," Egil nodded. "We'll need them. And don't worry, Nilsa, look at it this way, you'll have a chance to improve by practicing in a real combat situation," he smiled at her to lessen the tension.

"Thanks for the support, but I'm still not at ease…" she replied, balancing from one foot to the other, unable to stay still she was so nervous.

Ingrid put a hand on her shoulder to calm her and so she would stop moving.

"I'll do what I can…" she said with a shrug and her eyes on the ground, quite unsure of herself.

"Fantastic," Egil went on. "When night falls, we'll make a nocturnal incursion on the keep, and there we'll put the finishing touches on the mission if everything goes according to plan."

"Viggo and I will do that," Astrid said determinedly.

"Hey, don't volunteer me," Viggo waved his arms and took a step back.

"Why are you complaining when it's always you saying how you lack action and are bored to tears," Astrid retorted.

"Well, yeah, but I meant a couple of fights here and there, for fun, not taking a blasted well-protected keep. That goes over the fun line and falls into the insane category. Doing crazy things isn't my cup of tea."

"Well, it's your lot, so you shut up. See if you could learn not to be so cocky, because when push comes to shove, the first difficulty we encounter makes you cringe," Ingrid chided, cutting out his protests.

"I don't cringe at anything. I'll go into those ruins and I won't leave a single Dark Ranger standing," Viggo replied, offended. "A cocky fighting rooster, that's me," he stated and beat his chest with his fist before imitating the crow of a rooster.

Everyone laughed at the joke except Ingrid, who rolled her eyes and hid her face in her hands.

"You're hopeless."

"Yes, my precious," he smiled at her, all charm.

"Wonderful then," Egil said, clapping his hands together. "We'll use that approach and follow the plan I've thought out. Everything will come out right. I hope."

"Wouldn't it be better to go to the nearest big city and ask for help from the City Guard or even the king's army and let them lay the siege and take the keep? That way we save ourselves this mess and move on to better things," Gerd asked all of a sudden, after having been thoughtful and quiet for quite a while.

"Yeah, that could be a good idea. The army will deal with them," Nilsa nodded.

"I thought about that," said Egil. "The thing is that when we call upon the Guard, the army, or both, there will be a lot of noise, and that noise will reach the keep."

"What noise?" Gerd asked with his head to one side.

"Gossip," Ingrid explained. "When the army moves it generates all kinds of rumors, and most likely someone from this group is currently in the city and would find out, or they might have paid informants to warn them of something like that."

"Exactly," Egil agreed. "By the time we laid siege to the keep, its occupants would have already fled."

"Well then, that plan is no good," Nilsa reasoned.

"I think we can do it ourselves," Astrid said confidently, looking nonchalant.

"Of course we can," Ingrid agreed and winked at her. Astrid smiled back.

"Sometimes you scare me with all that confidence you exude, it's infectious," Viggo said appreciatively.

"Then we go back to the original plan, right?" Lasgol guessed. "I agree that we can succeed if we plan in detail and don't take any more risks than absolutely necessary. Act carefully and be prepared for any eventuality."

"Yes, we go back to the initial plan," Ingrid said. "Gerd's suggestion wasn't bad, but it's not feasible."

"Fantastic, let me explain the details. Lasgol, we'll need Camu's and Ona's help," Egil said, waving at them. They both stood at attention at once.

"Okay. Let's hear those details," Lasgol said.

Egil started to explain what they had to do in detail.

Chapter 7

By early evening everything was ready. Egil went over the details once more and gathered them all around to give them final instructions.

"Okay, it's time to begin the siege," he said. "Be very careful and follow the plan. Try not to improvise too much," he warned them, "deviations from the original plan are usually costly."

"If we get into the kind of big trouble we usually do, I swear I'll start improvising like crazy," Viggo told him.

"You stick to the plan and don't do anything foolish," Ingrid ordered him in a scolding tone, but with clear signs of concern. "We're not going to bury you here today because of another reckless act of yours we don't want to witness."

"No burying me," Viggo replied, shaking his head. "Someone as remarkable as me deserves a funeral at sea. Lay out my body in a Norghanian assault ship, set it on fire, and send me to the ocean. That's how I see myself going to the realm of the Ice Gods."

"You're more and more hopeless every day," Nilsa said, shaking her head. "Crazy as a loon."

Gerd was covering his face with a large hand and shaking his head too.

"But I don't feel like dying today. It's a perfect day for a bit of entertainment under the snow, so don't worry," Viggo smiled from ear to ear and spread his hands so the snowflakes would land on them.

"I'm glad you don't feel like dying today," Lasgol told him, slapping his shoulder. "I don't feel like you dying at all. My life would become very dull if that happened."

"That's for sure!" Viggo laughed and Lasgol joined him.

"Everybody ready?" Egil asked his friends, looking into their eyes.

"Ready," Ingrid confirmed while she watched the others arm and otherwise equip themselves for the taking of the keep.

"Fantastic. Let's go," Egil said, climbing onto his horse.

"Be careful," Lasgol begged him. "What you're going to do is extremely risky, even more than usual…"

"I will, don't worry about me. I've calculated the risk. Everything will come out according to plan. Take your positions and await my signal."

They all nodded, and Ingrid handed Egil the improvised flag they had made, furled around a stick.

Egil took it and left. He headed to the keep. The others ran to their positions, loaded with the equipment they were going to need for the operation. Lasgol signaled Camu and Ona and they followed him at once.

Egil advanced slowly under the winter snow that kept falling from an overcast sky. There was no threat of a blizzard though. He was following the path that led to the keep; the men at the bulwark must have already seen him, since he was the only figure in sight in the whole valley. The Panthers were taking a long detour to position themselves on both sides of the keep without being seen. Crossing a snow-covered valley without being spotted by the watchmen in a fortress at the center of it was quite complicated to achieve. But, Egil knew that his comrades would do it. They were all wearing winter-white hooded cloaks, which would help them blend into the snow-covered surroundings.

The forest north and east of the keep would also help cover their advance. The most exposed area was south, and that was where Egil was at that moment. It was not feasible to approach from the southern route without being seen, so he had opted to use this fact as a distraction. Nothing like a ruse for things to go well. That played a major role in their chance for success, of any plan he had ever conceived—fooling the enemy, confounding them to gain an advantage. That was what he was about to try now. He hoped it would work.

He reached the long stretch of road that led to the bridge which crossed the river before the keep. He stopped and scanned the bulwark. He was out of shooting range, so for now he was safe. But he *was* within sighting range, and the occupants were no doubt watching him, wondering what on earth he was doing there, why he was standing under the steadily falling snow. It was cold, though not too much, and the wind, the deadliest enemy in winter, was not blowing hard, so he could bear the snowfall without trouble. And although he was not as strong and large as the average Norghanian, that did not mean he could not bear the cold as well as anybody else in the realm.

He huddled in his hooded winter cloak, took out the flag, and unfurled it. It was a white banner they had just made, and he lifted it high so it would be fully visible from the keep. It was the international sign for parley or surrender, depending on the situation. The wind blew the flag above Egil's head; the Dark Ones could see it perfectly well. He waited to see if it worked. He imagined them wondering what he was doing there with the flag. It was not an aggressive action per se, but it might be taken as such. A white flag implied conflict, and the Dark Ones would want to know what it was. Besides, it indicated that he knew they were hiding there, and they were not going to like that.

He did not have to wait long. The portcullis of the keep rose and a rider crossed the bridge in his direction. The distraction was working; while everyone in the keep was looking his way, his friends would hopefully be reaching their positions unseen. It was still too soon to be sure, but Egil hoped they would not encounter trouble.

The rider reached Egil and stopped five paces away. It was without a doubt a Ranger. He was dressed and armed like one, a strong, weathered man. A veteran, over fifty, closer to sixty, with a silver mane under his hood and gray eyes that were looking at Egil from head to toe.

"I know who you are," he said hoarsely. "You're one of the Olafstone, the youngest."

"That's right," Egil confirmed with a nod. "Who do I have the pleasure of speaking to?"

The veteran was thoughtful. Recognizing Egil had considerably taken him aback.

"Does it matter? If you're Egil Olafstone you're with the Rangers, the Royal Eagles from what I've heard. That means you've found us, you know who we are, and you're here to hunt us down and take us to Thoran."

"It matters to me, and yes, your guess is absolutely right."·

The veteran shook his head.

"It was bound to happen sooner or later. Pity it isn't later," he said with regret. "My name is Henerik Maltheson."

"A pleasure to meet you. These aren't the best of circumstances, it's true, but I believe we can reach an agreement. If you and your people at the keep surrender, there will be no need for bloodshed."

"And you think we'll surrender and come with you simply because you ask nicely?" Henerik asked sarcastically.

"One can always hope …"

"Well, that's not going to happen. We won't surrender. I don't intend to give Thoran the pleasure of hanging me in the main square."

"It doesn't need to be that way. I can offer you forced labor in the mines if you surrender quietly."

Henerik laughed hoarsely. His laughter was sincere.

"At my age I wouldn't survive forced labor for long. No, I'm going to pass on that offer, and none of those with me will take it either. We won't surrender."

"Sorry to hear that… I would've preferred a peaceful solution to this."

The veteran shrugged.

"Once certain lines are crossed, as is our case, there's no looking back. We made the decision to become Dark Rangers and we must face the consequences."

"May I ask what made a reasonable man like you make that decision? I find it hard to understand."

Henerik smiled ruefully.

"In my case it was the gold. At my age all one thinks about is retiring and enjoying what's left of life in style. That wasn't going to be the case with a Ranger's pay, if I ever reached retirement. I was nearly killed in my last mission before I turned to the Dark Rangers. Age and a desire to live well in my last years rather than dying in a mission or retiring with a miserable pension made me decide."

Egil nodded. "I understand. I thought it might have been because of Thoran, but your reasons are something I can understand, although I don't share them."

"Don't get me wrong, I hate Thoran as much as everyone, but that's not something that keeps me awake. Norghana's had bad kings for a long time, and that's not something that's about to change. This bad king will be followed by another one equally bad, or worse."

"Perhaps, but let's hope not. If it's within my power, I'll try to make sure there's a good king after Thoran who will lead a strong Norghana."

"Good luck with that."

"Yeah, I'm going to need it."

Henerik glanced around. "I understand you're not alone. Where are your comrades, the rest of the Eagles?"

"Taking up positions in case I don't manage to persuade you," Egil replied casually.

"You're not going to persuade me. The solution to this situation is the hard way. I appreciate the attempt, but you haven't succeeded. We must take risks in this life. This may be the last one I take, but I'll take it nonetheless. I'll withdraw. If you want to take us you know where we are."

Egil saluted him with a slight nod.

Henerik turned his horse round and galloped back to the keep—he knew they were going to be attacked and he wanted to prepare the defense.

"Pity…" Egil said regretfully under his breath, and he started waving the flag up and down. He did it for a few moments to make sure all his friends saw the signal.

Then he dismounted and got his bow ready for combat.

The first fight was not long in coming. A big arrow from a longbow flew to the upper part of the keep from the east. It was followed by one from the west. The two archers could not be seen because they remained concealed and at a distance which the archers from the keep could not match, unless they had equally long bows, which was not common among Rangers. Bows that size were difficult to wield and uncomfortable to carry, so they were not commonly used. The composite bow was what all Rangers carried with them, unless they were on a special mission that specifically required longer ones.

The arrows reached the upper part of the keep. The tips broke on impact and there were small flashes followed by discharges that caused arcs as they bounced off the metallic parts of the rivets and protections. They were Air Arrows. Ingrid and Nilsa had made large ones for the longbow with the components of the Air Arrows, which was uncommon since Elemental Arrows were only used with composite and short bows. The watchmen out on the balcony crouched, covering their heads. Several even leapt to one side to protect themselves from the arcs that were spreading along the upper part of the iron railing.

The Dark Ones aimed at the spot where the arrows had come from. They shot composite bows, and even with the height advantage, they did not manage to reach the archers. Nilsa and Ingrid were already nocking new arrows to punish the balcony and roof of the keep. This time they used Earth Arrows. Their intention was not so much to hit their opponents, which at that distance and with longbows was highly unlikely, but to keep them busy. The arrows broke against the inside of the balcony, and again the Dark Ones were forced to quickly move out of their path.

Nilsa's and Ingrid's punishment on the keep was not demolishing, but it was effective. Ingrid even managed to hit one of the Dark Ones before night came, which was a real feat. The defenders would not abandon the fortification if they were as smart as Egil expected. But, as with all plans, sometimes things did not turn out as you hoped they would, no matter how logically and reasonably they had been planned. From one of the repaired battlements, three Dark Ones let themselves down on ropes. At a crouch and under the cover of night that was already falling, they headed to Ingrid's position. Three others did the same on the other side and headed toward Nilsa to kill her.

The plan was beginning to flounder. This was not the move they had expected the Dark Ones to make. Or, was this a strategy of Henerik's upon discovering who he was up against? Had he opted to avoid a siege and instead act swiftly to take them by surprise? Whatever it was, they would have to adapt their original plan to the situation.

The three Dark Ones advancing on Ingrid's position moved fast on the snow that covered the land. They were unquestionably Rangers—it was clear by the way they moved and the ease with which they traveled over the rough terrain. They were armed with composite bows and would soon be within shooting range to bring down Ingrid.

The same was happening on Nilsa's side. The Dark Ones were rapidly closing in on her over the snow and almost had her within range. The redhead was nocking the arrow she was going to release at the keep on her longbow. She raised it and drew the string; she calculated the arc it needed to reach the upper part of the structure and was about to release when she glimpsed movement in the shadows before her. She aimed her bow in that direction, glimpsed a figure— the first of the three attackers—and released without hesitation. The figure, armed as well, raised his bow to release at her. Nilsa's arrow caught him right in the chest with such force that he fell backwards as the Earth Arrowhead broke.

"I'm under attack!" Nilsa cried and threw herself on the snow to her right. Two arrows brushed past her body.

The two Dark Ones moved in swiftly to finish her. Nilsa was crawling through the snow as fast as she could, looking for a nearby tree to hide behind to avoid the two archers. She reached the tree and went around it. It was a relatively thick oak, so she was able to conceal herself behind its trunk. She drew her knife and axe. She was panting. She knew she had to control her breathing and nerves. The two Dark Ones would come around both sides of the tree most likely. She would have to hurl herself at the first one and hope that the second one would miss. It was too much to hope for, but she had no choice. If she tried to get away with them so close, they would bury two arrows in her back before she reached the next tree. And if she revealed herself to fight she would get an arrow in her chest. Getting one of them with the longbow had been an awesome feat, or good luck, but she would not repeat it—Nilsa was painfully aware of that.

She relaxed her breathing and managed to calm down and overcome her initial fear, then prepared to act. She heard a soft sound to her right, as if someone had stepped on a branch under the snow. She took a deep breath, flexed her knees, grasped her weapons hard, and came out from behind the tree toward the origin of the sound. She met one of the attackers who, seeing her, corrected his aim to her heart. Nilsa knew she would not get to him in time, so she lunged forward on the ground. The arrow brushed her head. She was two hands away from the Dark One, who dropped his bow, drawing his knife and axe in one smooth motion.

Nilsa wanted to get up to fight, but she knew that if she did, the other archer would get her. She was half buried in the snow, and that had saved her. Once she left the protection of the snow she would be lost. Unfortunately, if she did not defend herself, she would be too. She looked up and saw that her opponent was going to strike with his axe; she saw it coming down and rolled to one side, the axe hitting the ground. The attacker raised his axe to strike again and from her position on the ground she hit the man's supporting leg's ankle with her right foot as forcefully as she was able. She felt the jolt in her own leg and clenched her jaw, then saw her attacker loose his balance and miss the blow with his axe. She took the chance to strike him again with her other leg, but this time the Dark One saw it coming and lifted his leg. Nilsa missed. She was left awkwardly positioned, and her attacker jumped on her. They both rolled on the snow, fighting.

The Dark Ranger tried to bury his knife in her heart, but Nilsa blocked his arm with her axe. The man's axe sought her face and she blocked it with her knife. The Dark One was on top of her, using his weight to deflect her blocks and kill her. She was holding the man up, her teeth clenched, with all the nerve and strength she could muster.

"You're not... going to... kill me..." she muttered, more to herself than to him.

At that moment Nilsa saw a figure behind the Dark One; it was his partner. She felt her heart skip a beat—now she had no escape. But suddenly, the Dark Ranger stopped pressing her. Nilsa freed her weapons and was about to bury her knife in his side when he fell on top of her, unconscious. Nilsa pushed him off her and the figure was revealed.

"I almost didn't get here in time," a feminine voice said.

"Astrid!" she cried, recognizing her. "And the other Dark One?"

"Don't worry, I surprised him from behind when he was coming to finish you off."

"Phew...." Nilsa whistled in relief. "Thank goodness you came to my aid!"

"I realized something was amiss. I saw them come down the ropes, but I was far away. I came running as soon as I noticed."

"Well, you saved my skin, Thank you!"

"Oh it's nothing, I save you today, you save me tomorrow," Astrid winked.

Nilsa smiled and stood up with the brunette's help.

"Let's tie and gag these."

"Right, hey..." Nilsa put her hands to her head. "Will Ingrid be all right? If I was attacked, she must have been too."

"I don't know..."

On the opposite side, where Ingrid had been shooting from, an

70

odd combat was taking place. Three Dark Rangers with composite bows were trying to bring down Ingrid, who was armed with her short bow, *Swift*. From her waist hung the tiny one: *Punisher*. She had gone into a beech wood when she glimpsed three attackers coming at her.

"You'll regret having gone over to the Dark Rangers," she told them from behind a thick tree, two arrows buried themselves in the trunk. Ingrid took a quick glance and saw the exposed leg of one of the attacking Rangers. It was a difficult shot but it was worth trying. If she maimed him she would have an advantage. She nocked a regular arrow and counted to three. She poked half her body out from behind the tree and was about to release when she discovered a second archer aiming at her from her left and a little behind. If she released, she would have no time to get back behind the tree and the Dark One would hit her. She hid again. The arrow brushed past her shoulder. She immediately ducked back out, since she had a moment before the archer nocked again. She aimed at the leg of the other Dark One and released.

"Argh!" she heard the wounded man cry as he withdrew his leg.

Ingrid hid herself behind the tree. An arrow hit the side she had released from.

"Drop your weapons and come out with your hands behind your head!" she told them. "Or I'll kill you all!"

"You'll try, but you won't succeed," a voice to her left said.

Ingrid poked half a face out in the direction of the voice. She could not see the Dark One or his footprints in the snow because it was too dark, but at least she had an approximate idea of where he was. She changed bows and took out *Punisher*. She nocked a short arrow—arrows for this tiny bow were a lot shorter. They deviated at more than ten paces, but at this close range they were fine.

"Oh, I assure you I will."

"We'll see about that," the same voice said on her left. He had to be about three trees from her own position. She decided to go for him. Using a distraction maneuver, she flung *Swift* to the right of her position and at once three arrows flew to the spot where the bow had fallen on the snow. Ingrid came out from behind the left of the tree where she was hiding and saw the shoulder of the Dark One as he took cover behind another tree. He was four trees away. Ingrid sprinted on the snow—she had to reach him before the other two saw her. She dodged the first three trees that separated her from the Dark One, but the archer on the right saw her.

"Beware, Carlson! She's coming after you!"

Carlson came out from behind his tree with his weapon armed, but he was too late. He was met by Ingrid, who let her arrow fly. It hit the man's hand and his bow fell to the ground as he cried out in pain. His own arrow flew to one side and buried itself in the snow. Before he could recover from the pain, Ingrid reached his side and delivered a powerful right punch with all the inertia of her run; he was knocked out and fell backwards.

An arrow flew two fingers away from her side. It was the Dark One whose leg she had wounded. She went after him, zigzagging through the trees. The wounded man came out from behind the tree where he was hiding and tried to get Ingrid. He missed. His arrow fell two hands away from where she had swerved. He dropped his bow and drew a knife, but he did not have time to use it. Ingrid's arrow buried itself in his shoulder. He cursed under his breath as Ingrid reached his side and knocked him unconscious with a blow from her elbow to his temple.

There was only one archer left. Ingrid was surprised she had not seen him release as she approached the wounded Dark One. Warily, she went over to the position he had been releasing from. With lightning-fast reflexes, she slid sideways and passed the tree to discover the archer. She was about to release but did not do it. The archer was sitting against the tree, unconscious.

"I saved you the trouble of this one," a voice said.

Ingrid raised her gaze and saw Viggo up in the tree smiling nonchalantly.

"What are you doing here?"

"Helping correct this little deviation from Egil's plan."

"I didn't need your help."

"Well, just in case, I came to help."

Ingrid thought about it for a moment. "You made the right choice. They could've surprised me."

"That's what I thought. Besides, what kind of a boyfriend would I be if I did not come to the aid of my precious girl?" he said, all charm, beaming.

"Don't call me your girlfriend," Ingrid said, annoyed.

"Or my precious girl?" he said, his eyes bright.

"We'll talk about that later," she replied, a little weakened by Viggo's words. "This isn't the time or the place."

"Absolutely, my Blondie."

Ingrid muttered curses under her breath and shook her head.

"Let's tie and gag them. The plan goes forward."

"Okay. This is going to get interesting fast," he commented, a lethal gleam in his eyes.

Chapter 8

The next stage of the plan—which starred Ona, Camu, and Lasgol—now began in the darkness and silence of the night. They had placed themselves on the north side of the keep and were waiting for their signal. They were quite restless since they would have to act alone, without the cover of the rest of the group.

Everything's going to go well. Ready, Camu? Lasgol asked, with the added intention of instilling him with calm and confidence.

Ready, his friend messaged with a mixed feeling of joy and nervousness before the impending action.

Use your power to camouflage yourself and Ona.

Okay.

Lasgol felt a slight tingling at the back of his neck, which meant there was magic at hand. Camu had already activated his camouflage skill.

You can, can't you? Lasgol asked him to make sure. Camu tended to exaggerate everything he could do, both physically and magically.

Yes, I can, Camu assured.

Yeah, you always say you can do everything, but this is important. If you don't make all three of us invisible, whoever they see from the top of that keep will end up riddled with arrows. They're good with bows; remember, there are Rangers among them.

Only three, I can. Easy.

What do you mean 'easy'? As far as I remember you could only make yourself and one other person invisible.

I practice, skill improve, Camu explained proudly.

You've improved? In range of action or length?

Range. Reach more in a circle.

Wow... Lasgol was thoughtful, trying to understand what the creature was transmitting.

Yes, I can.

Then, can you camouflage everyone within a circle around you? Is that what you're trying to tell me? Or have I misunderstood?

Sure. I can, Camu insisted.

Wow, that's wonderful! Why did you not tell me? Lasgol transmitted, somewhat disappointed and hurt for not having been informed.

You very busy.

Yes… that's true… but well, for something as important as this I can always find time… Lasgol felt a pang of regret for not having paid more attention to Camu in the past weeks. Lately, with everything that had happened and then the mission to capture the last Dark Rangers, he had barely had time to be with Camu and Ona. He would have to make an effort to spend more time with them alone. When they were all together it was difficult to pay them the necessary attention because a thousand things were always happening at the same time.

Ona help, Camu told him.

Very well done, Ona, Lasgol transmitted to her and patted her on the side.

Ona chirped once.

She not like magic, but help.

How did she help you? I'm intrigued. How could she?

She stand in places, I try to reach Ona with power. First no succeed, then try harder. Not either. Then try more, no. Then keep trying. Trying many days, in the end succeed.

Lasgol was speechless—they were working together and learning together. It was something both incredible and beautiful. Not only that, it was smart. Camu had realized he needed to improve the range of his power and had enlisted his sister's help. It was simply amazing.

It's fantastic. Great work, you two, Lasgol said, petting them with extra affection. He was so proud he couldn't conceal it.

We great work, Camu messaged. Extremely happy and at the same time proud, he strained his neck and lifted his head to show it. Ona, seeing him, put her paw on his head and pushed him down. Camu tilted his head and eyed her, annoyed. Ona put her paw on his head in that unique feline way and pushed his head down again. Camu had to yield and bow his head.

Lasgol realized what she was doing and chuckled, covering his mouth so Camu would not see him. It was charming, how both worked together so well. He was grateful for their teamwork.

They heard the hoot of an owl three times in a familiar cadenza. It was the signal. It was time to act.

Come on, it's our turn, Lasgol told his two friends.

They began to approach the keep from the northern side. The watchmen were busy on the east and western sides where Ingrid and

Nilsa had been attacking the upper section and the defensive balconies. The northern side was not as closely watched. Although they were camouflaged by Camu's magic, Lasgol worried about the trail they were leaving in the snow. They were invisible, but their footprints were not. Luckily, in the middle of the night and from the top of the keep which was not well lit, the trail was not too discernible. Even so, Lasgol stopped every few paces to muddle their tracks. The less risk they took the better, even while using magic. Lasgol was cautious—life had taught him that lesson early. Magic had limitations and a price, and one could not always be sure it would work.

They arrived at the stone wall of the north section without incident. Lasgol felt the damp rock and sought the edge of the snow on the wall. Careful not to make any noise, he left his satchel on the snow-covered ground and took out the first trap he had prepared for the attack.

He looked up to see whether there were watchmen directly above them on the balcony and saw one walk past. He stood still. The Dark One could not see them because Camu's magic cloaked them, but even so, Lasgol waited for the man to go by. The odds of being discovered were low, but he wanted to reduce them further by not making the slightest sound that might draw attention.

Once the watchman had disappeared around the corner, Lasgol placed the trap on the wall. He fastened it with an especially strong sticky resin he had made. Eyra had taught them how to make it at the Camp. He found it ironic that now he was going to use it against her—or against her own, since Eyra was no longer among the living but in the realm of the Ice Gods.

He placed the second trap right beside the first one. He could not see Ona or Camu but he felt them beside him, expectant. It was funny that, within the circle of Camu's camouflage, not only could nobody see them from the outside, but they also could not see anybody inside the area covered by Camu's magic. Once again Lasgol marveled at how singular and precious magic was, both his and Camu's. Egil would surely have an explanation for it; Lasgol would have to ask him once they finished this mission. The various forms of magic he was discovering amazed him, and he hoped he would discover many more forms of it—both in himself and in Camu, as well as any other kinds of magic existing in Tremia of which he still knew nothing about. Surely they must be fantastic and interesting as well.

He carefully scanned their surroundings, but everything seemed calm. Night covered everything around them, the snow breaking up the darkness. Lasgol placed the third trap on the wall, using the remaining resin and putting it to the right of the first trap. After checking them, he decided they were well set.

Taking a deep breath, he concentrated, using his *Trap Hiding* skill on the wall to make the three traps vanish from sight. The watchmen would likely not see them, it being such a dark night, but he used his skill as an extra precaution.

Come along, I've already placed the traps, he told his two partners.

Camu messaged back*, Okay.*

We'll follow the wall to the west. Hug the wall, Lasgol told them, and they traveled silently. He stopped several times to blur their tracks in the snow. They turned the corner and went on. Lasgol scanned the wall for the best place to carry out the last part of their task—at last he found the spot.

We're here. Stay still until I tell you.

Yes, still, Camu messaged back.

Ona did not growl or chirp, but she put her paw on Lasgol's leg as a "yes."

It'll be ready soon, he messaged as he removed a black rope from his satchel, which he uncoiled. He had added a grappling hook to the end of the rope. Straightening, he examined the section of wall that had not been fully repaired. He calculated the launch and thought it feasible. Maybe not on the first throw, but with a couple of attempts he could do it. He left the rope and hook on the ground covered with snow and grabbed his composite bow.

It's time, he announced to Ona and Camu.

Ready, Camu transmitted, along with a feeling of joy and excitement for what was going to happen next. Ona put her paw on his leg and remained tense, her feline instincts alert, which always happened when the situation became dangerous.

Lasgol put his hands to his mouth and called out like an owl. He tried to make it sound as close to a royal owl as possible. In the keep there were Rangers who would be able to identify whether the hoot was some kind of signal. Egil had foreseen that though; the only difference was the last note, which would be higher pitched so they knew it was Lasgol and not a real royal owl. With a bit of luck, the defenders would not realize it was a signal. So Lasgol imitated a royal owl to the best of his abilities—and thought it came out quite realistic.

Let's go to the corner, he told his two friends.

They moved along to where the west wall joined the north. Lasgol aimed his bow, waited the stipulated time, and finally released.

The arrow flew to the three traps on the wall. The shot was poor—he missed, and Lasgol cursed under his breath. It was not a particularly difficult shot, but it was not easy either. In other words, he should be able to hit the target. He still had some time, so he took it slowly and activated his *Hawk's Sight* skill to see the traps clearly. Then he concentrated and called upon his *True Shot* skill, which took a while to activate and which he usually could not use in combat because it gave others time to hit him while it activated. The green flash that indicated magic ran through his arms and bow after a short while, although it seemed like an eternity to Lasgol. He released. The arrow flew straight and hit the trap in the middle. There was a light burst since he had used an Earth Arrow, and an instant later the trap exploded with a big bang. It was a Fire trap. At once the other two traps on either side of the first also exploded into great flames.

That's it, withdraw! Lasgol told his two partners.

They went back to their previous position, and Lasgol uncovered the rope and prepared to throw it. He made a first attempt to calculate the trajectory and the hook hit the wall below a crack halfway up that had not been fully repaired.

The watchmen's cries of alarm after the traps had exploded reached him, and he looked in that direction. He could not see them since they were on the north wall, around the corner, but he guessed they were looking for their attackers near the site of the explosion. The traps could not penetrate rock—they were not that powerful— but they were going to attract a lot of attention, which was the intention.

He tried launching the grappling hook again, and this time he was far more accurate—it nearly gained purchase. The watchmen were trying to deduce what had happened on the other wall, a column of black smoke climbing the wall from the Fire traps' explosions.

Lasgol tried once again, and this time he managed to hook the opening in the wall. A feeling of joy filled his chest at succeeding.

I'm going to climb, he told Ona and Camu.

I with you. Ona retreat, Camu transmitted along with a protective feeling, which touched Lasgol to the core.

Okay. Ona, withdraw carefully and lie low, Lasgol told Ona; he had no time to haul the panther up.

The big cat put her paw on Lasgol's leg and then crawled back along the snow. At night, and with her white fur which blended into the snow, nobody would see her. Besides, the Dark Rangers were too focused on the north wall, attempting to discover the source of the explosion.

He signaled Camu to follow and began climbing with the help of the rope. Camu went up beside him, clinging to the wall with his adhesive feet and climbing like a squirrel so well that Lasgol did not need to worry.

Can you maintain my camouflage? Lasgol asked Camu, who had been using his magic for quite a while to cloak both of them.

I can, came the creature's confident reply; Lasgol figured the response was based more on stubbornness than an accurate guess.

Are you sure you can? Your skill has been activated for quite some time now, and covering two people must be consuming more of your inner energy…

I can, I think… the creature replied uncertainly.

I assumed as much. See if you can conceal me at least until I climb through the opening in the keep.

Okay, Camu agreed, although this did not necessarily mean he would be able to.

Lasgol reached the opening in the wall and looked inside carefully. He saw one watchman with his bow ready, waiting for anyone to come by. This entrance was covered, but Lasgol had expected that. It made sense to place archers in the weak spots. Unfortunately for the Dark One, Lasgol could see him but he could not see Lasgol.

Camu, don't move, Lasgol said so his friend could still cloak him with his skill.

He entered without a sound and crouched. The feeling was weird, because he could see the armed watchman but the man had not noticed Lasgol's presence and was not aiming. He hesitated whether to take two more steps. He was not sure Camu's power would work through a wall—most likely not. But he decided to risk it and readied his bow. The shot was four paces off, so he measured his strength and distance and released.

The watchman took the blow in the chest. It was an Earth Arrow, and when the tip broke it burst with earth and smoke, blinding and stunning the Dark One. Lasgol clubbed him in the head with the back of his axe, leaving him senseless.

Camu, are you here with me? His power could not reach Lasgol from the other side of the wall, as he had guessed.

No. I come in. Now yes, I am.

Lasgol vanished again, Camu's magic cloaking him once more. *Good, don't leave my side.*

Not move much.

Don't move at all—this is a very dangerous situation.

Okay, Camu transmitted back, but it was clear he did not fully agree. He could not hide his doubt—so far Camu was unable to hide his feelings and emotions, which Lasgol thanked the Gods for, because otherwise, as difficult to control as Camu already was, he would become impossible.

Suddenly, Lasgol had a strange feeling, as if they were not alone. He looked at the door but it was deserted. Puzzled, he glanced at the window and saw a figure slipping inside. Lasgol started—he had not heard a sound. He reached for the weapons at his waist but a black knife appeared before his eyes.

He stood still as a stone statue.

Chapter 9

"You ought to be more careful," a biting, familiar voice whispered.

"Viggo! You scared the living daylights out of me!" Lasgol whispered back as he recovered from the shock.

"You should always watch your back," Viggo whispered with a triumphant smile on his face.

"You have to avoid scaring your friends to death," Lasgol chided him, wagging his finger at him in annoyance.

"It's so that you learn, weirdo," Viggo whispered with irony.

"I'm no…. You're…" Lasgol started to protest, but Viggo was already at the door that opened onto a long outer corridor.

Ingrid appeared suddenly at the opening. She walked into the room and looked around with a frown.

"Everything all right here?" she asked in her usual cold, efficient, and determined tone.

"Everything's in order," Lasgol replied.

Ingrid gave him a nod and went to the door where Viggo watched the outside.

Lasgol strode over to the opening and looked out. He glimpsed two figures coming through the snow. He started to worry.

Camu, how are you doing on power?

Fine, Camu said confidently.

You think you can go to Astrid and Nilsa and cover them? They're approaching us but they're visible, and the traps' distraction maneuver is likely not as effective by now. I don't want them to be seen when they come closer to the wall.

I try, Camu transmitted boldly, slipping through the crack in the wall to intercept them.

"We're going to clear this area," Ingrid whispered to Lasgol from the door.

"Ok, I'll wait for Astrid and Nilsa here."

Lasgol peered outside. Thanks to his *Hawk's Sight* skill he could see his two partners easily, which troubled him even more. Some keen watchman who realized the Fire traps were only a ruse could discover them. He took a deep breath, hoping his fears would not be realized. But not a moment after he thought this, a Dark Ranger started yelling.

"Two coming from the west!"

"Release!" cried a second voice.

Arrows flew right after, and Lasgol felt his heart skip a beat. Astrid and Nilsa threw themselves on the ground, trying to hide in the snow. The arrows brushed past them, missing them by a hair's breadth.

Lasgol snorted in relief, but the fear that they might be hit in the Dark Rangers' next attempt clenched his throat. He could not swallow. The archers were skilled—they would not miss a second time. All of a sudden, both Astrid and Nilsa vanished before his eyes.

Then he realized what had happened.

Way to go, Camu!

The creature had reached them and hidden them with his magic. Lasgol cheered up—Camu would protect them and they would arrive safe and sound.

"Where are they?" voices cried from the balcony.

"They've vanished!" another voice cried, sounding puzzled.

"That's impossible!"

The cries of alarm and disbelief came from the upper section of the keep.

But something troubling was happening. Lasgol could see the footprints of the three in the snow as they approached the western wall. He held his breath and hoped their attackers would not notice. Wishful thinking, he knew, but perhaps they would not see them. They needed a bit of luck.

"I see prints! Follow the prints!" cried a Dark One.

Luck was not on the Panthers' side that night.

"Release in front of the footprints!" another one ordered.

Lasgol's heart began to gallop. What if they were hit? The three were moving faster now; they had heard the shouts and knew they had been discovered.

More arrows flew. Lasgol had no way of knowing whether any had hit their target. He hoped not. He wished not.

The trail reached the wall. Lasgol took courage; they would not be seen there because they would not leave visible prints as they climbed the rope against the wall. But suddenly, the three figures were revealed.

"What…?" Lasgol muttered, terrified. Then he realized what was happening. Camu's power had run out. He had told Lasgol he had enough power, but once again he had exaggerated his abilities. They were now in a tight spot. Nilsa and Astrid were halfway up the wall and Camu was a little higher. "Keep climbing, you're visible!" he warned them, poking his head out of the crack.

Astrid looked up while she climbed with impressive speed and agility. Nilsa was further down, ascending slowly, her face red from the effort. Camu was looking at his own body, puzzled, as if he did not understand what had happened.

Climb quick! Your power, your inner energy, has run out! Lasgol warned him, seeing him bewildered.

Camu tilted his head and blinked twice, then he tilted his head again.

Tired…, he transmitted to Lasgol, along with feeling of great exhaustion.

Climb! Quickly! he urged, fearing Camu might have overexerted himself using his magic.

All right… Camu transmitted.

Lasgol waved at him to hurry. Several arrows tried to hit the three climbers. They hit the wall, almost reaching them. Things were turning ugly.

Astrid arrived at the top in a flash. She shot a fleeting look of joy at Lasgol and went in. Nilsa was climbing as fast as she could, breathing hard.

Camu was not moving.

Come on! Camu, climb!

The creature shut his eyes and fell to the ground.

Camu! No!

With a dull sound he hit the ground and stayed there, half-buried in the snow. Two arrows tried to kill him. Two others went for Nilsa. The redhead cried out in pain—she had been hit.

She lost her footing and hung from the rope, holding on with only one hand. She had an arrow in her leg, which she was clutching with her other hand.

Lasgol grabbed Astrid's wrist.

"Help Nilsa. I'm going to help Camu."

She nodded and gave him a warning look. "Be careful."

Lasgol nodded and let himself down on the rope. He reached Nilsa, and without a second thought pushed with his feet against the wall and let go of the rope, dropping past his friend who was clenching her jaw, bearing the pain. Astrid was climbing down behind him to help Nilsa.

The blow against the ground shook Lasgol's entire body, although the snow cushioned the fall up to a point. Luckily on his way down Lasgol had called upon his *Cat-like Reflexes* and *Improved Agility* skills, and they greatly reduced the impact. He lifted his head and saw two arrows heading straight at him. His *Hawk's Sight* skill allowed him to see them coming at great speed. He leapt to one side, imitating Ona. Both arrows brushed his back. He raised half his body in the snow, noticing Astrid helping Nilsa up the wall, then saw Camu unconscious a few paces away. Instantly, Lasgol crawled to his friend. Several arrows fell to his right and left as he snaked through the snow.

He reached Camu and grabbed his back legs. He started to drag him. His friend was so heavy he had to make a real effort to drag him and move him along the wall. Lasgol wanted to get to the corner and past it so the arrows from above would not hit them.

Inside the fortress, Ingrid and Viggo moved along the stairs that led to the upper section of the western wall. They crouched as they went, totally silent. Viggo reached the upper part, the balcony, and put his head out just enough to see what was going on. He turned to Ingrid, showing three fingers to indicate how many Dark Rangers there were. Then he pointed left and Ingrid nodded.

Viggo got down on the floor and began to crawl like a black snake along the wooden floor of the balcony. The three Dark Ones were releasing below, all their attention focused on getting Lasgol.

Ingrid glanced out. She decided to change her bow and took out the short one—Swift. She aimed at the watchman in the center while Viggo crept up behind them without being heard or seen. She waited until Viggo was one step away from the Dark Rangers before releasing. The arrow hit the archer in the middle, and when the tip broke there was a burst, followed by a discharge that left the man shaking and grimacing with pain. The other two turned with their bows ready to release, but Ingrid was already nocking another arrow.

They were about to release on her when Viggo leapt up from the floor at the attackers, catching them totally by surprise—they had not seen him. He hit the one on the left in the nose and the one on the right in the temple. The Dark One put his hand to his face in pain, but he recovered and tried to hit Viggo on the head with his bow. With a swift, nimble movement, Viggo stepped aside and the Dark Ranger broke his bow on the floor. Viggo kneed him in the stomach and made him double up, finishing the attacker with a blow to the back of the neck with the handle of his knife. The Dark One he had hit on the temple had recovered from the shock and drew his knife, but an Air Arrow from Ingrid left him convulsing on his feet. Viggo finished the two Dark Ones with blows to their heads.

He looked at Ingrid, smiled, and gave her a thumbs-up. Suddenly, Viggo crouched like lightning and an arrow passed over his head.

Ingrid looked south and saw the archer. She felt her quiver and realized she had no more Elemental Arrows. She would have to use regular ones. She changed bows fast and grabbed her composite one, Spot-On. She always carried the three on her: two slung across her back and Punisher at her belt. While she nocked the arrow she saw Viggo throw himself on the floor and slither off like a black viper. The archer's arrows brushed his bottom as he zigzagged, but he carried on like nothing had happened, although Ingrid suspected they had grazed him. He would be sore for a few days, which made her grin. She also could not help but notice that he had a very cute upturned butt. The moment the thought crossed her mind she could not help but worry that he might be hit and felt terrified it could be serious. Focusing on the archer, she aimed with a strong arm and released as she exhaled. The arrow flew in a straight line, parallel to the wall following the balcony, and hit the archer in his left shoulder as he leaned out to shoot Viggo.

Viggo saw the Dark One lower his bow as he was hit in the holding shoulder. He leapt to his feet to rush at the archer, sprinting with the strength of a leopard chasing its prey.

Ingrid was already nocking another arrow to finish their attacker off. She had hit him in the shoulder on purpose; at that distance she could have got him right in the chest, killing him, but this was not a killing mission—their mission was to capture the Dark Rangers and deliver them to the King. If it was possible, of course. If things got ugly they would have to kill them. Egil had asked them not to unless there was no choice, and she would follow his wishes, although she thought traitors deserved to die for what they had done. On the other hand, she understood it was not her place to be magistrate and executor; she was a Ranger, and her orders were to capture, not kill.

Viggo reached the Dark Ranger before Ingrid could finish her thoughts and knocked him out with a round blow with both hands to the man's temples. The Dark One fell to the floor as if all the energy had left his body.

Ingrid turned her bow and went to the opposite corner, seeking any remaining Dark Rangers. There did not seem to be anyone posted up there.

Viggo signaled that everything was clear on the other side.

Ingrid nodded. Since everything was clear she went to warn Lasgol. She looked over the railing and searched for him; for a moment she was unable to find him and was a little taken aback. Then she saw him buried in the snow. A smart move—since he could not drag Camu on account of his weight, he had decided to hide him and cover him with snow before covering himself as well. Only two bumps were visible, which were not so different from the rocks scattered around.

Ingrid put her hands to her mouth and imitated a raven's croak; Lasgol would know there was no danger. She waited while Viggo finished inspecting all the upper sections of the keep and the floors below. If there were any Dark Ones left he would deal with them. Ingrid feared Viggo might slit their throats if he was on his own. She hoped he would control himself.

Lasgol's head appeared in one of the mounds. He looked up. Ingrid waved at him to draw his attention. Lasgol saw her and made a questioning gesture. Ingrid replied with a signal that meant everything was under control.

Lasgol came out of the snow and started to dig out Camu.

Ingrid looked around—there was no danger, so she decided to leave Lasgol and keep looking. She went to the room where Astrid and Nilsa were. She arrived and rushed in; no sooner had she set a foot inside that a knife appeared at her neck. She stopped in her tracks and stood very still.

"Excuse me," Astrid said in a whisper and withdrew the knife.

"Nothing to excuse. You were right," Ingrid assured her friend, then noticed Nilsa lying in a corner in the shadows.

"What happened to her?" Ingrid asked, going over to her.

"She's been hit in the leg. It's the muscle," Astrid explained.

Ingrid knelt beside Nilsa and examined her wound.

Nilsa made light of it. "It's nothing."

"It's something. I doubt you'll be able to walk," Ingrid made a face.

"I can limp," Nilsa said with a pained smile.

"That's the spirit," Ingrid encouraged her, smiling and stroking her head.

"It's not serious, just annoying," Astrid confirmed. "I've already seen to it; she needs to rest for a while. I think she'll be able to walk in a couple of days. For now she shouldn't move that leg or put weight on it."

"Yeah, that'll be for the best."

"I can walk... I'll limp. That's all there is to it," Nilsa said, determined to go on.

"Don't move. The situation is under control. We'll deal with it," Ingrid told her.

"Fine... but I feel a little useless…. What luck."

"Getting wounded on a mission is nothing to be ashamed of. On the contrary," Ingrid said to cheer her up.

"Okay. Go on... and be careful," Nilsa said, indicating her own wounded leg.

Astrid and Ingrid left Nilsa resting with her back to the cracked wall, her shortbow ready on top of her stretched-out legs. It was most likely she would not get any unwanted visitors, but she was prepared just in case. They left and went out on the balcony; it was deserted, and Viggo was nowhere to be seen.

"Where did he go?" Astrid asked.

"He's already checking the lower levels, most likely looking for the chief," Ingrid told her.

"Yeah, that's what I'd do. Once the leader is eliminated all the trouble will be over. The rest will surrender or flee."

Ingrid nodded. "Let's search for the leader too so we can finish this."

Astrid poked her head over the west wall and saw Lasgol beside Camu, his bow ready to protect him.

Astrid signaled that everything was clear above.

Lasgol responded with gestures that meant he would stay with Camu and that they should keep going.

Astrid touched Ingrid's arm and they continued. They descended a flight of stairs inside and searched two floors of the keep. In one of the rooms they found two more Dark Rangers lying on the floor unconscious.

"Viggo's already been here," Astrid said, bending over to check them.

"And he leaves the dirty work for us."

"That's him all right," Astrid smiled and brought out the tying ropes and gags to secure the two Dark Ones.

They set to it, and by the time they finished they heard shouts near the entrance door to the keep. They went out to the courtyard and saw three Dark Rangers escaping on horseback. They had raised the gate to the keep and were fleeing.

"Cowards!" Ingrid cried at the sight of them riding away.

"They must be the last ones remaining. They're trying to get out of range," said Astrid.

Ingrid armed her bow and aimed, rage written across her face.

"I'm not letting them get away," she said.

She aimed for an instant, following the trajectory of the horse, and then released. The arrow flew and hit the first one riding on a white courser. He fell off into the river.

A shadow leapt onto the second rider from the raised portcullis and brought him down.

Ingrid nocked another arrow, but as she aimed, the third rider escaped at a full gallop over the bridge.

"That's Viggo," Astrid said, pointing at the figure who had brought down the second rider.

"Let's see if we can get the leader," Ingrid said and started running toward the gate, crossing the courtyard.

Outside the keep, Egil was watching a rider coming toward him at full gallop. He had foreseen that if the mission went well someone would likely escape, and there was only one way out of the keep: where he was standing. He armed his shortbow and aimed. He was close to the bridge; even he could make the shot at such close range.

The rider charged at Egil. If he changed course Egil would have an easy shot, since he was close enough to the bridge that it would be impossible for anybody to escape without offering a clear target.

He recognized who it was: Henerik. Egil knew he would not change direction. He was going to run him over, since that was the best chance to survive. Egil sighed, and as he exhaled he released.

The arrow flew straight at Henerik's chest as he spurred his horse to go faster and run over Egil.

The horse was almost on top of Egil when the arrow hit Henerik in the right forearm he had used to cover his chest.

Egil threw himself to one side, rolled on the snow like he had learned with the Rangers, and turned to see Henerik running away.

But he was not going to escape.

Suddenly, coming out of a mound of snow where he had been hiding, Gerd appeared. He tensed his bow and aimed at Henerik. The leader of the Dark Rangers opened his eyes wide as the Earth Arrow hit him right in the middle of his chest. He was stunned from the explosion and headed straight to Gerd. The giant removed Henerik from his horse, breaking the man's bow against his body as he passed by his side.

Egil smiled.

Nobody escaped the Royal Eagles.

Chapter 10

Viggo kept watch on the prisoners, who were all tied up and gagged in the center of the great hall of the keep, with an unfriendly glare. The Dark Rangers were resigned to their fate. They had been defeated and now did not pose any resistance. In any case, Viggo did not trust his prisoners' attitudes—theirs, or anyone's in general, with the exception of his comrades. This helped him not to miss any details of what went on and left him ready to act if necessary.

Egil, on the other hand, was healing Henerik's wounds and anyone else who had been wounded during the assault and capture of the keep.

"Don't you want me to put them out of their misery?" Viggo asked Egil with the coldness of an Assassin without a conscience.

"Not necessary. I'm sure our friends know how to behave regarding the new situation they find themselves in," Egil replied with a grin.

"And in case they don't adapt to the situation, I'll make sure they understand it," Astrid intervened from the other side of the group of prisoners, showing them her Assassin knives.

Ingrid and Gerd were looking after Nilsa, who was lying on an oak table at the far end of the room. Her wound was clean, sutured, and well-bandaged.

"Does it hurt?" Gerd asked her, worried.

"Not much," she said, turning her head.

"You'll be good as new in no time," Ingrid promised her.

"I hope there won't be any lingering problems…"

"I don't think so. The wound is clean. If it doesn't get infected, and I doubt it will now that we've cured it thoroughly, it shouldn't give you any trouble," Ingrid said.

"You'll see, you'll soon be running and leaping like a gazelle," Gerd said encouragingly with his honest smile.

"I hope so, leaping and running are my specialties," Nilsa joked, although she could not help but look concerned.

Lasgol was in an adjacent room waiting for Camu to wake up. Ona was with him, and she was troubled, moaning constantly and pacing the room.

He'll wake up soon, you'll see. Don't worry. There's nothing wrong with him, he just

overdid himself using magic and fainted, Lasgol explained to her.

But the explanation did not seem to convince her; she went on pacing around Camu with woeful eyes, moaning every now and then. The fact that Camu did not wake up had her distraught. She did not understand the reason why.

Egil came in to see how they were.

"Any news on Camu?"

"No, for now there are no significant changes. His breathing is stable and he doesn't seem to have sustained any injury or other harm."

"Then can we confirm this is most likely because of his excessive use of magic?"

"That's what I think. It's happened to me too on occasion. Then I learned to control it. You can't drain the well, or you faint and then you're left at the mercy of your enemies."

"You'll have to teach that to Camu, although in his case the well might be something entirely different. We don't know how he visualizes his inner power."

"I tell him it's like a well or pond of calm water. I hope he understands."

"So do I, for his own good. He's an amazing creature, and his skills are fantastic!"

"Yes, he is, and they are," Lasgol confirmed, looking at Camu, worried.

Suddenly, Camu opened his bulging eyes wide. He stared at the ceiling of the room.

"He's waking up," Egil noticed.

"Camu, are you all right?" Lasgol asked him.

Camu got on all fours and looked around. He seemed to recognize them after a while. He snorted hard and poked out his blue tongue.

We win? he asked Lasgol.

Yes, we won, but that's not important. Are you all right? Is anything wrong with you?

I very well. Rested.

Are you sure?

Yes, sure, he transmitted and started doing his happy dance, flexing his four legs and wagging his tail.

Seeing him, Ona lunged at him and started licking his head with long licks. Camu did not protest and kept dancing.

"He seems to feel just fine," Egil said with a big smile.

"My, he really scared me," snorted Lasgol.

"Magic and its limitations are something we must keep exploring," Egil suggested, "as much with you as with Camu."

"I know... it's the most sensible thing to do, or else we'll get into trouble at the least expected moment or the wrong time, like today," Lasgol commented with a snort.

"Let's find out what happened," Egil suggested eagerly.

"I'll ask him, see if we can get a clear idea, but I don't have much hope."

"Try anyway, we'll find out something positive for sure," Egil said cheerfully as he looked at Camu with interest.

Lasgol nodded, although he was not sure Camu would be capable of expressing what had happened to him or why.

Camu, can you explain to me what happened to you? he asked the creature.

Camu stopped dancing and looked at Lasgol.

I tired, very much. Then... I not remember more.

Lasgol turned to Egil, "He says he felt exhausted and then doesn't remember anything else."

"Ask him whether he experienced anything that might have warned him that he was overdoing his use of magic before he fainted," Egil told Lasgol.

Lasgol transmitted the question to Camu.

I understand Egil, he replied proudly.

I wanted to make sure you did, Lasgol transmitted back. He was aware that Camu was becoming better and better at understanding conversations between humans, but Lasgol was unconvinced he grasped everything. Of course, Camu would say he understood everything perfectly, of that Lasgol was certain—classic Camu.

Not feel anything before very tired.

"He seems to have felt nothing."

"Then we can safely say for now that there's no warning that you're using up all your power. It's the same with you, isn't it?"

Lasgol nodded. "I never know when I'm going to run out of

energy, I don't get any warning signals from my body or mind. The energy in my pool simply runs out and I collapse."

"Just like what happened to Camu. This is *most* interesting."

"Is it?" Lasgol's nose wrinkled. He did not find it at all interesting not knowing when he was going to run out of his inner energy and be left helpless.

"It is, because it points to a possible relation between human magic and that of the creatures of the ice."

"Hmm, I hadn't related them… well, it does seem to point out that the limitations of magic affect us similarly."

"We should figure out whether Camu feels the pool of energy like you or recognizes his magic in some other way. It's something that intrigues me," murmured Egil, his gaze lost in conjectures.

Pool energy? Camu asked Lasgol, transmitting a feeling of incomprehension.

Yes. You see, when I activate my power and search for the energy I'm going to use to call upon a skill, I see this energy in the form of a pool of blue water inside my chest.

Not understand.

Lasgol sighed. It was an advanced concept and he had doubted Camu would understand. His comprehension was not yet that of an adult, and it might not be for a long time.

When you use your power to camouflage us, how do you do it? Where do you get the energy to conjure the enchantment?

Camu put his head to one side and blinked twice.

Not know…

You don't see a well or lake of energy inside you?

No… no well. No lake.

Interesting…

Lasgol relayed the conversation to Egil.

"Fascinating. Truly intriguing. Our friend isn't yet aware of where his magic comes from."

"Do you think it's because he's still a pup?"

"Most likely. Yes, I believe Camu doesn't yet perceive the working and origin of his magic. In any case, it should be quite similar to how yours works, so he must have a pool of energy, even if for now he's unaware of where it is or how to access it. He must do it unconsciously when he needs it."

"That must be it. I'll try to help him understand that if he uses his power for a long period of time, he can use up his entire reserve of energy."

I understand, Camu transmitted at once.

Are you sure you understand?

Yes, I understand.

Ona chirped twice to indicate that Camu did not understand.

Yeah, Ona, I don't think he does either.

Yes, I understand. I smart.

And well-behaved, added Lasgol.

I very well-behaved, Camu nodded, moving his head up and down repeatedly.

"That's fantastic, he knows how to nod," Egil said cheerfully. "That's human conduct, not animal. It's curious that he's capable of assimilating it. It must be because he's growing up among humans."

"Ona is growing up around us too and she's not developing this kind of behavior."

"Very true, well noted. Big cats have their own behavior and it's very difficult to influence them. Their instincts prevail over learned behavior."

Ona chirped once.

Lasgol stroked her head. *You go on with your behavior, Ona, you're a dear. Don't worry,* Lasgol transmitted to her.

Ona laid her paw on his leg, and he patted her head lovingly.

Tired, bad, Camu transmitted as he watched Lasgol with his bulging eyes and a lost gaze.

Yes, Camu, if you suddenly begin to feel tired you must stop using your magic at once. It means you've run out of energy, and if you go on using it you'll pass out, like what happened tonight.

Tired, I stop magic.

That's right, Lasgol transmitted, feeling relieved because Camu seemed to finally understand.

Egil knelt to take Camu's head in his hands and look into his eyes.

"You're a very special creature," he told him. "In order for us to help you, you must always transmit what you're feeling—anything that you find strange—and we'll always try to help you understand."

Because we friends.

Yes, Camu, because we're your friends and we love you, Lasgol said.

"Never doubt that," Egil added, "We'll always look after you and do whatever is necessary to understand and help you," Egil promised.

Camu licked Egil's face with his blue tongue and Egil could not help laughing.

Ona, observing the show of affection, joined in, licking Egil's hair with her wide, raspy feline tongue.

Lasgol laughed out loud.

"They're making you look most handsome, Egil."

"Absolutely! I love it. I feel fantastic!"

Lasgol laughed again.

They let Camu and Ona rest and went back to the others watching the prisoners.

As Henerik saw Egil he made as if to speak but, being gagged, all he could do was grunt.

"Astrid, would you mind letting him speak?" Egil asked.

The Assassin took off Henerik's gag.

The leader of the group of Dark Rangers cleared his throat. "I knew you were good, that was the word, but I never thought you'd be *that* good."

"And today we've been a little clumsy," Viggo said acidly.

"That's true," Astrid nodded.

"Usually we're about three times as good as we demonstrated here today. The plan was not as good as other times," he said, eying Egil.

"One plans as best he can according to the situation and the enemy he must face. There's no perfect plan or a totally predictable enemy," Egil said defensively.

"What are you going to do with us?" Henerik asked.

"Deliver you to the authorities of Garnoga City so they can deal with you," Egil replied.

"But only if you behave. If you try any nonsense you won't live to tell the tale," Astrid threatened them.

"If you deliver us they'll hang us."

"Not all of you," said Egil. "Ask for forced labor and your lives will be spared."

"That's just another kind of death sentence," Henerik protested.

"You should've thought of that before betraying the realm," Ingrid snapped. "A Ranger never leaves the Path, never betrays the King."

"We'll see how long it takes the Royal Eagles to betray their king," Henerik said, staring at Egil.

"We're not going to betray the King. Not now, and not in the future," Ingrid said.

"That remains to be seen. This king will drive Norghana to ruin. We'll see how long you remain loyal."

"I don't think you'll ever see that," Viggo said acidly.

"No, I won't see it, but you'll remember my words when that day arrives."

"Until that day comes we'd better not hear any more," said Astrid and gagged him again.

"Tonight we'll speak privately," Egil told Henerik. "I need to make sure this matter is truly over."

"Lively chat with your little friends?" Viggo asked, raising one eyebrow and smiling coldly.

Egil tilted his head, thought for a moment, and finally nodded.

"Yes, I believe it's necessary to resolve my lingering doubts."

Astrid and Lasgol took over the first watch while Egil had a talk with Henerik. They exchanged complicit looks while they watched the prisoners huddled between them on the floor. Ona and Camu rested beside Nilsa; Gerd made sure the three were comfortable.

Ingrid signaled to Viggo.

"Come with me. We need to talk, you and I, privately."

Viggo smiled and nodded. They went to another room. The night was dark and cold, and an icy wind came in through one of the windows. They sat away from the draught.

"Yes, my precious?" Viggo said with a loving gaze.

"Let's make something clear," she said in a hard tone. "I'm not your precious, or your girlfriend, or anything else. I'm Ingrid."

Viggo was about to reply with one of his usual retorts, but he thought better.

"Does this mean there's nothing between us?" he asked uncertainly.

Ingrid was taken aback by his question.

"I… well…" she muttered, unable to finish.

"I understand that you don't want to tout it about," Viggo continued," but I have feelings for you, and you know it. I also believe you feel something for me, even if you deny it in front of the others."

"I haven't said one thing or the other," said Ingrid, folding her arms as her gaze shifted from hard to strange indecision.

"You can't deny you kissed me."

"It was an accident," she snapped.

"You tripped and accidentally fell on my lips?"

"No, you idiot, I thought you were dead and when I realized you weren't…"

"You threw yourself in my arms to kiss me because that's what comrades do, naturally."

"I don't know what came over me," she said in frustration.

"Perhaps you ought to meditate on it and see what your feelings tell you…"

"I'll do what I have to do. What I don't want is for you to get any ideas, especially your weird ones."

"About us, you mean?"

"I mean there is no 'us.' There's just you and me, two separate people who are fond of one another. That's all."

"So, we're fond of one another, and that's that… is that what you want me to believe, or what you want the rest of the group to believe?"

"Everybody, because it's the truth."

"I believe there's a lot more than fondness between us, even though you insist on denying it."

"Well, you're wrong," she snapped.

"Okay, then, what do you want us to do?" Viggo asked her, disappointed.

"Go on as we have until now, as always."

"Ignoring what's happened?"

"That's right," she replied firmly, her chin lifted.

"You know that will only make things awkward between us, don't you?"

"I don't see why they would be awkward."

"Because there's something unresolved."

"There's nothing to resolve."

"As you wish," Viggo shook his head with a resigned look, then left.

Ingrid remained alone in the room, staring out the window. The cold breeze reached her and she shivered. The frigid air wormed its way into her soul, and she felt bad, empty. She snorted and shook off the cold. She couldn't stop thinking about Viggo, and she felt awful.

"He's such an idiot…" she muttered, heaving a deep sigh.

Chapter 11

Two weeks later, the group of friends crossed the gate to the royal castle at the capital. They had delivered the last group of Dark Rangers and had gone to report to Gondabar that they had finished the mission the King had given them.

As they headed to the stables, they noticed they were attracting an unusual amount of attention. The soldiers on duty, even those doing exercises, were watching them curiously and whispering.

"Well, we seem to be famous," Viggo commented, leading his horse to the stables.

"I don't think we're famous, it's just that we draw attention," Astrid replied.

"It's bad manners to whisper and gossip," Ingrid said, displeased with the unnecessary attention. She preferred discretion.

"We're now Royal Eagles. That means we'll arouse interest, especially in this environment," Egil said from the saddle, curious about how they were perceived in their new role.

Lasgol had also noticed and was watching Ona walking behind Trotter. Camu was with her but in his invisible state. He had been hiding his sister until they arrived at the royal castle so as not to frighten the good citizens of the capital.

Gerd brought up the rear with Nilsa, who was scratching at her leg around the wound.

"Does it bother you?" Gerd asked her when he noticed.

"No, not at all. Don't worry, it just itches every now and then," she smiled.

"But you don't have any pain, right?" the giant wanted to make sure.

"No, the wound has healed well. It doesn't bother me and there isn't any permanent damage. I'm the same as before I was wounded. Really, I promise."

"Wonderful!"

"Isn't it? For a moment I was frightened, but it's healed perfectly with all your nursing."

"Now you have a story to tell of your adventures as a Royal

Eagle!" Gerd laughed.

"You don't say!" she joined in the laughter. "I'm going to be a sensation among the Royal Rangers with my stories. And, with a battle wound, even more so."

"I believe you're already a sensation among them," Gerd went on laughing. "You don't need stories or wounds."

Nilsa bowed her head and smiled. "Well, I think they'll help a little."

They left their mounts in the stables and Lasgol made sure Trotter was well looked after. As they walked to the Tower of the Rangers, they could see that, indeed, they drew many stares as they rode through.

"Well, well, we seem to have the famous Royal Eagles back."

"Hi, Kol!" Nilsa smiled mischievously at once; she knew Kol was interested in her and she led him on.

"I wouldn't say we're famous," Gerd told him.

"Well, believe it or not you are," Haines said, smiling, which did not improve his looks at all. He was an experienced Royal Ranger that Nilsa knew well.

"This is interesting," Viggo came closer to listen.

"We'll go up to speak to the quartermaster," Ingrid said, pointing to herself and Egil.

"We need arrows, traps, and to refill our belts with all the components we've used," she added.

"And other substances," Egil said mysteriously.

Lasgol glanced at Astrid, who raised an eyebrow with interest.

"You'll find the quartermaster at his post. I was there a while ago to get a new bow," said Kol.

"Did you break it? You're usually very careful," Nilsa said, surprised.

"Actually, I broke it on a thief's head—I've been on a 'cleaning mission,' ridding the northeastern coast of outlaws."

"Wow, then you're like Gerd. He also uses his bow that way," Nilsa giggled.

"It's very efficient, but expensive," Gerd said with a grin.

The four laughed.

"Yeah, that's true, the quartermaster wasn't happy at all when I told him. A good bow is expensive and hard to make."

"Well, we'll go and ask for a composite bow for Gerd."

Ingrid and Egil nodded and went on.

"What news around here?" Nilsa asked.

"Everything's pretty quiet for now. No invasions or civil wars, or mentionable attacks from subversive dark organizations," Kol said ironically.

"A real novelty if you ask me. It's been a long time since things have been so quiet," Haines commented.

"That's good news!" Nilsa was so delighted she clapped her hands and skipped.

Lasgol and Astrid stayed behind to hear the rumors; it was always good to be informed of what went on in the realm.

"You should know you're a celebrity around here now," Kol said, winking at Nilsa.

"Oh, really? Me?"

"You bet. Everybody knows you and that you've been hunting the Dark Rangers until there were none left. You've done a great job."

"Well, I didn't do it on my own..." she blushed. "My companions did almost everything. I was wounded..."

"Wounded?" Haines and Kol asked, shocked.

"Yes, in the leg, capturing the last group of Dark Ones. I'm still limping a bit," she exaggerated the limp to see their reaction.

"Then you're a heroine. They ought to give you a medal," Haines said.

"I volunteer to be your nurse until you recover," Kol offered with a charming smile.

Nilsa blushed to her ears.

"She certainly deserves a medal," Gerd said.

"And the nurse?" Kol insisted.

"We'll talk about that when I see how everything is," Nilsa replied.

"That means you want to see what your other suitors among the Royal Rangers say," Kol said.

"And among the Royal Guard," Nilsa said, laughing.

Kol rolled his eyes and shook his head.

"You've disarmed me," he said, waving his arms.

They all laughed heartily, and several Rangers stared at them as they were coming out of the tower.

"I'll see you all later, we're going to look for accommodations,"

Nilsa said, continuing on her way.

"Right. See you later, and welcome back all of you. It's an honor to have you back, and I'm sure I speak for everyone," said Kol.

"We appreciate everything you do," Haines said gratefully. "It's a difficult and unpleasant task. One never wishes to hunt down their own comrades."

"Thanks, though someone has to do it, and we're very good at anything difficult, and especially anything unpleasant," Viggo said in a sarcastic tone.

Astrid and Lasgol exchanged a glance and smile—Viggo was dead on.

They arrived at the tower, and the moment they went in Nilsa used all her charm and contacts. After several conversations, she got one of the large rooms in the lower section of the tower for their exclusive use. They went in to lay down and rest on the beds. They were exhausted after the long journey and the many weeks of hard work. Ona and Camu went to the back and, after playing a little in the new surroundings and being petted by Astrid, they relaxed and lay down on the floor, huddled against one another like two huge sibling pups.

Nilsa was unable to keep still, since upon her return she felt she had to resume her prior duties, even if that was not the case—at least until Gondabar decided their next move now that they had finished this mission.

"Could you be more quiet?" Astrid asked her.

"Yeah, you'd make a lazy bear nervous with all your pacing about," Viggo said, waving his arms, annoyed.

"Sure, says the one with the personality of a mountain ogre," the redhead snapped back.

Lasgol muffled a chuckle. At that moment Ingrid and Egil walked through the door. Ingrid laughed, but she raised her hand when Viggo began to reply.

"I'm not saying anything, don't worry."

Lasgol was surprised Ingrid did not carry on, and by Viggo's face so was he. He looked at her in silence.

"You have all the supplies?" Gerd asked.

"Yes, everything's in order. We could go out again at dawn if necessary," Ingrid explained.

"The quartermaster will get us everything we need by tomorrow,"

Egil added. "He asked us why we go through so many materials and components so quickly—he's certainly baffled."

"Because we work a lot and fast?" Astrid said with a smile.

"As we should!" Ingrid stated.

"Do you think we'll be sent on another mission again so quickly?" Nilsa asked, not sounding too enthusiastic.

"I hope they let us rest up a little before," Gerd said.

"Don't count on it, you'll be disappointed," said Viggo.

"If the realm needs us, we'll be ready to serve at once," Ingrid proclaimed.

"You need to be well-rested and fresh to serve the realm properly," said Egil. "Exhaustion and lack of energy can lead the bravest and most well-prepared defenders of the realm to the abyss."

"One day you should publish a book with all your wisdom," Viggo told him. "I'd call it *The Obvious Path*."

Egil smiled broadly.

"Maybe one day I'll write my memoirs. As for the title, I'm not convinced."

"Your wisdom will be legendary," Astrid said, "don't pay any attention to Viggo. Many would benefit from your knowledge, experiences, and deductions about life and the way to face it."

"Thank you very much, Astrid. It gladdens my soul you see it that way. I'll think about it and might write my story, when I'm older and more experienced."

"I'll read it day and night when you do," Viggo said ironically.

"You would definitely learn something," Astrid said.

Since Viggo respected Astrid's opinion he said nothing.

They rested a while and nodded off lightly. Then a Royal Ranger knocked on the door, giving his name.

Nilsa opened it.

"What's the matter, Erik?" she asked.

"Gondabar sent me to fetch you. He wants to speak with you. Official business."

"Okay. We'll go at once."

The Royal Ranger waited for all of them to come out and led them to Gondabar's rooms. The Leader of the Rangers welcomed them with a big smile. He still looked like a frail old man, but there was a renewed gleam in his eyes, a gleam of hope. They all knew their leader had endured rough times lately. Thoran had stripped him of his position, and it was only thanks to the intervention of the Panthers that he had recuperated his post. Just like Dolbarar, who was back at the Camp as its Leader.

"Welcome, it's a pleasure to see you all again," he told them from behind his office desk, spreading his arms.

"The pleasure is ours," Egil replied with a small respectful bow which they all followed.

"Truly, seeing you all safe and sound is a great joy."

"We got the occasional scratch, but nothing serious," Egil said.

"I'm glad they weren't serious wounds. The Ranger profession is always surrounded by dangers, and we must take extreme precautions when defending the realm from enemies."

"Especially internal enemies," Egil replied.

"All the Dark Rangers you captured are in prison awaiting the King's decision about their future."

"A very short, ill-fated one," Viggo said.

"I suppose that will be the case," Gondabar agreed. "Although our King's designs can be unexpected."

Lasgol and Egil exchanged a doubtful glance—what would Thoran do with them? Likely what Egil had guessed, but one could never be sure when dealing with the King and his brother.

"You've accomplished a daunting task for the realm, and the King is very pleased. He told me so and thus I pass it on to you."

"Thank you very much, sir. We do only our duty."

"With all the intelligence we've gathered—and we have several Rangers combing the realm, seeking information—the Dark Ones have been eradicated."

"Have we found them all then?"

"That seems to be the case."

"That's excellent news," Lasgol said cheerfully.

"Indeed. The threat is over. We can all breathe in relief now and leave this business behind and look to the future with optimism."

"Without forgetting the lessons learned," said Egil.

"Too true. This can never happen again. Something like this can never be repeated. That is why it's essential you continue as Royal Eagles, to ensure something like this never happens again."

"It won't ever happen again," Ingrid promised.

"We'll make sure of it," Nilsa said with enthusiasm.

Gondabar smiled, "I'm old now and my days are numbered, but

my mind is at ease knowing that when I'm no longer here, you will be and will look after the good of the Rangers and the realm."

"Our Leader will guide us for many more years still," Egil said.

Gondabar smiled, thankful for his words.

"I am grateful for your good wishes. We'll see what plans the Ice Gods have for their servant."

Lasgol expected Gondabar to live for many years and lead their people. But the frail look of the Leader indicated otherwise.

"What does the King want of us now?" Ingrid asked.

Gondabar looked at her and nodded.

"You are granted a rest after performing such a difficult task. The King has not indicated that he needs you for any other urgent mission, so for the moment you will not be sent out on a new assignment."

Nilsa could not hide her joy and skipped in place. Gerd smiled, also pleased to hear the good news.

Astrid nudged Lasgol, who looked at her and smiled.

"In that case, are we to resume our old duties?"

"I would be delighted if you could resume yours, Nilsa. It's always a joy to have you near, and you help me with so much…"

"But I won't…" she guessed by the way the Leader had spoken.

Gondabar nodded.

"Your next destination is the Shelter."

They all exchanged looks of surprise—and a couple of disgust. They had known this was a possibility, but they had not been sure until now.

"Is that the destination for all of us, my lord?" Egil asked.

"That's right. The Mother Specialist has requested the King to send you to continue your training and improvement. The King has agreed."

"He has?" Ingrid asked, surprised.

"He believes it will be good for the Eagles and therefore for the realm. The Mother Specialist was quite persuasive and promised the King advances in the development of Improved Rangers, something his Majesty approves of and endorses."

"Because we'll be better fighters?" Astrid asked, raising an eyebrow.

"Because you'll be Rangers with better aptitudes and skills, which will enable you to face more complex missions and enemies."

"It's understandable that our monarch wishes to have better prepared Rangers, capable of tackling future risks and dangers," Egil reasoned, eyeing his comrades.

"Especially among the Royal Eagles," Gondabar nodded. "Because of your achievements and potential, you'll be the perfect candidates for the studies the Mother Specialist pursues."

"And if we refuse those studies?" Lasgol asked. He did not want anyone experimenting on him or Camu.

Gondabar looked at him and smiled lightly.

"Sigrid only has the wellbeing of the Rangers in mind. It ought to be an honor for all of you to be specifically chosen. Isn't it?" he asked, a little taken aback. "Nilsa, Gerd, and Egil would be able to Specialize. Sigrid will give them specific training so it's more effective."

"What does specific mean?" Gerd asked.

"That you won't train with the rest of the Specialists, but that you'll have special sessions so they'll be more effective."

"That's interesting," Egil said, scratching his chin.

Lasgol was not convinced it would be so.

"And the three of you who are already Specialists will be given the opportunity to develop new specialties. This is something innovative and promising, I think."

"I consider it an honor to have been chosen," Ingrid said enthusiastically.

"I don't like the idea of the Shelter at all," Viggo protested. "Although, on the other hand, improving my skills as an Assassin is a benefit I wouldn't mind receiving."

"Will we have the option of leaving this improved training if we choose to?" Astrid asked, looking at Lasgol out of the corner of her eye.

"Absolutely. This isn't compulsory, it's a chance to learn new things and improve as Rangers."

"And what would the King say if we passed?" Lasgol asked, not believing for one moment that escape would be so easy. "Will he allow it? It's one thing if the Rangers do," he said staring at Gondabar, clearly alluding to him as the Leader. "But it's a very different thing whether or not the King will allow it."

"The King is occupied with other matters far more crucial to the realm. I doubt he has an opinion one way or another. It would be remarkable if he insisted on someone doing something they did not want to do anymore."

Lasgol could not debate that, but still, he did not find it so remarkable that Thoran might interfere in the business of the Panthers. In fact, he found it highly possible. He admitted that Gondabar was right—a king had much more important matters to attend to, and they were nothing more than a bunch of Rangers who served him. As long as they did not make too much noise, they would, hopefully, be left in peace.

"Rest today and think about it. I hope you will all accept. It's not a mandate of any kind. If any of you do not wish to go, he or she may remain here," Gondabar offered.

"Thank you, my lord, we'll think about this opportunity," Egil said.

"Very well. Let me thank you personally for the great work you've done before you leave. You have managed to unmask the traitors and wipe clean the honor of the corps by capturing the last Dark Ranger. As a Leader, it fills me with pride to have you among our people. On a personal level, you saved me… I will never forget it."

They all bowed their heads, "It was an honor," Egil said.

"Go, rest. You've earned it. You have my personal gratitude, as well as the kingdoms'."

Chapter 12

They withdrew to their room in the tower, where they would be left in peace and able to talk undisturbed about the new developments, and the consequences they might have on their lives. The decision they made now would significantly affect their futures.

"The King is sending us to the Shelter," Ingrid stated without beating around the bush as the rest sat down on the beds. "I see it as an opportunity to improve, to keep learning and developing our skills to become better Rangers."

Lasgol had gone over to pet Camu and Ona and sat on the floor with them. Hearing Ingrid, he said, "You know what I think of Sigrid and her experiments..." He shook his head. "I don't trust her. They're dangerous, and I don't really believe they have everything under control..."

"The Mother Specialist wouldn't lie about it," Ingrid told him, narrowing her eyes and folding her arms.

"I'm not saying she's lying, that wouldn't be in her character. She might be a cold, hard person sometimes, but she's honorable and upright. She's a leader with behavior beyond reproach," Lasgol said. "What I believe is that the Mother Specialist wants to keep all the experiments under control and make them safe. She's working on it, I don't doubt that, but I'm not sure she's managed to master them completely..."

"New paths are often hard to walk and making trusted advances in them requires a long march," Egil intervened thoughtfully. He sat beside Lasgol on the floor to stroke Camu.

"I don't understand what the know-it-all means," Viggo protested as he threw his dagger at the frame of the mirror on the wall. He had thrown it ten times in a row from different positions and always buried it in the same spot at the top of the frame.

"You might understand if you stopped playing with your little dagger all around the room instead of paying attention to what's being debated," Ingrid chided him.

Viggo smiled and threw his dagger backward over his left shoulder while looking over his right. He hit the same spot again with amazing skill.

"I may be just a man but, contrary to common knowledge, I can do more than one thing at a time and still do them well," he replied, still smiling.

Nilsa chuckled. "I doubt that very much. There's no man capable of doing two things well at the same time. Not even with blasted magic."

"What does that mean? That you women can and we men can't?" Gerd asked, catching the ironic tone of the statement. The giant was staring at the girls with an offended look on his face.

"Of course we can," Astrid intervened, watching the exchange from her cot. "Something you can't," she said, adding to the argument.

"Not even your boyfriend, the weirdo?" Viggo countered with a sardonic grin since he knew he had just put her in a tight spot.

Astrid looked at Lasgol, who gave her a look as if to say "you're not going to say I can't" and nodded firmly.

"Not even him," she replied, blowing a kiss at Lasgol.

Lasgol protested, as did Gerd.

"What do you mean I can't?"

"Of course we can!"

Nilsa was shaking her head and Ingrid was wagging her finger.

Very funny, Camu transmitted to Lasgol, along with a feeling of joy.

You understand what we're discussing? Lasgol asked Camu, doubting his friend could grasp the irony and meaning of what was being discussed. In general, Camu did not grasp irony and jokes with a double meaning.

I understand, Camu assured him.

Lasgol had expected he would say so, since the creature never admitted he could not do something. Often, Lasgol wondered whether Camu's character was due to the kind of creature he was or if it was his own personality, independent from the type of animal he might be. Probably both, although because he was so stubborn this was most likely a feature of his own individual personality.

Hmmmm... explain it to me then. Lasgol looked into his bulging eyes; he wanted to make sure he really understood.

Girls against boys, he transmitted, and Lasgol was left with his mouth hanging open. He really was understanding!

That's right, Camu. Very good.

I clever.

And rascally too.

More clever than Ona.

No, you're not cleverer than Ona, he assured Camu as he stroked the snow panther, who was looking at him with her deep eyes.

I be. Boys against girls.

No you're not, and boys against girls is nonsense. We're all the same. Equally capable, equally smart, equally brave, honorable, and everything good in the world.

Ona chirped once and put her paw on Lasgol's leg.

And the bad? Camu asked.

Well... those too. Equally bad. In fact, there's no difference between the genders. It doesn't matter whatever you are, boy, girl or anything else, because it doesn't make you better or worse. Or good or bad. You understand?

I understand.

Are you sure...? Lasgol kept looking into his eyes. Camu cocked his head to one side and blinked hard, which was not a very good indication. As a rule, when he did this, he was thinking hard about something, and it was usually because he did not fully understand some concept.

Yes. All the same. No difference. Boys, girls, dragons, all.

Yes... well, dragons... why did you mention dragons?

I dragon. Boy or girl?

Lasgol was taken aback.

Let's see... you're no dragon, and as to whether you're a boy or a girl... we really don't know.

Ona girl. You know. Camu, why not know?

Well... because Ona is a snow panther. That's a species we've known for a very long time and we know how to tell males from females. You on the other hand... we don't know what species you are... and so we don't know how to tell which sex you are.

You not know? Egil not?

Lasgol looked at his friend. Egil was debating the unlikelihood of men being less capable of doing more than one thing at a time and not doing said things as well as women. Gerd and Viggo cheered him while the girls had fits of giggles.

No, he doesn't know either. We've talked about it many times, and after examining you from top to bottom we can't find any indication one way or the other.

Camu closed his eyes hard. He kept them shut for a moment as if he were concentrating on something.

I think I'm boy, he transmitted to Lasgol.

Good, if you consider yourself a boy, then you're a boy. Perfect.

Camu tilted his head to one side and then the other, blinking repeatedly.

Yes. I want be boy.

Well then, you are, Lasgol said.

You tell others.

Very well, I'll tell them as soon as they finish up this silly discussion.

Discussion funny.

Yeah, you love these things.

Ona chirped twice, showing her disagreement.

Egil's defense seemed to demolish the girls' attacks, who were smiling watching the outraged faces of the men in the group.

"In any case," Viggo interrupted the argument, "what I wanted to say is that I don't understand what the weirdo is saying because he speaks in such a convoluted manner. It doesn't matter whether we're him or me or man or woman. No one but someone living glued to books and knowledge could understand him. And I have my doubts that anyone would want to."

Egil smiled. "I'll take that as a compliment," he bowed lightly to Viggo. He then carried on with his explanation. "What I meant to say is that advancing in any matter often requires traveling a long road filled with difficulties. The achievements, the discoveries, don't come as soon or as easily as one would wish. Study and the consequent advancement in certain areas of complex knowledge have required many years of effort by the most privileged minds of our continent."

"Saying it like that, it sounds as if the Mother Specialist and the Elder Specialists are going to have a lot of hard work before them to achieve the Improved Rangers they want," said Viggo.

"Not only them, but Sigrid's brother, Enduald, since she mentioned him. If I recall correctly, she commented he was helping her with the improvements," Astrid said.

"Most likely using his magic…" Nilsa added, making a face at the fact and what the use of magic meant in the process—which, one way or another, would surely affect them.

"Very true," said Egil. "We also must take into account that the

111

same can be said for the Path of Magic. It's a very difficult one which requires a lot of study, experimentation, and sacrifice. Therefore, Enduald and any other mage have had, and will have to go on working hard to advance in their magic, both to achieve new skills and to improve on the control and power of the ones they have already developed."

"Making advances in magic is no easy task, I can vouch for that," Lasgol commented. "No matter how hard I try to develop a skill, most of the time I can't manage to do it. The same happens when I try to improve the ones I already have or access the reservoir of magic I'm supposed to have and which I can't get to."

"That doesn't mean you won't manage to," said Egil. "What it tells us is that, as we'd already guessed, it's a very complicated path which requires great sacrifices. I'm sure if you keep working on developing your power, if you strive with all your heart and make it a priority in your life, you'll make it," he said encouragingly.

"I don't know…" Lasgol said, not convinced.

"I believe you will achieve it," Astrid echoed encouragingly, winking at him.

"With all this, it's quite clear that Lasgol is right and Sigrid, Enduald, and the Elder Specialists are making all the effort but there's no guarantee they have everything completely under control," said Ingrid.

"And therefore there's an evident risk, no matter how much they try to minimize it," said Viggo.

"But they're offering us the opportunity to become greatly improved," said Egil. "So, we must understand that the risk is weighed by the reward we'll receive in the end."

"In our case," Gerd said, "the risk can't be that much. I mean Nilsa, Egil, and myself, since we'll follow the Path of the Specialist like they did," he said, waving at Astrid, Ingrid, Lasgol, and Viggo.

"That's what I understand. We'll be taking most of the risk, since we're already Specialists," said Ingrid. "After all, it's us they want to turn into Improved Rangers."

"That's not entirely correct," said Egil. "The risk will be smaller for us, that's true, but from what they inferred, the way we'll be trained will be different from the way you were. Since we don't know the way and manner of this new training, we must be wary and assume there will be inherent risk."

"Oh my…" Gerd protested.

"And the risk will be especially high for Lasgol," Astrid said, "since they have already experimented on him and will want to continue doing so."

"We've also got to consider Camu," said Lasgol. "They might want to experiment on him too."

I not afraid, Camu immediately transmitted.

Not even if they experiment on you using magic?

Magic no fear. I cancel magic.

Yeah, there you're right… you can cancel magic, nullify the experiment…

"We'll absolutely refuse," said Gerd, folding his powerful arms over his huge chest.

"Let me remind you that it's not altogether imperative that we agree to this demand," Nilsa said, uncertain. "Gondabar has given us the choice of refusing it."

"But it is a great opportunity," said Ingrid. "We can all see that, right?" She looked at her partners one by one and they all nodded, even Lasgol.

"What we have to decide is whether the opportunity is worth the risk," Astrid reasoned, rising and looking out the window. "Do we accept the risk and seek the gain the opportunity offers us, or do we let the opportunity pass?"

Egil also rose. "In my case, and I speak only for myself, I think the opportunity is worth the risk. I think I can personally assume this risk. Just the experience of going to the Shelter and learning with the Elder Specialists is priceless. To become a Specialist would be an incredible asset which will help me face the challenges of the future much better prepared. But I don't mean to influence anyone's decision by this. I'm merely stating my beliefs. The training, in my case, is a desired reward, and I personally can't let the opportunity we've been presented with pass me by. The experience and knowledge I'll acquire is too important for me to reject the offer. I understand the risk, I see it, but the reward surpasses it by far."

"The knowledge motivates me, but most of all the experience of learning there," said Gerd. "The risk concerns me, especially because it's one I know nothing about, so I can't give it shape and that gives me the shivers and I start panicking…. But, like Egil, I think the reward ultimately surpasses the risk," he said, nodding and wiping the sweat from his forehead.

"I've always wanted to become a Mage Hunter," Nilsa said. "You all know that. It's always been my wish. That's why I became a Ranger. When I wasn't chosen to become a Specialist, my heart broke, I won't deny it. I thought I'd never have the chance—I'd almost renounced my dream. And now, all of a sudden, I have the opportunity, and I can't let it go by, no matter the risks."

"Well, we have three who want to go," Viggo said, rubbing his hands. "This is getting interesting. I've always thought that life without risk isn't worth living," he said, looking straight at Ingrid. "So, count on me. I'll go. A few experiments aren't going to pull me back. Besides, I want to be the best Assassin the Rangers have ever had or will have. A legend. For that, improving will be very good for me, very good indeed!"

"I won't even deign to comment on becoming a legend…" said Ingrid. "In my case, it's easy. I think it's an honor to be given the opportunity of becoming Improved Rangers, Specialists with more than one specialty. It'll help me reach my dream, which as you know is to become First Ranger of the Realm, so I'm going. Without a doubt. The risk is secondary—it's always been that."

"I don't want to be legendary like Viggo, but I do believe learning new techniques and obtaining new specialties would make me a much better Assassin," Astrid said. "Which also increases my life expectancy and that of my comrades. The better we are at our professions, especially me at my profession, the longer I'll live," she said and stared at Lasgol.

Lasgol watched his friends. They all wanted to go. They had made it very clear. Even Astrid. He heaved a deep sigh while they all looked at him expectantly, waiting for his opinion. He was the only one who was not convinced about going. He understood the benefits, what they could achieve and how much they would improve, which as Astrid had said would help them survive in situations they otherwise might not. But his previous bad experience made him hesitate. On the other hand, he did not want to deprive anyone of the chance, and he knew that if he refused to go, Astrid and maybe even Egil would not go in order to stay with him. That would rob them of an opportunity they wanted to take advantage of. He could not refuse to go and drag them along with his decision. No, he could not—he had to go.

"I have my doubts, but I'll come," he said at last.

Ingrid nodded.

"Very good, then it's decided. We'll all go!"

"It's going to be most amusing!" Viggo said with marked irony.

Lasgol watched his friends chatting about their decision and starting to plan the journey. He knew he had made the right decision. He knew for one reason in particular: he wanted to be there to protect his friends from the risks they were going to take; risks that, he had the feeling as clear as a summer morning, were very real.

Chapter 13

The following morning, they told Gondabar about their decision to continue their training at the Shelter, which seemed to greatly please the Leader of the Rangers. Since the Royal Eagles had accepted Sigrid's wish, there would be no trouble with King Thoran. Although Gondabar had made light of the possibility, Egil and Lasgol were all too aware there might have been a problem.

Gondabar sent word to Sigrid at the Shelter with a messenger owl, and once he received confirmation from the Mother Specialist, the group set out. Loke would come out to welcome them once they reached the Frozen Peak. The journey was quite pleasant. For once they were able to leisurely ride and enjoy one another's company without major worries. This was something they were unused to and it seemed odd to them.

They teased each other constantly, and a good mood reigned among them. Lasgol and Astrid rode a little apart to enjoy some privacy. Although never enough, since Ona and Camu went after them and every now and then the two joined them, or else Lasgol had to call the rascals so they would not stray with their games and mischief. Ingrid rode at the front, leading the group as she liked to do, and Nilsa rode beside her with a thousand questions and comments, mostly regarding weapons, war tactics, and the like. Every now and then she added a comment about some handsome Royal Ranger or a possible future romance, which completely threw Ingrid off. They chatted like two old friends and, to Nilsa's surprise, Ingrid seemed completely relaxed, which was rare when it came to her—she was always alert and tense, particularly when they traveled. She was not even teasing Viggo, who was riding behind them alongside Gerd and Egil.

The general good mood and harmony were a welcome change for all. Egil was commenting with Gerd on the different Specialties they would have access to according to their School, although he was not fully aware of how the Specialty selection process would go. Viggo teased them, telling them it was one thing to be invited to train and a very different one to manage to graduate in any of the Specialties. According to Viggo, a giant prone to panic and a puny know-it-all would never graduate. He was so sure he was willing to bet a year's pay. But when Gerd tried to accept the bet, Viggo withdrew it because, according to him, he did not want to rob his friends with such an easy win. He even granted double possibilities to Nilsa, who was clumsy and a nervous wreck but who had a chance to make it, whereas they had none.

During the journey in the evenings when they stopped to rest, Lasgol used the time to practice developing new skills with his Gift. The time when he had hesitated to use his magic had been left behind. The experiences he had been through—the mages, sorcerers, and healers he had met in his adventures—had opened his eyes, and now he had no doubts. He had to keep developing his skills and power. It was a must. The more skills he mastered, the safer he and his friends would be. Not only that, the greater his power was, the more likely he would be able to face significant challenges and difficulties and overcome them.

Especially the experience with the Turquoise Queen and the Star of Sea and Life had taught him that magic could be used for good, to protect those he loved, even an entire people if one was powerful enough, as Uragh was. Objects of Power were another area that fascinated Lasgol now, since their magic and power could be used to eradicate evil and face wicked monsters and enemy sorcerers. Egil shared his interest and was likeminded in this regard—they needed to study and develop Lasgol's magic and, if possible, find Objects of Power that might help them in the future.

Egil encouraged him to experiment and keep developing his magic; he even volunteered so his friend could try his skill on him, which could be somewhat dangerous. His friend also acted the part of scholar and wrote down all of their tests and discoveries about Lasgol's skills, and magic in general, in his travel journals. The same happened when they worked with Camu and his magic. But reaching conclusions with Camu was a tough task in itself. The creature tended to not give them the information in an objective manner but as he saw it, which on many occasions was wrong or simply exaggerated. Reasoning with Camu was no easy task either, so the progress they were making was rather poor. Still, they did not get discouraged and kept on trying.

That evening Lasgol was trying to develop his *Fast Shot* skill. It was one he wished to master because his archery was quite limited, no matter how much Ingrid and Nilsa helped him improve with their advice and techniques. Lasgol knew that if he managed to develop a skill that would allow him to release fast, it would give him a valuable advantage which would complement Ingrid's and Nilsa's skill with the bow. Unfortunately, he had tried to develop it on multiple occasions and always failed. In fact, it had propitiated the development of his *True Shot* skill.

But, in spite of everything, he was not discouraged. He would succeed. It was just a matter of time and perseverance. He picked his quiver and, after debating with Egil about how to provoke the yearned-for green flash which indicated he had done it, went over to a solitary tree in the middle of the snow-covered landscape to practice on it. He shut his eyes and concentrated, seeking his inner energy and finding it in the pond in the center of his chest. He could feel it, access it. Now it was a matter of generating the skill. He pictured it in his mind: releasing several consecutive arrows rapidly. Egil believed the key to accomplishing a goal was to visualize something concrete and definite. Otherwise, something fleeting or shapeless would materialize. The truth was, almost everything Egil said made sense, even when he was only theorizing, as was the case currently.

With this in mind, Lasgol pictured himself releasing arrows at the tree with a movement so fast it was barely visible. He opened his eyes and released: one, two, three times. Nothing. The flash did not come and the speed of the shots were unchanged. Lasgol snorted. It did not seem like he was going to make it this evening either. But he did not allow himself to be disappointed and kept trying. Camu and Ona watched him, lying under a tree near the fire where his comrades were warming themselves as they turned to watch him every now and then while they chatted. Astrid let him practice without interrupting him or interfering, since she knew how important it was for him to be left alone in this.

Lasgol thought about quitting for the night and going to get warm by the fire. It was very cold, and although releasing arrows as fast as possible made one warm, it was not enough to defeat the winter night chill. Since he still had about a dozen arrows in his quiver, he decided to keep going until he had none left or he froze, whichever happened first. He pressed on, and as he released the last three arrows something unusual happened. There was an alteration on the calm surface of his inner pond of energy. There was no yearned-for green flash or skill. But, that disturbance, as if someone had thrown a pebble in the lake, seemed significant to him. Yes, he had been on the brink of achieving it. Perseverance was yielding its fruit. Confident he was making progress and was near succeeding, he went to tell Egil and warm up a little, since he could not feel his hands or toes.

They continued their journey at dawn, and by early evening they reached the skirts of the Frozen Peak. A lone rider was waiting at the foot of the great lonely mountain. When they were close enough to identify him they realized it was Loke. The Specialist was unmistakable with his dark hair and the red skin of a Masig. His brown and white pinto horse also spoke of his origin. Norghanians did not use to ride prairie horses. Lasgol sent Camu a mental message to camouflage so the Masig Ranger would not see him. He was not sure whether Loke knew of the existence of Camu, and as a rule Lasgol preferred to keep the creature secret as much as possible. One thing he had learned was that discretion helped avoid problems, and he always tried to practice it.

"Welcome," Loke greeted them with a friendly smile.

"How are you?" Ingrid asked in return.

"Happy to see you again and in better circumstances."

"Yeah, because the last time we saw each other it was in an ambush by the Dark Rangers," Viggo recalled.

"An ambush we survived by the skin of our teeth," Ingrid nodded. "We did not see you afterwards at the Great Council," Ingrid said questioningly.

"I'm not a member, I can't attend," the Masig said, shaking his head.

"We didn't see you at the capital either," Viggo said.

"I don't like cities. Too much rock and too many people. I prefer the great plains and snow-covered mountains."

"Hear, hear. I'm with you," Gerd said.

"I serve the Elder Specialists. I remained waiting outside the capital until I was called."

"How are they?" Lasgol asked him.

"Well. They're all in good health. Elder Ivar has fully recovered from the wounds he suffered at the Dark Rangers' ambush."

"I'm glad to hear it," Lasgol nodded.

"At their advanced age, wounds take longer to heal," Viggo said with some irony.

"The Elders are unique—age is a secondary factor to them. Those of you who've had the privilege and good fortune to train with them know that better than anybody," Loke replied.

"Indeed, they're very special and age doesn't seem to weigh on them at all," Ingrid agreed. "I haven't seen anyone else with such vitality, physical strength, and mental prowess among all the Rangers. Certainly not among the new blood," she said, looking at Viggo meaningfully.

"They're amazing, that's true," Astrid said. "Besides, the knowledge and experience they possess are priceless."

Loke nodded. "They've sent me to fetch you. They're waiting for you." He pointed behind him at the Frozen Peak.

"Let's not make the Elders wait," said Egil with a gleam of excitement in his eyes. "It's bad manners, and besides, I'm looking forward to seeing the Shelter."

"That makes two of us," said Nilsa, who was rocking back and forth in her saddle, ecstatic.

"Follow me then," said Loke and, facing the skirts of the great peak, he began climbing one of the sides. The group followed one by one. Loke led them to the entrance of a huge cave; he went into it and they all followed.

"We'll leave our horses here. I'll look after them."

Ingrid nodded and dismounted.

The others did too. Lasgol said goodbye to Trotter and stroked his neck.

Loke will take good care of you. Rest, my friend, we'll meet again soon.

Trotter snorted and moved his head up and down. They left the horses in the cave and began the ascent to the Frozen Peak. It was already a complicated climb due to the steep incline and the difficulty of the rocky ledges, and the fact that it was winter and everything was covered in snow made it even more challenging.

"Tread carefully," Loke warned them as he led the climb. "It's quite slippery, and the air on the Peak is icy."

"Just what I was looking forward to doing today, climbing a snow-covered peak in a cold that freezes even your ideas," Viggo commented with his usual irony.

"A little exercise will be good for you," Astrid said, winking at him. "We don't want you to rust."

"I think a short nap by a campfire would be even better for me," he replied as he climbed carefully to avoid slipping.

"Do we have to go all the way up to the tip of the peak?" Gerd asked as he looked upward, his face red from the effort.

"Almost to the tip but not quite," Ingrid told him. "It's not as hard as it looks. Keep going, don't think about it, and you'll be there before you know it."

"I'll do that…" the giant replied.

"Nilsa, take it slowly, up there it's steep and slippery," Ingrid warned the redhead.

"I'll be careful," her friend said as she double-checked every step and hold.

They climbed after Loke toward the upper cavern almost at the top of the Peak. Egil delayed them a little since he had difficulty climbing, especially the last part where the air was so icy it was cutting. Lasgol brought up the rear, ensuring Egil could make it. Ona and Camu went up without any trouble after Lasgol, who was always impressed by how easily they both climbed mountains. Camu, of course, was capable of climbing any surface—his paws adhered to everything.

"We're here," Loke said when they reached the cavern.

They went in and, although it was still cold inside, they were protected from the wind that blew outside, which they all immediately appreciated. Loke led them through natural corridors and several caverns before they reached an enormous one with blue-white walls. In the center of the gigantic cavern they saw a colossal block of ice. Inside, frozen for all eternity, stood what seemed to be a mythical creature: a golden dragon.

"By the Ice Gods, it's a dragon!" Gerd cried, putting his hands to his head.

"You believe me now?" Viggo said reproachfully. "I told you I had found a dragon…"

Gerd was unable to reply. He was staring at the colossal creature with his mouth hanging open and he had gone completely white, as if all the blood had drained from his body.

"That… can't be a dragon," Nilsa said, shaking her head and going around the block of ice. "I refuse to believe it," she continued, so absorbed and nervous as she looked up at it that she tripped on a lump of ice and fell over.

"See? Even Nilsa has fainted in awe at the sight of the Frozen Dragon," said Viggo.

"I didn't faint! I tripped! Smartass! You idiot!" she yelled at Viggo as she jumped to her feet.

"This is truly fascinating," Egil said as he stepped over to the massive block of ice and, with his gloved hand, wiped a spot clear to be able to better see inside. "It's something fantastic. Definitely fantastic," he murmured, almost gluing his eyes to the ice in his eagerness to see what was inside. "A reptilian-looking creature with golden scales and two extended great wings. I see four claws, huge jaws open in an eternal roar, and a huge body with a long, crested tail. Definitely fascinating."

"As far as we know it's not a dragon but a shape that looks like one," said Lasgol. "I wouldn't rush to say it's a dragon."

Be dragon, Camu messaged him.

Of course, what else would you say?

I know it be dragon.

Ona, you're smarter and more intuitive, what do you think? Is it a dragon? The snow panther chirped twice.

Ona not know.

Oh sure, and you do.

Be like me. Dragon.

Apart from knowing it, do you have some way of proving it? Some reason why you're so sure?

Not know prove.

Then let's not jump to conclusions.

Be dragon. Not jump.

"Let's hope it isn't," Gerd said, shaking his head.

"I know it's a dragon, and one day it's going to wake up and then you'll see what happens," Viggo said, folding his arms.

"No! Really?" Nilsa said taken aback, unsure of what to think.

"Don't pay any attention to him," Ingrid said. "It's not a dragon and it's certainly not going to wake up. That's just nonsense."

"We can't dismiss the possibility that there really is a dragon trapped in that block of ice," said Egil. "It might very well have been frozen in a massive, ancient frost over four thousand years ago when dragons ruled over Tremia."

"Egil, you too?" Ingrid sighed reproachfully, shaking her head.

"We can't rule out that possibility without studying it properly. The likeness is manifest. It's possible it happened; not very likely, but not impossible," Egil went on.

"What you want is to study it," Ingrid said.

"I really would. I'll ask permission from the Mother Specialist."

"She doesn't usually grant it," Loke warned him.

"I'll ask her anyway," Egil insisted, his tone of voice clearly conveying his enthusiasm at the possibility of discovering something "fantastic," as he liked to say.

"It could also be a statue or a sculpture of a dragon made by men which then froze," said Astrid.

"True, we can't dismiss that possibility either," said Egil.

"It might also be an optical effect created by some kind of object or figure inside the ice," Lasgol ventured.

"Object?" Egil said curiously. "It might be, but I find it unlikely. To create such an optical illusion wouldn't be easy, and it would've had to be on purpose, since accidentally creating such an impressive sight or freezing it would be highly unlikely," Egil mused, walking around the great block of ice.

"You mean like when they set some mirrors against others and the images get distorted and suddenly you see things differently?" Gerd asked.

"And where have you seen that?" Viggo asked Gerd.

"At the Spring Fair in my village. Once a charmer came, and he had magic mirrors. They made you look fat, or tall, or even like a dwarf. The best was when he set several mirrors in different positions inside a dark tent with gas-lamp lights and you completely lost yourself. You couldn't get out the way you went in."

"Maybe that's because you're so dumb, instead of the mirrors playing tricks," Viggo mocked him jokingly.

"Maybe I'll give you a bear hug and show you how much this dumb one loves you," Gerd replied, spreading his arms toward him.

"No, not that, it's the worst of tortures!" Viggo cried in mock terror as he ran to the other side of the frozen dragon to escape Gerd's hug.

Lasgol felt the hair at the back of his neck stand on end as he stared at the dragon.

"I mean an Object of Power," he specified. They all stared at him—they knew the implications of such a possibility.

"A magic object?" asked Astrid.

"I don't like this at all," said Nilsa seriously.

"This is a place of Power," said Lasgol, sweeping the cavern with his gaze. "The Mother Specialist knows. The Elders are aware of it. Either the cavern or the Frozen Dragon has Power, I guarantee it."

"Of course it has Power," said Viggo, poking his head out from behind the great block of ice. "Because it's a real dragon!"

"That remains to be proven," Ingrid said. "As you can see, there are different opinions."

"Yeah, yeah, I'll buy Gerd's mirrors, that's the most convincing one," he said sarcastically.

"This place is indeed a place of Power," Loke confirmed. "As is the White Pearl."

"Have the Mother Specialist and the Elders confirmed that?" Egil asked Loke.

"Yes, they have. As has Enduald, who is an Enchanter and can feel the Power."

"Well, that makes it all the more interesting, and it'll be fantastic to be able to study it," said Egil.

Lasgol was not thrilled that his friend was so keen to study the Frozen Dragon.

"I think this evening, when we're alone, I'll tell you what happened to me here during the Experiment…" Lasgol muttered, wanting his friends to realize the danger of interacting with the Dragon and the power of this place.

"You already told us," Ingrid said.

"Yes. But maybe I didn't stress enough the role of magic through the whole process and how dangerous it is."

"More than stress, I believe what you want to do is emphasize the danger," Egil winked at him. Lasgol knew his friend *did* understand what he meant to transmit to them about this place—the power it emanated, its danger. And what it meant to experiment like Sigrid had done with him here.

"It wouldn't be a bad thing if you told us everything that happened to you again with as much detail as you remember," Ingrid said. "If there's latent danger in this place, we should know about it and be ready."

"For the last time, I'm telling you," Viggo insisted. "We're standing before a frozen Golden Dragon. Of course there's danger here. A huge one!" he shouted, waving his arms high and wide at the block of ice.

Gerd's and Nilsa's faces were the starkest: his of pure terror and hers of total loathing.

"I'm sure the Mother Specialist will provide you with a necessary explanation about this place and its power," Loke said to ease them.

"I'd love to hear it," Egil said.

"Let's continue," Loke indicated one of the corridors and went into it. The group followed. They arrived at the end of an elevated tunnel which opened into an immense valley, the end of which could not be seen. The valley, partly snow-covered, was surrounded by a range of mountains that extended in all directions, and in it were forests, rivers, and lakes.

"Wow. It's beautiful!" said Gerd, gasping at such a beautiful landscape.

"You don't say," Nilsa said, joining him as she looked down, a hand shading her eyes.

"Nilsa, Gerd, Egil, welcome to the Shelter," Loke said.

Chapter 14

Loke led the group through the valley toward the Lair. They crossed several forests and some rivers before they faced the final stretch. Nilsa, Gerd, and Egil were alert, looking all around and enjoying the great valley the Shelter was, filled with wildlife and plants they did not know. Despite being winter, the temperature was quite mild, and although everything was snow-covered, they were able to walk without trouble. The mountains surrounding the landscape protected it from the icy winter chill.

They arrived at a great hill surrounded by a thick forest where the snow had barely settled, which was surprising. But what was really incredible was the enormous white sphere sitting on top of the hill. It was thirteen feet in diameter and looked like a huge, polished pearl shining with an arcane aura.

The Masig Specialist stopped and addressed the group.

"For the new ones, this is the White Pearl."

Gerd gave a long whistle. "Wow... it's awesome..."

Nilsa snorted, "It's as if one of the Ice Gods had set it here..."

Egil could not take his eyes off the Pearl. The great white sphere had him spellbound.

"This is fantastic. Is it my imagination or does it really give off a magical aura?" he asked, staring at the object.

Yes, ancient magic, Camu confirmed.

Can you feel it? Lasgol was surprised.

Yes. Before little, now more.

Wow, it seems your perception of magic continues to develop.

I develop much. Yes.

This, or everything in general?

Everything in general.

Lasgol rolled his eyes. He had asked to see whether Camu noticed the irony but, once again, he had not.

Beside him, Egil saw his face and stared at him.

Lasgol noticed. "You're not mistaken," he confirmed.

"The White Pearl, like the Lair which is right below it, oozes energy or power if you understand it better," Loke said, avoiding the word magic. "The Lair is an enormous cave inside the hill with a set of singular smaller caves, each with a specific purpose you will be learning about."

"Is it where the Mother Specialists and the Elders dwell?" asked Egil, who was still staring at the Pearl absolutely fascinated.

"Exactly," Loke confirmed, pointing at one side of the hill where they could see an opening in the rock. It will also be your home while you're here."

"How cozy," Viggo said with irony.

"Let's continue and not make the Mother Specialist wait," Loke said.

Sigrid welcomed the group with open arms—and a smile of satisfaction—in front of the entrance to the lair, where she had been waiting for their arrival. She was wearing her usual green-hooded cloak with large brown streaks and a scarf of the same color which covered her mouth and nose. In her hand was a long wooden staff with silver engravings which she leaned on. She pulled down the scarf to speak and when she did steam came out of her mouth.

"Welcome, Royal Eagles. It fills me with joy to see you here today," the leader of the Elder Specialists said.

"And it's a joy to be back at the Shelter," Ingrid replied with a respectful bow.

"This place brings back many memories," Astrid nodded.

"Good ones, I hope," Sigrid said with a mischievous smile which rejuvenated her face, marked by the passing of time. The more than seventy springs she had seen could be appreciated in her looks, which still retained the essence of past beauty.

"Almost all exceptionally good," Viggo replied with heavy irony.

Sigrid smiled, but this time her smile was somewhat harsh.

"The Path of the Specialist is a difficult one to follow. There is nothing worthwhile in life that is easy to accomplish. If it appears so it is an illusion or a deceit. Most likely the latter. Always mistrust and work hard to achieve what you want in life."

"Very accurate," Egil said, nodding. "The words of the Mother Specialist aren't only true but also quite inspiring."

"I am glad you see it that way, Egil Olafstone," she addressed him. "I have heard positive things about you."

"I hope they came from respectable people with good judgment," Egil replied half joking, "I don't usually receive compliments, and I have few friends outside this group," he said with a wave at his comrades.

"Enemies you certainly have, and many are at court. You know that and I know that," she said with a wink. "However, the words that praise your intelligence and good work come from a very dear old friend who has my full trust and whose judgment I value greatly: Dolbarar."

"The Leader of the Camp is too kind and benevolent with me…"

"I doubt it. Dolbarar is not one to praise someone unless he or she deserves it. He does so only when someone truly impresses him. You have done that, which does you credit and which I value."

Egil bowed, accepting the compliment gracefully.

"Thank you, ma'am, I'll try not to disappoint that trust."

"I am sure you will disappoint neither Dolbarar nor myself," Sigrid said confidently. "At the time you were unable to enter the Shelter as a Specialist, but your trajectory as a Ranger and Royal Eagle, besides the potential we see in you and how intelligent we know you are, means you will fit in perfectly in the Shelter."

"Thank you for your kind words. It's an honor to have been invited to train here," Egil said. "More so taking into account that I was rejected previously and that there are few who are offered a second chance once rejected."

"Only those who truly deserve it, which are usually not many," Sigrid replied, raising an eyebrow. Her face took on the look of an evil witch, something Lasgol knew all too well and that his friends would experience soon. The Mother Specialist went from being a kind, good witch to an evil one in the blink of an eye, and when this happened it was scary.

Egil noticed the expression on her face and the change in her tone.

"It makes it yet a greater honor," he said gratefully and humbly.

"I have plans for you," Sigrid told him, as her expression turned back to being kind and pleasant. "I am sure you will find a home in the Specialties of Nature where you will be able to train and develop a promising career which will lead you to a successful future among the Rangers."

"The Mother Specialist makes me blush. I don't know whether I'll be able to reach   such high goals," Egil said, seeming touched by Sigrid's high expectations and kind words.

"Or perhaps the path you must follow will not be among the Specialties of Nature. You might find your destiny in those of Expertise or even Archery."

"I'm positive it won't be in Expertise or Archery," Egil said with an uneasy grin. "The bow isn't my forte, and as to physical combat, I'm hopeless I must admit, much to my own chagrin."

"I can vouch for that. He's utterly useless," Viggo said. "If you take him away from his books he's as lost as a penguin from the Frozen Continent in a Nocean Empire desert."

"I see your friends know you well…" Sigrid said, cocking her head and looking at Egil from top to toe as if she were weighing whether Viggo's words were true or not. "In any case, we shall see what the Harmony Test determines in your case. There have been surprises in the past," she fixed her gaze on Lasgol as she said this. "Am I right?" she asked, inviting him to speak.

Lasgol remembered what had happened to him and how he had ended up with two Specialties instead of one like everyone else who had specialized with him.

"Yes… great surprises…" he admitted.

Sigrid smiled at him. "I have hope and confidence that this special group will provide us with new interesting surprises. I understand that if you are all here today it is because you wish to go on learning and improving as Ranger Specialists."

"Yes, Mother Specialist," Ingrid said with a slight bow of respect toward Sigrid.

"If the Mother Specialist believes we're worthy of training as Specialists..." Nilsa said hesitantly.

"We've come to accept the invitation the Mother Specialist made to us..." Gerd said.

"Of course I believe you are worthy of training as Specialists. You have proven this with your actions in the missions you have carried out—saving the King and his brother, freeing the kingdom of frozen monsters, and capturing the Dark Rangers as Royal Eagles. You more than deserve it, which is why I invited you, and I absolutely maintain the invitation. You have impressed me out there," she pointed her hand beyond the Frozen Peak.

"We appreciate it," Nilsa said, blushing. She made a small curtsy, but since she was so nervous she almost lost her balance. Luckily she did not disgrace herself in front of Sigrid with her usual clumsiness.

"It's an honor we deeply appreciate," Gerd added, putting his hand on Nilsa's back to steady her.

"Will we join the rest of those selected this year then?" Egil asked with a nod at a group of Rangers trotting by in their physical strength lesson. They were running in pairs and one ran with the other one on his or her back. He noticed a white tiger running after them with unfriendly intentions by the looks of the runners. When he saw the tiger lash out at the last one, he swallowed.

"Oh, I see you have noticed Snowflake. They are doing one of my favorite exercises. I'm sure your friends remember it well..." she said, eying Astrid, Ingrid, Lasgol, and Viggo as they instinctively put their hands to their backsides.

"We do remember well, some of us have scars that will remind us forever," Viggo moaned.

"More than well," Lasgol corroborated.

Sigrid smiled, "There are experiences in life you never forget. They teach us and remind us how important certain lessons are. A Specialist who does not look after his or her body, no matter how good they are with weapons or even using their head, is doomed to end up dead in combat, at the bottom of a cliff or frozen on a mountain because of their lack of physique."

"We've learned that well, and its' something we believe and never neglect," Ingrid said.

"The constant challenges we've been faced with keep us in shape and with a mind as sharp as a Ranger's knife," Astrid assured her.

"I believe you, mostly because you have managed to survive so far and you do not seem to have sustained serious injuries."

"We have been wounded," Nilsa nodded.

"Yes, we have, most of us," Lasgol joined in, "but nothing too serious, at least so far, and we hope it will continue that way."

"The additional training you will receive will help you continue to remain safe and avoid greater evils. Always and as long as you listen and internalize the teaching you will receive. As to your question, Egil, you will not train with them," she said with a wave at the group who was running away with Snowflake making them keep up the pace.

"We won't? Then who will we train with?" Egil asked, interested, looking toward the inside of the Lair, dying to go in and see for himself whether everything the others had told him about that enigmatic and surprising place was true and not an exaggeration.

"The three of you will train together and away from the rest who will follow the traditional system. You will learn under a new training method we have designed specifically for you. The idea is to design this new method to produce faster and better results in the Rangers we train here."

"Then we'll be the first to follow this new system?" Gerd asked, unable to hide from his expression the fact that being the first to take part in an experimental training program upset him deeply.

"You will be, and we are hoping it will be a success," Sigrid said, opening her arms and throwing her head back.

"Being the first at something implies, as a rule, more problems and even losses, at least until stabilizing the goal is achieved," Egil commented thoughtfully, his head bowed.

"Wow... that doesn't sound so good..." said Gerd.

"Some risk gives thrill to things," Nilsa said. "Isn't that what Viggo is always saying?"

"If you're going to be led by what I say, you ought to think again," Viggo said with a look that said even he did not follow his own advice and sayings.

"It will certainly be quite interesting, that I can guarantee," Sigrid said. "It will be a little harder and more complicated than the traditional program, but it is necessary in order to obtain better results and, in particular, to speed up the process."

"So we'll pay the price for being the first with our flesh and our minds," Egil guessed.

"There is no gain without suffering, all Rangers know this," Sigrid said. "In any case, I do not wish you to participate in the new process of training if you do not want to. You may join the rest, although they have been training for some while and you will have to catch up quickly."

Nilsa, Gerd, and Egil exchanged doubtful glances. Gerd was afraid of jumping into a new training program they did not know. Nilsa wanted to be the first one to graduate from the new system, but she was concerned about what it would entail. Egil was certain there would be risks and it would be hard. On the other hand, something new and innovative drew his attention and he wanted to try it out. Their glances expressed these feelings. Egil glanced at Nilsa, and she finally decided and nodded repeatedly. Then he looked at Gerd who, with a loud snort, shrugged and nodded. Egil smiled and nodded at his friends.

"We'll do it," he told Sigrid.

"Wonderful. I did not expect any less of you," Sigrid told them.

"And what about us, Mother Specialist?" Viggo asked. "What about those of us who are already Specialists? What awaits us?"

"I see you are as straightforward as always."

"A bit more. I improve with time, like a good wine," Viggo said, full of sarcasm.

Sigrid nodded, smiling. "As I already mentioned at the Council, I have been working to improve the training to achieve Improved Rangers. The goal is to make Rangers with several specializations who will be an unstoppable force in the field. Imagine what it will mean to have a hundred Ranger Specialists, all with several specializations."

"That would be amazing," Ingrid said, nodding enthusiastically. "They would be almost impossible to stop."

"That is precisely the idea—to create a force of Specialists so outstanding they will be capable of facing up to any challenge."

"That sounds good. I would make them all the same Expertise, Assassins to be precise, and set them loose at night to finish off all the enemies," Viggo said. "Yes, I can see it now. By dawn, half the realm's enemies would be dead," he said, his gaze lost in the overcast sky.

"The King also believes this is something we ought to pursue. It would grant him an important advantage on the battlefield. Besides, he would gain great prestige with such a force—he would instill fear and respect in enemies of the realm. Additionally, it would give him the opportunity to fill the crown's chests by leasing the services of these mighty Rangers to other realms."

"For that it would be necessary to develop multiple Specializations, and so far only Lasgol has done that," Astrid said, wrinkling her nose.

"That is true," Sigrid nodded. "It is true that Lasgol is an anomaly, but I have been working on being able to replicate it."

"Through experimenting…" Lasgol said, not at all happy.

"That is correct," the Mother Specialist admitted. "I received permission from the King to continue my experiments and studies. Being able to put it all into practice with four extraordinary specialists is what I have been waiting for."

"We are extraordinary," Viggo agreed, "especially me. But all this talk of experimenting doesn't sound at all good..." he shook his head. "No, not good at all," he shook it again.

"I promise you I will be extremely careful and watchful so that everything goes well. Besides, my brother Enduald will assist me at all times. He has formulated a way to reduce the risk in the experiments significantly, controlling them with enchantments. We will also use the help of another mage to make sure everything goes well."

"Magic... this gets more complicated still," Viggo said, shrugging as if to shake it off.

"The experiments did not leave me with a good aftertaste... I'm not much in favor of them," Lasgol said directly.

"I know, and I understand why. But, let me assure you that this time they are very different and, as I have already explained, we will be taking many safety measures," Sigrid insisted.

"Safety measures that use magic for experiments that use magic," Lasgol said, unconvinced. He folded his arms over his chest.

"Trust me," Sigrid looked into his eyes, trying to transmit confidence and trust, which Lasgol noticed but which did not really touch his soul.

"We're used to risk and what it entails," Astrid said. "That's why we assess situations cautiously."

Sigrid nodded heavily. "I do not deny there is risk, but think of the reward which this risk you think you are going to take will bring you. You will gain dominion in several Specialties simultaneously, which is something formidable. Furthermore, if everything goes as I expect it to and the new system works and I can develop it even more, you will even be able to achieve specialties in different Schools."

"That sounds really interesting. To be able to combine specialties from different schools is a dream I would love to attempt," said Ingrid, nodding as she looked at Sigrid.

"Which could become true..." Sigrid replied, waving her staff in circles.

"I'm only interested in Expertise," Viggo said with a condescending nod at the other schools. "I will obtain all the specialties of Expertise and become a legendary Assassin."

"That is a lot to wish for," Sigrid said, raising an eyebrow. "I do not know whether that is even possible, but we can certainly try. I can offer you all of this if you accept to follow my program and participate in my studies and experiments."

There was silence. They were all evaluating Sigrid's words. After a moment they began to nod. All except Lasgol, who was still troubled. But he was keenly aware that the benefit they could have by working with Sigrid was too great to let this chance pass.

"If the Mother Specialist believes the risk is under control, I think we ought to try," he yielded at last. The rest of his friends joined Lasgol in accepting.

"Very well, your decision pleases me greatly," Sigrid said. "I hope you have brought your mischievous companion with you," she told Lasgol and looked at Ona, trying to guess where her brother might be.

Before she finished her sentence, Lasgol was already feeling afraid for Camu. If the Elders experimented on them they would do so too on Camu. His heart shrank. No, he would not let them experiment on his friend.

"He's with me, yes. But he stays out of all of this."

Sigrid made a face and her evil witch expression appeared again. She was about to say something but she thought better of it and shut her mouth.

"Of course, Lasgol, of course," she said, and her good witch face came back.

Chapter 15

Snow was beginning to fall heavily over the Lair and in all that part of the valley, and with it, night also fell over them as they were talking without their realizing it. All of a sudden there was the sound of stone grating on stone and with a slow, sliding motion, the round stone door shut on the entrance, preventing passage into the great cave.

"Well, it would seem the Lair doesn't want us to come in," Viggo commented acidly. "Are you sure we're welcome, Mother Specialist?"

"You are, I promise. The door shuts with the arrival of night, you know that well, since you have lived among us, young Assassin," Sigrid replied.

Viggo nodded and then shrugged.

Ingrid eyed the door with a thoughtful look on her face.

"I seem to remember it shutting later, didn't it?" she asked Sigrid.

"Your memory does not fail you, dear Archer. The door used to shut later, but for some reason we still have not been able to understand, now it does so earlier, at sundown," Sigrid explained.

"This is new. It seems significant, doesn't it?" Lasgol noted, surprised. "A change the Rangers haven't forced upon the Lair: there must be some arcane reason…"

Door shuts because magic, Camu messaged him.

That's what I was thinking too. Did you feel the magic?

Yes, magic be very ancient.

Can you guess how ancient? Lasgol asked, surprised.

Yes, now I can better.

That's great. Your power and sensitivity are developing, they're growing. That's very good news.

I know. I clever.

Lasgol had to hold back an ironic remark. Camu would not understand it anyway, so best not to say it.

Be alert to any magic you feel while we're here, regardless of the kind. I think that both the Lair and Sigrid, and particularly her brother Enduald, will use magic.

I always alert to magic.

Good boy.

I cancel magic.

But before cancelling it, we examine the situation. Don't make the decision alone. It could be dangerous.

Situation? Camu asked, transmitting his inability to understand the concept.

I mean where we are, when, who is with us, who or what generates the magic—these

132

factors will determine whether we should interrupt it or not.

Better interrupt it. Ask later.

No, no, no. That's like shooting first and asking questions later. It's not right. We must think and speak first.

Viggo says shoot first and ask afterwards.

Don't pay attention to what Viggo says. Half the time he's wrong and the other half he says utter nonsense.

Viggo fun.

Yes, that he is, but he's also a bad example to follow. You heed me and ask me before accepting as good whatever Viggo says, or we'll have big trouble.

Okay.

Lasgol did not find this "okay" very convincing, but he knew it was the word Camu showed agreement with, even if he was not planning on doing or following whatever he had agreed to.

"The reason the Lair is acting differently is a mystery to us. We are studying it, but for the moment we have no explanation whatsoever," Sigrid explained.

"When something changes there's usually a reason for it," said Astrid, who was also staring at the huge stone door that had fitted itself on to the entrance to the cave.

"Yes, there is. That is why we are investigating it. We wish to know what is happening and why this and other changes are taking place in our beloved Shelter."

"Other changes?'" Lasgol asked, raising an eyebrow. "What other changes?" he wanted to know and was unable to stop himself, even though he knew his tone was a bit strong. If there were other changes in the Shelter they should know about them to consider what they might mean.

"We will comment on the changes we are seeing at leisure. You have just arrived and this is not the time. We had better go inside. This incessant snow is beginning to soak our clothes and it would be unfortunate if you became sick upon your arrival. Or I for extending the welcoming," Sigrid said, shaking off the snowflakes that already covered her shoulders.

"Of course, Mother Specialist," Loke said and went over to the door.

Lasgol was left with the longing to ask further questions, but he knew the Mother Specialist, and if she did not wish to talk right then she would not, so he did not insist.

Sigrid followed Loke and then the rest brought up the rear. The Masig gave three short whistles and in reply there was a dry *crack*, followed by the sound of stone grating on stone. A large part of the rock shaped like a circle slid to one side, revealing a large opening in the rocky wall and a warm light coming from inside.

The Mother Specialist went in followed by Loke. Then the others entered.

"Welcome to the Chamber of Runes," Sigrid said. "Those of you who are already familiar with it, welcome back, and those who are setting foot here for the first time, I assure you that your stay here will change your lives forever."

Nilsa, Gerd, and Egil were looking at the place, eyes wide with wonder. The great cavern was lit up with torches and the flames made dancing shadows on the walls of rock which were strangely curved, including the floor and ceiling.

"Mother Specialist …" Egil started to say as he stared at the chamber, impressed.

"Yes, Egil," Sigrid said encouragingly with an expectant gaze.

"Lasgol told us the runes in this chamber still hold power…"

Sigrid nodded. "That is correct, and being as you are of a scholarly mind and also a good observer, I guess you want to see them, am I right?"

"If it's not too much inconvenience and the Mother Specialist has no problem with it," he replied.

"I see no inconvenience. It is no secret. I must warn you I will not have answers to your questions once you see them, since we know almost nothing about them. There is a great deal of information about these runes that escapes our knowledge and understanding."

"Understood," Egil said, nodding.

"Very well." Sigrid showed them the staff of power. She circled it around her head in a whirl and hit the rock under her feet with the bottom of it. The silver engravings on the staff flashed powerfully, as if activating an enchantment in it.

They all watched Sigrid's actions—some like Egil and Lasgol with great interest, and others like Gerd and Nilsa with fear or dislike.

Magic in staff, Camu warned.

An instant later a silver flash came out of the staff, bathing its surroundings with a silver light from the floor to the ceiling, spattering the walls around them and even themselves. The burst of light made them cover their eyes with their arms and hands so as not to be momentarily dazed. When they focused on their surroundings, they discovered something incredible: above the door, on the walls, on the floor and the ceiling, silver runes impossible to understand had appeared.

"Fan… tastic…" Egil muttered in awe.

"And… fabulous…" Gerd added.

Magic runes, very ancient.

Don't try to cancel it. Let Egil examine them and then he can tell us what he thinks of these runes.

Okay.

Lasgol was not sure Camu was able to cancel the magic of the runes in this place. It felt like ancient and powerful magic. In any case, Lasgol did not want him to do it. There did not seem to be imminent danger of any kind, and he wanted Egil to be able to study them in peace and see what conclusions he reached.

"Truly enigmatic," Egil said, somewhat recovered from the shock and now examining the runes more carefully.

"It is. I will let you enjoy the runes and the power emanating from this mysterious place, and I will retire," the Mother Specialist said. "I have duties waiting for me I must see to."

"Of course, Mother Specialist," Ingrid hastened to say. "We don't wish to keep you."

"Make yourselves comfortable. You know the place. Loke will help you with whatever you need. Let me tell you once again how delighted I am that you decided to accept my offer," she told them, nodding as she headed for the Winter Cave.

"Yes, let's go to the Spring Cave—we can leave our equipment and get comfortably installed," Ingrid said, shifting her traveling backpack on her back, as well as the three bows she always carried.

She started to move but noticed that Egil was glued to the spot. He was still absorbed, contemplating the runes as if hypnotized by the silver gleam of the engravings on the rock.

"Fascinating, this cavern is truly something exceptional," he commented, watching with eyes wide open at the colossal cave around them. "Not only because of these runes of arcane power, but because of the cavern's structure," he said in an analytic tone.

"Structure?" Astrid asked, following Egil's gaze.

"Absolutely," Gerd replied before Egil could. The giant had not moved either. "It's... as if a huge sphere had grown in here and had been taken outside..."

"It's very weird, yes..." said Nilsa, who, like Egil and Gerd, was looking around without moving. "And you're right about what you commented regarding this place, it gives the impression that the great pearl out on the top is right above this one inside..." Nilsa eyed the curved walls of the cavern.

"You're right... this doesn't look like a coincidence," Gerd joined her in studying the whole interior of the cavern illuminated with the torches.

"Very good guess," Egil congratulated him.

"You don't think it's a coincidence either?" Gerd turned to ask him.

"Irrefutable, my dear friend, irrefutable. Such exactitude in the position and similarity of shapes can't be a coincidence. Furthermore, we know there's magic in the walls of this cavern and probably in the pearl as well, even if we haven't seen it yet."

"Does anybody know the purpose of this cavern or its origin?" Egil asked, then realized Sigrid was no longer with them—he had been utterly absorbed analyzing what his eyes transmitted to him of this singular place. "Oh, she's gone. It's obvious this isn't something the Rangers built, Lasgol told me the place was found like this when they explored it."

Loke nodded.

"The Rangers discovered this place, but nobody knows its purpose or origin," he explained.

"Fantastic," Gerd said with a smile.

"Fantastic?" Nilsa was surprised.

"Yes, because it gives us the chance to study this unusual site. Nothing better than a good mystery to stimulate the intellect," he said, putting a finger to his head.

"There's no mystery to solve here," Viggo said bored.

"Isn't there? I'd say there is," Egil said, looking at him intrigued. "Why do you say that?"

"Because I've already solved the mystery," he said proudly, folding his arms over his chest.

"What mystery have you solved?" Ingrid asked him, cocking her head with a look that meant she did not trust Viggo's words.

"That of this cavern and its magic runes, something none of you were able to do, which shows that apart from being the best Assassin in the realm, the most good-looking and charismatic, I'm also very intelligent," he said nonchalantly.

They all stared at him, but after a moment they burst out laughing.

"Isn't he vain!" Nilsa laughed, holding her stomach.

"And most unpretentious too," Gerd said amid guffaws.

Ingrid rolled her eyes and shook her head.

"You can laugh all you want, but it's the truth," Viggo insisted seriously.

"Fine, fine, enlighten us with your intelligence. What's this mystery you've solved?" Ingrid said at last.

"Very simple. The Lair is really a dragon's lair. The dragon that's frozen at the entrance of the Shelter to be precise."

"What nonsense!" cried Nilsa. "No way. Impossible!"

"Your explanation is a tad fantastic," Gerd said, shaking his head.

"I've heard you say many silly things, but this one is right up there with the best of them," Ingrid said, waving her hands about.

"Say what you want, I don't care. I know what this place is," Viggo replied, not caring what anyone said—he was not going to change his mind. "And you know it too, even if you don't say it," he accused Lasgol, jabbing his finger at him.

Lasgol shrugged.

"I think we need to find out a lot more before we jump on a theory like that…"

"You know perfectly well what's at the end of the Cave of Winter."

"Yes, but what we discovered doesn't prove your theory…"

"It's an interesting theory…" Egil said suddenly. "Not all that farfetched," he went on thoughtfully.

"Egil, please, don't encourage him or he'll never stop this nonsense," said Ingrid.

Nilsa joined her friend's protest. "Yeah, don't encourage him, that's all we need."

"I think it's a horrendous theory," Gerd said. "Just thinking that a dragon once lived here makes my knees knock. Well, to be honest, just thinking that one day I might see a dragon makes even the hair on my legs shiver."

"I doubt that will ever happen," Astrid smiled at him warmly, "so don't fret. Dragons and men have never met. Or so the history tomes say."

"Of course you'll never see a dragon—they don't exist," Ingrid said. "They're mythological creatures invented to scare poor naïve people too gullible for their own good."

Dragon yes exist, Camu protested.

Do you know for sure? Humans have never seen one, or at least there's nothing written about it, Lasgol transmitted.

Sure. I dragon.

Oh yeah, I was forgetting that small fact, Lasgol replied with a resigned look on his face.

"We mustn't dismiss any theory or supposition, no matter how farfetched it might look, until we have certain basic facts proven and ascertained," said Egil. "Until then all theories are possible."

"Possible they might be, valid, not so much," said Ingrid.

"In any case, we're not going to solve it tonight," Nilsa added.

"Yeah, we'd better rest," Gerd agreed.

"Follow me, we've prepared suitable accommodations for all of you," Loke said, gesturing for them to follow him.

"They'll surely be fit for a king," said Viggo sarcastically, staring at Loke with an ironic smile.

The Masig did not bat an eyelash. "This is what the Path of the Specialist teaches," he corrected him in a serious tone. "You'll share accommodation with this year's other contenders in the Cave of Spring."

Viggo wrinkled his nose in distaste.

"Well, it might be what the new Path of the Superior Specialist teaches," he said mockingly.

"I doubt it, and that path doesn't exist," Loke said.

"If Sigrid succeeds in her experiments, have no doubt it will exist," Viggo assured.

Loke did not reply.

"I believe so too," Astrid supported Viggo. "Sigrid spoke before the King about Improved Rangers, but she did mention Superior Rangers…"

"And she already had that idea when we were training here," Lasgol added. "I already knew it."

"Whatever the Mother Specialist has in mind is a mystery to me," said Loke, "but it will be good for the Rangers and the realm."

"We hope…" Lasgol said, raising an eyebrow. "We hope…"

Chapter 16

They found the Cave of Spring just as they remembered it. But there was a significant difference: a quarter of the whole space had been reserved for them. It had been separated with long, high folding wooden screens upholstered with green fabric to give them some privacy, keeping them away from the other contenders.

"Well, I like this new setting," Ingrid said, looking around and at how they had situated her group.

"They've given us some privacy," Astrid said, though by her tone it was clear she would have liked more. "Pity we don't have individual rooms…" she said, looking at Lasgol playfully.

"That's not possible at the Shelter," Loke said. "This is the only place fit to receive guests."

Viggo put his head between the screens to see what was inside. He found there were four sets of bunk beds for them with their corresponding trunks. There was also a kitchen area and another set aside for their toilette—all very rustic with wooden stools and no additional comforts.

"Well, put it on your list of things that ought to improve in the Shelter, because it needs it," Viggo grumbled as he pulled his head back and looked at Loke wrinkling his nose and shaking his head. "This is no suitable accommodation for someone of my stature. Not even for theirs," he said, jabbing his thumb at the rest of the group.

"Viggo…" Ingrid started to say.

"No 'Viggo,' are we or are we not the famous Royal Eagles?" he went on. "We deserve special treatment and a much more decent place to rest. This half-solution isn't what we deserve and least of all of what *I* deserve," he said, lifting his chin and looking offended.

"You may choose between the accommodation here or camping outside in the open," Loke replied in a harsh tone. He was not one to stand for nonsense.

"They're very dignified accommodations," Lasgol said to make peace. "We appreciate the effort made to provide some privacy."

Loke nodded.

"I must take care of some things. I'll come back later. If you need anything you can ask me then."

"Thank you, Loke," Ingrid said.

The Masig Ranger nodded and left at a quick pace.

"What little sense of humor that one has," Viggo said with a look of incredulity.

"He's an exceptional Specialist and upright as an arrow," Ingrid said. "An example you might follow," she told Viggo.

"And have that vinegary face? No way." He shook his finger. "I'm charisma personified."

"Yeah, you have the charisma of a shark," Nilsa told him.

"I see him rather like a porcupine," Gerd said with a smile.

"Very accurate, both of you," Ingrid agreed, nodding with her hands on her hips.

Astrid laughed but said nothing.

Viggo lion, Camu transmitted to Lasgol. Ona, who was close to Lasgol, growled twice.

Ona doesn't agree.

Ona not know.

Lasgol did not know what to say to that—Viggo was an indescribable mixture of different animals.

"Say what you please, but the history books, troubadours, and poets, they'll all talk about me as a legendary character," he said, puffing out his chest.

"As a character for sure," Ingrid said, and she could not keep a smile from appearing on her face, which she tried to hide by looking the other way.

"Let's settle into our new home and unload weapons and satchels," Lasgol suggested. "We can rest for a while."

They went into the enclosed space the screens provided and prepared to get comfortable. Ingrid chose the upper bunk on the left set. Nilsa watched Viggo's reaction to see what to do. Viggo seemed to be heading for the bunk Ingrid had chosen but at the last moment he changed course and climbed onto the upper berth beside Ingrid's with great agility. Astrid, with equal nimbleness, climbed onto the third upper bunk more to the right.

Nilsa settled on the bed under Ingrid's, Lasgol did the same under Astrid's, and Egil got onto the upper one in the fourth set. Gerd looked at the two remaining beds, the one under Viggo and the one under Egil. For a moment he hesitated about which one to choose but finally decided on the one under Egil.

Viggo grunted. "Better. The last time you nearly suffocated me with one of your gluttonous farts."

"Oh, yeah, as if yours smelled like roses."

"Me? My sweat smells like jasmine!"

"Yeah! Exactly!" Nilsa guffawed and the others joined her.

"I'll have to study this condition of yours, it sounds most stupendous," Egil said, laughing his head off.

"You should study everything about me so future generations might improve," said Viggo with his hands under his head as he stretched out on his bunk, most satisfied.

They laughed louder before they relaxed and finally rested somewhat.

Loke came back later with some changes of clothes and food to prepare for themselves.

"This courtesy is an exception, don't get used to it," the Specialist told them.

"Thank you, we appreciate it." Lasgol said. "Is there a problem with Ona staying with us?"

"It's not common for a familiar to share accommodations with its specialist, but the Mother Specialist has said you can do so."

"My gratitude to the Mother Specialist," Lasgol said, eying Ona and Camu—who although invisible, was right beside her—out of the corner of his eye.

"I'll tell her. Have a good night. Tomorrow you'll begin your training. I recommend you rest well," Loke said.

They nodded and thanked him, and he left them to dine and rest.

"I still think they ought to treat us better. Now we have to prepare our own dinner," Viggo grumbled the moment they were alone.

"Let me remind you that you'll have to hunt, fish, and gather your own food," Ingrid said. "You know the rules of this place, don't act as though you'd suddenly forgotten."

"We'll have to too?" Nilsa asked her.

"You? Absolutely," Ingrid replied, "and I understand we'll have to as well."

"Wow… at the Royal Castle we have a canteen and cooks…" Nilsa was thoughtful lost in memories.

"Well you can say goodbye to all those comforts here," Astrid said. "It strengthens your character and helps you feel better, since every task accomplished is an achievement that feeds and pushes your self-esteem."

"I'll try to see it that way…" Nilsa said, sounding unsure that she would view it in the same light as Astrid.

While they were preparing their dinner, the sound of muffled voices and murmurs reached them—the other contenders were coming back after finishing their day's training. Viggo looked through the screens.

"Nilsa, Egil, Gerd, come see this, it's most enlightening," Viggo said with great sarcasm.

The three looked through the screen to see the group who was arriving absolutely exhausted. Their faces showed fatigue and even some despair.

"It seems to me we're going to have a tough time…" Gerd said, looking troubled.

"Irrefutable, my dear friend," Egil agreed. "The training's going to be hard. That's to be expected. We'll be trained as Specialists—it's bound to be more difficult than what we did at the Camp to become Rangers. Otherwise, they wouldn't achieve such optimal results."

"Let me remind you we barely managed to graduate as Rangers…" Gerd said, fear in his voice.

"I remember well, it's an experience I'll never forget," Egil replied. "We suffered, but in the end we did it, and here we are now. We should anticipate difficulties and great pain, but I believe that, just as we did at the Camp, we'll emerge victorious from this."

"That's right! Well said, Egil!" said Nilsa, clapping her hands excitedly. "We'll do it, one way or another!"

Gerd was watching the contenders who could barely stand, and did not feel as optimistic as his two comrades. It was going to be tough, and there were no guarantees they would manage. If they did not weather the training, Sigrid would not graduate them, no matter how much she wanted the new system to work. It was one thing to put all her work and wisdom into creating a new program, and a very different thing to pass them if they did not perform well. The Path did not allow for shortcuts or tricks—they would have to walk the Path filled with every obstacle and difficulty they encountered and keep going with pure determination and obstinacy. Only then would they reach their goal.

"Ufff…" he snorted. "This is going to be extremely complicated, I can feel it."

"Your feelings are spot on, big guy," Viggo said. "I'm going to have fun seeing you three suffer." He laughed and patted Gerd's shoulder.

"Don't be such a troll," Nilsa said reproachfully. "You should be a better friend and cheer us up instead of laughing at us."

"I am being a good friend, I'm warning you of what's coming. What else do you want from me? I can't graduate again for you… I already went through all of this. I hope you will too…." He smiled from ear to ear.

"Don't pay any attention to him. Everything's going to be all right. Don't give up, whatever happens, and you'll make it," Ingrid said encouragingly. "If he made it, you can do it too," she said, pointing her finger at Viggo.

"It'll be hard, but you'll get through," Lasgol said optimistically. "Always keep your goal in mind and that'll help," he added.

"I want to become a Mag Hunter," Nilsa said confidently. "I'll always keep that in mind."

"That's the attitude!" Lasgol said. "Never lose sight of that."

They chatted a while longer about the experiences Ingrid, Astrid, Lasgol, and Viggo had been through in the Shelter, sharing them with Nilsa, Egil, and Gerd so they would be warned and understand what they were up against and how to face it. The experienced gave the others a lot of advice according to what each of them had been through during their training there in the hopes it might serve them.

And finally they slept. Nobody really rested well—their dreams were filled with expectations of what they were going to experience during this new stage at the Shelter, those who were there for the first time and those who were returning. For some reason, they all had the feeling they were going to be powerful experiences, and their dreams were all restless.

They woke up before sunrise, like the rest of the contenders. A little rested and recovered, the contenders began to be curious. They did it unobtrusively, peeking in between the screens to catch glimpses of what went on inside. Lasgol had to come out to take a good look at their living quarters to verify which part of it was completely out of sight from the contenders so Camu could remain visible in order to recover his energy.

Camu, always stay in this area so you aren't seen, he told Camu, indicating the space that was fully out of sight.

Ona also watched, but it was not a problem if she was seen. In fact, it was a good thing, because nobody would dare poke their noses where there was a snow panther.

Ona, make yourself known and growl a little to those people out there, let them know they can't come in here, Lasgol transmitted to her.

Ona put her paw on his leg and stepped out through the opening between two screens that served as a door. She stood right in front of it and did as Lasgol had told her. Then he came out and stroked her head so everyone could see she was his familiar. The contenders, some young and others more weathered, watched them furtively but said nothing and went on getting ready for another hard day. Lasgol waited a while, stroking and petting Ona and watching the contenders, then returned to his friends.

They got ready and waited. Loke appeared at dawn and led them to the Chamber of Runes where Sigrid was waiting for them. She was not alone. A man of restricted height was with her: her brother Enduald. Lasgol wondered how solid their relationship would be now because, from what they had heard, it had used to be quite rocky.

"Good morning, everyone," Sigrid greeted them cheerfully.

"Mother Specialist," they all replied with a small bow.

"Today we will begin your training," she announced. "As I told you, it will be somewhat different from what you experienced when you were here," she said, looking at the four veterans. "To begin with, and as I assured you, we will closely supervise the training. That is why my brother Enduald is here today," she added, inviting him to step forward.

"I have created a Training Medallion for each of you," he said in his usual unpleasant tone, as if he were cross at them. The fact that he always dressed in black did not help him appear more pleasant. "You must wear it at all times within the Shelter," he said and showed them a leather pouch. From it he took out a round medallion, very similar to a Ranger's. But unlike a Ranger medallion, this one was metal instead of wood and the engraving was also different—a small sphere over a larger sphere in the middle. It seemed to symbolize the Pearl above the Lair.

Medallions have magic, Camu warned Lasgol at once.

What kind of magic? Can you feel it?

I can feel, but not know. Be Enduald.

You can feel that? You know the source of the magic?

Yes, I feel, be his.

That's very interesting. It's certainly an improvement. Lasgol felt cheered.

Not know what kind of magic, Camu said, annoyed.

Don't worry. You'll become more sensitive to the magic and then be able to discern more about it.

Sure?

Well, I'm not completely sure, but I think that's what'll happen, or what I hope will happen, seeing as you're getting more sensitive…

You not know.

Well, no… I wish I knew what was going to happen as you grow up, but the truth is I don't have the slightest idea.

Maybe dragon wings come out.

I'm almost one hundred percent sure that won't happen.

You not know.

Lasgol did not know what was going to happen, that was true, but Camu was not going to sprout wings, that much he was sure of. Even so, arguing with Camu was a waste of time, so he let it go and looked at the medallion as his friends were doing. By their expressions, they were quite intrigued and a little frightened.

"We already wear Ranger medallions as well as Specialist ones. How are these medallions going to help us?" Ingrid asked, raising an eyebrow.

"What are they for?" Astrid added.

"Our women Specialists are very keen and perceptive," Sigrid said with a malicious grin. "What you really want to know is whether these medallions are special, is that not so?"

"Are they magical?" Nilsa asked directly.

"Yes and no," Sigrid replied in an enigmatic tone. "They are because they are enchanted. That is to say, my brother has placed enchantments on them to help you with the new training and ensure you are protected. And no, they are not magical since they have no magic per se, beyond the enchantments Enduald has set on them."

"Fascinating," Egil commented, taking the medallion from Enduald's hand and studying it closely. "Are they metal because it's easier to enchant than wood?"

"Yes, that is true," Enduald grunted. "Wood is difficult to enchant and it loses the enchantment sooner."

144

"Fantastic. That's what I had guessed," said Egil, staring at the object with analytic eyes.

"You will not see anything odd in them. They look like simple metal medallions," Sigrid warned.

"Until one of the enchantments is activated," Lasgol commented as he looked at the medallion. He did not see any flash that might indicate a spell or enchantment was taking place, which meant the medallion was not active at the moment.

"That is correct, my young and talented friend," Sigrid said. "The medallions have very specific functions, and until the right conditions are given the enchantments remain inactive," she explained.

"I don't like these medallions at all. Can't we train like the other contenders?" Nilsa asked, feeling irked.

The Mother Specialist shook her staff in denial.

"No, you cannot. You will participate in the new training program. The first requisite is to wear these medallions Enduald has prepared. It has taken him a long time and a lot of work to create the enchantments and then set them in the medallions. In fact, he is exhausted and has used a lot of his magic in doing so. It would be very rude on your part to not use them now that they are ready."

"Very rude," Enduald insisted in a bad temper and glared at them as if he meant to bite their heads off.

"Could we at least know what enchantments they have?" Lasgol asked, interested in their identity and purpose.

"I fear that would be counterproductive," Sigrid said. "You would not understand the function or the purpose. My brother and I have thought and created the enchantments very carefully and with specific purposes. The most important of all is to safeguard your lives. Keep that thought in mind."

The explanation did not convince Lasgol, but he had been expecting something of the sort from Sigrid. Before he could protest, Egil put the medallion around his neck.

"I don't feel any different," he told his friends.

"It is perfectly safe to wear them," Sigrid assured them. "Put them on so we can begin."

There was a moment of doubt. Looks were exchanged, some unsure and even afraid. Finally Ingrid reached out her hand. Enduald gave her another medallion, which she hung around her neck without a second thought. Viggo, seeing Ingrid put hers on, reached out and accepted another medallion from Enduald, which he put on. Gerd, his hands shaking, put his on. Astrid followed suite, looking at Lasgol who, seeing her putting it on, had no choice but to do the same. Nilsa was last, and she put hers on, grumbling and looking disgruntled.

"Perfect. That is done. Now the new training begins."

Chapter 17

Lasgol felt weird with the Training Medallion around his neck. He was expecting to see a flash of color come from the object at any moment, indicating it had been activated, but he could not sense anything abnormal, nor did he feel anything strange, apart from the restlessness that wearing the blasted enchanted medallion gave him. He did not know what the object would do, and he was not at all at ease. Not that the magic made him excessively nervous—what did make him anxious though, was that it was part of Sigrid's global experiment with her new training system.

Ona growled beside him. She could feel Lasgol's state of mind.

"Now that you all have your medallions it is time to begin," the Mother Specialist said, and Lasgol became even more restless. "The three Rangers will go with Loke, who will be in charge of the first part of their training. The four Specialists will stay with me."

"We're getting split up?" Gerd asked, glancing at his friends with fearful eyes.

"Yes. The training must be different for the Rangers than for the Specialists, although both groups will follow the same program," Sigrid explained, pointing her finger first at Nilsa, Gerd, and Egil, and then to Astrid, Ingrid, Viggo, and Lasgol.

"Don't worry. We'll meet again in the Spring Cave," Ingrid told them cheerfully. "Everything will be fine," she said, trying to ease them.

"Wonderful…" Nilsa said doubtfully as she stared at the medallion hanging around her neck.

"An enchanted medallion… this is fantastic…." Egil was studying it with avid eyes. He did not even seem to be paying attention to what was being said, he was so excited.

"Learn as much as you can. It will serve you well, I'm telling you," Astrid assured them. "Becoming an Assassin here has changed my life."

Gerd appreciated his friends' words and some of his elusive courage returned to his great heart.

"We will, thanks," he said.

Loke appeared at the entrance to the cave.

"Go with him," Sigrid ordered.

Nilsa, Gerd, and Egil said goodbye to their friends and went with Loke, leaving the others with the Mother Specialist. The Masig stopped under the snow in front of the Lair and the three looked at him, alert and a little tense.

"We'll start the training right away," the Specialist said.

"Right now? Like this?" Nilsa asked nervously.

"Without preparation or anything?" Gerd opened his arms wide.

"Yes, we're going to train thoroughly and without pause," Loke told them.

"Well, that's great..." Nilsa grumbled.

"We haven't even had time to get used to the idea," Egil said. "We thought today would be a day of introductions."

"In the new system you learn everything as it comes. No long and tedious explanations," Loke told them.

"Well... doesn't sound so bad," Gerd said with a shrug, somewhat cheered.

"I see you're wearing winter gear. Very good. You're going to need it. It's quite cold and it seems like we'll have bad weather today. Follow me and I'll take you to the place of the first stage of training," Loke said.

"We're not going to train here?" Nilsa asked, noticing several contenders leaving the cave. Outside it was dawning and the day was crisp. "Like them, I mean," she nodded toward the group.

"No. Your training has been designed differently from the one they follow. In fact, it's very different. They're going hunting, fishing, and root gathering before their physical session with Snowflake. Here, at the Shelter, it's compulsory to be self-sufficient and very fit. You'll see them return to the Summer Cave with what they have caught."

"And what do they do at the Summer Cave?" Nilsa asked, cocking her head. She remembered what Ingrid had told her but wanted to hear for herself.

"That's the second of the Caverns, and it's where we have the workshops and kitchens which we all use at the Shelter. I'll show it to you later. I'll also show you the Autumn Cave, which is devoted to the Skills and divided into four quadrants where the Elder Specialists have their gear beside posts and workshops where they carry out their explanations and practical lessons."

"When will we be able to enjoy lessons at the Autumn Cave?" Egil asked, his eyes lighting up. "I can't wait to see the workshops and the wonders the Elders treasure in them, from tomes to weapons to all kinds of potions and advanced compounds."

"I see you've been told about it," Loke said, nodding. "Your comrades will have told you how the Lair is structured and the way we work."

"Yeah, they've told us many things about this place," Egil said. "Which makes us look forward to being able to discover and experience it all."

"I understand that, it's natural. I must warn you that before you begin to train with the Elder Specialists, you must first pass the physical training with me."

"Wow..." Nilsa could not help herself and immediately shut her mouth when she realized she had said it aloud.

"Any comments?" the Masig asked her.

"I thought that since we weren't going to train with the others, we'd go straight to learning with the Elders... to go faster, of course, not to cheat in the training," she said with a mischievous half-smile.

"That's not possible. Without a fit physique you won't be able to become Specialists. That's a requirement everyone must overcome, you more than anybody else—there won't be any shortcuts for the Royal Eagles. That's something the Mother Specialist insists upon: that both your training and that of your already Specialist comrades must follow the most rigorous rules. There won't be any help for you, because that would ruin the Mother Specialist's goal."

"To create Improved Rangers?" Gerd asked.

"Exactly, and for that we must follow a strict training program, which is what matters in the end. If the program works, it will be used by others. If there were any kind of cheating, it would be counterproductive and undermine the accomplishments of the new system."

"We're active Rangers. We're quite fit," said Nilsa, checking herself from head to toe and then her partners.

"Well, I disagree very much with that opinion." Loke shook his head. "I find you quite soft."

"Soft?" Gerd felt his strong arms with his hands. "There's nothing soft in here," he assured Loke.

The Masig remained firm. He felt Gerd's stomach and legs, squeezing hard.

"Let's not fool ourselves, I don't think those legs supporting the weight of that belly can bear what a good Specialist bears. Am I wrong?"

"Well... if it's a Tireless Explorer..." Egil intervened as he looked down at his own body, all too aware of his own limitations.

Nilsa cleared her throat. "Well... I... I've spent a lot of time in the capital as a messenger and liaison for Gondabar and of course I haven't been working on my fitness... if that's what you mean."

"That's exactly what I mean."

"I, on the other hand, have been outdoors most the time," said Gerd. "Patrolling the southern frontier mainly," he added, puffing out his chest.

"And would you say you're fit? Could you compete with me in a long distance race through the snow?" Loke challenged him.

"Well... as for competing... and with snow... I'm a very large guy," he said apologetically.

"Body size is irrelevant when it comes to being in good shape," Loke replied. "Large or small, tall or short, we can all be in shape if we train enough and maintain that training."

"I guess so..." Gerd blushed.

"You guess correctly."

"I'm a bit puny. I always have been, though I understand that in my case the idea is the same as for Gerd," said Egil before Loke could repeat himself.

"You understand correctly," Loke said and looked into Egil's eyes. "The three of you will soon be in perfect shape. That's my responsibility and my part in your training. I will accomplish that. You won't set foot in the Autumn Cave or learn under any Elder until you have my approval."

"I bet it's not going to be easy to achieve," Nilsa giggled.

Loke shook his head.

"There's one thing we have in our favor," Egil told his two friends, who looked at him in disbelief.

"And that's…?" Gerd asked.

"Experience," Egil said, nodding hard. "Few have lived through the experiences we have. Perhaps they haven't toned our bodies as much as might be desired, but one thing I will say, they've toned our minds thoroughly, and that's to our advantage."

"Yeah… that might be true… we've had to face very strange things and even stranger experiences," Nilsa agreed.

Egil shrugged. "I hope it'll help with this."

"I'm sure it will," Loke said. "As Egil has said very wisely, the experiences you each have lived through strengthen the mind and character. Things you'll need to work on here."

"Well, that's something…" Gerd said, somewhat cheered.

Loke looked inside. "Since you've already been told about the Shelter and the Lair, you'll know what place is forbidden…"

"The Winter Cave," Nilsa replied. "Although I'd love to see the Elders' quarters, and Sigrid's."

"Which is precisely why it's forbidden to enter—everyone would love to see them. You'd do nothing but bother them and they need to rest, especially when they withdraw to their quarters."

"We understand," Egil assured him. "I'm very jealous of my privacy, and when I withdraw to read I hate to be interrupted."

"The Elders and the Mother Specialist feel the same. Remember: no breaking the rules and going into the Winter Cave. I promise, the Mother Specialist is as fierce as she is wise. I wouldn't advise bringing out her irascible side."

"We wouldn't even dream of it," Gerd said.

"We've heard things, yeah…" Egil said; he knew of Sigrid's two faces from what Lasgol had explained about his past experiences with her.

"Very well. Wrap up and hang your composite bows across your backs. It's time to begin your training. We'll start with a quick march to warm up."

"Will it be long?" Gerd asked, who was already hungry before even beginning. They had not broken their fast and his stomach was about to start groaning.

"You'll find out."

"Oh…"

"One more thing. I'm now your instructor. As long as your training lasts you'll address me as 'sir.'"

"Yes, sir," said Nilsa.

"Absolutely, sir. You're a Specialist and we're Rangers," Egil said respectfully.

"No need to be so formal. Just adding 'sir' at the end of your sentence will suffice."

"Very well, sir," said Gerd, wondering what other Norghanians would think about having to call a Masig "sir." Surely many would not be in the least pleased. Luckily for him and the rest of the Snow Panthers, a person's race or origins were totally unimportant—what counted was their heart, whether they were honorable and honest or not.

The three friends exchanged looks of uncertainty, wondering what Loke would deem a quick march and what pace he might set. In marches, distance was not the issue unless it was really long, but the rhythm marked. They also noticed that the weather was against them. They were being whipped by strong icy winds befitting of a winter storm that had settled over that part of the Shelter's huge valley and threatened to bear down heavily on them.

The Masig Specialist set an insistent pace, heading north. At first they followed him without much difficulty, but they soon began to feel the effects of the challenging pace as the snow reached their knees and made progress even harder. Following Loke at the pace he set became a very difficult task, particularly when he went uphill. They soon realized he was not going to stop to rest or even drink water and least of all eat—he was wearing them out against time.

The Specialist seemed to feel neither the cold nor the harshness of the route. He went through snow-covered forests and up and down mountains, always at the same rhythm as if this were no more than a morning stroll to whet their appetite. What impressed them more was the fact that they had already been marching for over half the day and the Masig did not seem to feel it in the least.

Nilsa, Gerd, and Egil followed him one by one. The only things they could see were the back of the Specialist, who never looked back to see how they were faring, and the steam as he breathed, it was so cold. Thankfully, their winter gear's protection was good and they were well covered with their hooded cloaks and seal skin boots. The real problems were the roughness of the terrain and the snow, which were wearing them out completely. If they did not stop soon, and Loke did not seem to plan on stopping any time soon, they were going to run out of strength long before they arrived at wherever he was leading them.

"Loke... sir..." Nilsa muttered.

But the Specialist did not stop or turn to look at them. He just continued marching.

"If we don't rest soon we'll drop from exhaustion," Gerd told Egil.

"Loke doesn't seem to want us to stop," Egil replied, pointing at the Specialist who was marching on into a forest.

"Do you realize he's been taking us up the mountain?" Gerd asked between deep huffs, indicating the slopes before them covered with snow.

"Yeah... everything's uphill from the Lair. He's chosen this path on purpose—it doesn't appear too steep, but we're always climbing," Egil said, huffing, exhaustion setting in.

They went on without stopping. The storm did not break upon them but drifted further east, for which they thanked the Ice Gods, but the endless march went on and it was already mid afternoon. They bordered two beautiful lakes, one of them fully frozen and covered with snow, the other only partially frozen.

"I feel like stopping and diving headlong into that lake," Gerd said, looking at the water as he trod heavily on in the snow.

"That wouldn't be a good idea..." Egil countered behind him.

"At least my legs would cool off. They hurt horribly."

"Mine too. I'm starting to have cramps," Egil said.

Nilsa turned and saw them eying the lake. They were barely moving.

"Come on! Keep going!" she cried, looking at Loke who was already halfway up the steep hill, which was covered with snow and ice in several rocky places. The redhead's face was almost as crimson as her hair from the effort and was breathing hard in the cold winter air of the frozen mountains.

Egil and Gerd nodded and, drawing strength from their meager reserves, followed Nilsa, stepping where she or Loke had so it would be easier to advance. Even so, they were beat and about to collapse with exhaustion, an exhaustion that would keep them down for a full season.

"I... can't... go on..." Egil muttered; he could barely stand, and each step was followed by terrible pain.

"Come on... hold on... it's nothing more than a stroll..." Gerd said mockingly, although he was about to collapse too.

At last, Loke stopped at the top of a hill between two oaks, behind which stood a hunter's cabin. He looked at them with his hands on his hips, shaking his head.

"I see we're not in as good shape as we thought, are we?" he said without irony, his tone making it clear he meant every word he said.

Egil had his tongue out and was panting. In fact, he could not even climb the last slope. Gerd was not much better, and halfway up he had to stop. Every time he inhaled the air of the mountains his lungs burned with exhaustion and the cold air, and his legs hurt so much from the effort that he could not continue. Nilsa was the only one of the three who still seemed capable of climbing a little longer, but then she also had to stop because her body refused to keep going.

Nilsa managed to reach Loke and dropped down on her face in the snow. She rolled onto her back and lay there, looking up at the sky covered with dark clouds. Making a colossal effort, Gerd arrived at the end of the ledge and, throwing himself on the ground, dragged himself the last few paces until he reached Nilsa. Egil could not make it and remained halfway up, lying on the ground.

"Well, that wasn't so bad. I thought you'd do worse," Loke told them.

"Yes… sir…" was all Gerd could utter.

"I'll… go help Egil…" Nilsa offered, although she could barely stand.

"I… I'm coming…" Egil muttered.

Loke waited patiently for all three to reach him without making fun of them.

"Very well, I see you've finally arrived," he looked up and sought the sun, which was already setting. "It's taken us too long," he told them. "A Specialist in perfect shape can do this route in half the time."

"Half the time?" Nilsa repeated, her eyes wide with incredulity.

"A Specialist in a particularly forced march, you mean," said Gerd.

Loke did not smile; he remained serious.

"This first experience should help you understand what you need to improve."

Egil nodded several times. He was lying on the ground in the snow and could not even get to his feet. He had cramps in his legs and back.

"We understand."

"I'm glad you do, because the true training begins now."

"Now? True training?" Gerd said blankly.

Loke brought out a small leather pouch and opened it. He took a ring out and showed it to the three friends. It was a simple silver ring without ornamentation or precious stones. Some strange inscriptions were visible inside it.

"This is the ring Enduald created to improve the learning system," he told them.

"I don't understand…" Nilsa said, "What's this ring for?"

Loke remained serious. Very slowly he put it on his index finger, sliding it down to the knuckle.

Suddenly the ring flashed blue.

In reply, Enduald's medallions flashed too with a blue light.

Nilsa, Gerd, and Egil looked down at their chests, where the medallions were hanging, with fear.

"Welcome to the Improved Learning System."

Chapter 18

While Loke took charge of Nilsa, Egil, and Gerd, the Mother Specialist, together with Enduald, took Ingrid, Astrid, Lasgol, and Viggo to the White Pearl. They went up the hill that housed the Lair to the great sphere that always shined with a whitish glow. It gave the impression that the light was reflected off the polished surface and that its white color was due to that reflection. Curiously, it also shined at night. The hair on the back of Lasgol's neck stood on end, which meant there was magic close by.

Pearl, power, Camu warned him.

Yes, I can feel it too, Lasgol messaged back as they arrived at the top of the hill and looked upon the mysterious, great sphere.

There is more, Camu warned again.

What do you mean more? More power than the magic coming from the Pearl? Lasgol was taken aback.

Magic of Enduald, Camu transmitted.

I understand. The medallion or something else?

Something else.

Lasgol looked over at Ona, who was right beside him. Camu was most likely just a little behind his sister. Sometimes Lasgol could not resist turning to look at the creature, even if he did not see him. It was something his subconscious made him do, and by the time he realized he had already looked. Of course, on many occasions, like this one, Camu was camouflaged and Lasgol could not see him.

They went around the Pearl until they were standing facing north. And then Lasgol saw it—the origin of the additional magic Camu had sensed. Before the great marble-like sphere they saw an arcane metal rod with silver engravings, taller than a man and crowned with a crystal sphere, standing in the ground. A big chill ran down his back. What was that rod for? That it was enchanted Lasgol guessed at once. If it had Power and it was Enduald's … it could only mean that the Enchanter had cast spells on it with his own magic.

Sigrid and her brother stood beside the rod. Lasgol noticed the arcane metal rod was three times Enduald's height, so he guessed the dwarf was not going to use it like he and Sigrid used their staves, which they both held in their right hands. The great rod was fixed in the ground, and Lasgol stared at the strange object, trying to guess what it had to do with them and their situation.

"This is a new twist," Viggo said under his breath in an acid tone. "That rod looks like bad news," he said, making a face and putting into words

Lasgol's thoughts.

"We don't know what it's for, let's not get ahead of ourselves," Ingrid murmured as she watched the object fixedly. She was trying to keep her usual confident expression, but this time a tic in her right eye gave away the fact that she did not like   anything the rod stood for.

Ona growled twice to show her annoyance.

"Poor Ona also feels this might be dangerous," Astrid said and hastened to stroke the panther's head to soothe her.

The Mother Specialist was looking at them with eager eyes.

"I see restless glances in my dear young Specialists," she said kindly. "I promise you have nothing to worry about. Everything we have prepared for you and that you will gradually discover we have studied intensively and prepared cautiously."

"Intensively and cautiously," Enduald repeated in his usual rough tone.

"And what is that, exactly?" Viggo asked, gesturing toward the arcane object. "Are we going to dance around that metal rod while we offer tribal chants to the great pearl?"

Sigrid laughed out loud.

"You are funny. You have always had a spark. That is a quality one is born with. Learning it is very complicated and very few are capable of it. Were you aware?"

"No, but I guessed as much. There are very few with my spark and I don't think anyone can replicate it," Viggo replied, proud of himself.

The Mother Specialist's expression hardened.

"Yet that is not a quality we appreciate here. It is a lot better to be like her," the Mother Specialist, said pointing a long, crooked finger at Ingrid.

"Oh, that's for sure," Viggo nodded. "There's no one like her," he said, and his admiration was not fake, nor was he trying to be funny. He was completely serious.

Ingrid looked at him with a fixed gaze. She had been surprised by his answer. She had been expecting to hear one of his sarcastic remarks, not something sincere.

"This place oozes Power," Sigrid told them. "That is why we have chosen it for the first part of your training. We call this the Experience Stage, in which the goal is to get you to experiment and learn as many specialties as you possibly can."

"The Mother Specialist means that we will learn other specialties of our School?" Ingrid asked with great interest, since that was exactly her wish and she wanted to see it through already.

Sigrid nodded repeatedly.

"That is correct. You may experiment with all the specialties of your School and study them later on."

"All of them? Is that even possible? Or will we be given only basic knowledge like the traditional system and a new Harmony Test will determine the additional Specialty we'll choose if we're capable?" Astrid asked with narrowed eyes as she tried to envision what the training process would be like.

The Mother Specialist took a deep breath.

"It is possible. That is what I am looking for, and I believe all of you in particular will be able to do so. What I want to accomplish is that you train in all of your School's specialties, if possible. I am sure you will be successful."

"If possible?" Lasgol asked, raising an eyebrow. He did not like the sound of it not being proven whether it was indeed possible.

Sigrid looked at him and smiled peacefully. "I cannot assure success because this has never been tested before. The four of you will be the first to take part in the Higher Training System."

"The name is extravagant, I like it," Viggo said, nodding, his face revealing his admiration. "What I'm not clear about at all is that it'll work. Managing to get one Specialty was a triumph. Getting more than one I frankly find highly unlikely, no matter how advanced your new system might be."

"It will work," Enduald said, annoyed, as though insulted by the mere insinuation of failure.

Viggo looked at him and raised his hand.

"If Enduald the Enchanter says so…" he smiled ironically.

"I say it and reaffirm it myself," the dwarf said, and by his look he would have liked to bite Viggo for his insolence.

"We have, of course, done preliminary tests," Sigrid said reassuringly. "I must say Lasgol helped us a lot."

"Me? How?" he asked nonplussed, since he had not participated in the creation of the new training program.

"You are the key to my new system," Sigrid told him. "It is based in fact on what we found out when we studied you, and in particular when we experimented on you. In the Test of Schools at the Camp you passed the four tests—you could have chosen any of the four Schools. This fact, unheard of as it was, gave me the idea of experimenting whether something similar might be done with the Specializations. On that matter your Harmony Test was very revealing. Obtaining two Specialties simultaneously was something I had been after for a long time, and you did it before my own eyes. Considering these two facts was how I decided to experiment by having you repeat the Harmony Test here, at this same place of Power. Do you remember what we discovered?"

"I remember…" Lasgol said, somewhat embarrassed.

The Mother Specialist observed how his friends were looking blankly at Lasgol.

"What we discovered was an incredible revelation: you aligned with all the specializations, every single one, of any of the four Schools. It was fabulous, a grand surprise which opened my mind to new possibilities I had never contemplated before."

"It was intimidating... overpowering..." Lasgol said, looking at Astrid out of the corner of his eye as she looked at him, concerned.

"We discovered that, potentially, you could obtain all those Specialties, although we did not know how to do it then. You also were not prepared to train in all of them at that moment, but it opened the door to a new path of learning. Those discoveries gave us the ideas we have followed to create this new system of learning and training."

"The two Specializations I obtained were very hard to finish. The training was very tough. I'm convinced I would never have been able to cope with another Specialty," Lasgol admitted honestly. "That's why I find it so hard to accept that this new system will manage to do more than what I did that day."

Sigrid smiled, and her face looked kind and optimistic.

"Of course you will manage. That is the reason why you are here, to achieve multiple Specializations. And not only you, my special friend, but them as well," she said, pointing her staff at Ingrid, Astrid, and Viggo.

Ingrid took a deep breath and looked at Lasgol and then at Sigrid.

"We all know that Lasgol is someone "special." He has the Talent, and that's why he might have aligned with multiple specialties, but we don't have the Gift," she said, waving her hand at Astrid and Viggo and then at herself. "We don't have the Gift. We won't align like him."

Sigrid's smile turned predatory.

"That, my brave Archer, is what we are going to try and find out. Lasgol, with his Gift, has opened a new path. It need not be exclusive for those who have been blessed with the Gift like Lasgol or Enduald."

"The things Lasgol and Enduald can do escape logic," Astrid pointed out, siding with Ingrid's point of view. "We can't do those kinds of things. We'll never be able to, no matter how hard we try."

Viggo cleared his throat loudly. "Well, speak for yourselves. I'm with the Mother Specialist. If this weirdo can obtain several specializations, I can too. Of course I can," he said, folding his arms over his chest.

Ingrid rolled her eyes.

Sigrid nodded.

"There is some truth in what each of you are saying. It is true that, by yourselves, without my help, you will not be able to succeed. That is practically guaranteed. But with the system I have created you will indeed. It will help you succeed. That is the goal of the new path we will take. Lasgol has shown us that the goal is within our reach. You will make it true, and you will make it possible for all those who, like you, do not possess the

Gift. Of that I am absolutely sure. It will be something incredible: a wonderful achievement for the Rangers and for all Norghana."

"On the one hand I see it as feasible, more than anything because I see myself with more than one Expertise Specialization on my back," Viggo said, lifting his chin. "On the other hand, I have a lot of doubts about the process and whether it will really work, no matter how much Enduald insists on it."

The Enchanter threw him a wary glance.

"It will work," he barked, and his staff, also of reduced size, flashed with a silver glow.

"That eloquent explanation doesn't convince me, honestly," Viggo protested. Like Lasgol, he had his reservations about what Sigrid meant to do and the means she would use to accomplish it.

"The process, the means that will be used, are what trouble me," Lasgol said, looking at the rod.

"Let us go by stages," Sigrid said, waving her staff to quell the protests. "Allow me to explain the process and the stages. That way you will better understand and there will be less to fear."

"Please go ahead, Mother Specialist," Ingrid said eagerly.

Sigrid nodded. "You will first pass the Experience Stage. This will be followed by the Expansion Stage, where you will be able to experiment in other Schools' specializations. Then will come the Higher Harmony Stage, which will determine the specializations you will each train in according to your alignment. Once you have trained and learned, we will have the Higher Proficiency Stage. As you will see, the new system is based on the traditional one but has been expanded and improved. I promise you will find it familiar and will finish the training and end up with several specializations."

"Sure, that's the only possible result," Viggo replied, disbelief written all over his face.

"The complexity of the stages and how they will be executed is what concerns me," said Astrid.

"I assure you we have studied them thoroughly. We have thought about this and worked on the process a lot," Sigrid insisted. "And it has not been the two of us alone," she added, looking at her brother. "We had the inestimable help of the Elder Specialists." Sigrid hit the ground three times with her staff, and a silver flash rose into the sky.

In response to that signal, a moment later the four Elder Specialists appeared, climbing the hill in their direction. Ivar, Elder Elite Specialist of the School of Archery was accompanied by Annika, Elder Elite Specialist of the School of Nature. They were followed by Engla of Expertise and Gisli of Wildlife.

Lasgol watched them approach. With each step they emanated an air of wisdom and, in spite of their age, power and agility. It seemed that vitality and youthfulness dwelt within them, like a flame that got smaller but never went out. They looked as wise, capable, and intelligent as he recalled. It felt good to see them again. They gave him a sense of safety, that everything was going to be fine. Although now, after the Dark Ranger's ambush and what had happened, that peaceful feeling had cracked, leaving a gap, failure and even death could creep through.

He snorted and prepared to greet them. Unfortunately, they had been able to see for themselves that the Elders were not semi-gods as they had once seemed, but well-prepared men and women with great knowledge who were also only mortal. They could die at the hands of enemies, and because of this, so could Lasgol and his friends. He would listen to what they had to say intently—he knew it would be important.

"Elder Specialists," Sigrid greeted them with a kind smile and welcoming, open arms.

"Mother Specialist," Annika replied with a slight bow.

"My dear friend," Sigrid returned the gesture before greeting each of the other Elders in turn. "Thank you all for answering my summons."

"They have come," Engla said, raising an eyebrow at Lasgol and his comrades. "I did not think they would."

"We always go where there's danger and the chance to obtain glory," Viggo said proudly, bowing deeply at Engla, his Expertise Elder.

"Or where the King or the Leader of the Rangers need us," said Astrid in a humbler tone as she bowed to Engla.

"I did not think they would come either," Ivar said and greeted Ingrid with a nod of appreciation.

"Master, I could not let an invitation from the Mother Specialist pass. It's an honor to be back in the Shelter and share time with my Elder Master. I couldn't let the chance of new learning pass."

"Your words fill me with pride," Ivar said, grateful for the acknowledgment.

"I had hopes they would come," Gisli said, greeting Lasgol with a wink.

Lasgol felt honored by his courtesy and greeted the Elder with a small bow.

"It was a joint decision," Lasgol specified without revealing that he was not overly pleased to be there.

Gisli bent over and opening his hands, addressed Ona.

"Do you remember me, Ona? Won't you come and say hello?"

Ona, who was always on Lasgol's right, expectant, chirped once.

"Go and greet Elder Gisli," Lasgol told her.

The snow panther stepped up to the Elder and let him stroke her head.

"You're such a beauty," Gisli said, smiling, pleased.

"I have summoned the Elder Specialists so they can personally tell you about their experiences, since they have participated in the creation of the training and learning program you will experience."

"It has been an extenuating task, one with such an innovative approach it will leave you with your mouth hanging open," Annika assured them. "I am certain the results we will obtain will surpass everything we have achieved in the last few years, which has been a great deal."

"That is my dream," Sigrid said, her eyes shining with desire.

Annika smiled at Sigrid. "This is not the fruit of the work of one season. The Mother Specialist and each of us, the Elders of the Specialties, have been continuously working to improve the way we train the Specialists that have come to the Shelter. And before us, the Elders we replaced when they left their post."

"Only with steady improvement can we reach excellence," Engla said. "Of that we are absolutely certain."

"Disagreement over how to innovate is what divided us in the past," Ivar remarked. "Some paths entail more risks than others…"

"And produce better results in the end," Sigrid hastened to say. "Without risks there are no significant advances. We all know this."

"This is what we all wish for and bet on," Annika said. "I am positive we will achieve our goal—Higher Specialists with several Specialties around their necks."

"It is indeed our wish," Gisli agreed. "I also believe we will succeed. Especially with this group, which has already overcome the expectations for any Ranger Specialist. Your successes speak for themselves, and I congratulate you."

"Thank you, Master," Lasgol said, pleased with his Elder's acknowledgment.

"Our young Specialists are nervous. They foresee the risks implicit in the training," said Sigrid. "I would appreciate it if you tried to calm their fears," she told the four Elders.

Ivar nodded. "I will speak first, since I have always been reluctant to change and leaving aside the traditional Path of the Specialist which has given us such good results in the past. But, after many discussions with the Mother Specialist, I decided to help her because I saw she was determined and I wanted to make sure nothing bad happened to anyone who followed this new path. I volunteered for the first experiments, so I can speak firsthand. I have experienced parts of what you are going to go through in my own flesh. I will not lie to you, it is not pleasant and there is risk. But, I think Enduald has done a fantastic job with the safety measures and the risk will now be very limited."

"It is minimal," Enduald assured them as he leaned on his staff of Power, which stood a bit taller than him.

"I was also reluctant to this new path of learning," Engla said, "and still am. But, after trying it and participating in its creation, I can say it is safe enough. You might not like it—in fact, I am almost sure you will not, but that is part of the process of learning. As for safety, you can rest easy."

Sigrid spread her arms wide "More at ease, my young Specialists?"

Ingrid nodded. "I sure am, Mother Specialist."

"The Elders have eased my mind considerably," Astrid said, nodding as well.

"I don't trust it at all, but if Elder Engla says it's safe, I'll take her word," said Viggo.

Sigrid eyed Lasgol—he was the only one who had not spoken up.

"Fine…" he agreed at last with a deep sigh.

"Wonderful! We will begin right away!" the Mother Specialist cried excitedly.

Lasgol felt another chill run down his spine. He was not going to like this at all—that he knew.

Chapter 19

Nilsa, Egil, and Gerd were watching Loke expectantly. They had sat up in the snow, frightened by the medallions glowing with a blue light.

"That ring is enchanted," Egil guessed, staring at it, fascinated by the blue glow Loke's finger gave off.

"Correct. It's part of the new training method the Mother Specialist has created and in which I myself have taken part. The ring has been enchanted by Enduald and will help, together with the medallions, to control how we train and improve the results," the Masig explained.

"Fantastic," Egil said, thrilled to find out what spells Enduald had created and how they were going to work.

"I'll say it straight out. I don't like this magic at all and it makes me very nervous," Nilsa said, shaking her head ostensibly.

"I don't like it either…" Gerd said, inspecting the medallion with eyes where fear had no place to hide.

"Your suspicion is understandable," Loke said. "It's natural to fear and be wary of what we don't understand. In the case of magic, even more so because of the rejection it generates in the minds of many people, as I can see is your case. But, I can assure you it's safe, since I have tested it myself."

"Even so, I don't like it at all," Nilsa insisted. "Couldn't we train like it's always been done?"

"With the tiger Snowflake?" Gerd asked; that idea horrified him even more than using magic in the training.

"I'm sorry. We'll train following the new program," Loke said in a serious tone, leaving them without a choice.

"I think it'll be a fantastic experience which we'll all learn a lot from," Egil told his two friends. "Besides, we have the assurance that Loke's tested it and he says it's safe. I would like to try, and I think you ought to do the same."

Nilsa and Gerd looked at one another. Gerd nodded questioningly, and Nilsa took a deep breath.

"Fine, but if things get too weird, I'm quitting," she said.

"Let me remind you that if you quit the physical training you won't be able to try to become a Specialist."

Nilsa snorted. "That's not fair. There shouldn't be a need for magic to do this."

"Life is rarely fair," Egil reminded her. "But it gives us opportunities to do great things. When an opportunity appears, as in this case, we must take it, even if it implies risking getting into deep waters or arcane territory."

"You're getting bolder by the day," Gerd told Egil. "I'll have to keep a close watch on you so you don't drown in those deep waters or vanish forever in one of those arcane territories."

Egil gave a chuckle.

"Okay, big guy, you watch me."

"And while you're at it, watch me too," Nilsa said as her angry face took on a lighter mood.

Loke was watching the exchange without a word.

"I'm worn out and freezing," Gerd said. "Wouldn't it be better to go into that cabin over there and warm up a little?" He looked at Loke pleadingly.

"Do you accept then to train following the Improved Learning System?"

Egil looked at Nilsa, urging her to accept.

"Fine, I accept," she hung her head, resigned.

Gerd nodded.

"We accept," Egil said to Loke.

"Very well. Let's go into the cabin. We'll spend the night in it. Tomorrow at dawn we'll begin training."

"Great. I'm dead and I can't feel my feet," Gerd said, starting to walk on the snow.

Loke took off the ring, and in so doing the medallions stopped glowing.

"Better…" Nilsa muttered as she walked up to the cabin tiredly.

Loke waited for Egil and then headed to the small cabin, which at that moment and with night falling seemed like a palace filled with unthinkable comforts. Loke opened the door and they went in. Of course, what they found was no palace at all, but it was functional and would shelter them for the night. It had a low hearth with a fireplace and the back wall was stone which would protect them from the cold. The rest was made of wood and appeared to be well-built and solid. The kitchen was tiny, and there were no toilets, so they would have to go outdoors to relieve themselves.

"I'll take care of the fire," Loke said. "At the back there are four bunks—you're lucky, you won't have to share. But don't get used to this luxury, because it's the only one you'll enjoy."

"Wow, and I was expecting a whole turkey for dinner," Gerd said, rubbing his stomach which growled loudly.

"Food will be rationed the whole time you're training. You are forbidden to eat anything other than what I give you to eat."

"Are you going to starve us to death?" Nilsa asked, opening her eyes wide.

"I said nothing of the sort. You'll eat five times a day, but only what I give you and when I give it to you," Loke explained.

"Five times! That sounds a lot better," Gerd cried joyfully, smiling broadly.

"I'm afraid, my dear friend, it won't be either as much or as tasty as you imagine," Egil warned him as he patted his shoulder.

"Wow... way to send my joy down a well."

"I think you mean down the drain," Nilsa said.

"Yeah, that."

Loke had a fire going in no time, and after unloading the gear and weapons at the back of the cabin, they sat before the fire on small stools. Because Gerd was so big he sat directly on the floor.

"I'll get supper ready," Loke said and left them warming up and enjoying the fire.

"It's going to be fantastic, you'll see," Egil insisted so they would be at ease. "We're going to come out of this training more fit than Ingrid and Astrid, I'm sure."

"You really think so?" Gerd asked him dubiously.

"More than Viggo for sure," Nilsa said with a mischievous smile. "I don't understand how he can be in such good shape and have the physical capacity he has with such little training."

"That comes naturally for some people, like Gerd being so strong," Egil explained.

"Or the urge to eat everything he sees," Nilsa said with a guffaw.´

Egil and Gerd joined in the laughter.

Loke returned to them. "I see the heat is doing you good."

"It cheers the spirit besides warming the body," said Egil.

Loke nodded. He put a rustic pot on the fire and began to prepare a spiced broth.

Gerd could barely contain himself. He looked as if he wanted to drink the whole pot straight from the fire. Nilsa read his intentions.

Don't even think about it," she said, holding his arm.

"It smells delicious! And I'm starving!"

"It will be ready soon," Loke said as he added some herbs and some yellow, powdered plants.

Egil was observing the ingredients Loke was using.

"This is a strong broth, it will restore part of the energies spent today,"

"Part? And the rest?" Gerd asked, looking at him with a hungry face.

"First the broth and then the main course."

"I hope it's a stew!"

"You'll see soon enough," Loke told him, but from his serious tone it did not sound as if it was going to be a delicious stew, exactly.

Loke poured out the broth in wooden bowls and gave each a spoon. They all gulped it down—Gerd did not even use the spoon, he had already drunk it in long draughts.

"It tastes of roots and herbs and something very spicy. It burns my tongue and lips," Nilsa said, making a face.

"It's not delicious, but I understand it's made with beneficial herbs and plants," Egil commented. "The hot spice is to warm the body and favor the digestion, if I'm not mistaken."

"You're not mistaken at all," Loke said. "It'll give you energy and you'll recover your strength, apart from warming you up."

"I'm still hungry, can I have another helping?" Gerd asked.

"No, you can't. The ration is the same for all of you."

"But I'm twice as big as Egil…"

"And you have fat we must burn and turn into muscle. Until then, same serving."

"When it's all muscle will there be more helpings?" Gerd wanted to know.

"Then there will be, in order to maintain that muscle. Now you're only maintaining the fat."

"Then let's make that muscle, I want double rations." Egil and Nilsa laughed. The ghost of a smile appeared on Loke's face and was instantly gone. He brought them the main course. Gerd looked on, licking his lips in anticipation. His joy evaporated at a moment's notice. They were in for a disappointment.

"What's that supposed to be?" Nilsa asked, staring at a piece of something rectangular and dark brown. It was the size of a hand and half as thick, compact and rough to the touch.

"Are we going to eat an adobe brick?" Gerd asked with eyes as big as saucers. "I don't think it will agree with us."

Loke looked at them and explained: "It's a mix specially prepared for this training. It's made of dry meat, roots and beneficial plants, and other nutritional substances.   It's then all pressed and dried with some medicinal compounds, hence its shape. We call it an Improved Ration."

"Are you sure this isn't used to build houses or bridges?" Gerd insisted with the compact brown rectangle in his hand, looking at it from every angle.

"That can't be edible," Nilsa said, shaking her head.

"It is," Loke said, picking his helping and biting an end. He began to chew slowly.

The three friends stared at him, unable to believe he was eating it so nonchalantly.

"It's a lot better than the chow they feed the Royal Army, and I assure you it's healthier than the dried meat we Rangers are so fond of."

"But that's when we're on a mission or traveling…. We could hunt or fish something more nutritious and better tasting that this," Gerd said, looking at him with an odd face.

Loke swallowed the piece he was chewing. "You must consider this part of the training as if it were a mission. In fact, it is."

"A mission? And what's the target?" Nilsa asked, not daring to try her helping as she eyed it with a look of disgust.

Loke stared at her. "The target is to reach an enviable physique that will allow you to join the Specialists Training Program in the least amount of time."

"The one our comrades are already in?" Egil asked, greatly interested. "It would be wonderful to be able to participate in that training."

"Exactly," Loke confirmed as he took another bite. "They have an advantage over you, both physically and in the specialization training, since they've been through the experience of obtaining a specialty already. That makes it a must for you to go through an accelerated training so you're not left behind, and so you'll be able to join them in the last stages of training."

"Understood. We'll do everything possible to not lag behind and be ready as soon as possible," Egil said. "For us it's a dream to become Specialists."

Gerd took a huge bite out of his helping and swallowed it almost without chewing, then another.

"Well, after a couple of bites it doesn't taste so bad. You get used to it."

"That's what you say. To me it tastes like goat dung mixed with grass for ponies and dried mountain roots. The taste and texture are really not very accomplished."

"We won't die from eating the Improved Ration," Egil said as he ate his helping, chewing thoroughly as it was quite tough. "We'll get used to it. If it's not too much to ask, I'd like to know the ingredients and learn to prepare it."

"There are some ingredients you won't like…" Loke warned him.

Nilsa and Gerd stopped eating and looked at Loke.

"Such as?" Egil insisted.

"Certain worms and several very nutritious insects."

Nilsa spat out the piece she was chewing with loathing on her face. Gerd shrugged, apparently unfazed, and went on eating, unconcerned.

"Fantastic. I'd like to know which and the way to prepare them," Egil replied.

They went on eating, and when they were done, already well warmed, they slept. With dawn they would undergo their first training session, and the three friends were as nervous as they were excited. What would it be like? What part would magic play in all of it? Would they suffer as much as they feared? Would they manage to finish the training and join their comrades? These and many other questions plagued their dreams, and none of the three managed to rest as well as they would have liked.

Chapter 20

The Mother Specialist looked at each one of the four friends and opened her arms.

"It is time to begin. Today is a historical moment for the Rangers. The four of you will be in the history books for the success we will achieve here today. You will be heroes among the Rangers, the first of a new class of rangers—better, stronger, more resilient, nimble, with more knowledge and many skills. We will write a new path, and it all begins here and now."

"It will be a great achievement," Enduald iterated with a grunt.

"Everything is ready to begin," Sigrid said and glanced at Annika. "If you would be so kind…" she asked.

The Elder Specialist stepped forward and nodded at Sigrid.

"To facilitate the learning, I have prepared an empowering potion you must take," she told the four with a kind smile.

"What a surprise, one of those disturbing potions," Viggo commented acidly.

"I assure you, its function is simply to facilitate the process by preparing your mind so it can adapt to the new process better," Annika said.

"Of course, Ma'am," said Ingrid, glaring at Viggo and stepping up to take Annika's potion.

"Drink it all at once. The taste is unpleasant," she advised and took out a phial from her Ranger's belt and gave it to Ingrid, who nodded and downed the contents as the Elder had told her.

"Let's see if it's as bad as the last ones we had," said Viggo. As he came over to receive his dose, Annika gave it to him with a reproving glance. Viggo smiled at her and downed it in one gulp.

Lasgol was next. Annika smiled at him sweetly as she gave him his phial.

"Everything will be all right," she said to ease him.

"Thank you, Ma'am," he said and drank.

The last one was Astrid, who nodded at the Elder and drank the contents of the phial quickly.

"You will feel your mind go a little hazy. But that is natural—that mental state will make it easier to assimilate knowledge better. Do not be concerned," Annika said reassuringly.

Viggo made a face.

"My mind is always in a hazy state," he said, joking.

"We can all swear to that," Ingrid commented, nodding resignedly.

The Mother Specialist thanked Annika for her help and the Elder withdrew.

"Now we can proceed, the preparations are concluded. But, in order to be able to do so we still need a very important figure."

The four friends exchanged puzzled looks. Lasgol, especially, did not like this last-minute surprise at all. Who was missing? And more important still, what was this missing figure? The four Elder Elite Specialists were there besides Sigrid and her brother Enduald. What was going on?

"More surprises," Viggo whispered ironically to his comrades.

"Not exactly the best moment for them," Astrid protested, also in a whisper.

"It must be something important," said Ingrid, who trusted the Mother Specialist and therefore her new system.

The Mother Specialist hit the ground with her staff three times again and a new silver flash shot into the sky.

"We'll just have to wait and see, the anticipation is killing me," Viggo said sarcastically and then yawned.

Astrid smiled. Ingrid, on the other hand, shook her head. Lasgol looked around, trying to find who would join them next.

After a moment they saw him appear, coming up the hill toward the White Pearl. He wore a finely made hooded cloak and under it they could glimpse elegant clothes. They could not see his face properly, so they did not know who it might be. He was thin and not too tall. He walked elegantly and had a firm poise. He did not look like a Ranger. Lasgol felt it was someone they already knew, but he could not say who.

The figure reached them and, with a nod to the group, went to stand beside Sigrid and Enduald.

"Welcome, my good friend," Sigrid greeted him.

"Mother Specialist," he replied and uncovered his head.

Lasgol recognized him then. It was Galdason the Illusionist Mage who had participated in the Test of Schools at the Camp. He looked the same as the last time they had seen him—he still looked recently turned forty, his blond, long hair perfectly combed, as were the goatee and moustache adorning his uncomely face. He looked at all of them with deep gray eyes above a prominent nose. Lasgol eyed him, then Enduald's staff, and he began to guess what was going to happen. His skin turned to goose flesh.

"That's the 'nightmare cook,'" Viggo said, not happy at all to see him. "That's all we needed."

"Yeah, that's the Illusionist Mage who created the Test of Schools," Astrid said, also displeased with the situation.

"Exactly—Galdason. He's one of us, both Dolbarar and Sigrid trust him. We've got nothing to fear," Ingrid assured them.

"Sure, just wait until he starts doing strange things… tell me then," Viggo replied. "Or have you forgotten?"

"No, I haven't forgotten, but I trust our leaders," Ingrid snapped back.

Lasgol had the same bad feeling as Viggo.

Mage with Power, Camu transmitted to Lasgol.

Can you tell what kind of Power he has?

No, only that have Power.

Fine. Stay alert but don't intervene in whatever is going to happen, even if they use magic.

Not cancel magic?

No, it's friendly magic. Don't cancel it. Let them do their spells and charms. If I need you I'll message you.

Okay.

Lasgol was somewhat relieved. If things got complicated or turned out badly, he could tell Camu to undo the current magic and cancel any new spells. With that the situation would be solved. Or that was his hope.

"Dear Galdason, are you ready?" the Mother Specialist asked.

The Illusionist Mage showed her his staff. "I am. We can begin whenever you wish," he said.

"Very good, in that case the time to begin is now," said Sigrid, and she looked at Enduald. The Enchanter began to cast a spell, uttering unintelligible words under his breath and waving his short staff before him in circles.

Lasgol looked at Astrid, who gave him an uncomfortable glance. Viggo and Ingrid exchanged a look of concern. The four were quite used to magic after all the experiences they had been through, but whenever a stranger cast a spell, they could not help stiffening, feeling deep in their gut that something was wrong, their throats dry. In this case, Enduald was not an actual stranger, but given his surly and secretive character, he did not exactly inspire trust.

With one last sentence of power he finished his spell. With his staff he touched the rod to the ground. There was a burst of silver light, which went up the rod to the sphere at its tip. Four beams of light issued from the sphere, which projected to the ground, creating four silver circles a pace away from the rod. The light the sphere emitted lit up the four circles, which were each big enough for a person to step into.

"My dear young Specialists, stand in the circles that have been summoned," Sigrid told them.

Lasgol sighed. The moment had come. He wished with all his heart that everything would go well. A little unsteadily, he stepped into the nearest circle. A beam of silver light from the sphere bathed him from head to toe. Astrid stood in the circle on his right. Ingrid occupied the next one and, finally and reluctantly, Viggo stepped into the remaining one.

Ona growled twice—she did not like what she saw and felt.

Easy, girl, everything's fine. You wait with Camu until I call you.

The good snow panther chirped once.

Lasgol was beginning to feel weird. His mind, as Annika had told them, began to turn hazy. He had already experienced that feeling before during the Skills Test and knew it was normal. It was due to the potion he had drunk and which was beginning to affect his mind. He had always thought it a dangerous practice and he felt anew the risk enveloping him. He had to trust Sigrid and the Elders, but they were playing with their minds and using magic in a way that had not been done until then among the Rangers. The results could be disastrous if things went awry. For the good of all he hoped they would not.

"Close your eyes and empty your minds. Relax," Sigrid told them.

Lasgol glanced at Astrid before following the instructions. They smiled at one another and Astrid nodded reassuringly and they both shut their eyes. Lasgol tried to empty his mind, but he had the feeling it was going to be practically impossible. All kinds of thoughts were coming to his mind, from fear for his comrades' lives or his own, to fear of what was going to happen next. His mind seemed a little numb, drowsy although not stunned; he was able to think clearly and precisely, but less quickly, as if ideas had a harder time taking shape than usual. It was as if every thought came more slowly and remained in his head longer—he found it strangely fascinating. He was afraid something bad would happen to Astrid, and that thought seemed to have been with him for a long while, even though he was sure he had just thought it.

He tried to calm down and empty his mind, as the Mother Specialist had requested.

"Come on, my pups, relax and empty your minds. There must be space for new ideas, for new lessons of life, for new knowledge," Sigrid coaxed.

Lasgol took a deep breath and slowly and consistently let all the air out in an attempt to relax. He was not fully successful though. He took another breath while he tried to stop the thoughts that kept assaulting him. All of a sudden he began to think about his mother, Mayra. He recalled the last time he had seen her alive and a feeling of sorrow flooded him. He clenched his jaw tightly. The feelings surrounding his mother's death enveloped him, how he had lost her…. One day he would avenge her. He would find Asuris, the Arcane of the Glaciers, who had betrayed and killed her from behind, and finish him. He could see the violet eyes of that loathsome being without scruples as if Asuris was right before him. He felt such rage, such hatred, that he thought his guts would burst inside him.

"Annika's potion and Enduald's spells will help you perceive and feel with greater intensity. Stay calm and control your thoughts, emptying everything in your mind," the Mother Specialist told them.

Lasgol noticed he was growing enraged precisely for those reasons. What he did not know was why he had been thinking about his mother when the ones who were really in danger were themselves. He tried to empty his mind and regain the serenity he needed to maintain. It did not work, it immediately brought back new thoughts, this time of his father and memories of the past—many of them good, although they turned bitter and painful as they were substituted by the memories of Dakon's death.

When his attempt to leave his mind blank failed, he chose to think of great darkness. It was hard to push his thoughts away and create a dark wall before his mind.. Slowly he banished the bitter thoughts of his past and focused on leaving his mind in unfathomable darkness.

"Go ahead, Enduald," Sigrid told her brother.

The Enchanter grabbed his staff and touched the rod three times as he uttered some words of power. There was a blue flash that ran up the rod to the crystal sphere at its top. Four beams of light issued from it and bathed Astrid, Ingrid, Lasgol, and Viggo. Enduald's medallions which they wore around their necks, resting on their chests, became activated with blue flashes too.

The Mother Specialist warned them, "You will feel your medallions activating. Do not worry, they will protect you and make sure you do not run any risk," she explained.

Lasgol realized that, even with his eyes shut, he had felt the blue flash of the medallion.. He tried to stay calm and expel the thoughts of unease trying to flood his mind. He wondered how his comrades were faring

"Galdason, if you will be so kind," Sigrid asked with a wave of her hand, granting him leave to start.

"Of course," the Illusionist Mage replied, and he began to mumble words of power while he moved his staff beside the rod. The Elder Specialists watched both very closely: what the mage was conjuring and what went on with the four friends. Galdason finished the spell a moment later, and a rosy beam came out of his staff and went up the rod to the sphere, where it divided into four pink beams that bathed the four friends standing inside the circles.

Lasgol began to feel strange, as if the haze that affected his brain were dragging him to a place he still was not able to glimpse. He felt like he was being taken, that some force was dragging him to a distant but familiar place. He did not know what all this meant, what was happening, but in an unconscious way he resisted being dragged wherever his mind was taking him. The haze was becoming thicker and the force that pushed him into himself was growing stronger by the moment. He began to see the haze turn into a spiral as he was dragged inside it by a force he could not manage to tame. He could not see what was at the end of that spiral enveloped in mist, but he felt it was nothing good.

The Mother Specialist addressed the Elders now.

"It is your turn, my dear friends."

The Elite Elder Specialists nodded and came closer. Gisli stood in front of Lasgol. Ivar stood in front of Ingrid, and Engla moved to stand between Astrid and Viggo also in front of them. But Annika remained a few steps behind. She did not move, she just watched.

"Ready?" Galdason asked.

The Elders nodded almost at the same time. "We are ready," they confirmed.

"Very well. Place your hand on their medallions," Galdason said.

The Elders did as they were told. Engla held both Astrid's and Viggo's medallions, one in each hand. At once both beams of light, blue and pink, leapt onto the Elders and bathed them in their shades.

"Everything all right?" Sigrid asked, looking at Enduald and then Galdason.

"Everything is going as we expected," Enduald confirmed.

"Everything seems to be going accordingly," Galdason said.

The Mother Specialist smiled, pleased.

"In that case, I here declare the Experience Stage initiated. Galdason, if you will do the honors."

"It would be a pleasure," the Illusionist replied and went over to Ivar. He put one hand on Ivar's head and the other one on Ingrid's. He cast a spell. A purple-rosy aura appeared above both the master's and pupil's heads. He repeated the same spell with Engla and Astrid, then with Engla and Viggo next. Finally, he cast a new spell for Gisli and Lasgol, joining their minds. The linking auras shone in purple and pink hues, indicating that the minds were joined by Galdason's spell.

Suddenly, Lasgol felt the force he had been resisting finally taking him, and he shot out through the end of the spiral to a place in the mountains. He tried to understand what was going on but could not.

He lost consciousness.

Chapter 21

Nilsa woke up and leapt to her feet with the first light of dawn. Loke had already dressed and was preparing his weapons by the fire whose coals he kept alive. The Masig saw she was up and motioned her to come over.

Nilsa began to get ready. Egil opened one eye and looked at her.

"Is it morning?"

Nilsa nodded. "Come on, time to get up," she told him, muffling a yawn.

Egil sat up in his bunk and looked at Gerd, who was snoring like a mountain Troll.

"How can a human being make so much noise when he sleeps?" Nilsa asked, shaking her head. "For a moment I thought he was going to blow off the roof with his snores."

Egil laughed and shook the giant hard.

"Wake up, my friend. Time to begin the day. It's going to be fantastic."

"Eh... oh..." Gerd mumbled, still drowsy, turning his huge body to the other side.

"Come on, get up. Breakfast is waiting and we're heading out," Loke ordered.

It did not take them long to prepare to face whatever Loke had in store for them. The Masig Specialist offered them their Improved Ration.

Egil took it with a smile and began to eat as if it were a delicious breakfast made by the royal cook.

"You have a water skin right over there," Loke told them with a wave at the kitchen table, "To help you digest it."

Nilsa waved her ration away, but Loke gave her a stern look.

"That's not food, sir, it's something disgusting," she protested.

"That's the only thing you're going to eat while you're training with me, and without eating anything... you know what'll happen. So the sooner you get used to it, the better for you."

"The only thing?" Nilsa asked, seeking an alternative.

"The only thing," Loke confirmed in a tone that made it clear he was serious.

"Okay..." Nilsa muttered, getting the hint. If she did not eat she would become weak and be unable to cope with the training. She thought of her goal: to become a Mage Hunter. She would do it, and if in order to achieve her purpose she had to eat worms, so be it.

They all ate in silence, trying to get used to it. Once they finished, Loke made them grab their backpacks with the gear and their composite bows and they left the cabin. The day was clear, although quite cold and the snow and frost covered everything the eye could reach. Some black clouds in the east seemed to be moving toward them. When the storm arrived it would likely break over them, which would not be at all pleasant.

Loke took a deep breath. "It smells like mountains in winter," he said cheerfully. "Nothing better for a good training session."

"Are we going to go on another march today, sir?" Nilsa asked, afraid to repeat the experience of the first day.

Loke smiled, which was rare for him.

"Oh… oh…" Gerd said, fearing the worst at the sight of the Specialist's smile.

"We're going to go on a march, yes. To the Moaning Peak and back," he said, pointing at one of the western peaks quite far away.

"Hmmm… that peak is very far away. Will we have time to get there and come back before nightfall?" Nilsa was looking at the distant peak uneasily.

"I promise we will," Loke took Enduald's ring out of the leather pouch where he carried it.

Nilsa stiffened. "What are you going to do with the ring, sir?" she asked, distressed.

"Don't you worry. Leave the medallions in the open."

The three took out Enduald's medallions. Loke put the ring on his index finger, sliding it down to the knuckle. It flashed with a blue glow. The medallions responded with flashes of the same hue. Nilsa and Gerd were very tense and watched what was happening with fear in their eyes. Egil, on the other hand, was delighted and did not miss a detail of what was going on.

"The ring will serve two main functions—improving your physical shape and controlling your body so you don't run excessive risk," Loke explained in a soothing tone.

"Excessive risk? That sounds bad," Gerd said, making a face.

"You're going to drive your bodies to their maximum capabilities. The training is designed so that you improve quickly. For that, you'll work like you've never worked before. The medallions will keep you from going beyond the point of no return."

"He means death," Egil told his comrades.

"Exactly. Now don't worry about the medallions and the ring. Make sure you follow my instructions and everything will be all right."

"Yes, sir," Nilsa replied unsurely.

Gerd murmured a fearful "yes."

Loke began to march and the three friends followed him. He set a very hard pace, similar to the day before. It did not take them long to start feeling tired in their legs and lungs. Snow began to fall as they went up a small mountain with few trees. Loke whispered something to the ring, and there was a more intense blue flash. At once the three medallions flashed the same hue.

"What was that?" Nilsa asked her two friends, restless, because Loke was not looking back and was continuing up the mountain at a back-breaking pace.

"Magic, but I don't know what for, which I hate," said Gerd.

"Loke has probably activated the enchantment which ensures nothing bad happens to us. Take it easy, I'm absolutely sure everything's going to go well. It's comforting to know that magic is making sure our bodies don't betray us." Egil said.

"This isn't one of your plans. This is magic..." Nilsa said. "Something always goes wrong with magic. I don't find it comforting at all. Rather the opposite."

"Let's hope nothing goes wrong," said Gerd as he looked down at his medallion, which was emitting a faint blue gleam.

"If you feel anything different, tell me. I want to gather all the information I can about this new system that utilizes magic. I find it fantastic—and more than that, it's fascinating!" Egil smiled, very pleased.

Nilsa made a face. "You just wait, you'll change your mind in the end."

They went on; the snow was falling more heavily and the terrain became abrupt and steep. Egil began to have difficulty keeping up with his comrades. Every step he took, treading in the snow, the more he lagged behind. Before noon he was quite a ways behind them.

Loke noticed it and whispered something to the ring again. A second flash went from the ring to the medallions.

Egil started to feel his legs picking up the pace, although he could not go any faster with the effort he was making. It puzzled him. How could his legs go faster than he could? His heart began to race due to the additional effort. But he did not feel as tired as he ought to, which puzzled him even more. He tried to go slower, but he could not.

"Wow, this is certainly interesting," he muttered under his breath, wide-eyed with surprise.

Gerd was also beginning to lag and, after noon, Egil caught up with him. They both went on at the same pace.

"Something funny's happening to me," Gerd commented, looking at his own legs with a horrified expression.

"The pace... is... faster than what you're capable of going at," Egil told him, huffing from the exertion.

"Yeah... my legs are moving faster than they should..." Gerd said, shaking his head.

"How's your heart?" Egil asked him.

"Like a herd of wild horses." Gerd shook his head.

"Mine too, and I'm sweating under the snow that's falling, which means additional effort or overload."

Nilsa, who had been a little ahead, also began to lag. Her two friends caught up to her, and she managed to keep up with them.

"We're... all marching at the same pace..." Egil commented.

"I can see that... so?" Gerd asked, his face red from the effort.

"We shouldn't be... each of us should go at a different pace, that which our bodies can manage..."

"That's because of... the magic," Nilsa said, wrinkling her nose and panting.

"Yeah... he's forcing us to keep up a more intense pace than we ought to be able to bear..." Egil reasoned.

"I'm going to try and go slower," Nilsa said.

Gerd and Egil watched her. She could not manage to decrease her speed.

"You can't?" Gerd asked her.

"No! The blasted magic makes me keep going at the same pace!"

"Wow, that's fascinating," Egil said. "This is fantastic,"

"Fantastic? How can it be fantastic?" Nilsa cried, raising her fists to the sky.

"This is very intimidating," Gerd said, looking at his legs.

Egil was at the limit of his strength and could barely speak.

"Because... it makes us... go faster than what we're actually capable of..."

"That can't be good!" Nilsa protested.

Gerd was not talking—he was panting with the effort of maintaining the pace.

Egil was also panting. He was white as if he had been drained of all his blood.

"This way... they'll get the body to develop..."

"This is madness! They're going to kill us!" Nilsa shouted.

The protests did nothing to affect the Specialist or decrease the rhythm. He did not even let them stop to eat their ration; they were forced to eat it on the go, without stopping, which was in itself a real ordeal.

The Masig Specialist began to climb the first ramps of the peak. He went up as if for him this were a simple stroll that did not require the least effort.

Halfway through the afternoon, in the middle of the climb, Loke turned and saw them about twenty paces behind him. He whispered to the ring again. There was another flash.

"What now?" Nilsa asked, growing more annoyed with the use of magic.

Then suddenly they felt less tired, as if they had been imbued with new energy to keep going.

"I feel much better!" Gerd cried, very pleased. "A moment ago I couldn't cope with my soul and now I can!"

"I also feel a lot better," Egil confirmed. "The medallions are affecting our mind."

"Our mind? Now it's the mind!" Nilsa cried, outraged.

"It has to be our mind, because we couldn't feel better any other way. We haven't decreased the pace a bit and we're climbing the mountain after a whole day of heavy marching. The only answer is that the magic is tricking our minds to make us believe we're not exhausted."

"But the mind controls the body! If magic tricks it, it will kill us!" Nilsa cried, staring at each step she took on the snow with horror and rage.

"That's true. But it won't kill us, will it?" Gerd asked, very frightened, feeling his heart as he climbed.

Egil was looking at his medallion with each step he took, trying to come up with an explanation.

"No, it won't. I think therein lies the secret of this accelerated training… drive the body to the limit to obtain a quick benefit. In order to do that, they trick the mind."

"But that's dangerous!" Nilsa protested.

"It is," Egil agreed.

"But Loke said it's the medallion that controls it, that nothing bad will happen to us," Gerd said, hopeful.

"Don't believe everything they tell you!" Nilsa snapped, furious.

"The medallions control it," Egil said. "What remains to be seen is whether they really work or not and how they've been designed."

"And if they don't work well?" Gerd asked, already guessing the answer.

"I'm afraid our hearts will burst from the effort," Egil said.

"Blasted magic!" Nilsa yelled as if it had already happened to her.

Once again, Loke ignored their protests, nor did he give them any explanation. He just told them to keep climbing. A little later he gave them their ration with the order to eat and also hydrate from the water skins they were carrying.

Loke went on and reached the top of the hill. He turned to watch them ascending and waited for them to arrive.

"Now stop and begin your resting period," he ordered.

"But can we stop?" Gerd said, lifting his arms.

"You can. You have to leap forward with your feet together. Don't do it until I tell you to."

"This is very dangerous, sir," Nilsa said.

After a brief respite Loke said, "You're doing very well. Keep going, there's no danger."

Once at the top Loke began the descent. Nilsa, Gerd, and Egil followed him. They stopped talking as the afternoon wore on and evening fell. They followed the same route back. The feeling of wellbeing faded away and exhaustion and pain filled their minds.

All of a sudden, Egil's medallion shone with a blinking red gleam. Surprised, Egil stared at the medallion on his chest.

"Sir... a red glow," he told Loke, who turned to him at once.

"Stop," he ordered Egil.

"I'll try..." Egil leapt forward with his feet together and stood still right where he was. He suddenly felt his mind explode with pain, and a terrible ache ran through his whole body.

"Agh..." he groaned.

"Easy now, it's natural. It's due to the overexertion. It will pass. Now it's important that you don't stop, just walk slowly toward the cabin. We're close now. You'll make it. Just walk slowly. Step by step, without effort."

"I'll... try..."

Loke nodded and went on with Gerd and Nilsa who, as they moved, kept glancing back at Egil to check if he was all right. Egil was doubled up with pain. He tried to walk but was unable.

"Don't worry about him, he's fine," Loke promised.

"Sir, he doesn't look it..." Gerd said, concerned. "I can help him," the giant offered.

"You won't be able to. Keep going. You'll have to trust me."

"Are you sure he'll make it?" Nilsa asked anxiously.

"Positive. Don't stop."

Nilsa and Gerd kept going, looking back every few steps. Night had fallen on them and it was too cold to bear. Luckily all the effort they were making kept them warm under their winter clothes.

With the cabin in sight in the distance, under the moonlight that slipped through the dark clouds, Gerd's medallion began to blink red.

"Sir... the medallion..." he said.

"Stop," Loke ordered.

Gerd leapt and landed on both feet, stopping at once. He groaned with pain and doubled up like Egil.

Nilsa went on toward the cabin. She turned several times to see how Gerd was doing. Loke gestured for her to keep going. They left Gerd trying to recuperate.

"Walk very slowly to the cabin," Loke told Gerd and continued with Nilsa.

She was now the only one able to keep going. The cabin was in sight and she only needed to go up one last steep stretch to the hilltop where the cabin was. Nilsa took two steps on the hill and at the third the medallion began to blink red.

"Stop where you are," Loke ordered her.

Nilsa gave a small hop, and as soon as her feet touched the ground she felt a great pain throughout her body and she fell over.

"Don't stay on the ground. Shake off the ache by walking slowly, you'll feel better."

"Arghhhh… everything hurts…"

Loke nodded. "It's only natural, the overexertion has been great."

"This is insane… dangerous…" she said, trying to get back up.

"Every shortcut has its price," Loke replied. "Come on, keep walking, you're already at the cabin."

Nilsa did as Loke said. Very slowly, dragging her feet, doubled up with pain, she managed to climb the hill and reach the cabin. She stopped at the door to wait for her comrades.

"Come in and recover," Loke told her.

"I want to wait for my friends, sir…."

Loke nodded. "Very well."

Gerd arrived after quite a while. He was broken. His face was the picture of suffering. When he managed to reach her side, Nilsa gave him a tight hug at the entrance to the cabin. They both waited for Egil. Loke was waiting too, a short distance away with an inscrutable look on his face, scanning the night that hid Egil.

They waited. Nilsa and Gerd could barely stand and had to sit down on the floor at the entrance, worry and pain on their faces. They finally glimpsed Egil approaching. He was taking gradual, small steps, going very slowly, so much that he appeared not to be moving. Loke went to meet him.

"You're almost there. One last effort and you're done."

"I… I will… make it…" Egil coughed out as he walked, dragging his feet almost bent from the pain he felt.

He approached the cabin very slowly, every step an agony.

Nilsa and Gerd stood up and hugged him when he reached them.

"I… I did it…"

"The three of us did it!" Nilsa said triumphantly.

"Nothing can defeat us!" Gerd cheered.

Loke came to them. "Come in and lie down by the fire. I'll teach you some back and leg massages you must give each other before you fall asleep."

"Now, sir?" Nilsa asked blankly.

"Yes, now, otherwise you won't be able to move tomorrow."

"Can't we rest tomorrow, sir?" Gerd asked. "We're beat."

Loke shook his head. "Tomorrow we start the true training. Today was just an exercise to attune the medallions to your bodies."

Nilsa, Gerd, and Egil exchanged horrified looks and dropped down before the fire.

This was going to be insufferable.

Chapter 22

Lasgol woke up in the middle of a snow-covered hillside. He was lying face up, half-buried in the snow that fell heavily from a covered sky. He shook his head. There was still a foggy mist in his mind which made him see everything around him as very far away, though it was right there. It was the weirdest feeling. He picked a handful of snow in his gloved hand and squeezed it, simply to make sure it was there and real. He was not at all sure it really was.

When he squeezed it he felt the coolness of the snow and how it compacted. It seemed to really be there, that it was real. He shook his head to clear it and get the fog out of his mind, but he could not. On the contrary, he was stunned and had to wait a moment to recover.

"Well, that was a bad idea," he muttered and put his hands to his temples. He felt as if he had a terrible migraine, only without the pain. The mist in his mind made him see the surroundings as distorted, although he knew he was there and that it was real. It was quite strange.

He observed the landscape. It was familiar, yet he could not manage to recognize it. What was he doing there? How had he got there? Why was he alone? All of a sudden, he felt as if he were in a nightmare. Perhaps it was just that, a nightmare he would soon wake up from. He tried to remember where he had been a while ago and to his surprise he was unable to recall anything. He thought that very strange. Why could he not remember anything about what had just happened? Suspecting something was going terribly wrong, he made an account of what he did remember. He knew he was Lasgol Eklund. He remembered his childhood, his parents, friends, his training as a Ranger, his friends, his training as a Specialist and all the adventures he had had until coming to the Shelter again for the new training. The last thing he could recall was arriving at the White Pearl with Sigrid and Enduald. From then on it was all a blank..

He snorted. This could not be good. He had heard Egil say in one of his memorable speeches about matters related to the human memory that people who could not remember things had suffered heavy trauma or blows to the head. Egil had read this in several tomes of knowledge. Lasgol was thoughtful. Which of the two might have happened to him? He did not know, and this troubled him. He looked around for some clue, but he was alone. There was nothing nearby that gave him any information.

The snow kept falling, and although it was not very cold, he thought the best thing in his state would be to find shelter. He saw a forest to the east and started walking towards it. Perhaps he would wake up and feel better by the time he reached it. He was tempted to shake his head again to get rid of that dopey feeling. He decided not to for fear of being stunned again. His head felt full of cotton with the strange fog that did not seem to go away.

At least he was in perfect physical condition. He had no pain, or wound, or blow. He thought that perhaps the reason he could remember nothing was that he had hit his head badly. A strong blow—he put his hand to his head and felt it to make sure he was fine.. He found nothing.

He stopped. And his magic? Could he use his skills with his mind in this weird state? He tried. He concentrated as hard as he could, but it was not enough because his dulled mind was not working properly. He sought his pool of power in his chest. He found it. He tried to call upon his *Cat-like Reflexes* skill he used so often and which in general he could summon almost unconsciously. Yet, it did not work. The green flash that covered his body when the skill activated did not come.

"What's going on here?" he muttered under his breath.

He tried again, this time with his *Improved Agility* skill, another of the skills he called upon all the time and usually activated without any problem. He could not. There was *no* green flash. Lasgol began to worry. *Why aren't my skills working?* He looked around in case there was some sorcerer canceling his magic. No, he was alone before this beech forest.

He shook his head again; he wanted to get rid of this mental fog and recuperate his magic skills. He felt dizzy and keeled over. He fell on his side and lay there absolutely stunned. He decided not to move and wait for the dizziness to pass.

"Resting when you should be training?" a familiar voice asked.

Lasgol opened his eyes and tried to sit up. The dizziness continued, but it was more bearable now. He looked toward the forest and saw a familiar figure coming closer. It was Elder Gisli.

"Master? What's happening?" Lasgol asked, confused. "My head's not working properly…"

"Don't worry, that's natural. Your mind needs to be in a foggy state so the training can be successful. Otherwise we couldn't be here now."

"I'm not sure I know what that means, Master…" Lasgol said blankly.

"You'll understand in time. What's important is that you know that right now we're training."

"Training? Here? Now?"

"That's right, my keen pupil. I'm here to train you in the remaining Skills of Wildlife."

Lasgol finally understood that Elder Gisli was there to teach him. He was going to train him. What Lasgol could not understand was how he was going to do so in the other Skills of Wildlife. He already had the Specialties of Beast Whisperer and Tireless Tracker, and it had taken him the whole specialization year to do so. And he had by the grace of the Ice Gods, since two specialties in one year had nearly killed him. It was simply not viable that he train in the remaining ones. His mind might not be fully working, but he could calculate the time and effort *that* would take perfectly well.

"Master, that's not possible… You no doubt mean to train me in an additional third specialty, right?" Lasgol said, thinking he had not understood and that what Gisli really meant was that he would teach him one other specialty of Wildlife to add to the two he already had.

"It is possible here," Gisli assured him, spreading his arms and twirling under the snowflakes that steadily fell from the sky.

"Here? Where are we, Master? This place looks familiar, but I'm not sure where we are."

"It is familiar because we're really inside your mind."

Lasgol's eyes opened wide..

"Master? Is that even possible?"

"Through normal means it isn't and that's why it seems outrageous to you. It would be really weird if you thought otherwise," Gisli winked at him. "But it's possible with the help of magic. The training you're about to receive will take place here, which is no other than your mind."

Lasgol was trying to understand and assimilate what Gisli was telling him, but he was having serious trouble doing so.

"And how come my Master is here with me if we're inside my mind? How did you get here?"

"That's a good question. I see that, although a little hazy, your mind is still working well. The reason why I'm here is that Galdason has put me in your mind through his illusion magic. It's the way we've designed the training."

Lasgol fought the urge to shake his head. None of this made much sense. It sounded like a mixture between madness and a nightmare.

"I wouldn't be sleeping, would I?" he asked Gisli.

The Elder smiled.

"No, you're not. We're really inside the White Pearl, and with us are Sigrid, Galdason, and Enduald, who have designed this system and keep it working through enchantments."

Lasgol looked around. He saw the snow-covered mountains in the back, the forest beside them, and a frozen lake further to the east.

"All of this looks so real… are you sure we're not really here?" he asked, bending over to pick up some more snow with his gloved hand. Then he put it to his mouth. "It tastes like snow, it's cold like ice, it's ice," Lasgol said, offering it to Gisli.

"It is, since everything must be as real as if we were really here," Gisli explained. "Only thus will the training and teaching have the results we want."

"I'm confused, Master," Lasgol admitted. "Where are Camu and Ona? Why aren't they here with me?"

"They're fine, don't be concerned about them," Gisli assured him. "They're at the Pearl. Beside us. They're not *in here* because they'd interfere with the training, and that's the opposite of what we're trying to do. You can't have distractions or concerns: all your attention must be focused on assimilating what I'm going to teach you."

"It always is, Master."

"We need to accelerate the training, and any distraction goes against this maxim."

"We're trying to accelerate the training?" Lasgol asked, surprised by this discovery.

"That's right. It's one of the main goals of the new system, since only by accelerating the training will you be able to learn multiple specialties."

Lasgol thought about this, looking up at the covered sky.

"Master, accelerating the training isn't going to produce good results. Nothing done in a hurry ever comes out well. I'll never make it."

Gisli put his hand on Lasgol's shoulder.

"That's very true, my young Specialist. That's why the way to accelerate the training is precisely by stopping time."

Lasgol was flummoxed.

"Master, time can't be stopped, it would be…"

"The end of days, yes, I know. Take it easy, that's not what we've managed to do," Gisli said in a soothing tone.

"What have you managed?" Lasgol asked as he slowly grasped where Gisli was going with his explanations.

"We've managed to make time go a lot faster than in the real world. One afternoon there is a whole week here."

Lasgol was petrified as he tried to rationalize what Gisli was saying and then started to understand.

"If time goes a lot faster here, in this world… then… we can train much longer than in the real world…"

"Exactly. I'll be able to explain and teach you lessons that would take several days in the real world in moments, since we're doing it here, in this world within your mind, and here time flows much faster."

Lasgol put his head in his hands and looked in the four directions. He thought for a long moment while Gisli watched him curiously.

"I think I understand, Master," Lasgol said.

"I didn't expect any less of you."

"How long will it take me to train in the Specialty of Tireless Explorer?"

"Four or five seasons is the required time, both here and in the real world."

"I see… but if I do it here, in my mind… how many seasons will go by in the real world?"

"We don't really know exactly, but we calculate close to one season in the real world."

"Wouldn't it be less?" Lasgol, who had already calculated it in his head, asked. Even if his mind was dulled, he could still make the calculation well enough.

"It would be if we trained you every day in the real world, but we can't do that."

"Why not, Master?" Lasgol suspected something was wrong.

"Precaution. We can't saturate your mind with daily steady training because we might hurt it."

"That doesn't sound at all reassuring…"

"Don't worry, we've taken measures so that nothing bad might happen. We'll only allot one morning or one afternoon every couple of real days to training. We don't want to strain the mind more. We'll let it rest sometimes so it doesn't suffer and has time to recover."

"That sounds sensible. Straining the mind doesn't sound good at all."

"We don't want it to be strained. Galdason will do regular check-ups to make sure your mind is in perfect condition."

"That eases my mind…." Lasgol said, although he really was not at ease at all. "And how long will it take me to become a Man Hunter?"

"Another four or five seasons."

"Additionally, right?"

"That's correct. We don't believe we can accelerate the process much more. Not without risks. We won't do parallel trainings."

"Then for Beast Master it'll be another five seasons, here, in this world."

"That's right," Gisli confirmed.

"In all it'll be about three seasons in the real world."

"It might be less. We're not sure. Since it hasn't been attempted before, we only have estimates and conjectures. What we know about the experiments we've done and in which I myself have taken part, is that time occurs between five to ten times faster than in the real world, and it's what we're going to use to train you."

Lasgol snorted hard.

"Yeah… at last I understand it, Master. I hope it works. It would be a great breakthrough, a huge one. But, I wonder whether the knowledge acquired here will be the same as that acquired in the real world. What if it's not so? What if I don't manage to retain the knowledge? What if I lose it once I'm back in the real world?"

"That's something we'll have to watch and study. Every day we'll return to the real world and evaluate whether the knowledge acquired during the time here, in the training world, remains or not in the real world. We believe it does. The first experiments and studies we, Elder Specialists, underwent prove it so, but we have a lot to learn and improve."

"What will happen to my mind? Will it be capable of telling when I'm here and when I'm in the real world? Furthermore… won't it become confused with the times? With which time it is in each place, I mean? Since they flow at two different speeds…"

"We haven't been able to study extensive periods of training, only brief intervals, so I can't answer that question. It's possible you might feel confused and that your mind won't be able to adapt well to the time passed in each world. We'll have to see how your training evolves and the secondary effects of it on your mind and body. It's going to be very interesting."

Lasgol did not think that suffering secondary effects from the training was "interesting," but he did not complain.

"All right, Master."

"Which of the remaining Specialties of Wildlife would you like to start with?" Gisli asked him.

"I'm not sure…"

"Let me present them to you and you may choose whichever you want."

"I think that's fine, Master."

"We have the Specialty of Man Hunter; a favorite of kings and nobles since its function is to capture, dead or alive, fugitives, criminals, and enemies of the realm. We prefer to capture them alive, although we don't always manage to do so. Since you're already a very good tracker, you'd have to improve your fighting skills and also traps designed to catch men. Really this Specialty is a combination of Wildlife, Archery, and Nature, although it is under my School because it's mainly Wildlife. As I always say, to catch someone you must find them first, and that's usually the most difficult part."

"I know…" Lasgol muttered.

"A Man Hunter may use hounds, hawks, and owls to help him, and this requires a very good hand with all of them. Since you already have a familiar, besides a creature from the frozen continent, we won't need to train you in the use of more animals, although hounds and hawks are quite often used. Always keep in mind that this specialty is difficult and dangerous, since it's about catching criminals. Death awaits the Man Hunter at the end of the trail, because the quarry will try to kill him or her rather than get caught."

"I understand, Master. My friend Luca is a Man Hunter. I've talked about it with him in the past."

Gisli nodded and went on.

"The next Specialty is that of Tireless Explorer. Its main function is to explore and gather information, day or night, rain or shine or snow, without ever wavering. It is sought after by the army to sight the enemy and avoid ambushes or traps. They're also used to explore unknown or foreign territories. When it is a matter of exploring, revealing enemies, dangers, new lands or mysteries, you call the Tireless Explorer."

"I like this specialty a lot. Exploring, seeing new lands, I'm very drawn to it. I remember that ponies, horses, and all kind of mounts are essential for this specialty, am I right, Master?"

"That's right. It requires creating a strong bond with one's mount."

Lasgol thought about Trotter and how well his pony understood him and behaved.

"I already have that."

Gisli nodded. "And finally, the most difficult of the Wildlife Specialties, since it's the one which requires the most knowledge; one you acquire with time and patience."

"Beast Master," Lasgol said.

"That's right. The Beast Master, capable of dealing and communicating with birds, great cats, horses and all kinds of animals thanks to the knowledge they possess of the skill of Wildlife as a whole. It requires a lot of study, both from tomes of knowledge and practice in nature."

Lasgol nodded.

"I'd love to have all that knowledge."

"Very well. Which of the three do you want to start with?"

"Man Hunter," Lasgol replied.

"Very good, Man Hunter it is then," Gisli said and pointed at the forest. "Let the training begin."

Chapter 23

The days went by for Nilsa, Gerd, and Egil at the hunting cabin, training with Loke and following the Improved Training. There were days of sweat, pain, and development. Every morning they went out to train and did not get back until dusk. The Improved Ration they ate five times a day provided them with enough energy to bear the harsh training.

The tasks they had to accomplish every day seemed oppressive, and it was also hard that they did not see their friends and had no news of them. They had not set foot in the Lair since Loke had taken them to the hunting cabin. The daily routine barely left them time to think, since all their energy was focused on surviving the daily task Loke had set for them.

Most days, Loke had them work on their physical resilience. They had started with endless walks that lasted weeks and now had become long distance races on the snow. He made them run at a light trot through the whole central valley of the Shelter. They had been doing this exercise now for four weeks, and the truth was they knew the training was working because at the beginning none of the three could finish the long runs they were now doing without too much effort.

During these long runs they were allowed to stop, but only when the medallions gave out red flashes, which all three knew meant they had overexerted themselves. Egil was fascinated by the medallions and the spells Enduald had put on them. Every evening he asked Loke about them. This evening was no different. They were having their "delicious" ration before the fire with a resigned look on their faces.

"I wonder…" Egil began to say as he observed the medallion hanging from his neck and resting on his chest.

"What do you want to know?" Loke asked, guessing Egil wanted to inquire about the medallion.

"I understand that Enduald, being an Enchanter, is capable of casting spells on objects like the Rangers' cloaks, these medallions, or the ring that controls them," he said, indicating Loke's index finger, although he was not currently wearing the ring.

"It's what he's been studying and developing all his life," Loke replied. "He's a renowned Enchanter in the magic community."

"I did not know there was a magic community," Gerd said, chewing hard.

"Not as such. But Mages, Sorcerers, Enchanters, Shamans, and others blessed with the Gift are in touch with one another, at least those of the more advanced and civilized kingdoms in Tremia. I don't know much about this, but I do know they're familiar with each other and some have a very good reputation while others not so good."

"Certainly interesting," Egil said. "It would be fantastic to meet members of this magic community and exchange ideas with them."

"As a rule, they only speak to those who are like them," Loke said.

"Well, that's a shame, I would've loved to talk about magic matters with them," Egil said, although he was really thinking about Lasgol. He should interact with these mages and learn from them.

"You'd better stay away from them," Nilsa recommended, "lest you end up enchanted," she smiled and poked her tongue out at him.

"I'd gladly take that risk," he replied, also smiling.

"I'm sure you would," Loke said as he put more wood onto the low fire.

"Going back to the medallions…" Egil continued. "I'd like to understand something …"

"Ask away. I'll answer if I can, but it's not a discipline I master so I can't promise I'll have the answers."

Egil nodded. "I understand Enduald can enchant objects like these." He looked at his medallion. "What puzzles me is how he can enchant them with healing spells, because they are healing spells, aren't they?"

Loke looked at him for a moment, thinking.

"They are. They are in charge of watching and controlling your bodies, your health."

"And how can Enduald do those spells? It's one thing to enchant a cloak so it's more resistant, but it's quite different to use healing spells."

"That avid mind of yours will take you far," Loke said.

"Or it will plunge him into the sea," Nilsa said.

"Let's hope it's the former," Egil said with a guffaw.

"Enduald can use healing spells in his enchantments because he works with a Healer's help," Loke said.

"Edwina," Egil said, nodding repeatedly. "Now I understand. Enduald goes to the Camp and works with the Healer Edwina."

"That's right. They don't do it openly, but I think I can share this information. After all, you're putting your lives in the hands of these enchantments and spells."

"You can trust us, sir. We won't mention it to anyone," Gerd promised as he searched for some crumb to put in his mouth in the folds of his clothes.

"You can trust us completely, sir," Nilsa said very seriously. "We're totally trustworthy."

Loke nodded.

"The Healer has been working with Enduald for years on different experiments related to the enchantment of objects that can heal or at least be beneficial for the health. These medallions aren't a new concept. They were developed years ago. What they've been doing is calibrating them and making sure the healing spells work as planned. The ones you're wearing around your necks are the fruit of many years of work for both of them."

"A real treasure, then," Egil said, acknowledging their value and staring down at his own with admiration. "They're fantastic, yes."

"That's right," Loke agreed.

"Can I have another serving, sir?" Gerd asked.

Loke looked at him and nodded. "An additional half ration."

"Thank you, sir!"

"You're welcome. You've lost all the fat you brought with you. You may eat a little more."

"I feel very well, a lot more resilient and strong, sir" Gerd told Loke as he ate his additional half ration.

"More resilient without a doubt. Somewhat stronger too, because all this training has created some additional leg and back muscles mainly, which is what we were after."

"I also feel surprisingly resilient and strong," Egil said.

"In your case the improvement has been frankly remarkable. I never thought you'd improve so much. I'm surprised, because you didn't have that much physique to begin with."

"I'm a lot better now," Egil said, squeezing his thighs and calves, which had toned up considerably.

"I feel more or less the same, although I'm five times more resilient," Nilsa said.

"You arrived a lot more balanced, and you have a wiry, powerful body."

"Does this mean we've improved enough to go back to the Lair, sir?" Gerd asked.

"You still have a few weeks left of training and then you'll be able to go back and see your friends."

"Same training, sir?" Nilsa asked with a wave that meant she was tired of running around clearings and mountains.

"No," Loke shook his head. "Now we'll work on strength, without neglecting resilience of course."

"Of course, sir" Nilsa said, making a horrified face.

"I have enough strength," Gerd said, his mouth so full they hardly understood him.

"Yeah, you were born with a lot of muscle."

"If Viggo were here he'd say and with little brains." Nilsa laughed.

"You bet," Gerd laughed too. "They'll be all right, won't they? Our friends I mean."

"They will be. Don't worry about them but about yourselves."

The three friends nodded. That night they dreamed they had finished the Higher Training and rejoined their friends. They celebrated their reunion with hugs and laughter. They were all perfectly well and the training was going smoothly.

The following morning, Loke woke them up with the first light of dawn. Hauling two enormous leather bags on his back, he took them to a steep hillside covered with snow about half a day from the cabin—and of course they had to run there to stay in shape. The hill had a small fir forest on the lower part of the slope. Loke told them to stay among the firs and rest from the race.

"You'll remember this place forever," he told them in a dry tone which made them all very nervous.

"Well, that's nice, sir..." Nilsa trailed off.

"Here we're going to do one of my favorite exercises," Loke told them. "I can't say I invented it though; it was one of the Elder Specialists who's long passed away, but I did help perfect it."

"He didn't pass away from the exercise, did he?" Gerd asked, alarmed.

"No, he died of natural causes, old age..."

"Phew, thank goodness," Nilsa said, wiping perspiration from her forehead.

"It's an exercise that not only builds muscle but also character," Loke explained.

"This is going to be painful... I know it..." Gerd moaned.

"Well, if it's going to be painful for you who are a mountain of muscle, imagine what it'll do to me," Egil said, horrified.

Loke looked at the steep slope.

"See the top of the hill?"

"Yes, sir, that's quite a slope," Gerd said.

"But it's not that far..." Nilsa commented, surprised. They were now used to running very long distances—a slope was a piece of cake for them given the great physical shape they were in.

"No, it's not, but remember that we're here to work on our physical strength."

"Ohhh... and how will we do that?" asked Gerd.

Egil was staring at the slope with analytical eyes.

"Were going to have to drag something up that slope..." he predicted.

"Exactly. You do have a good head," Loke told him.

"Drag? What?" Nilsa asked, looking around. "There's nothing here but snow and trees."

"Not snow..." Egil said, already guessing.

Nilsa cried in horror. "Nooo!"

"What?" Gerd asked, not catching on yet.

"You're going to drag a tree up to the top," Loke said.

"You've got to be kidding!" Gerd said in disbelief.

"I'm not kidding," Loke said very seriously. "One each." He took three felling axes out of the bag on his back. He went over to one tree and marked it.

"This one's for you, Gerd."

"It's huge!" the giant protested.

"A match for your strength," Loke replied.

Gerd stared at the robust tree, despondently.

"This one's for you, Nilsa, and that other one is for you, Egil."

"Those are smaller!" Gerd protested.

"You have twice the muscle I have," she accused him, jabbing his torso with her finger.

"And thrice mine," Egil said, shrugging.

"That won't be the case by the time we finish this stage of the training," Loke assured them as he took out some odd looking ropes with harnesses from his bag.

"And what's that supposed to be for?" Gerd asked warily.

"Once you've felled your tree, you'll tether it with these ropes, put on the harnesses, and lug it up the slope to the top."

"Is that an order or wishful thinking, sir?" Gerd asked in complete disbelief.

"Very funny," Loke replied with a serious look. "Begin."

Nilsa, Gerd, and Egil looked at one another, their expressions halfway between puzzled and horrified.

"You cut the tree down, you know how to do that. Once it's felled I'll help you with the harness."

They began to cut down their trees. It took them quite a long while to do so and a lot of effort. Gerd's was the first one to fall to one side in the midst of his warning cry.

"Good. Now it's time to drag it," Loke told him as he tied the ropes to the tree and then put the harness on Gerd. "Try," he told him.

"Aaagh!" Gerd pulled with all his might, but he could not move the tree more than a couple of paces.

"Let me help you a little," Loke said. He took out the ring and put it on. He murmured words of command and the three medallions flashed blue.

Suddenly Gerd started dragging the tree with a look of intense effort.

"Now I can…" he said, clenching his jaw.

Loke turned to Egil and Nilsa.

"Hurry up, the hill's waiting. You'll be back in the Lair in no time."

"In no time…" Egil snorted, knowing full well he was going to suffer horribly before that moment arrived.

Chapter 24

The Experience Stage continued for the rest of their comrades, and it was not going as well as they had expected.

Viggo was protesting irately.

"I don't understand why we have to do this training inside my head!" he cried, taking an attack stance with his knives ready.

"Because that's how it's been designed, so it's as efficient and effective as possible," Engla replied.

Viggo watched the Elder Specialist of Expertise who, standing on a tree that crossed over a river of fast white waters, prevented him from passing and threatened him with her own Assassin's knives.

"We've been training for weeks, and I have so many things inside my head that I think it's going to burst," he said, raising his voice to be heard above the roaring of the river.

"I doubt very much that it will burst, and if it did, I doubt whether we would find much thinking matter."

"Yes, Ma'am," Viggo replied, and he lunged a combined attack, seeking first her forward foot and then her left arm.

The Elder defended herself with a very light hop backwards on the tree trunk and blocking both attacks easily with her own knives.

"I do not see you progressing adequately. You should already be able to defeat me and overcome this exercise and I see we are stuck. It is my duty to remind you that until you pass this test we cannot go onto more advanced matters."

"It's the river. It makes me nervous. The current is very strong."

"And I've thrown you in ten times, so you should be used to it."

"One doesn't get used to being carried away by the water and nearly drowning!" he protested, attacking again with a leap forward and a swift slash followed by a thrust.

Engla saw the attack and defended herself once again, preventing Viggo from cutting her.

"The good thing about this new training is that we can take you to the utmost limit, because, since everything happens in your mind, the physical consequences are not real."

"What does that mean? That it's okay if I drown in the river?" Viggo asked as he retreated on the trunk, trying to keep his balance as he defended himself from Engla's attack.

"We had already foreseen that the training might be taken to the limit, what we did not know is how it might affect the pupil's mind."

"That's awful! How do you think drowning feels?" he protested, leaping backwards from a combination of diagonal and vertical slashes from Engla.

Engla stopped and looked at him from head to toe.

"How many times did you drown?"

"Four!" Viggo cried. "It's a horrible experience!"

"But you are still alive and training. I think that is a masterstroke," Engla said with a smile of satisfaction.

"Ma'am, the fact that I don't drown for real but in my mind doesn't mean I don't suffer when I die!"

"Well then make an effort not to die so much," Engla snapped.

"I'm making an effort!" Viggo shouted and attacked again with rapid slashes and thrusts while he advanced on the trunk, forcing the Elder to retreat while she blocked and avoided Viggo's thrusts.

"Wait a moment..." Viggo stopped in the middle of the trunk. "There's a catch here."

"A catch? What do you mean?" Engla asked, looking innocent.

"How come I can never beat you?" he asked, raising one eyebrow. "I should be able to defeat you, here on this trunk or anywhere else."

"If you say so... the truth is quite different. You have not defeated me once since we began the training, and a season has gone by."

"A season where? There or here?" he tapped his head.

"Here, but at the rate we are going it will be one outside as well, and you are progressing slowly," Engla said, shaking her head.

"That's because this is driving me crazy," he replied with a wave of his knives, "and because there's cheating here."

"What do you mean by cheating?"

"The difficulty of the exercise. I should've already passed it. I should've defeated you already, Ma'am. How come I can't?" he asked, looking suspicious of some anomaly.

"Because you are stubborn and quite clumsy?" Engla snapped again.

Viggo shook his head.

"There's trickery here," he said and attacked once more with unstoppable speed. But Engla was able to avoid his attacks with movements suited to a younger person with great agility.

"You missed again," Engla said.

"Your agility and movement speed are better suited to Astrid. It's not possible that my Elder moves as well as Astrid."

"No? And why is that?"

"Because of your age!"

"I feel sensational, as fit as when I was a young girl," she replied and countered at lightning speed, managing to cut Viggo in his left forearm.

"Arghhhh!" he cried between rage and pain.

"Does it hurt?"

"Of course it hurts! How can a deep cut in the arm not hurt?"

Engla shrugged.

"Since it only happens in your mind, I cannot know for sure."

"My mind feels the pain as if it really happened!"

"But it is not real."

Viggo showed Engla his blood dripping on the trunk.

"It looks pretty real to me, Ma'am. Very real in fact."

"If you say so..."

"This training system is badly designed. It should take place in the Elder's mind and not the pupil's," he complained.

"That is an interesting proposition. It is something we considered and discarded. Since the pupil is the one who needs the benefits of the training, we thought it best that it took place in his or her mind."

"Well, it's a mistake! Between the mental fog, the constant confusion with time and place, and these bloody exercises, my mind's going to burst!" he protested again.

"So, let me end your misery if you are feeling so bad," Engla said and attacked him with such speed that, although Viggo managed to block the first attack and then the second, he could not stop the third. Engla's right knife plunged deep into his stomach.

"Arghhhh!" he cried out in pain and frustration.

"It seems you failed the exercise again."

Viggo's medallion flashed red.

"I know what it is... the Elder Specialist is faster and more agile than in real life..."

"That is a good guess, my leathery apprentice. That way we are able to help you improve a lot more."

Viggo squinted in rage.

"That's cheating..." he muttered and fell into the river, which took him away with the strength of its current to drown him a little further down.

Engla watched Viggo dying with a smile on her face.

"I think he *is* making progress," she said to herself.

In another landscape inside Ingrid's mind, she and Elder Ivar were training determinedly. Ingrid was hidden in the snow, half buried, and Elder Ivar was beside her, also lying covered in snow. Before them spread a beautiful lake with a bluish-white surface.

"Take a deep breath and let the cool air fill your lungs. It will make aiming and keeping your arm steady easier," he told her.

"Master, this shot is especially difficult,"

"You have been able to hit the bull's eye at four hundred, four hundred and fifty, five hundred, and five hundred and fifty paces. I do not see why you cannot hit another one at six hundred paces," Ivar said to cheer her.

"The distance is huge. Five hundred already seemed so far…"

"And you managed to hit the center."

"After weeks of trying…" Ingrid complained.

"You will be able to make it. Forest Sniper is one of the most difficult Specializations to achieve since it requires a hawk's eye and remarkable dexterity with the longbow. You have the qualities required to reach this specialty—I can see it and I feel it, otherwise I would not waste my time training you in it. There are other Archery Specializations we can try instead."

"Thank you, Master, it's just… that… between the wind, the falling snow… the distance of six hundred paces, and that I barely see the target, I'm not at all sure."

"Remember that we can repeat the training as many times as necessary. We are in your mind. This is a great advantage over the real world, where we would have to leave it for another day and the conditions would vary. Here the conditions and time remain more constant and we can repeat the exercise over and over."

"That's true."

"May I ask why of all the Archery Specializations you wanted to begin with this one?" Ivar asked her.

"Being as I am an Archer of the Wind, which is short range Archery specialty, I preferred to start with its opposite—the longer range of the Sniper."

Ivar nodded.

"I see. It makes sense."

"If I manage to master this specialty, I'd like to continue with Natural Marksman or Infallible Marksman."

"And why is that?"

"They're two specializations I should be good at, since they're similar to Archer of the Wind."

"Similar does not mean they will be easier. Natural Marksman is a short-range specialty, true, but it requires some instincts that not everyone possesses. A Natural Marksman achieves such a strong connection with the bow that he or she is able to release and hit the target almost subconsciously. A Natural Marksman releases faster than speech and makes a bull's eye almost every time."

"Yes, Master, and it would be a great complement to the specialty I already have. I hope to have the skill to do so."

"We will find out when we get down to it," Ivar replied and made a sign to keep aiming with the special sniper's bow.

"But in case you are unable to develop the Natural Marksman skill, you have Infallible Marksman, which, from what I have seen of your technique—which is frankly very good—I do not think you would have any trouble achieving."

"That specialty is extremely technical; I guess that by practicing and practicing I could manage," she said.

"The Infallible Marksman's only goal is to not miss. Every shot, whatever the situation and the bow used, must hit the target. Always. The training used to achieve that focuses on making true shots with different bows, mainly the composite which is the favorite for this specialty. The shots are taken with time and concentration, no haste at all."

"The opposite of a Natural Archer, then," Ingrid guessed.

"That is correct. One releases on instinct, the other through concentration. One releases immediately, while the other takes all the time the shot requires."

"Like me now..." she said and snorted.

"With targets at no more than two hundred paces away."

"I understand."

"And what about Mage Hunter or Elemental Archer? Are you not interested in them?"

"To be honest, Master, not really. My friend Nilsa, who is currently participating in the Improved Training, wants to become a Mage Hunter, so we're fine with one in the group."

"I see. I hope your friend makes it."

"Yes, so do I. It would make her very happy and the rest of us as well. As for Elemental Archer... it brings back bad memories."

"Why is that? Some loss?"

"Something like that, Master. A friend betrayed us. I get the shivers every time I think about it."

"That is natural, betrayal is a difficult wound to heal. It requires time. Luckily, if everything goes well and the new system is a success, you will be able to come back later on and specialize in it if you change your mind."

"I'll think about it."

"Very good. Now, you have been calibrating that shot long enough. I will count to three and then you release," Ivar said.

"Right. Let's hope I hit the target," Ingrid tried to cheer herself.

"One, inhale," Ingrid did so.

"Two, hold that breath and do not lose sight of the target."

Ingrid's bow was ready to release and her eye was fixed on the target.

"Three let go."

Ingrid released the large arrow which flew with great strength. Tracing an arc, it flew over the frozen lake at great speed. Ingrid followed the flight of her arrow, almost willing it to the target. It reached the other side of the lake and headed to the Ranger's Scarf tied to a stake that was the target. Her arrow reached it squarely, breaking the stake.

"Bull's eye!" Ingrid cried, raising her arm in victory.

"Magnificent shot," Ivar congratulated her.

"Will I be able to achieve the Forest Sniper Specialty?"

"Thirty more like this one and you will."

"Thirty?" Ingrid looked horrified. "It'll take me an eternity."

Ivar made a face that meant that would not be a problem.

"One thing we do have here is time."

Ingrid nodded.

"I'll make it, Master."

Ivar nodded. "Let us keep working."

In another mind, in another place, Astrid was practicing with Engla. They were in a castle with high walls and two central towers. It was the dead of night and the moon beams drifted through the clouds. Up along one of the towers a shadow was climbing, hiding from any light that might reveal her. It was Astrid. She reached a window at the highest part of the tower and looked down. She was over sixty feet high. She swallowed. She was a pretty good climber and heights did not faze her much, but she respected them. One slip or a wrong hold and she would fall to her death in the bailey. Just thinking about it made her shiver.

She strengthened her hold to be able to maneuver. Taking out a lock pick from her belt, she proceeded to force the window open without a sound. She managed to do it without being discovered by the castle guard patrolling the battlements below.

She slipped into the tower. She found herself in a room that was without a doubt the study chamber of the lord of the castle. It was exactly where she had wanted to land. She had not erred in her guess as to where the Count's working chamber would be. Everything was going fine. The most important thing was not to make a mistake now. If she was caught off guard she would be finished. They would sound the alarm and she would not be able to escape from the castle. And if she could not escape… she could not be caught alive… those were King Thoran's orders.

She crouched and approached the carved oak table. The room was in shadows, so she had to use extreme care as she moved since knocking anything over would draw the attention of the guard watching, on the other side of the door, in the hallway. She took out her knife and began to work on the drawer until she managed to force it open. There was a light *crack* of the wood as it yielded. Astrid stood still, listening, in case that tiny sound had caught the guard's attention.

All of a sudden, the door of the room opened and the light from the hall flooded in. Astrid pressed herself against the desk and made herself as small as possible. A massive soldier came into the room and swept it with a glance, searching for the source of the sound. Astrid remained hidden, blending into the shadows. The soldier took another step into the room and swept it again until he was sure there was nobody there. Astrid did not even breathe.

He did not see her. He turned round and went out.

"Everything in order?" the other soldier asked.

"I thought I heard something, but I saw nothing."

"Must have been a rat."

"Most likely."

Astrid waited a little for the two soldiers to be distracted in their thick-minded chit-chat and slowly put her hand into the drawer she had forced open. The documents she was seeking ought to be there. Her fingers recognized a dagger, an ink flask, and nibs. At the far end she touched something leather. She felt it carefully and noticed it was a cylinder, used to hold maps or letters. She took it out and inspected it. It was long enough to keep rolled-up documents inside.

She had found it! The compromising document Thoran wanted was surely inside of it. She grabbed the end with the leather cap and twisted it to remove the cap and reach the documents.

She felt a prick in two of her fingers.

She brought the container to the window, and in the light of the moon she found what had pricked her. When she had taken the cap off, she had triggered a mechanism inside the container and a dozen sharp needle points had sprung out, piercing her glove and reaching her finger tips.

"A trap in the container..." she said, and by the time she guessed what had happened, her medallion flashed red and she collapsed on the floor.

Engla appeared suddenly.

"You failed the exercise," she said with a piteous look.

Astrid was trying to mutter something but she could not. The poison was killing her; she had blood at the corners of her mouth.

Engla looked at her, bending over her.

"I hope you have learned the lesson. Stealthy Spy is a very difficult Specialization and an extremely dangerous one. Their mission is to spy, gather information, and always keep to the shadows. They never let themselves be seen or caught and must always be alert to traps and enemy ambushes, because the enemy will protect their secrets to the death."

Astrid opened her eyes wide, and with one last convulsion, she died.

Chapter 25

After a few more weeks of training, Loke finally gave his approval, and Nilsa, Egil, and Gerd finished their Improved Training. The news caught them by surprise one morning when they were getting ready to practice. They were beside themselves with joy.

"At last!" Nilsa yelled to the sky with her arms raised.

"We did it!" Gerd cried, so happy he could not stop smiling from ear to ear.

Egil's body ached all over from the extreme effort of the training, but like his two friends he was overjoyed. The three hugged, jumping with glee and laughing as if they had passed the greatest of tests.

"Let me remind you that this part of the training was just to get you in good shape," Loke told them. "The important part starts now when you join your comrades in the Specialist's training."

"I think this has been more than just getting us in good shape," Nilsa replied.

"I doubt anyone in the whole realm is in better shape than us," Gerd said.

Loke smiled without a word, although they were sure they were right.

"Sir, in my opinion, the Improved Training program has been a success," Egil told Loke. "Will other Rangers follow this training? Future Specialists?"

Loke examined them from head to toe.

"That's not my decision. I'll share the success achieved by the three of you with the Mother Specialist and the Elders, as well as the risks I've identified. They will decide whether to continue with the program or not."

"They might need more groups to undergo the training before making a decision," Nilsa ventured.

"Yeah, I'd try with two or three more groups," said Gerd.

"Not everyone's like us," Egil said with a certain pride in his voice he did not bother to hide.

"Exactly," Nilsa agreed. "There are few like the Snow Panthers," she said laughing.

Gerd and Egil joined her infectious laughter.

Loke watched them. "The truth is that I must admit you're right. I have never met any Rangers like you."

"Does that mean we can leave this cabin and rejoin our team in the Lair?" Nilsa asked, hoping the reply would be positive.

Loke nodded.

"That's awesome!" Gerd cried.

"Fantastic!" said Egil.

"We'll clean up things here, lock the cabin, and go back to the Lair," Loke said.

"Will we return at a normal pace this time?" Gerd pleaded.

"I'll let you decide that. If you want to take it as a stroll we can. If you prefer to do one last racing session, we can do that too."

The three friends exchanged glances. They were very sore and tired from the effort of the last weeks.

"I think one last race would be good for us," Egil said with a mischievous grin.

"The sooner we get there, the better," said Gerd.

"Well, then, a farewell race it is," Nilsa agreed.

Loke smiled and nodded. "So be it."

The joy of the Panthers as they were reunited was indescribable. The Spring Cave filled with laughter, cries of joy, hugs, more joy, and affectionate greetings and camaraderie. Gerd nearly broke Viggo's back with a tremendous bear hug. Lasgol and Egil also hugged with big smiles and a thousand questions and comments which would have to wait for a better moment. Nilsa hugged Ingrid and Astrid tight and they all beamed at being together again.

Ona and Camu also received countless petting which they enjoyed, delighted. Even Nilsa stroked Camu, even though in the past she had always kept her distance. Gerd had picked up Ona in his arms, showing off how strong they had become. The snow panther growled at first, but then she chirped, enjoying the attention. The other Rangers who shared the Cave did not know what was going on behind the screens, but they became infected with the joy that filled the Cave. For one evening, everyone there enjoyed something similar to a party, one of reunion, companionship, and friendship.

In the days following the reunion, they spent time catching up with everything that had happened to each of the groups. They were all perplexed by everything they were discovering. When Ingrid, Astrid, Lasgol, and Viggo explained what each of them had been through in the training and the way the lessons had been taught, Nilsa, Gerd, and Egil listened in astonishment. And something similar happened when the others recounted their experiences with Loke. There were thousands of questions and clarifications, mostly from Egil, who was absolutely fascinated by everything his friends told him.

Egil was dying to join Lasgol and the others in the Training as soon as possible. He tried to persuade the Mother Specialist, who told them they first had to study the results Loke had gathered and evaluate the risk of beginning the training so soon after finishing their Improved Training. Egil guessed from the Mother Specialist's words that they would have to wait and, although he was itching to start, he had to resign himself and wait for the Mother Specialist's approval.

A few days later it was Ingrid's, Astrid's, Lasgol's, and Viggo's turn to rest. They could not strain the mind beyond what had been stipulated, since there was a risk of suffering mental disorders. That was what Galdason told them, and he made sure they did not force themselves too much in the training and rested every day when necessary. He also did a quick check-up whenever they were resting, as was the case now.

"The macabre Illusionist Mage will come presently to look into our noggins," Viggo warned them as he spied through the screens of the Spring Cave to see what went on outside the resting area.

"He's not macabre," Ingrid chided as she sat on her trunk getting Punisher ready.

"What do you mean he isn't? Do you think what he does to us is *normal?*" Viggo asked her, spreading his arms in disbelief.

"I admit it's not normal, but I don't consider it macabre either," Ingrid countered. "This training and teaching is being given to us in a unique manner."

"Wow, at least I'm half right," Viggo smiled at her as he went on spying through the screens.

"I must admit that I find this system of training us directly inside our minds dangerous to say the least," Lasgol said in a troubled tone as he petted Ona, who was lying beside his bunk like a huge kitten.

Galdason and Enduald together, lot of magic, Camu transmitted to him from where he was lying on the floor, all stretched out with his blue tongue lolling out.

Yes, they use a lot of magic with us and it's dangerous.

Dangerous? How? Camu wanted to know at once.

They use it to enter our minds and project knowledge to us.

Not understand.

Lasgol realized these concepts were a little advanced for Camu. He decided it would be easier to make the explanation simpler.

They mess with our heads.

Ah. That bad.

But for now don't stop it. I'll tell you if you must do so. It might be dangerous to interrupt the training sessions abruptly.

Okay.

"I find it fascinating and innovative," Egil remarked as he studied several tomes of knowledge which Annika had lent him to study. Egil had asked Annika to let him get on with the subject while they waited for the approval to join the Training, something the Elder Specialist had found wonderful. Few pupils arrived at the Shelter asking for extra study material. But Egil was no ordinary Ranger—he was obviously special. The Elder Specialists and the Mother Specialist in particular were well aware of this.

Viggo spun around and snapped, "Fascinating? You've got to be kidding!"

"No, I'm absolutely serious," Egil replied.

"I wonder if we haven't made it sufficiently clear that in this training you end up dead. And not figuratively, but literally, with a knife buried in your heart," Viggo told him, making a face of horror and disgust.

"Or poisoned to death," Astrid said, raising her eyebrows.

"I find it so innovative that it seems hard to reach all the possibilities. In what other training can you force the limit so much? None, because if they pushed to the limit, it would bring on precisely death. They have created a system that forces you to improve by pushing you to the limit of death."

"Well, the weirdo doesn't think it's okay either, and as a rule he always agrees with this kind of thing," Viggo told him.

"I always said that Sigrid's experiments were dangerous, and I warned you about them," said Lasgol. "What we're going through seems to me something completely against nature. But I'm not surprised it has come to such an extreme. Training until we literally die—I think it's too much and that it'll have some negative consequences."

Egil shut the tome he was reading. "I find it fantastic, and it could lead to extraordinary advances in training which future generations will be able to benefit from and use to achieve goals that for us are simply dreams. Furthermore, the advances they achieve with us will be used in other areas—I see multiple possibilities."

"Mainly military ones," Ingrid added. "Imagine if they could train soldiers this way and teach them different ways of fighting with this system. They would be much better prepared soldiers than those we have now."

"And that the other kingdoms have," said Gerd, who was lying in his bunk eating green apples he had brought from the Summer Cave in his Ranger's belt. "We'd eat the Zangrians if we had soldiers like that."

"That's true," Ingrid agreed. "If we managed to teach them several fighting types and make them as fit as they're demanding you to be, they'd be capable of fighting against the Wild Ones of the Ice themselves without trouble."

Astrid leapt to the floor from the top of the bunk and on landing, rolled over her shoulder to her right in an evasive movement she used and practiced often.

"Imagine if Rangers and Specialists were able to train like this. And not only that, all the time that might be saved too. They could probably be trained in half the time," she said, bringing out her Assassin's knives and proceeding to slash and cut the air, practicing.

"All of that sounds very good, I'm not denying that," said Nilsa as she paced around the space within the screens. "But you forget a little detail. They're using filthy magic!" she exclaimed angrily. "The whole system is based on magic. Without Galdason and Enduald, this wouldn't work. And sooner or later we'll have to pay the price for using magic. Something will go wrong and one of us will pay dearly."

Viggo nodded repeatedly. "Freckles here is quite right. Playing with magic is dangerous, we all know that, even the weirdo who's not capable of mastering his own."

Lasgol looked at Viggo with narrowed eyes.

"I do master my own. I master it perfectly," he said, defending himself from Viggo's barb.

"Do you? Really? Then why can't you manage to develop the skills you're always trying to achieve? Don't think we don't notice. Every time you have a free moment, wherever you are, you're always trying to develop some new skill, and you never manage to."

Lasgol frowned. "One thing has nothing to do with the other. Just because I can't develop new skills doesn't mean I don't master my magic. The skills I have developed I control perfectly well."

"Yeah... that pool of energy you say you have and which, according to Edwina, is a lot deeper than even you can see, all that sounds like you aren't mastering it."

"And your verbal incontinence sounds to me like you speak nothing but nonsense, which means that up there something's very wrong," Ingrid told him, jabbing his head with her finger.

Viggo shrugged and cocked his head with a smile.

"I wouldn't say you're that wrong," he smiled and made a crazy face.

Ingrid rolled her eyes.

"He even admits it now."

Astrid leapt, then pirouetted and ended up beside Lasgol, kissing him on the cheek.

"Don't pay any attention to foolish Viggo. You know what he's like."

Lasgol smiled in spite of himself. "Yeah, like a toothache."

Toothache bad. Viggo good. Funny.

Don't defend him. You know perfectly well what he's like.

Ona growled twice.

See? Ona knows.

I fun. Viggo good.

Egil saw Lasgol looking at Camu and guessed they were communicating.

"Lasgol and Camu have magic, and that's something wonderful," he said, waving at them, "something we can't manage to understand. That doesn't make it bad. It's our fear of being unable to understand magic that makes us think it's something bad. But, intrinsically, there's nothing wrong in it. We simply don't understand."

"You're always defending magic and anything arcane," Nilsa said accusingly. "Your opinion is biased. In this group there are others who don't think like you. Gerd, Viggo, and I believe magic is dangerous and that whoever uses it ends up paying a steep price."

"Your fear isn't sustained with real facts," Egil replied. "In all the times that Lasgol and Camu have used their magic, nothing bad has happened, and it has helped us survive on numerous occasions. Therefore, your discourse is invalid or at least in doubt."

"The fact that it hasn't happened yet doesn't mean it's not going to," Nilsa said adamantly.

"In any case, Nilsa, you had already come to a favorable view on magic. What's made you go back to your negative position?" Ingrid asked her.

Nilsa pointed at Enduald's medallion on her chest and then at Viggo's head.

"All this semi-magic method of training is what's making me go back to my initial beliefs. We're going to suffer from this experience. Give it time—you'll see."

"Don't be so pessimistic. Nothing's going to happen," Ingrid told her.

"Don't say I did not warn you," Nilsa said and lay down on her bunk, frustrated with the current situation.

Egil came over to stroke Camu, who licked his hand.

"I don't mean to create more dissension," he said, looking at Lasgol, "but I'm dying to get permission to join your training. It'll be fantastic. I can't wait to experience what you're already doing."

"Beware of what you wish, our dear know-it-all. It might come true and you may have a worse than bad time," Viggo said.

"A few bad experiences forge the character," Astrid told Egil, ruffling his hair affectionately.

"I'm not so thrilled to be joining you," said Gerd. "I'm having a pretty hard time just thinking about your training," he said, snorting.

Nilsa grunted from her bunk. "I'd better not say anything. I'm in a pretty foul mood already."

At that moment Galdason came into the Spring Cave and headed to their location.

"Here comes the marvelous Illusionist," Viggo said and looked at Ingrid with a broad smile.

She gave him a look of "you're hopeless" then smiled a little, which Viggo counted a personal victory.

Chapter 26

Galdason came into the private area. Lasgol did not have to say anything to Camu—he had camouflaged himself as soon as he had heard Viggo announce the Mage. Lasgol was not sure whether Galdason knew about the existence of Camu or not, but just in case, and out of caution, he preferred that his friend remain out of sight.

"Good morning, everyone," the Mage greeted them amenably. He was holding a staff in his right hand with rosy-colored inscriptions.

"Good morning," Egil greeted him back. The others either gestured or muttered greetings, Nilsa with a slight snort.

"I have come to see how you are doing," he told them.

"We couldn't be better," Viggo replied, flexing his muscles.

Galdason smiled. "I mean how you are in here." He touched his head with his staff.

"Oh, up there it couldn't be worse. But it's not because of all the magic—we were like this already, before we started all this weird stuff you're doing to us," Viggo said.

Galdason laughed. "A sense of humor is a good sign."

"So, you mean that as long as I'm making jokes I'm not cuckoo?" Viggo made a crazy face.

"I would not put it in such simple terms, but yes, as long as you have a sense of humor and you show it, it's a good sign, as a rule."

"Then the one you do need to examine is Lasgol. Lately he's not being funny at all," Viggo said.

"I thought you said I had no sense of humor," Lasgol said.

"That's right, how distracted of me. Then he's okay," Viggo rectified, making a comic face.

"In any case, I must examine the four of you. The Mother Specialist wants me to keep iron-tight control. We cannot risk anything happening to you."

"We appreciate it, sir," Ingrid said, stepping forward to stand before the Mage." You can start with me."

"Thank you. It will only take a moment. You will feel no pain," the Illusionist assured her.

"Go ahead, I don't fear pain," Ingrid said.

"Sit on the stool, please," Galdason said, indicating the one beside him with his staff. "There is nothing to fear. I am only going to check the state of your mind. It is not anything that intrusive."

"Sounds terribly comforting," Viggo said, making a horrified face.

Ingrid sat down and tied up her hair in a ponytail so her head was easily accessible to the Mage.

"I'm ready."

"Very well, let us begin." Galdason produced a strange crystal prism about two hand-spans long with several facets totally transparent. He held it in his left hand above Ingrid's head. He began to cast a spell, moving his staff in small circles before him.

They all watched, wavering between troubled and intrigued by what the mage was doing. Then suddenly, a rosy light issued from the prism in Galdason's hand and bathed Ingrid's head. The mage put his eyes to the prism while he went on conjuring in a quiet voice and moving the staff with his right hand. Several images appeared on the transparent facets of the prism. Galdason studied them carefully as if seeking to understand them. They were blurry images that came and went. They did not seem fully shaped and it was difficult to see what they were really showing.

"Leave your mind blank and relax, please," Galdason told Ingrid.

"I'll try."

Viggo was watching attentively. He was concerned about Ingrid, although he tried to hide it with his comments.

"Nothing easier than thinking about nothing when your brain's being probed with an arcane crystal that projects a pink beam on your head…"

Astrid nodded. Viggo was not wrong. Leaving your mind blank in that situation was extremely difficult. Having a mage using magic directly on your head would make the most courageous Norghanian nervous.

Galdason studied the images he was getting from Ingrid's mind. He took his time, as if he had all day to do so, which made them all the more nervous still. After a long while he seemed satisfied and stopped the exam.

"You're perfectly all right," he told Ingrid.

"As I had expected," she said confidently.

Galdason smiled. "That's the spirit. You can get up now. Next

209

one, please."

Astrid took a step forward, but Viggo beat her to it.

"I'll be next. We should take advantage of this streak of good luck," he said and winked at Ingrid.

It took Galdason even longer to examine Viggo, so Astrid and Lasgol had to wait patiently for their turn.

When he finally finished his exam, the Mage commented, "Well, this mind was very difficult. The images I got were hard to decipher."

"That's because I'm a mystery," Viggo joked, puffing his chest.

"Rather because you're wrong up there," Ingrid corrected him, tapping his head with her finger.

"Next one, please?"

Lasgol gestured Astrid to go first.

She winked at him and sat on the stool.

The Mage examined her for a long while, but he took much less time than with Viggo.

"I don't see any reason for concern," he told Astrid.

"Thank you, sir," she said and gave her seat to Lasgol, who sat down and prepared for the examination.

Cancel magic? Camu's message reached him.

No, he's only going to check that I'm all right. I don't see any problem with that—it's good that they check up on us just in case.

Okay.

Galdason began to examine him. Lasgol did not feel anything strange beyond a tickling sensation in his mind. It was a funny feeling. He could tell something was going on, but it was so light that he could not identify what it really was. It did not confuse him and neither did his mind fog up, something he was grateful for. It was just as if his head itched lightly, but on the inside.

The Mage took his time, and when he finished at last, he gave Lasgol's shoulder a friendly slap.

"Everything is fine. It does not appear that the training is causing your minds any damage," he said.

"What a relief it is to know that," Viggo snapped at once in a very acid tone. "If I find my head wandering I'll let you know, sir."

"If you should notice anything odd such as headaches, difficulty sleeping or strange confusion, let me know," Galdason said, ignoring Viggo's barb.

"Will do, sir," said Ingrid.

"Very well. I find you apt to continue with the training. Good luck."

The Mage went out, and Lasgol was left wondering whether by the end of the training process they would show any mental strain and what it might be. If they were being examined it was because there was a risk. What he could not put his finger on was how much risk they were taking. This troubled him.

"How nice that we can go on training. I can't wait to see Engla again and die at her hands over and over," Viggo said sarcastically.

"The truth is that their teaching system is excruciatingly painful," Astrid said, agreeing with Viggo's feelings.

"Have you already decided which among the Expertise Specializations you're going to choose?" Lasgol asked with curiosity.

"I'm thinking about Stealthy Spy," Astrid said. "It's an Expertise Specialization very much in demand by the King and also at Court to spy on rivals and also the enemy, both in and outside Norghana. Besides, based on what Engla told me, it's for those who prize honor and loyalty to the realm above all else."

"Bah!" Viggo dismissed the idea with a wave of his hand. "Chameleon Stalker is much better. They're capable of blending into the environment and vanishing completely as if they really were human chameleons. Their function is to stalk the target and catch or kill them. And it has nothing to do with all that nonsense of being faithful to the realm etcetera. You'd be like 'the bug,' but human," he said, pointing at Camu who was once again visible and listening to the conversation.

Astrid was thoughtful for a moment. "For that I'd rather become a Forest Assassin. It's said they have no rival in forest or mountain. If you go into a forest where one is lurking you don't come out alive. Engla has told me there's no Mage, soldier, Ranger, or Wild One that can beat a Forest Assassin in the forest. Their weapons are stealth and invisibility among the foliage."

"I don't really like that specialization…" Lasgol said. "It's about being an Assassin, so their main mission is to kill in the forest."

"And what's the problem with that?" Viggo asked, opening his arms and looking blankly at Lasgol.

"Well, exactly that—it's being an Assassin," Lasgol insisted.

"The best of all professions," Viggo replied with a broad smile.

"Don't worry so much, Lasgol," Astrid said affectionately. "I'm already an Assassin." She winked at him.

"Yeah… but if you obtain another Assassin's specialization, you'll have more missions of this type…"

"You really are a softie, weirdo," Viggo teased him.

"A sweetheart is what he is, and he worries about me," Astrid replied to Viggo, looking lovingly at Lasgol.

"Yeah yeah…" Viggo said. "I'm going to see what my little sweetheart's doing." He left to try and talk to Ingrid and see whether he could make some progress in their peculiar relationship and present situation.

"I bet she's dying to speak to me," he smiled as he walked away.

Astrid and Lasgol exchanged glances and smiled.

"Sure," Astrid said, unable to erase the smile from her face.

Chapter 27

A few days later the Panthers woke up with the arrival of dawn and were getting ready to face the day.

"How long have we been here?" Viggo asked all of a sudden, looking confused. He was looking at the ceiling of the Spring Cave with a lost gaze.

"I believe he's definitively beginning to lose his head," Nilsa said, watching him, amused.

"Don't make that assumption. Time passes differently for us than for you," Astrid said. "It's confusing. It's hard to know how much time has passed when you come back."

"Don't worry, we'll keep track of time for you," Gerd told them with a friendly smile. "We're about to finish Spring and start Summer. We arrived at the Shelter in Winter, so we've been here for two full seasons."

"Ufff…" Viggo snorted. "It seems to me that we've been here at least ten seasons, if not more."

"Not here, but in training we have," Ingrid told him. "We've been here for only two. It's the great advantage of the new system that allows us to train for long periods of time without much time passing in the real world."

"Advantage? What advantage? My hair's going to turn white and I'll get all wrinkly if we keep spending all that time in training," he said, pointing at his own head.

"That would be in that world. Not in this one," Egil corrected him. "From all you've told us—which I can't wait to experience—the time spent in training passes much slower compared to the real world," he said, pointing a finger at the rocky floor of the cave.

"Yeah, but it's beginning to get all mixed up in my head. Now I have no idea how much time's gone by here, which is a bad sign, right?" Viggo asked, frowning.

"You've never been very well in your head, so your present confusion isn't an indication of anything," Ingrid said.

"Oh, no? So, you don't get mixed up between there and here? Don't you get confused when you think about how long you've been here or what season we're in?"

Ingrid was about to reply, but she stopped before speaking. "Sometimes..."

"Aha!" Viggo jabbed his finger at her. "It's not just me, then."

"Only rarely," she corrected.

"Yeah... rarely... sure..." Viggo said, folding his arms over his chest. "I'm getting more and more confused, and no matter how much Galdason looks into our brains and assures us we're fine, I have serious doubts. I'm getting all confused about time."

"That's a very natural reaction of the mind," Egil commented. "I see no reason to worry. If you're in two different worlds where time flows at different rates, it's only natural that it would create some confusion in your mind, especially considering that when you come back from the training your mind has to readjust to the new reality. It must receive a shock every time that happens—it has to calibrate two different realities at the same time. It's very complex..."

"I have no idea what the book-head just said, but it's given me a terrible headache," Viggo said, holding his head in his hands.

"I keep track," Astrid told him. "That helps me. I write down how much time has gone by here and how much in the training. It helps me keep it separate. Try it, I think it'll help."

"How neat, now I'll have to write things down like this bookworm just to know what time I live in!"

Lasgol had been listening attentively, and now spoke up:

"Not only in what time, but also in what world. What I do, apart from writing down the time—which is an excellent idea—is to stay clear about which world I'm in, the real one or the one in my head. That way I get less fuzzy and I feel in control of the situation a little better. You have to always ask yourself. 'Where am I? Which time is this?' And if you're able to answer both questions, everything's fine."

Viggo snorted and made a face; he did not like Lasgol's idea very much.

"And when I don't know which time or world I'm in, what then?"

"Then you'll be declared crazy as a loon," Nilsa said with a chuckle. "Something we all know will inevitably happen, because you're awfully wrong up there."

"I fully agree with Nilsa," Ingrid joined in.

Viggo looked affronted and made as if to bite them.

"Don't pay any attention to them and listen to what you're being told," Astrid recommended. "It'll help you not get mixed up and your head will be better focused."

"Oh, I'm listening, but doing what you say is something else," Viggo replied. "I'm only saying that by the time we spend four seasons here, we're all going to be way crazier than loons."

"You were born that way," Nilsa told him. "So you really can't complain."

"Laugh all you like, you'll soon regret it. When do you say you start the training?"

"The Mother Specialist told us that we'll begin in a few days," Nilsa said excitedly. "She seems quite happy with Loke's reports."

"Yeah, it looks like we're ready," Gerd said, showing off his strong arms. "I've got so much muscle and so little fat I think I even weigh more."

"Yeah, but you have three times the stamina you had before," Nilsa pointed out.

"Yup, that's right. My strength and resilience have improved a lot. Loke knows what he's doing."

Egil stood up, stretching.

"Not only does our Masig Specialist know what he's doing, but the new training system with the medallions really works. It achieves physical improvement in a time I'd deem unthinkable through traditional means. It would've taken us an eternity to become this strong and gain all this stamina. In fact, in my case, I doubt it would have even been possible only following the traditional training methods."

"That's because you're such a puny little man," Viggo said scornfully.

"Not anymore. Want to check?" Egil challenged him.

"Of course I want to check. I'm not going to believe your claims just because," Viggo replied, taking a mock fighting stance.

"I'm warning you, he's improved greatly," Nilsa warned him. "We all have. I think we even surpass you!"

"No way. You three can't kiss the sole of my shoe in anything. And least of all in strength and stamina," Viggo replied daringly.

Egil took a step forward.

"A bear fight? Until one brings the other one down?" Egil asked, challenging Viggo to the type of fight they had been taught in their second year at the Camp.

Viggo's eyes widened.

"You're serious, aren't you?"

"Yes, very serious," Egil said confidently as he stood in a fighting position.

"Unbelievable. I'm going to give you what for, you know-it-all. I'm going to send you flying, my friend."

"That remains to be seen," Egil replied, full of confidence.

Viggo came to stand right before Egil. They each grabbed hold of the other's Ranger's belt with both hands.

"I'll be the judge," Gerd said as he hastened to check their holds. "Everything looks fine. Ready?"

Egil and Viggo nodded.

"Very well. Go!" Gerd cried.

The fight began. Viggo pulled hard, expecting to lift Egil from the floor easily and throw him to one side. To his surprise, Egil withstood the pull, exercising his strength to counter it. Viggo assumed Egil had been lucky and pulled hard. Once again, Egil was able to withstand the pull and Viggo did not manage to move him an inch. Egil countered with a swift, strong pull that caught Viggo unawares. He fought back with all his might. Egil could not move him, but he came close.

"Well…. It looks like the Great Assassin can't shake the puny little guy off," Nilsa said ironically.

"This puny little man… has taken a potion to increase his strength…" Viggo said, clenching his jaw while he tried to topple Egil unsuccessfully.

"I haven't taken… anything… it's the result of the Improved Training…" Egil replied, also making a great effort.

"Wow, this is interesting, it seems we're not as strong as we thought we were," Ingrid said, smiling from ear to ear.

Viggo put his hip in to try to unbalance Egil and knock him over, but again the scholar held fast and countered with strength on his part, keeping his balance. Viggo tried several different pulls and shoves, followed by an attempt to topple Egil, but he was unsuccessful.

"Well… it seems I'm out of shape…" said Viggo, unwilling to admit Egil was right.

"Actually, the one who's in good shape is Egil," said Ingrid.

"He… won't hold… much longer…" Viggo said as he used all his strength and resistance to try and defeat Egil by sheer exhaustion.

But he could not do that either.

In the end they were both left with their tongues hanging out, unable to go on, and Gerd stopped the fight.

"The result is: a tie!" he cried.

Nilsa applauded loudly and Ingrid and Astrid joined her.

"Magnificent demonstration," Ingrid admitted to Egil, impressed.

"That was really good," Astrid told Egil with a slap on the shoulder as he recovered from the effort.

Viggo ill? Camu messaged to Lasgol with a feeling of surprise.

No, he's not ill, Egil's improved a lot.

Not believe.

Well, you'd better believe it. It seems that the new Improved Training works very well.

"If you want you can try besting me," Nilsa challenged Viggo. "Once you've recovered, I mean. Right now you look pretty worn out."

Viggo growled at her.

"No thank you. I see you're all very strong."

"For the sake of finishing the show…" Gerd said and grabbed Viggo by surprise from his shirt front with one hand. He lifted him off his feet and held him hanging in the air.

"Will you put me down, you brainless giant?"

"What's that?" Gerd asked without lowering him.

"Put me down, my very dear friend and comrade," Viggo corrected himself, smiling, all charm.

"I could keep you up there until dinner time, just so you know," Gerd said.

"I believe you, there's no need for any more demonstrations."

Gerd put him back down and smiled at him.

"It was meant to convince you."

"Oh yes, I'm more than convinced."

At that moment someone came to see them. It was Annika.

"Come with me. The Mother Specialist wants to see you."

The seven friends exchanged uncertain glances. Annika's tone was serious, and if Sigrid requested their presence something bad was afoot.

They all nodded and followed her out of the Spring Cave. The

Mother Specialist was waiting for them in the Chamber of Runes. There were two other Elder Specialists with her besides Enduald and Galdason.

"Wow... This doesn't look so good," Nilsa commented in a whisper as they approached. She grew nervous seeing them all there standing with somber expressions.

"You don't say," Viggo whispered back, "it looks like a funeral. Has anyone died?"

"Let's hope not, but what serious faces," Gerd said under his breath.

"It must be related to the training and that's why they're all here. Don't worry so much," Ingrid said, waving aside the others' worries.

Lasgol was also worried and glanced at Astrid. The brunette gestured to him to be calm. Ona was at his side and could also feel the tension. Camu must be somewhere at his heels, not far. For some reason Lasgol felt like something horrible was about to happen.

Chapter 28

They reached the Mother Specialist and the Elders and greeted them respectfully.

"Welcome," Sigrid said, opening her arms wide.

"Mother Specialist, Elders," Ingrid said for the Panthers, and then they waited, expectantly. Sigrid looked stern, troubled, so Lasgol guessed something bad had happened, not that they had done anything wrong.

"I have serious, urgent news to communicate to you," she told them directly, which made everyone pay attention to what she said next. "King Thoran requests his Royal Eagles. You must leave at once for the capital and present yourselves without delay."

"Mother Specialist, what's going on?" Ingrid asked, surprised that King Thoran would summon them so urgently.

"What we have been told is that the capital has been under attack since a few days ago."

"That's terrible!" Nilsa cried.

"Are the Zangrian attacking us?" Gerd asked before he could stop himself.

"No, it is not the Zangrians," Sigrid shook her head.

"The Nocean Empire?" Egil asked, raising an eyebrow. "I can't imagine the Kingdom of Rogdon attacking us. King Solin isn't bellicose, or so I've heard."

"No… no rival kingdom is attacking us. It is not a conventional attack…" the Mother Specialist trailed off.

"Not conventional? Then what?" Ingrid asked, even more intrigued.

"We are being attacked with Magic," Sigrid told them, looking grave.

Lasgol was nonplused. The capital being attacked with magic? He found it difficult to imagine.

"Who? How?" he mumbled almost incoherently.

The Mother Specialist looked at him, nodding.

"Those are the questions we are all asking ourselves. The information we have is scarce and not particularly detailed. We know that the capital is under what appears to be a colossal winter storm. Its origin is unknown and we do not know who has summoned it or why it is attacking the capital. It has been over Norghania for nearly a week, and it is completely freezing the land. The temperatures are so low and the storm so extreme that the city has had to be evacuated. People have frozen to death, I am afraid…"

"Evacuate the capital? Dead? Wow! Then it must be an awful storm… it sounds really bad…" Gerd said, shaking his hands.

"They are calling it a Killer Winter Storm," Sigrid continued explaining. "It has wreaked havoc. The population has fled the city and the surroundings. Not all of them managed to escape in time and the storm… has taken them…"

"That's terrible news," Astrid said.

"And King Thoran? And the Court?" Nilsa asked.

"King Thoran took refuge immediately in Skol, his brother Duke Orten's fortress, but we have just received news that he is now outside the capital with his army," Sigrid added. "The members of the Court have gone back to their own counties to shelter in their fortresses and prepare for a possible war."

"I'm sure the possibility will have already been dismissed but, couldn't it be a simple storm with nothing arcane or magical behind it?" Egil asked, narrowing his eyes. "It wouldn't be the first time a great winter storm bears heavily on a certain part of Norghana that looks as if it had been sent against us as a punishment from the Ice Gods for some offense or other."

"At first that is what was thought, that it was a winter storm off cycle since we're in summer, which although it might occur, is a rare phenomenon. But after three days of suffering and studying it, the King's Ice Mages reached the conclusion that it is not a natural storm. It has been conjured, and for now it is not losing strength."

"But to conjure such a great storm that lasts for days you would need great power…" Lasgol reasoned. "Tremendous power, in fact. Who has such power?"

"I believe that is precisely why King Thoran has summoned you. He most likely wants you to investigate. You must report to the Royal Camp outside the capital and receive new instructions."

"That sounds great…" Viggo whispered to Astrid under his breath. "You'll see the mess they're going to land us in…"

"We must act at once," said Ingrid. "We must find the enemy and end the threat."

The Mother Specialist nodded.

"Our realm needs you," she said to Ingrid.

"And we will not fail," she replied determinedly.

The Panthers exchanged troubled looks. The news was bad, and they would have to face a situation they had never encountered before.

"What will happen to our training and learning, Mother Specialist?" Egil was eager to know. He did not like the idea of leaving the training at all.

"You will resume the training as soon as you come back from the mission King Thoran gives you. The results are very satisfactory both in the Improved Training and in the Experience Stage. My greatest wish is to continue with the system as planned. Go and serve your King and do your duty as Rangers, when you return you will continue your training."

"I can't wait..." Viggo whispered ironically in Astrid's ear.

"Don't be like that—deep down you're delighted with all we're learning," she whispered back.

"Thank you, Mother Specialist," Egil said gratefully. "I can assure you that in my case I'm looking forward to the Experience Stage."

"Me too," Nilsa said.

"And me..." Gerd joined in, albeit with some reservations.

"It pleases me greatly to witness your eagerness and motivation. Be assured that the doors of the Shelter will remain open to continue improving your training. You are ready to pass into the Experience Stage and I wish you to do so as soon as you return."

"We appreciate it, Mother Specialist," Egil said, happy to have the certainty that they could train as Specialists upon their return. Besides, it would be in the new system which was something he personally was looking forward to, especially after what Lasgol, Ingrid, Astrid, and even Viggo—in his own way—had told him.

"Go now. Do not stop until you reach the capital. You are expected at the south of the city. You will find the King's army and the Ice Mages ready."

"Very well. We'll go at once," Ingrid said decisively.

"Before you leave, my brother Enduald wants to give you a gift," Sigrid said and gave way to the Enchanter.

"Since the threat is a winter storm, I have prepared these hooded

Rangers' winter cloaks with added protections," he said, handing them a satchel.

Lasgol accepted it and took out one of the cloaks. It was snow-white and had thick wool lining inside.

"They're very good quality. Are they enchanted?" Lasgol asked, already guessing they were, being a gift from Enduald.

"They resist low temperatures and give warmth to prevent whoever wears them from freezing to death. I hope they will serve you well. Given the situation you will be facing, I am sure they will."

"Fantastic," said Egil, pulling one out and happily putting it on; not feeling anything special, he looked at Enduald.

"The enchantments they have will only become active when the temperatures become unbearable to a human being. I have also put the usual spells of vitality and strength in these cloaks that I put in the regular ones, so they will help you in difficult times when the body fails you."

"Thank you very much, Enduald. Any and all help against the enemy is welcome," Ingrid said, bowing her head gratefully.

Nilsa, who disliked magic so much, said nothing, but even she knew they would be of great help and accepted hers. Astrid and Viggo did the same.

"Go now, Royal Eagles, and defend the realm," Sigrid said in farewell.

The journey to Norghana was quiet, except for the natural restlessness they all felt for having been summoned to the capital so urgently. All except Viggo, who was delighted to leave the Shelter—they rode as fast as their mounts would go but without forcing them to their limit. They had no idea what they were going to find when they arrived, and it would be better to have fresh horses just in case. Ona and Camu accompanied them close behind, wandering away occasionally but remaining in sight.

They reached the southern part of the walled capital and watched from a hill at a prudent distance. What they saw struck them dumb. The city was completely frozen: the walls, the battlements, towers, houses, streets, the Royal Castle—every rock and stone of the great city was covered with ice and frost. It was as if the Ice Gods had decided to freeze it with their icy breath to punish the Norghanians for some sin against the Gods. Only that was not the work of the gods. A colossal storm rose above the city with a voracious appetite, so lethal and intimidating that no human being crazy or brave enough would dare approach.

Huge black clouds, horribly fat and darkly shaped and threatening rose above the city. It looked as if part of the sky had burnt and broken and was now pouring an icy horror over the capital. Countless lightning bolts and freezing rain fell over the city. The buildings were hit by terrible hurricane winds, so cold that everything they touched was immediately frozen. The storm covered the whole city and rose to the sky in several icy columns that never stopped pouring their punishment convulsively over the now abandoned city; large clouds and ferocious winds imploded and others emerged again from the dark, frozen heart of the storm.

"Wow… that takes away all the courage of a man," Gerd said, gulping hard as he watched the horrendous storm.

"Come on! We'll stop whoever has created this monstrosity." Ingrid said.

"I'm telling you now that I'm not going there for all the gold in the world," Viggo said, shaking his head hard.

"It doesn't seem like a promising tactic to go into the heart of that evil storm," Egil replied. "We'll have to find more plausible alternatives."

"I'm warning you that I'm not going in there, just to be clear," Viggo repeated, shaking his head.

"We have Enduald's cloaks," Ingrid reminded them. "They'll protect us."

"Not even if we had a ball of fire protecting us," Viggo refused, folding his arms over his chest.

"Let's not be hasty," said Lasgol. "Let's go and see what orders we have," he added, pointing at the King's army a little to the southeast of the city.

"There are over a thousand military tents in that camp," Astrid counted.

"Imagine what it must've been like to evacuate the city under that storm," Ingrid said. "They must've been working nonstop."

"Look, there's another camp further east," Lasgol said, pointing in that direction. This was no army but rather all the people who had fled from the city and had nowhere to go. It was enormous and went into a forest, where they could glimpse a river which the poor wretches had completely taken over. There were some army tents, but many families had also made their own improvised tents with boards and canvas. They could appreciate the precarious situation of the several thousand people there. Soldiers from the army on carts were delivering blankets and food to the people.

"It's terrible… poor souls, I guess a lot of people will have died," Gerd said sadly.

"I guess so, because by the time they realized this was no passing storm it was probably too late to escape for many," said Egil. "Besides, if you look carefully at the city gates you can see they made a run for it, leaving their possessions behind."

"Yeah, you can see belongings and utensils scattered everywhere," Nilsa said.

"There are corpses by the gates," said Lasgol, who had used his *Hawk's Eye* skill and was able to see them properly, whereas his friends could not because of their distance from the capital.

"Poor people. To die like that, feeling that monstrosity… It's awful," said Astrid.

"I hope most of the citizens managed to escape and are either safe with relatives or in that improvised camp the Royal Army is tending to," Ingrid said wishfully as she put her hand to her eyes to see better.

"What seems unbelievable to me is the strength of that storm in the middle of summer. It should die out with the high temperatures, but it does not," said Nilsa, "which means it's due to some kind of magic."

"Can Camu feel anything about this magic?" Egil asked Lasgol.

Do you feel anything?

No, very far. See, no feel.

"He says we're too far away for him to feel the storm. We'll have to get closer."

"No way. I'm not going anywhere near that monstrosity," said Viggo.

"In any case we have to go down to the Royal Army camp. Let's go and see what else they know," said Ingrid.

Camu, Ona, stay here. Down there, there are too many soldiers. I would guess a couple thousand—it's dangerous for you.

Soldiers fools.

Smart they certainly aren't, at least most of them, that's true, Lasgol admitted. Norghanian soldiers had a reputation for being strong brutes but not for being intelligent.

We wait.

That's right.

They went down to the camp and at once felt the cold. About twenty infantrymen surrounded them, armed with axes and round shields. They seemed nervous, which was not strange given the circumstances. They could see the great storm in all its splendor from where they were. They introduced themselves as the Royal Eagles of the Rangers and the officer in charge of guarding the perimeter went to find a superior.

"I'm Captain Albertson."

"Captain," Ingrid saluted diligently.

"You can leave your mounts here. Sergeant Losten will take charge," he said and made a sign to an aged quartermaster.

"Yes, sir," the sergeant replied, and once the seven had dismounted he took the horses away with the help of four plain soldiers.

Easy, Trotter, They'll look after you well, he transmitted to his faithful pony.

"Come with me, please. They're waiting for you at the command tent," the captain told them.

"They're waiting for us?" Egil was interested.

"Yes, I have orders to take you there the moment you arrived."

"Orders from who?" Ingrid asked.

"Orders from King Thoran. His Majesty has come to direct the operations himself. General Ikerson and the Ice Mages are with him."

"I see. Has Duke Orten arrived?"

"The King's brother is on his way with an army of five thousand soldiers. He has been gathering the forces of the loyal counts and dukes."

"Fine, but I doubt soldiers can do much against that monstrosity. It won't hurt to prevent problems though," Ingrid said.

"That's what General Ikerson thinks. He's in command of the

army here. He also makes sure that King Thoran is well guarded, as we don't know the origin of the attack or what might happen next. The Ice Mages are studying and watching the storm, and they seem to be on the brink of an important discovery."

"In that case we seem to have arrived just in time," Ingrid said, exchanging a complicit look with Egil.

The Captain led the way and they followed. The great command tent was right beside the Royal Tent—unmistakable because it was by far the largest in the camp. They were both in the middle of the large square the army camp formed. Lasgol noticed that almost all the soldiers here were heavy infantry: large, ferocious, and armed with axe and shield. He also glimpsed the Invincibles of the Ice, the King's elite infantry. Of course his Royal Guards and Rangers would also be there, protecting the King as was their duty.

They passed by a multitude of soldiers, who stared at them inquisitively. Ignoring the looks, they followed the Captain to the command tent. The officer asked to see the General and the Ice Mages, and after a small exchange with the guard at the entrance of the tent, they were allowed inside.

In the large red and white canvas tent they found the General, four Ice Mages sitting in large armchairs, and a hunched figure whose head was covered by a white fur hood sitting on a chair.

"Come in, Royal Eagles," General Ikerson said in a powerful voice.

They remained by the entrance and bowed respectfully.

"General, Ice Mages," said Ingrid.

"We've been waiting for you," the General told them.

"We came as soon as we were informed," Ingrid assured him.

Ikerson nodded and began to pace around the tent with his hands at his back in front of the Ice Mages who remained seated and silent, watching them.

"As you can see, the situation of the capital is, for lack of a better word, devastating. The Killer Winter Storm has frozen it to the core and all the population has had to be urgently evacuated. Many have perished because we weren't fast enough," the General said regretfully.

"We warned King Thoran of the danger of the storm once we reached the conclusion that it wasn't natural but was the product of powerful magic," one of the four Mages said, who looked the oldest.

"His Majesty refused to order the evacuation at first because it meant a defeat before an enemy, a humiliation of the Norghanian pride," said the youngest of the four.

"No Norghanian King who has ever had to give the capital to the enemy has lived to tell the tale," the General said in defense of the King's position.

"Nor will he ever," Thoran said in his powerful voice, coming into the tent.

Chapter 29

Lasgol and his comrades turned and got down on one knee when they saw the King walk in with several Royal Guards.

"Your Majesty, it's an honor," Ingrid said.

King Thoran strode past them to a big chair at the far end of the tent where he sat. The Royal Guard stood behind him.

"The Royal Eagles have just arrived, Your Majesty. We were informing them about the situation and sent word to you," General Ikerson said.

"Well done, General," King Thoran stared at the seven companions with narrowed eyes; he seemed to be studying them. "As you can guess, the situation is serious," he went on, addressing them this time. "More than that it is an outrage, an unacceptable mockery. I have been thrown out of my own city, the capital of the realm. It is an embarrassment I cannot allow. They have attacked my honor, attacked the honor of the realm, and they will pay for it. They will pay with their lives! Nobody throws me out of my city! Nobody attacks me in my own house without paying for it with their life!"

King Thoran's voice rose to a scream that must have been heard throughout the camp.

"We'll find the culprit and make them pay," General Ikerson said.

"You and your men will not!" Thoran shouted. "They will," he said, pointing his finger at the seven friends. "They will be the ones to do that."

Lasgol swallowed. The King wanted them to find those responsible for this attack. But they had no idea who that might be, and worse still, it was probably some powerful sorcerer. And if that was the case, it was more than likely a formidable enemy they would have to face.

"Your Majesty, what is required of us?" Ingrid asked.

"Rise," he said, and they all did. "I want you to find whoever has conjured this abomination over my city and finish them."

"Eliminate them, sire?" Ingrid wanted to be sure.

"I want him dead! With seven arrows in the heart!" he said, pointing a finger at each of them. "I want him to die for the insult done to myself! For the injury against my kingdom! Against all Norghanians! Whoever is responsible must die!" he finished, banging his fist on the arm of his chair so hard it nearly broke.

"So be it!" Ingrid promised in a firm voice meant to appease the King's wrath.

"Your Majesty, do we have any clue as to who might be behind this attack?" Egil asked softly without raising his gaze.

The King glared at the most veteran of his Ice Mages.

"Explain to the Eagles what you have discovered."

The Ice Mage nodded and looked at the group.

"We don't know who the creator of the attack is, but we do know it's an attack because it's a great offensive spell that has been cast. We have analyzed the storm and found concentrations of magic in its core that are keeping it active and pouring over the city."

"Can't those concentrations of magic be attacked and destroyed?" Ingrid asked, staring at the Ice Mage.

"We've tried. But there is a problem. It is the same type of magic we use: Water Magic. When we attack the core of the storm to destroy it with our magic, the storm absorbs the attacking magic and uses it to stay alive."

"That is to say, the Water Magic feeds it and makes it stronger rather than weakening and finishing it," another of the Ice Mages said.

Ingrid and the others nodded.

"It is pathetic that my all-powerful Ice Mages cannot destroy a winter storm which they themselves would be capable of conjuring up," Thoran said, disgusted and enraged.

"Our combined power could create a similar storm, Your Majesty," the most veteran said, "but we could not maintain it active for so long, or make it so aggressive and powerful."

"Then how is it that this storm remains active!"

"It must have been conjured up by a great power and maintains an important magic remainder in its core from which it feeds."

"So destroy the core!" the King yelled at them.

"We have tried, but it devours our attacks… our Water Magic makes it stronger. If it were a sandstorm, Earth Magic or Fire Magic, we could counter it with our Water Magic, but because it is the same kind, we can't, Your Majesty…"

"You're not good for anything! You're useless!"

"And can't other Mages be summoned with a different type of Magic that might counter the storm?" Egil suggested.

"The realm's magi have no magic capable of countering that of Water…" said the veteran Ice Mage. "We would need Fire Magic, a lot of it, to put the storm out. Fire would counter it. Another option is Dark Magic, which could be used to devour the core where the remainder of power it feeds from lies."

"Unfortunately we have no Fire Mages in Norghana," said another Mage. "And it is also not advisable to use a Sorcerer or Dark Mage. They are extremely dangerous and we could not trust them."

Lasgol thought about his own magic and how to fight against the great storm and he found it impossible. His magic was related to nature but not to the four elements, so he saw no way to affect the Magic of Water. Besides, he did not even possess Attacking Magic like the Ice Mages and least of all Dark Magic or something similar to destroy other Magic.

"And asking other kingdoms for help?" Egil suggested. "I understand that the Kingdom of Rogdon has a very powerful Mage of the Four Elements—Haradin I think is his name."

"We know about Haradin and his power…" the veteran Ice Mage said.

"Nobody is going to ask another kingdom for help!" Thoran howled, wrathful. "It would be an absolute embarrassment! Nobody is going to laugh at me! What happens in my kingdom we fix in my kingdom! I will not be the laughingstock of our rival realms!"

Lasgol did not understand why the King was reacting this way. If the realm had a serious problem and was unable to solve it, he did not see how asking a kingdom such as Rogdon—who they had a peace treaty with—for help would be embarrassing.

"My rivals cannot know of our weakness! Or do you think they will not use it against me in the future? I will not submit to the shame of asking Solin for help or giving him any clue as to how he might attack me in the future. Nobody will talk to any foreign mage or sorcerer. This we will fix ourselves. It is a Norghanian problem, and we Norghanians will fix it," Thoran sentenced.

"Absolutely, Your Majesty," Egil said. Lasgol, though, saw in his friend's eyes that he did not agree with the decision. He did not either. If this Haradin could help, they should call him. A Mage of the Four Elements must be someone well versed in arcane magic and power if he was capable of using all four elements of Fire, Water, Earth, and Air to cast spells. Lasgol wished he could meet such a renowned mage one day. Who knew, one day their paths might cross.

"If we can't stop the storm and we don't know who conjured it, what clues do we have left to follow?"

"We know where it comes from," said one of the Ice Mages who had remained silent until then.

"Where it comes from? It hasn't been conjured up here?" Egil asked, intrigued.

"No, it has not been conjured up here. The storm was created far away and directed toward the capital where it remains anchored."

Lasgol and his friends exchanged looks, nonplussed. They had not been expecting this. The situation had taken another turn, one which might become unforeseeable and dangerous. Astrid and Lasgol looked into one another's eyes, wondering what might happen.

"Where was it created?" Ingrid asked, raising an eyebrow.

"In the Frozen Continent," the veteran Ice Mage replied.

"Well, that's neat…" Viggo muttered under his breath.

"Are we sure of that?" Egil wanted to make sure the information was accurate.

"We are," said the figure who had remained in a corner wrapped in a bearskin cloak and hood and who had not intervened until this moment. Lasgol realized the voice belonged to a woman, and it sounded cracked.

They all looked at her.

"We Ice Mages do not possess the skill to trace the origin of the Magic, but our sister Brenda Noita does."

Brenda Noita pushed back her hood, revealing her face. Lasgol remembered seeing her at the Rangers' Great Council. She had been introduced as a counselor to the Ranger leaders. She was dressed in the same white bear skin and he remembered her white hair gathered in a number of tiny braids that fell on both sides of her face. She really looked like a Snow Witch. Lasgol shut his eyes and recalled what he had heard about her. Her Specialty was Magic and everything related to it. She was summoned when there was some magical situation, which justified her being here now. He also recalled there were rumors that, apart from knowing the magical world, she was also said to be a seer and could tell people's futures or at least glimpse them.

"Yes, I do possess the ability to detect Elemental Magic and trace it back to its origins," Noita said in her cracked voice.

"She is the one who has traced the origin of the spell back to the Frozen Continent," Thoran said. "Those bloody savages of the ice without a brain have not learned the lesson I gave them. They continue to defy me even after being defeated twice!"

"Defeat them—if that's what you call defeat... I wouldn't call that what he did..." Viggo whispered into Ingrid's ear.

"Shhhh! You're going to get us into trouble," she snapped back also in a whisper.

"I am tempted to organize a new invasion of that blasted continent and destroy them once and for all. Curse the savages of the ice!" cried Thoran.

"Now's not the time, Your Majesty.... We must see to our people. They're suffering..." General Ikerson told the King very gently with eyes that showed fear of upsetting his lord.

"It is never the bloody time!" the King roared.

"If you will allow me, Your Majesty..." Brenda said all of a sudden. "I believe I have an idea that might be the solution to this problem."

"Well, if you have one, hurry up and share it, we do not have all day," Thoran snapped, urging her with a wave of his hand.

"My power is not as big or comparable as that of his Majesty's Ice Mages. But it has certain advantages..."

"We know that you are a Snow Witch. You may speak openly," the veteran Ice Mage told her.

"Thank you. I suggest that we trace the origin of the magic with my power and travel to the Frozen Continent to stop whoever created it."

"Finally a wise idea I like!" cried Thoran.

"Well I don't like it in the least," Viggo whispered to Ingrid.

"Shut up, the King's going to hear you..."

"Thank you, Your Majesty," said Brenda.

"I'll send my army and destroy that sorcerer and all who have helped him!" Thoran shouted, clenching his fist hard.

"Your Majesty... if we send the army, the creator of this evil will see us coming and will disappear among the glaciers. We won't be able to capture him," Brenda said.

"They would see us coming from leagues away," General Ikerson said.

Thoran made a face and sat down in his chair.

"What do you suggest, Snow Witch?"

"I suggest that a small group travel to the Frozen Continent in a single boat and hunt down the Shaman who has caused this storm."

Thoran was thoughtful.

"An incursion and target elimination mission with a handful of specialists might work," General Ikerson commented.

"Let me guess on whose heads this mess is going to fall…" Viggo whispered.

"Shut up, you should be proud to be chosen."

"Yeah, so proud…"

"That is exactly what we will do," said Thoran. "Royal Eagles, you will accompany the Snow Witch to the Frozen Continent. You will locate the Sorcerer and eliminate him. It will be an incursion and target elimination mission. Get in, eliminate the threat, and get out. I want it done in the blink of an eye."

"Of course, Your Majesty, we'll do that," Ingrid said confidently.

"Shouldn't one of the Ice Mages come with us? If everything points at the problem being of magical origin, they're the highest authority and possessors of knowledge," Egil said, seeking magical support for the mission in case things got complicated.

Thoran waved his hands in refusal.

"The Ice Mages are necessary here. They must defend their King. I am not going to send them on a mission to the Frozen Continent while this blasted storm remains here. We do not know what else that Ice Sorcerer might have sent or what is to come."

"How brave…. What a surprise…" Viggo muttered.

"Very well, Your Majesty. We'll find and eliminate the threat," Ingrid hastened to say, covering up Viggo's comment.

"Leave right away. General Ikerson, make sure my Royal Eagles have everything they need for the mission."

"Straight away, Your Majesty," Ikerson said with a bow.

"Go, and do not fail me." King Thoran dismissed them.

Chapter 30

The ship sailed the Norghanian northern sea in the direction of the Frozen Continent. It was a sea of freezing water and white, cold, foamy waves. It was relatively calm since it was summer, and the storms and winds were few at this time of year in the area.

General Ikerson had gotten them a Norghanian assault ship with a single sail—a fast and discrete vessel. It was piloted by the veteran Captain Tomason, who was as silent as his ship. The crew was made up of a dozen Norghanian soldiers, weathered and experienced. From their moves and how well armed and armored they were, they seemed to know how to defend themselves and to have been in more than one battle, at sea or on land. Their mission was to escort the Royal Eagles to the Frozen Continent and make sure they got there alive.

"I can't believe we've been sent on this mission, just like that," Viggo complained as he crouched at the prow of the ship, holding onto the figurehead, trying by all means not to get seasick and throw up, which he had already done twice.

"It's an honor that King Thoran has chosen us for such an important mission," said Ingrid, who was beside him. She did not take her eyes off Viggo as if she feared that, dizzy as he was, he might fall overboard.

Nilsa and Gerd were looking at the sea from starboard.

"The truth is that it's a great honor to be sent," Nilsa said. "I take it as recognition of our good work."

"I agree with you a hundred percent. Besides, the situation is serious. We have to free the city of that storm and help all those people return to their homes," Gerd sighed, thinking of all the poor wretches at the camp outside Norghania.

"And we also have to return our beloved King Thoran to his Royal Castle and the throne hall he leads us from," Astrid added with a wink.

"Yeah, because he does it so fantastically well…" Viggo said with great irony as he retched.

"I didn't say that, but he's our King and it's what we have to live with," Astrid said with a shrug.

"We must help the people and safeguard the King," said Ingrid. "This mission is perfect for us. We'll do both things, and besides, there's no one in the whole realm better than us to carry it out."

"If you... say so..." Viggo said and leaned over the board with half his body hanging out as he was sick again.

Ingrid grabbed him by the back of his collar so he would not fall into the sea.

"Careful... even if you're a smart-ass if you fall in the water it won't be good for you."

"Well, at least we didn't have to go into the city into the midst of the storm," Nilsa said, stroking the enchanted winter cloak Enduald had given them and which they all wore.

"Yeah, I thought we were doomed to do so," Gerd snorted in relief. "It would've been insane."

"This... is going to be... worse..." Viggo forewarned.

"Don't be a bird of ill omen. It won't be worse," Ingrid said as she pulled his head over the railing. "Don't pay any attention to him, everything's going to be fine."

Astrid made a face meaning she was not at all sure.

"Let's hope so... the Frozen Continent isn't exactly the safest place for us..."

"Of course it isn't. The moment the Tundra Tribes lay eyes on us they'll come to skin us alive," Viggo said, throwing up overboard once again.

Ingrid shook her head.

By the mast, oblivious to the conversation, Egil and Lasgol were sitting among sacks of food. Ona and Camu were with them, Camu invisible. Lasgol was worried because the ship had no place to hide Camu when he became visible. The warship had nothing but a small hold, which was already full of barrels of drinking water as well as weapons. They would have to improvise something.

Brenda, the Snow Witch, walked over to them from the stern and sat between Lasgol and Egil, joining them as if she had known them forever.

"This Captain Tomason is duller than the soup at the Blue Pony Tavern."

Lasgol and Egil looked at one another and smiled.

"He's not a talker, no," Lasgol agreed.

"Feels like talking to a rock," the Snow Witch complained.

"There are some quiet ones, and we've landed one," Egil said, smiling and shrugging. "Sometimes it's preferable."

"That's a beautiful panther," Brenda said, nodding at Ona who was lying beside Lasgol.

"Her name's Ona, and she doesn't like the sea much."

Ona moaned.

"It's natural, cats don't exactly like water. Salty water even less," the Witch chuckled with her particular voice.

"How is it possible that a person can pick up the trail of magic? And follow it? If I might ask?" Egil asked, unable to contain his curiosity.

"You needn't be so formal, I'm already old enough to have you addressing me so respectfully."

"Oh, sure, but I didn't want to be rude," Egil said.

"Respect me with your actions, not your words," she said and smiled. Her face lit up.

"Obviously," Egil smiled too.

Lasgol nodded, observing Brenda's creased face.

"Well, you see, very few can, my young Ranger, and I am one of those few. You need a certain kind of power that most people don't have."

"Isn't the Gift similar for everyone? Where there's a Mage of one kind there's usually another..." Lasgol said, wanting to know more.

The Witch raised her arms and dropped them down.

"Oh, no, my young friend!"

"Oh... but all Mages have the same type of base magic, right?" Lasgol went on.

The Snow Witch shook her head.

"Well, there are two theories about this matter, which has been debated over a lot among erudites and scholars of the subject. Some say that indeed all magic comes from the same base, the same source. They hold that those who use magic use the same underlying type, the only existing one, to help you understand. Then there are others who say this isn't so, that there are at least two different types of magic which come from two very different origins."

"Wow, that's fascinating!" Egil cried. "I've always thought that magic was universal and unique."

"Well, there are erudites who believe there are two different

236

magics which form the base for the magic we have now."

"Different in their origin?" Lasgol asked.

"That's right."

"And what are those two origins?" Egil wanted to know. "This is most intriguing," he added eagerly.

The Witch smiled. "Well, you two like to ask questions, huh? You like to know things, don't you?"

"We don't have many chances to speak to and learn from people with magical knowledge," Lasgol said.

"And it's something that fascinates us and that we're passionate about," Egil added.

Brenda smiled and chuckled, which made her really look like a good witch in a Norghanian mythological tale.

"Curious, most people fear magic and everything related to it and the arcane world."

"We don't," Egil said seriously. "We want to know, to come to understand the mysteries that rule it."

The Witch nodded repeatedly, "You see, my curious young friends, it is said—and there's no conclusive proof, one way or another, at least that has been found—that the most extended magic, that of Mages, Sorcerers, Shamans and the like, that we know of comes from the Gods."

"From the Ice Gods?" Lasgol asked, surprised.

Brenda shook her head.

"It can't be the Ice Gods, because those gods only exist in the culture and beliefs of the north. The other peoples of Tremia have other gods, and there's magic and Mages all over Tremia," Egil said.

"You have a very good head. That is correct," she said.

"Then, the magic originated from what gods?"

"*Part* of the magic," Brenda corrected. "These are Gods believed to have lived in Tremia when the first men arrived at this continent."

"And what happened to them?"

"They vanished with barely a trace about three thousand years ago."

"I've read something about that…" Egil said, trying to remember.

"And were they the ones who gave magic to humans?" Lasgol asked.

"That's the most widespread theory."

"It's usual to find in different mythologies that the gods grant gifts to humans. Magic could be one of those gifts," said Egil.

"And the other theory?" Lasgol asked.

"The other one is a little farfetched. The one that says that it wasn't the gods who granted magic to humans, but other creatures, more powerful than the gods themselves."

Dragons, Camu transmitted to Lasgol.

You think so?

Be dragons.

"Dragons?" Lasgol asked, somewhat embarrassed—it sounded crazy to him.

"Why! I did not expect you to guess. It appears you're smarter than I thought," the Witch said and laughed with strange cackles.

I know.

It sounds weird.

Be true.

"What an interesting theory," said Egil. "Dragons are mythological beings of great power, terrifying creatures with Magic. Yet, there's not much knowledge about them, and it's certainly not mentioned in any tome that they might have granted magic to humans."

"There are many things that aren't in any tome and many others yet to be discovered," the Snow Witch replied with one of her cackles.

"Yes, that's very true," Egil agreed. "The mysteries of our world are many and difficult to solve."

"I don't know whether this idea of the dragons giving magic to humans convinces me. I don't find it very likely. Why would they? Weren't they enemies?" Lasgol said, thinking aloud.

"Not at all. In fact, it is said that dragons and humans never lived at the same time in Tremia. It would appear that dragons vanished over four thousand years ago, right before the arrival of humans in Tremia," Egil said.

The Snow Witch shrugged.

"There's a lot we don't know. I'm only telling you the theories of others. Nobody knows what really happened. I don't either, so I can't clear your doubts."

"In any case, it's most interesting," Egil said, delighted by what she had told them.

"Also consider that the fact that dragons vanished doesn't mean they didn't remain among us, hiding their presence," Brenda said.

"Hmmmm. That opens another door to another mystery," Lasgol said. "How did they manage? How did they live among humans without being found out? And why?"

"Good questions. There's one theory that can explain that. It's just another hypothesis, so I can't say it's true, but there is a certain group among the scholars that believes that dragons and gods were actually rivals, declared enemies who fought for the supremacy and control of Tremia. The Erudites say that gods and dragons fought to the death for a millennium and the gods won in the end," the Snow Witch said.

"And that's why the losers, the dragons, hid among humans," Egil guessed, nodding.

"How did they manage? I guess they might have hidden and shifted their shape using their powerful magic."

Brenda shrugged.

"It might be both things in fact. There's no proof of either of these theories, this I want you to understand. Everything we're talking about is conjecture and theories."

"And that's why the Ice Mages can't trace the origin of this Magic and you can?" Egil said, raising an eyebrow. "Because you use different types of magic?"

"That's right. Their intent is on creating attacking spells," the Witch sighed and shook her head. "They only want to kill and destroy, not understand the essence of magic. They spend their lives specializing their power to freeze and kill spiders." She laughed with a hearty guffaw. "Then, in the hour of truth, unless they're needed to skewer someone with an ice stake, they're not much good," she mocked.

"Wow, I see you don't like them very much," said Lasgol.

"I don't like them at all. I tolerate them and they tolerate me, but we don't get along particularly well. We rather try to keep our paths from crossing. I manage a lot better with the Rangers. Sigrid, Gondabar, Dolbarar, and Edwina are people with ideas similar to mine. I really like them and they like me. Thoran and his relatives… I'd better not say in words what I think of them… your ears are still too young and not used to hearing such ugly terms," she laughed again.

Lasgol and Egil smiled at one another. "We understand," Lasgol said.

"There's one thing I'd like to witness, if possible," said Egil.

"How I track the magic's origin?" Brenda guessed.

Egil smiled. "Yes, exactly that."

"You'll soon see."

"Will we?" Lasgol was very interested too.

"I will do it in mid-afternoon, when the sun is in a better position for me."

"Fantastic!" Egil cried, delighted.

"We'll see what direction it leads us," she said. "I'll need human blood for the ritual. We'll have to sacrifice someone."

"Sac…rifice…?" Lasgol muttered.

Egil's mouth hung open, and he was unable to utter a word.

The Snow Witch began to laugh heartily.

"You're so gullible!" She went on laughing her head off.

Chapter 31

At mid-afternoon Brenda asked for the stern of the ship to be cleared. The crew moved back in a hurry. The truth was they always moved away from her, wherever she went on the ship. They backed away as if the Snow Witch had an infectious disease.

Lasgol and the rest of the group though did not act like this. In fact, Egil was at her side all the time, asking her innumerable questions about all kinds of matters which to him were very interesting. Nilsa was the most reluctant to be near someone with magic, but for some reason she liked the old woman and she made her laugh. Gerd was more anxious than usual, but he did not avoid Brenda either. Viggo had no time to talk to anybody with how the journey was disagreeing with him, and Ingrid kept an eye on him unobtrusively.

The sea was quite ruffled, which made the warship rock more than desired. She sank her bow in the waves to climb again with abrupt movements. There was a wind blowing which was becoming icier and icier—they were approaching the Frozen Continent.

Brenda looked up at the sky and, ignoring the sea, sat down with her legs crossed on the deck by the sea snake-shaped figurehead at the bow, looking straight ahead into the infinite sea. From inside her white bear coat, she took out a ceramic bowl with strange engravings and started to cast a spell with a long stick from which hung numerous ugly looking decorations: rabbit feet, animal eyes, pieces of snakes, toads, and even giant spiders. Other decorations were unidentifiable but also looked grotesque.

Lasgol and Egil were watching her closely, holding onto the railing and trying to prevent the icy breeze that lashed their faces from affecting their vision. The others had withdrawn to the mast and watched from there. Luckily, Viggo had stopped being sick. According to him, it was because he had vomited his stomach out to sea and so had none left in his body. Camu and Ona had retreated astern and were avoiding even glancing at what was going on, as if they might go blind just by watching what the Snow Witch was conjuring.

Brenda took out a phial from the folds of her coat, and while she went on conjuring she poured a dark liquid into the bowl. Then she took out a sachet and poured some gray powder into the bowl as she murmured an incomprehensible litany. All of a sudden, a dark violet column rose from the bowl. The Snow Witch poured two other components into the bowl before her on the deck and the column of smoke turned dark brown.

Everybody was watching the ritual in a trance, except the Captain and the crew, who now not only did not look but who turned their backs to the ritual and all looked at the sea from the stern of the ship. Luckily, practically no other kingdoms sent ships to sail these waters, and the dwellers of the Frozen Continent were not good sailors, otherwise they could have attacked the ship and the crew would not have even noticed.

The litany became some kind of mystical chant, and the column of brown smoke seemed to thicken and rise steadily, reaching high up, not fading as it was carried away by the sea breeze to vanish. It began to bear the wind, as if it had a life of its own. It appeared to be an arcane entity which rose and sniffed the winds. Lasgol did not want to miss any detail, so he called upon his *Hawk's Sight* and *Owl Hearing* skills.

Brenda raised her weird staff with all its horrible pendants and drew several circles above her head, seeming to command the arcane entity to search for something. She continued chanting. The entity turned around about thirty feet up and then suddenly split into three.

One of the branches headed to the Frozen Continent, to the northeast, following the course of the ship. The second branch went straight to Lasgol's chest. With eyes like saucers, he saw how it reached his torso and stayed there as if glued to it.

"What the... what's this..." he whispered, fearful.

The other branch went to the mast. Nilsa and Gerd cried out in fear seeing it come straight to the group. Viggo hunched down and Ingrid took a defensive stance. Astrid stepped away with a pirouette. The tip of the branch seemed to go straight toward Ona, who leapt to get out of the way, but at the last moment it turned and seemed to hit something that was not there. It had hit Camu, who was camouflaged and unseen.

Brenda turned and watched the proceedings as she continued her chanting and staff twirling. She stared at Lasgol for a moment, then at the spot where Camu was and squinted, as if trying to see him without succeeding. For a while the three-part entity remained active. Lasgol looked down at it touching his chest with a look of disgust on his face, although he did not feel anything weird. It was certainly not attacking him.

Are you all right? he asked Camu, concerned for him. He could not see him but he was sure the thing had found him.

I well, magic find me.

Yes, that's really peculiar.

Not like, I cancel magic.

No, don't! it'll be worse.

Why worse?

Because Brenda will realize something's wrong if her magic is cancelled. I don't want her to know about you.

Not trust her?

I still don't know whether we can trust her. She seems trustworthy, but we've been fooled before. Better wait and see.

Okay.

Brenda continued with the ritual for a while longer and then, all of a sudden, she was silent. The brown entity began to fade as if it were smoke, carried away by the sea breeze. A moment later it had vanished completely.

Lasgol snorted in relief. He had not liked being singled out by that thing at all or that it had also honed in on Camu. Egil looked at him as if reaching conclusions about the experience they had just had. Beside the mast Gerd also snorted in relief.

"It just gets better and better with every spell and instance of witchcraft we experience," Viggo said bitterly.

"I completely agree with you on this," Nilsa said with her hands on her hips. She looked quite peeved.

"It's what it means to be a Snow Panther—things never stop happening," Astrid said, coming over to Lasgol to see how he felt.

"And we can't even tell how often since we've become Royal Eagles!" Viggo replied. "I can't wait to land on the Frozen Continent and see what new mess we get into."

"Don't jinx us!" Ingrid said. "And don't let go of the mast or you'll get sick again."

"I'm going to marry this mast," Viggo said, holding onto it tight. Then he kissed the mast with mock passion.

Ingrid rolled her eyes. Nilsa giggled and Gerd laughed. Even Ona chirped, amused.

Brenda rose, stumbling. Egil went to her side and grabbed her arm.

"Do you feel all right?" he asked her, concerned as he noticed the Witch's fatigue.

"A little exhausted. Those spells require a lot of my energy and at the end even my bones ache."

"We'll make you comfortable beside the mast."

"I'll be comfortable among the sacks," she said, pointing at them.

"Fine, let's go then." Egil helped her sit down and covered her up with a blanket.

"Tell Captain Tomason to maintain the course, northeast."

"I'll tell him, don't worry."

A moment later Brenda was sleeping peacefully.

Night fell on the war ship and the crew prepared to rest. The Panthers did the same. Since Camu could not maintain invisibility indefinitely they covered him up with two thick blankets and hid him among the sacks on the other side of where the Snow Witch slept. Lasgol, Astrid, and Egil sat surrounding Camu so that it would be even more difficult to see him. Ona climbed onto the sacks and threatened any of the crew who dared to come close with jaws wide open.

They dined on the food supplies for the journey.

"This is truly a proper supper!" Gerd cried as he gulped down dried meat from one hand and cured cheese from the other, taking alternate bites from both.

"You're right, this is a thousand times better than the Improved Rations at Loke's cabin," said Nilsa. "Simply remembering them makes my stomach turn."

"Mine too," Egil smiled, enjoying the cheese with black bread.

"Bah, you complain for nothing. You'll see how well you feel when you get killed repeatedly in Sigrid's training, it's most enjoyable," Viggo told them.

"Killed? Why do we have to get killed?" Gerd asked and stopped eating when he heard that.

"Because, according to sadistic Sigrid, only by taking us to the limit will we train efficiently and quickly."

Ingrid elbowed him. "Don't you dare speak ill of the Mother Specialist. What they've managed to accomplish is something exceptional, and you know it."

"All I know is that my head's going to burst," Viggo moaned.

"Well, it would not be such a big loss," Nilsa said, giggling.

"Yeah… yeah… you can laugh all you want, but you'll see when they pierce your heart with an arrow how quickly you stop laughing."

"They're not going to do that to me," she protested and looked at Ingrid, seeking her denial.

"I've been hit in training on occasion, yes…" Ingrid admitted.

"And it really hurts?" Gerd asked, looking unhappy.

"It hurts just as much as in real life—a lot! The only difference is that the medallion shines with a red light and you don't really die. But it hurts the same," Viggo told him.

"You don't really die," Lasgol intervened. "Well, you do, but only in your mind. The medallion keeps you alive."

"The medallion must prevent the body from believing it has died, although the minds says the opposite. That way the body goes on living, the heart beating, even if the mind believes it's dead," Egil wondered aloud.

"It also makes you leave your mind at once," Astrid explained. "Once you die, let's say that you come out of the state you're in. The medallion expels you. It must be a mechanism to preserve the body and not harm it."

"Yeah, yeah, whatever, but they don't protect the mind, I'm telling you," Viggo commented. "You're all going to end up cuckoo, you'll see."

"You? Don't you mean we?" Nilsa asked mischievously.

"You. You are. Me, of course not," Viggo said, folding his arms over his chest.

"Of course, because you are already," Ingrid said.

They all laughed and Viggo pretended to be offended, but soon enough he joined in the laughter.

At midnight, Brenda woke up as if emerging from a terrible nightmare. Egil, who was beside her, held her by the arm and tried to soothe her.

"Easy, you're among friends," he told her.

She opened her eyes as wide as they would, looking around her and recognizing where she was.

"The ship… the Royal Eagles… the Killer Storm… the Frozen Continent…" she muttered.

"Yes, all of that," Egil said in a soothing tone and smiled. "Everything's fine."

Brenda sat up and, feeling the cold of the night in the Northern Sea, she huddled in her white bear coat. Egil helped her by wrapping the blanket around her shoulders.

"Call Lasgol, I need to speak to him."

"Now? It's midnight…" Egil said blankly.

"I know. I need to speak to him."

"Very well…" Egil nudged Lasgol a couple times to wake him up. Ona eyed him curiously, and Egil smiled at her.

"Don't worry, it's nothing, beautiful."

Ona chirped once and Lasgol woke immediately.

"What's up?" he asked sleepily.

"Brenda wants to speak to you."

"Oh… fine."

The two friends went back over to Brenda, on the other side of the mast. Astrid woke up as soon as Lasgol moved away from her and watched in case anything bad happened.

Lasgol and Egil sat down in front of Brenda.

"You wanted to see me?" Lasgol asked.

"Yes," The Snow Witch nodded. "You possess the Gift and you didn't tell me."

"It's something I don't usually mention… out of caution."

"That's all right. There are many in this world who don't understand or accept our talent. Better not to proclaim it to the four directions. It avoids unwanted situations. But even so, knowing that I am a Witch you should have confided in me."

"I don't grant my trust easily."

Brenda smiled. "I like this young man," she told Egil.

"I like him quite well," Egil smiled back and patted his friend's back.

"Thank you both," Lasgol replied, smiling too.

"The seeking spell I used today searches for traces of magic and if it finds them it points them out. It pointed at you," the Witch explained.

"I have the Gift, yes," Lasgol admitted.

"What kind of magic can you do?" she asked him.

"My skills are related to nature, animals…"

"Well, isn't that curious?"

"Curious? Why?" Lasgol asked, surprised.

"Because that's usually more in line with someone like me: a Witch."

"Oh… I don't consider myself a Mage or Witch or anything like that. I'm a Ranger who has developed skills that aid me in my job. Or at least I try to develop them so they help."

"What kind of skills?" she asked.

Lasgol told her about his *Hawk's Sight, Owl Hearing, True Shot, Trap Hiding, Dirt Throwing, Animal Communication,* and others.

"Well, well…." Brenda was thoughtful. "This is even more curious. I don't know anyone like you. As a rule Magic is what marks the path we follow. An Ice Mage is such because his Magic is of water and very powerful. A Mage of the Four Elements—and there aren't that many—is such because his Magic is Elemental. He can't do what you can with his Magic."

"Lasgol's special," Egil said, emphasizing *special.*

"We'll have to investigate this Magic of yours. I'm intrigued," Brenda said.

"I could do with some help," Lasgol admitted.

"Good for you," Egil looked at him and nodded. He was happy that his friend was going to let someone help him with his Magic.

"I'll see what I can do for you. I'm old and have seen and experienced many things throughout my life, many of them magical. I hope to be of service to you."

"I'm sure you have, and you will!" Egil said. "We have a thirst for learning arcane knowledge."

"I can see that perfectly well," Brenda smiled. "The spell, the Tracker, also found another source of Magic, but I couldn't see its origin. What do you know about this? It was beside your familiar, the panther, Ona."

Lasgol and Egil exchanged concerned glances.

"I can't help you if you don't trust me. I might be a Witch, but I can assure you we're not as evil as we're described in the mythology and tales told to scare the Norghanian children."

"We can imagine…" Lasgol said.

"I'm a Counselor of the Great Council of the Rangers. That

should be enough to trust me, since your superiors do so. And besides, I'm here with you on this mission to free the capital of the realm and end this threat."

"That's true…" Egil told Lasgol. "And she's no friend of Thoran or the Ice Mages."

"No, I'm not."

"Okay… I'll trust you. I hope I won't regret it."

"You won't, young Ranger Specialist. I promise. I might not be much to look at with my white hair and these braids that reveal my wrinkled face and ugly nose, but I can assure you that my heart is beautiful."

Lasgol had a good feeling about Brenda. He felt he could trust her, which was not usually the case. He decided to follow his instincts. If he was mistaken, they would be in trouble, but he hoped they would not.

Camu, are you sleeping?

Not now.

Can you come?

Can't camouflage.

Lasgol looked around; he only saw a couple of crew members at the stern.

Crawl over here with the blanket on.

Okay.

Camu crawled around to where they were.

"This is Camu," Lasgol introduced him to Brenda.

The Snow Witch lifted the blanket that covered Camu's body and looked.

"Wow…! I really wasn't expecting this!" she cried. "Does he have power?"

"Yes, he does," Lasgol confirmed.

Brenda looked into his bulging eyes and stroked his head. Camu licked her hand with his blue tongue.

"This creature… isn't from Norghana. He's from… the Frozen Continent."

"That's what we believe, yes," Egil confirmed.

"A magical creature from the Frozen Continent. This really is a surprise," Brenda said as she studied him, squinting and continuing to stroke him.

"Almost as much as the tracking spell the Snow Witch cast

today," Egil said with a wink.

Brenda laughed. "If today is a day of surprises, tomorrow will be even more so."

"Tomorrow? What happens tomorrow? Lasgol asked, worried.

"Tomorrow we arrive at the Frozen Continent. We'll begin the Hunt."

"Oh…" Lasgol looked to the figurehead, but the night did not let him see anything past it but water and darkness.

"Will it be a complicated Hunt?" Egil asked, raising an eyebrow.

"The Magic we're after is very powerful. I think it will be a very complicated Hunt,"

"Let's hope we come out unscathed and victorious," Egil said wishfully.

"Let's hope so…" the Witch said, looking ahead, to the northeast.

Chapter 32

At noon, a week after leaving the coast of Norghana, the ship dropped anchor at a beach on the Frozen Continent covered with ice and snow. The journey had been swift and without incident. They had not encountered storms, and the few icebergs they had met they had been able to dodge easily.

The Panthers grabbed their gear and weapons and landed at a signal from Captain Tomason. Ona and Camu followed the group. Camu had his energy once again after sleeping all night, so he was camouflaged. The Captain would wait for their return right there. But he would not wait longer than two weeks. If they had not come back by then, he would leave without them, considering them dead. Viggo thought it was a most heartfelt and promising farewell.

As soon as they set foot on the Frozen Continent, they felt the icy beauty of that harsh, primitive land. The first thing they felt was a cold so intense it seemed capable of penetrating their winter clothes. The temperature was low even for a Norghanian. The fact that it was summer muffled it somewhat to the point where they could just bear with it. Seeing no threatening clouds in the sky cheered them up. The freezing beauty of the landscape spread before them, so white it hurt their eyes, and it was only broken by some scarce polar vegetation, some blue, frozen lakes quite separated, and the great glaciers on the horizon.

For a moment they stood contemplating the freezing beauty of the landscape. The glaciers, with their unfathomable heights, were awe-inspiring. Their ice walls in turquoise-blue tones, even white, almost transparent, left them breathless.

"Wow, I don't know why we don't come here more often on holidays," Viggo remarked, looking around with his hands on his hips. "I love the warmth of the scenery and how welcoming it seems."

"Yup, it's just like the Turquoise Realm, I don't know why you're complaining," Astrid said with a smile as she adjusted her hood and the white Ranger scarf to protect her face from the icy wind.

"Some legends say it is here that the Ice Gods dwell when they come down to Earth," Egil commented as he huddled in his white cloak and also adjusted the Ranger's scarf to protect his face.

"Well, I understand why they say that perfectly well," Gerd commented. "There's nothing but frost, snow, and icy wind wherever you look."

"You're forgetting the glaciers and the icebergs," said Nilsa, pointing at them in the distance. "They are pretty, but I wouldn't call them welcoming."

Ingrid went forward to explore.

"I'm going to check whether we have company," she said as she left them. As she walked her boots sank in the snow but soon found ice beneath it.

"A harsh land," Brenda commented, scanning the tundra with yearning eyes. "It holds many secrets... some of them ancestral... buried under layers and layers of ice or among the frozen columns of the walls of those immense glaciers that take one's breath away."

Lasgol looked at Brenda. He did not know what she meant, but she was probably right. He felt weird setting foot on the land that had been his mother's home for so long. He wondered how she had come there, who she had known in that frozen land, and how she had managed to become the Leader of the Peoples of the Frozen Continent.

"Keep your eyes open," Ingrid told them when she came back. "Let me remind you that this is the land of the Wild Ones, the Tundra Dwellers, and the Arcanes of the Glaciers, and all of them will try to kill us as soon as they set eyes on us."

"You're forgetting the Semi-Giants," Viggo said as he went over his knives.

"Those are really scary," Nilsa said, "almost as much as the Creatures of the Ice they have."

Gerd snorted. "Better not think of all that! We have enough with surviving in this frozen tundra."

"Get your weapons ready," Ingrid told them. "If any threat appears I'll tell you what to do."

"Is she the leader of the group?" Brenda asked Lasgol when she saw Ingrid take charge of the situation.

"Yes, she usually is," Lasgol confirmed.

Brenda smiled, and her face filled with little wrinkles. She did not wear a scarf like the others. "I like this group of yours very much," the Snow Witch said. "It's something really rare."

"That's because we're special," Nilsa said with a giggle.

"You've no idea how much," the Witch said.

Ingrid scouted the surroundings without finding a trace of any enemy. Visibility was good—they could see as far as the different levels in the terrain allowed. In some areas it was as if several layers of ice had overlapped because of the weather, and instead of mountains they had those square blocks of frozen slabs that did not let them see beyond. On the other hand, any trail would vanish quickly in the falling snow and with the wind.

"It looks clear. Where are we headed?" Ingrid asked Brenda once she was sure they could start walking. There's no trail to follow."

"Not one of footprints. But one of Magic, yes," she replied, looking up at the sky.

"All magic leaves a trail you can follow?" Egil asked, very interested. "Or is it that this trail is, let's say, special for some reason?"

"Good guess, my curious friend," she admitted. "It is both. Magic can be traced if it's produced nearby. If the distance increases you lose the trail. But this trail is special, and that's why I can follow it even through the sea and tundra."

"Interesting. And what makes it so special?" Lasgol wanted to know also, equally intrigued.

"It's an ancient power, archaic and of this land."

"So we're chasing after an old geezer from this area?" Viggo said. "Well, that's better, it'll be easy to slit his throat."

"I didn't say it was an old man. What I sense is the essence of the Magic, and this is very ancient Magic."

"But, if it's ancient it'll be less powerful, won't it?" Gerd asked.

The Snow Witch shook her head and smiled.

"You young people don't understand the value of the old. You believe only what's modern is good and powerful. I swear this Magic I'm sensing is a lot more dangerous and powerful than any of the modern ones like that of King Thoran's Ice Mages."

"Oh bother..." Nilsa moaned, unhappy. "Now we'll have to go very carefully. It's not enough that I don't like modern magic," she said, glancing at Camu as he walked beside Lasgol without camouflage, "now I have to face ancient magic."

"This creature's Magic isn't modern," the Witch corrected her, "it's ancient Magic."

"Camu's?" Egil asked, looking at the creature.

"Indeed," Brenda confirmed. "His Magic is really ancient. I can't sense where it comes from, but I'd say its origin can be traced back thousands of years."

"That's fantastic. Our Camu has powerful, ancient Magic," Egil said, excited by the implications and possibilities this brought up.

"And very likely of this continent," Lasgol said. "I know from my mother that she got him here, in the Frozen Continent, the egg Camu was born from."

"Well, this makes the adventure even more interesting," Brenda said.

"This isn't interesting at all," Viggo protested. "My... nose... is freezing... and we've only been here for a short while."

"Don't complain so much, the temperature is most agreeable for this continent," Ingrid snapped at him.

"Yeah... yeah... But I don't want to be in this frozen ice world longer than is strictly necessary, or my thoughts will freeze in my brain."

Ingrid was about to make a sharp reply but she let it go.

I not feel magic, Camu transmitted to Lasgol with a feeling of frustration and sadness at not being able to sense the trail Brenda could.

It's curious that she can sense it and you can't. I wonder whether it's because of what she said about distance. Perhaps whatever we're after is too far and that's why you don't sense it.

Yes... that, Camu replied, not convinced.

"You'd better tell us which way to go, Brenda," Ingrid said.

"Absolutely, but I'll need to repeat the ritual."

"Must you?" Ingrid asked her. "That thing you conjure, the tracking smoke that rises and points in the direction of the magic, is too visible. It'll be seen from a great distance, especially in all this white expanse."

"I call it the Tracker. It's created through the ritual and it's taken me half my life to perfect it so it works well. I can't change it now because it's inconveniently visible."

"Hmmmm... well then, everybody remain alert and in a watchful position, I don't want any surprises," Ingrid told the rest of the group.

253

"Yes, ma'am," Nilsa said and ran to take up a spot. Gerd followed, then Astrid and Viggo.

Egil and Lasgol remained beside Brenda in case she needed protection.

The Witch sat down on the tundra ground and took the bowl out of a bag she carried on her back.

"Can I ask you something that intrigues me?" Egil asked her.

"You can, but once I begin to conjure I won't be able to answer. I enter a mental state that isolates me from my surroundings and focuses on directing the Tracker."

"Oh, that's all right. The question has to do with your Tracker. How does it know which magic it has to go after, or does it track any magic?"

Brenda smiled. "My Tracker traces all the magic around it. But if I want it to trace specific Magic, as is the case now, I can also direct it to that end. It's more costly, of course, both in the effort and energy it takes to cast the spell."

Egil made a face and looked around at the great tundra stretching before them.

"And how do you direct it here? What if it picks up some other magic that's not the one you're looking for? There are Arcanes of the Glaciers who also have magic, as well as Creatures of the Ice who wield magic. Won't it get all mixed up and point at one of those instead of whatever created the storm?"

Lasgol was listening, interested. "Yeah, I was wondering the same thing."

"The spell works very similarly to what you Rangers do when you follow a trail. Once you find it you follow it, and if others cross it, you are able to tell the difference and follow the original. My Tracker recognizes the original Magic and will follow it to its origin, although other magical sources may cross its path."

"How does it recognize the original Magic?" Lasgol asked.

"Like this," she said and showed them a large phial she took out of her bag. She took the top off and a gray, foggy substance issued from it. Brenda took it in her hand and put it in the bowl, covering the phial again so no more substance would escape.

"You took a sample of the storm," Egil said.

"Very clever, my young Ranger. That's right. For a hound to follow a trail it must smell it first. The Tracker works exactly the same," Brenda said, smiling, "and now, forgive me, but I can't waste this sample since I don't have much."

Egil nodded apologetically and moved back.

The Snow Witch got ready to cast her spell with her strange stick with its horrible amulets. She took out a container and poured a dark liquid in the bowl as she went on conjuring, then some gray powder from a small sachet. She went on casting her spell, looking up at the sky and moving the stick with circular movements. As had happened the last time, a dark-violet smoke rose from the bowl, forming a column. Brenda poured the remaining components and the smoke took on a brown hue.

The Witch raised the stick-staff while she continued the spell and circled it above her head several times. The entity that was the column of smoke began to turn on itself, searching for the trail of magic. It was steady for a while, slowly twirling as if not picking up any trace of magic.

Egil and Lasgol exchanged concerned glances. Brenda, though, did not seem to mind and continued her chanting. Ingrid kept looking back—the column of smoke was now thirty feet tall and too visible in that snow-white world.

Hurry up, Brenda!" she said, "That thing can be seen from leagues away on this terrain."

The Snow Witch did not seem to hear Ingrid and went on with her ritual. After a while, suddenly, the foggy entity seemed to pick up something. It started moving in a northeasterly direction, as if it were following a trail. It became thinner as it moved, as if it consumed its thickness to turn it into length and be able to move forward.

Lasgol was watching the ritual when he noticed something odd about Camu. He was lying down beside Ona but his eyes were closed, as if he were sleeping. He thought it odd. Camu would not miss a magic ritual, particularly in case he needed to intervene.

Are you all right, Camu? Lasgol messaged him. To his surprise, his friend did not answer.

Ona looked at her brother and put her paw on his head to wake him up.

Camu, are you tired? Lasgol asked him, thinking that perhaps he was weary from the journey, although it seemed unusual.

I… sleep… Camu replied drowsily.

You feel tired?

Yes... very tired...

Is it because you used your magic to camouflage on the ship? Lasgol asked. Had he been using his power for too long on the ship, unable to rest except for part of the night to recover his magic energy?

Not know...

Wow, that's curious. But you feel well?

Yes, well... only tired....

Lasgol was perplexed; this was new. Why was Camu tired? He was worried.

Are you sure you're not ill or that something's wrong?

No ill. No pain. Now better.

Lasgol was not convinced. He was about to tell Egil to see what he thought when a shout startled him and he froze on the spot.

"Alert!" Nilsa warned the group with a shrill cry. "A patrol of Wild Ones of the Ice!"

"Curse it!" Ingrid cried, running to Nilsa's position. "Are you sure?"

"Quite!" she replied, pointing in the direction the danger was coming from.

Ingrid watched them. They had seen Brenda's Tracker as she had feared. They were staring at it, intrigued. The Wild Ones they could see were huge, over six feet tall with overwhelming muscles and physique. The skin was smooth with that unmistakable ice-blue shade, the same as their hair and beard of a bluish blond that looked frozen. Ingrid could not see from where she was but she remembered the eyes, such a light, pale gray that they looked completely white without an iris.

"Definitely Wild Ones of the Ice," she said.

"How many?" Astrid asked.

"About thirty," said Nilsa.

"Do we kill them?" Viggo said.

Ingrid thought for a moment. "We're here for something else, This isn't the time to start a futile confrontation with enemies it's better to avoid."

"Is that a no?" Viggo asked.

"That's a no," Ingrid ratified.

"Pity, I wanted to test everything I've been learning in the Shelter," he said, disappointed.

"I'm sure we'll have some other occasion," Astrid said with a wink.

"True, the fun's just begun," Viggo admitted. "Knowing us, we're still going to get into deeper trouble."

"A lot deeper," Astrid stated with a chuckle.

The Wild Ones of the Ice had seen them and were now coming toward them at a run.

"Brenda, finish the ritual! We have company! We have to move!" Ingrid shouted.

The Witch was in a trance, directing the Tracker she had created to follow the trail of the magic they were after.

"Brenda, we have to leave!" Egil said urgently.

Seeing she did not react, Lasgol opted for shaking her, and did so hard.

The Snow Witch looked at them, coming out of her trance suddenly.

"We have to leave! The Wild Ones of the Ice are coming!" Lasgol urged her.

"Oh shoot, how untimely," she said, standing up slowly. She gathered her things as if there was nothing wrong while she watched the Tracker begin to vanish, fading in the icy wind.

"Run!" Ingrid ordered them. "So they don't catch up with us!"

Chapter 33

They ran off in a southwestern direction. Shortly after Brenda started to lag behind; at her age she could not be expected to run like the Panthers. Ingrid hung back beside her. She watched the Wild Ones of the Ice in the distance. They would not be able to lose them with the witch holding them back.

"I'll take care of her," Gerd said, doubling back to them.

"Are you sure you can?" Ingrid asked him, doubt visible in her eyes.

"Of course I can. My strength and resistance are now awesome. Let me show you," he replied, handing his bow to Ingrid.

"Okay, let's try," she said, accepting Gerd's bow and slinging it over her shoulder with her own.

"Come on, Brenda, I'll carry you piggyback." He bent his knees, took hold of the Witch's arms, and put them around his neck. Then she jumped onto his back and he put his hands under her legs, straightened up, and ran off as if he was not carrying anything at all. "Everything'll be okay," he told Brenda, who was holding on tight.

Ingrid stayed a little behind to measure their distance from the enemy. Luckily the Wild Ones of the Ice were not carrying bows or spears—they had their large axes and shields, and they were not fast. They had trouble moving their big bodies with all that muscle. If they did not meet any obstacles and Gerd held up, they could leave them behind.

Nilsa was running ahead, followed by Egil and Lasgol with Ona and Camu. Lasgol did not lose sight of Camu, who for now seemed to be holding up fine. Next came Astrid and Viggo, waiting for Gerd to catch up with them. Ingrid came last, measuring the distance from the pursuing group. To Viggo's and Astrid's surprise, Gerd caught up with them pretty quickly and set his pace to match Nilsa's, which was pretty fast.

The escape continued for several leagues. The Wild Ones of the Ice could not get close but they did not hang back completely. Unfortunately, there was practically nowhere to hide or lose their pursuers in that tundra.

"Nilsa, head to those rocks to the east!" Egil said, indicating a mound of snow and ice under which there seemed to be a group of quite large rocks. It was the only place that offered any possibility of hiding for several leagues.

Nilsa did as Egil told her, veering east without changing her pace.

"Those blue thugs are on our trail!" Viggo cried, looking back.

"They're like huge two-legged bloodhounds!" Astrid corroborated.

"Don't slow down, we've almost lost them!" Ingrid said from the rear.

"Gerd, how are you holding up?" Lasgol asked him, running on his right side.

"Perfectly," the giant replied, and Lasgol saw he was not exaggerating—he was totally unaffected by the Witch's weight.

"How are you doing, Brenda?" Egil asked from the giant's left side.

"I'm great. We'll have to do this more often," she said mockingly, but her face showed signs of exhaustion from hanging on.

Lasgol and Egil exchanged a worried look. Gerd seemed to be holding up well, but Brenda, sooner or later, would not be able to keep her hold.

"I have an idea," Egil told Lasgol.

"I'm all ears!" he replied as they ran on.

"Couldn't Camu hide us all? You told me his ability to camouflage had increased."

Lasgol shook his head. "It's increased, yes, but not enough to hide eight people. Not yet, anyway. Two or three maybe, but not more."

"Oh…"

"Anyway, let me check with Camu."

Camu, could you hide us all with your power?

Not know. I try.

Can you try while we're running?

I try.

Lasgol waited to see if anything happened. But he did not detect Camu's magic activating. Even if he could not cover them all, he should be able to hide at least Egil and himself as they ran beside him. But this was not the case.

What's the matter, Camu?

No magic.

What do you mean no magic? Lasgol asked him, puzzled.

Magic not activate.

That's very strange. Do you feel anything weird?

Only tired.

You're tired and your magic won't respond?

Yes, not know why.

Hmmm, try to make only me vanish.

I try.

Lasgol did not feel Camu's magic activating.

You can't?

No. Magic not work, Camu transmitted along with a feeling of worry.

Take it easy, it's probably nothing.

Be something.

We'll find out what's wrong with you. Don't worry now. Can you keep running?

Yes, but tired.

Lasgol was puzzled—Camu was never tired and his magic always worked. Something was not right, not right at all.

"What's Camu saying?" Egil asked.

"It seems he can't use his magic now."

"Wow, that's weird," Egil said, looking at the creature.

"Something's wrong with him," Lasgol whispered to Egil.

"Any idea what it could be?"

"He says he's tired and I've seen him asleep in the middle of the day. He seems exhausted."

"Curious. We must investigate. Something must be quite wrong with our dear Camu," Egil said, troubled.

"Besides, we have another problem, come to think of it. Even if Camu could manage to hide us all we wouldn't be able to hide our footprints. The Wild Ones of the Ice would find them at once in this terrain."

"Oh, too true. Our tracks would give us away wherever we hide."

They both kept running, thinking about a way to lose their pursuers and what could possibly be happening to Camu.

Nilsa maintained a strong pace and reached the rocks. She went around them and stopped behind. The Wild Ones could not see them from the direction they were traveling. Lasgol arrived and without stopping he climbed onto the rocks. He looked around and activated his *Hawk's Sight* skill. He swept the whole landscape in search of somewhere to hide and lose their pursuers whom he saw in the distance.

"Head north," he said to the others. "There's a hollow. We can lose them if we use these rocks as an obstacle to cover our flight so they can't see us from afar. Then we can hide in the hollow."

"I don't see a hollow," Nilsa said, shaking her head, looking troubled.

"You can't see it, but it's there. Keep going," Lasgol said.

"We keep going!" Nilsa cried as she ran north like an arrow.

The rest of the group ran after her, although Astrid hesitated, looking at Lasgol.

"Go, I'll be all right," he promised. "Take Ona and Camu with you."

"Are you sure?" she asked doubtfully.

"Yes, don't worry, I'll see you all in a moment."

Astrid nodded and gestured to Ona and Camu to follow her.

Go with Astrid, I'll be with you shortly, Lasgol told them.

We with you, Camu transmitted.

No, go with Astrid. Don't argue. There's no time.

Okay, Camu transmitted although not too pleased.

"Come with me," Astrid told them, and the three ran after Nilsa and the others.

Ingrid reached Lasgol's position.

"I'll stay behind, you keep going," he told Ingrid.

"No way. I'll stay with you," she replied. "I don't leave anyone behind."

"Fine, but don't distract me."

"What are you going to do?"

"I'm going to try and cover our trail. Those Wild Ones are going to follow our tracks to the other side of the continent. I know."

"Yeah... that's likely. And how do you propose making our tracks vanish? There are seven pairs of footprints plus two sets of animal tracks. It seems impossible, besides, in this terrain of snow and ice they're at least three times more visible."

"It'll be hard, I'm going to improvise."

"That doesn't sound promising," Ingrid said, shaking her head.

"I'm going to use my skill to hide traps and see if I manage to erase the tracks."

"Laying traps on top of them?"

"That's right. I can't think of anything else, and we need to lose them…"

Ingrid was thoughtful. She looked back and glimpsed several blue dots moving. They were the Wild Ones of the Ice, who were not giving up.

"We have some time. Go ahead and try it, because those two-legged sperm whales don't seem ready to give up."

"They're in their own habitat. They're used to it," Lasgol said.

"Even so, they're quite resilient."

"It must be their race," Lasgol said and began hiding the tracks their friends had left.

Ingrid watched Lasgol with her composite bow ready in her hand, an arrow nocked.

Lasgol stepped in his comrades' prints, looking to the rocks so as not to make a new set of tracks. He told Ingrid to step in the existing footprints like he was doing, and Lasgol placed one of the traps he carried in his traveling bag right on top of his comrades' tracks. Then he called upon his *Trap Hiding* skill and made it vanish on the snow. Just as he had expected, as he made the trap vanish, the tracks also disappeared under the trap.

"Wow, it works!" Ingrid said, surprised.

"Yeah, it looks that way. I'll place some more."

Lasgol placed the six traps he had carried with him and invoked his skill, hiding them all, covering up the prints underneath.

"It works… yes… but it's not enough," Ingrid said, wrinkling her nose.

Lasgol checked the land; Ingrid was right. He needed to hide another stretch so the tracks would be invisible from the rocks. He bent over a stretch of prints and called upon his *Trap Hiding* skill, but because there was no trap to hide the skill failed. The green flash did not occur and Lasgol felt that part of the energy in his hidden pool was consumed in a failed attempt.

He cursed under his breath.

He did not give up and tried again. He began to summon the skill, using part of his inner energy but, once again, as there was no trap to hide, it failed again. Lasgol snorted. He was staring at the tracks, sitting on his haunches.

"Better to keep going," Ingrid said. "We can still get away without being seen."

"The trail we leave will give us away…" Lasgol said, frustrated. He focused on the tracks. He visualized them in his mind and then imagined them vanishing, just as they had when he had set the traps. "Come on, I have to be able to do this," he muttered, concentrating as hard as he could on the tracks. He called upon his *Trap Hiding* skill once more, only this time he changed the final goal and instead of a trap focused on the tracks. He felt the skill beginning to activate and some more of his inner energy was consumed. He wished with all his being it would work. The green flash came.

"Lasgol…" Ingrid insisted.

"Give me a moment…"

Ingrid sighed and let him work.

Inhaling the icy air of the tundra, Lasgol concentrated and tried again. He focused on the tracks and forced his mind to imagine the tracks disappearing, just as the traps had.

"Vanish… they have to vanish… or they'll find us. They can't find us, they have to disappear…" he concentrated harder and, he tried again. He saw in his mind the tracks vanishing before his eyes as if it were real. He searched for his inner energy and willed the tracks to vanish. All of a sudden there was a green flash in front of him. Their trail was gone.

"Yes!" he cried joyfully.

"Did you do it?" Ingrid asked him with disbelief.

"I think so! I'm going to try again. "Lasgol concentrated. He took a few steps back, stepping into the already existing footprints and once again willing them to disappear. There was another flash and the prints vanished.

"Impressive!" Ingrid congratulated him. "They've disappeared completely!"

Lasgol tried again and another stretch of prints vanished before their eyes.

"I've developed a new skill! I'm going to call it *Trail Erasing*."

"Egil's going to love this!" Ingrid told him.

"He'll find it fantastic!" Lasgol laughed.

Ingrid smiled. "Oh yeah. Now you'd better hurry. You have a long trail to hide and the Wild Ones will be here soon."

"You're right, let's go."

Ingrid and Lasgol went on, stepping backwards as he invoked his new skill *Trail Erasing*. It took him a long time to hide the whole stretch to the hollow, but he did it. He got there with barely any inner energy left for any other skill.

"Lie low!" Ingrid warned as she saw the first Wild One of the Ice reach the rocks.

Lasgol did as he was told and she did the same.

Ingrid indicated the hollow, and they both crawled until they got to the rim and rolled down into it. Gerd and Viggo stopped their fall.

"Hide and keep silent, they're coming," Ingrid whispered to them.

They all lay down at the bottom of the hollow and were silent. Snow started falling heavily. Lasgol was grateful—the snow would cover any trail he had not been able to. He had gone so fast he was not sure he had hidden it all.

After waiting a while, Ingrid asked Lasgol to send Camu up to check.

Camu, camouflage yourself and go up and tell me what the Wild Ones are doing.

I go.

You can, can't you?

Yes, I can.

Lasgol saw Camu vanish and followed his trail as he climbed up the slope of the hollow.

Wild Ones go east.

They're not coming here?

No, go east.

All of them?

Yes.

Okay, watch a little in case someone heads here.

Okay.

All of a sudden Camu became visible.

Camu! You're visible!

Magic fail.

Come down quick!

Camu came back down to Lasgol.

What's the matter with you, my friend?

Not know.

Well, be careful. It looks like your magic isn't working properly.

I careful.

Lasgol felt distressed. He told Egil, who in turn was worried too.

Something was wrong with Camu, and they did not know the reason.

They waited a little longer while the Wild Ones moved away and then decided to keep running.

"We'll follow the gully east and then run north," Ingrid said.

"Let's go!" Nilsa said and ran off like lightning.

They ran until they came out of the gully and then north. Nilsa set the pace and they went on till nightfall. Finally they stopped, the darkness covering them along with some vegetation they found. They were exhausted, but they had lost the Wild Ones of the Ice and were safe for the time being.

"Really... I don't know what they've done to you in this Improved Training... but I'm thinking about joining up and doing it twice..." Viggo said panting, bent over almost unable to breathe and staring at Gerd, who had run with Brenda on his back the whole way.

"I'll... join him..." Astrid said as she tried to recover from the long run and found it hard.

"Truly surprising," Ingrid said. "It turns out that now you're stronger and more resilient than we are. That's a real feat!" she said, pleased.

"Well... no need to exaggerate... they're better... but not by much," Viggo refused to admit the truth.

"I... think... they've improved a lot..." said Lasgol. "They're in better shape than us."

"Because we've been probed in the head instead of improving our physical shape."

"I thought you were already in perfect form," Nilsa said mockingly.

"And I am," he said, unable to straighten himself, his hands on his thighs, panting.

"You're the spitting image of physical prowess," Ingrid said, who had already recovered from the effort.

"I know, thank you," Viggo said, raising his hand.

"What do we do now?" Lasgol asked.

"We'd better rest and recover our strength so we can keep going tomorrow," said Egil. "We can set up a couple of tents right here and rest. Brenda can't go on. She's exhausted. And so are the rest of us, we need to rest."

"I was thinking the same. We'll spend the night here," Ingrid said. "Besides, I don't want to risk going on at night with no visibility."

They set up the two winter tents they carried and settled in them. They ate from their supplies and drank from the water skins. Thus, they recuperated some of their strength and Ingrid allotted the watches. The night was going to be cold. They all remembered the freezing temperatures of that land. They could not have a fire since that would draw attention, so they had to use human warmth. They all piled up in the two tents and the last thing they heard, before Gerd's snores, was Ingrid whispering to Viggo:

"If you get fresh with me I'll cut your ears off," followed by Viggo's chuckles.

Chapter 34

The night was cold, but not as cold as the ones they had spent during their previous visit to the Frozen Continent, something they were all grateful for. Viggo still had both ears and his nose, which he was also grateful for. The morning was clear, and although the wind was freezing, there was no threat of a storm, at least for the time being.

"We have to keep going," Ingrid said. "Those Wild Ones of the Ice must have warned others of our presence here, and other groups will be looking for us."

"Yeah, we can count on that," said Egil. "They'll search for us. They're not going to let a few Norghanians wander about their land. It's unfortunate that things are like this, but that's the way things are. Perhaps one day there'll be peace between Norghanians and the Peoples of the Frozen Continent, but I'm afraid that day is still very far away."

"Yes, it's a shame," Lasgol agreed; he was all too aware that the existing hatred between both peoples would only bring about death and destruction.

"Let me conjure the Tracker so it tells us the way," Brenda said, and calmly and parsimoniously she started the ritual again.

While the Snow Witch cast her strange magic, the rest picked up the tents and prepared to leave. Ingrid sent Nilsa and Gerd to explore the surroundings and make sure that when they set out they would not come across another patrol of Wild Ones of the Ice, Tundra Dwellers, or Arcanes of the Glaciers.

Ona moaned, and Lasgol turned to her. She had her paw on Camu's back, who was still sleeping stretched out on the ground. He came over to see how he was.

Still sleeping? We're all ready to leave, he messaged him.

Ona moaned again.

Camu, are you getting my messages?

Seeing his friend was not answering, Lasgol shook him. Camu opened one eye and looked at him sleepily.

Camu, wake up! Lasgol insisted.

The creature opened his other eye and stared at him and Ona.

Much sleepy, he transmitted along with a feeling of being exhausted.

It's daylight already. You slept all night, you should've recovered.

I sleep. Tired still.

That's strange. Can you go on?

Camu got up and took a few steps.

Yes, I can.

Let me know if you can't.

I let know.

Troubled, Lasgol went to tell Egil. The two friends commented in whispers what was going on with Camu, but they had no idea what it might be.

Brenda was directing the Tracker which indicated northeast again. She ended the ritual and prepared to go on.

"But how far will we have to go? If we keep going we'll end up traveling from one end of the continent to the other!" Viggo protested. "And it's a huge continent!"

Ingrid turned to Brenda. "Can you gauge the distance?"

"Approximately. If I'm not mistaken, it's in those glaciers to the northeast," said Brenda, pointing at the tall blocks of blue ice that looked like mountains on the horizon.

"It's going to take us at least two days at a good pace to get there," Ingrid calculated.

"A little longer," Astrid said, indicating Brenda unobtrusively.

"You're right," Ingrid agreed. "Let's get going. The sooner we arrive, the sooner we'll be able to finish this mission and return home."

"The sooner the better. One's ideas can freeze in this land," Viggo moaned, shaking his arms and legs to get warm.

Ingrid was about to say something about Viggo's ideas but she held her tongue.

"Nilsa, you lead the way. Gerd, you look after Brenda, don't let her delay us."

"I'll take care of that," Gerd replied.

"Thank you for looking after me," the Witch said to Gerd gratefully. "At my age, long marches are exhausting."

"Don't mention it, it's my pleasure," Gerd replied.

They started and, as if they were explorers trying to cross that frozen land, they went forward, treading with care on the ground covered with snow and ice. They walked at a good pace all morning and stopped at noon to eat and rest. They all ate in silence, looking at the icy landscape around them, scanning for the presence of some possible enemy.

They glimpsed a couple of polar bears, huge ones. They also saw a pack of beautiful arctic wolves. But what surprised them most was a herd of white woolly animals similar to buffalos that passed by in the distance. It was clear to all of them that the animals in this land were huge, a lot bigger than what they were used to, with long white hair.

Lasgol and Egil looked after Camu, but they were unable to find the cause for his weakness. They gave him a potion with a strengthening remedy for sick Rangers; Egil even prepared an antidote against common poisons in case he had eaten some poisonous plant growing around. But nothing seemed to work. Camu continued feeling tired and weak. Lasgol thought about using his *Ranger Healing* skill. This allowed him to fight magic in his mind. Although he did not know whether it could do anything for Camu, he decided to try anyway. First he used his *Aura Presence* skill and was able to see Camu's three auras: his mind aura, body aura, and that of his magic power. He already knew them; he had seen them and examined them before, and what worried him a lot was that none of the three shone with the intensity they usually did.

"His three auras are quite dimmed," he told Egil.

"All three?"

"Yes, it's as if they were being consumed... as if they were fading..."

"Very curious. The body aura being affected or even the mind aura could be because of some illness. But his magic power shouldn't be affected."

"They're a lot less potent as usual, that I can see clearly."

"I see... try to heal them. We won't lose by trying," Egil told him. "It might not work, but do it anyway."

Lasgol tried, but he could not detect anything abnormal in Camu's three auras. They seemed to be all right; although they were less bright, they still shone in the natural shade that was characteristic of them and there was no other presence affecting them as far as Lasgol could detect. There was nothing to apply his *Ranger Healing* skill on.

"I can't, I don't see anything to heal…" Lasgol said regretfully.

"Well, that's weird," Egil said. "Perhaps the fact that you can't see the damage is because it's physical and not magical. You developed this skill to heal the effects of other magic on your body."

"Or maybe it's another type of magic I can't detect."

"It might be that, yes. In any case it's bizarre, but something's definitely wrong with him. Let's watch him closely and see how he evolves. It might be something temporary, like a cold or a fever for us."

They resumed their march and continued crossing the tundra without fail. The weather was cold, but they were holding up pretty well, at least during the day. Things changed at night, but their tents protected them well enough. So far they had not detected any enemy presence, so it seemed fortune was being kind to them. But the tundra was endless—leagues and leagues of frozen land spread in every direction so theoretically they should not have any more encounters.

Gerd was carrying Brenda piggyback once again. The Witch had run out of strength quickly and could no longer walk so she had climbed onto the giant's back.

"I regret being a burden. When I was young I could cross this tundra as you're doing now. It's a pity age punishes the body so."

"Don't worry, and you're not a burden. Without you we wouldn't know where to go and we'd be doomed to wander lost in this tundra."

"You're a special group of people and intelligent. I doubt you would have wandered for long," Brenda said with a giggle.

"I'm not so sure," Gerd replied, scanning the white frozen immensity that surrounded them: a flat landscape only broken by occasional mounds of frozen rock and the ever-present glaciers at the end.

"Those glaciers to the north, with their different heights and lengths seem to form mountain ranges like in our land," Gerd said, looking at them.

"Only they're more rectangular and made of ice instead of rock," Brenda replied.

"Why are there more glaciers to the north than in this area? Because of the temperature?"

"See how you're a very sharp group? That's exactly why. The

270

more to the north you go the colder it is, and the colder it is the more it favors the formation of glaciers and icebergs, which you'll see when we reach the coast."

Gerd nodded. "There are also glaciers to the east," he said, pointing at the great masses of ice, snow, and rock, "but they're smaller. Where you don't see them is to the south."

"This continent has been frozen for a long time. What you see now is the result of that effect."

"I don't know how the races that live here can survive the winter in this icy world."

"Because they've learnt to survive. Do you see any villages? Houses? Any cities?" Brenda asked him, looking around.

"No, none."

"Then… where do the peoples of the Frozen Continent live?"

"They do build houses in the north of Norghana, but not here…. Because they'd freeze in winter, they live underground," Gerd concluded.

"That's right, underground and in caves. There they can survive the low temperatures—apart from the fact that they are already capable of withstanding the cold a lot better than us, being tribes from this continent."

"You know a lot," Gerd said admiringly.

"I'm old, and with age experience makes you wise," she said with another giggle.

At nightfall, when the temperatures started to drop, they stopped in a small hollow that offered some protection against the piercing night winds. They set up the two tents, with Nilsa, Gerd, Ingrid, and Viggo with Ona in one, and Astrid, Lasgol, Brenda, and Egil with Camu in the other so as to occupy them equally. Ona's and Camu's already considerable size made them comparable to adults for sleeping space. In reality, they were quite bigger than an adult and took up more space.

They ate and drank in the dark. They could not light a fire for safety reasons. One of the few good things about night in the Frozen Continent was that because of the aurora borealis there was enough light that they could manage without additional light. This was not possible in Norghana, at least in the central and southern parts. Way to the north there was more light, especially in the territories where the Wild Ones of the Ice lived.

"Brenda, could you examine Camu with your magic?" Lasgol asked her.

"What's wrong with the creature?" the Witch asked.

"He's ill. We don't know exactly what kind it might be, but something's definitely wrong with him," Lasgol told her.

"He's exhausted all the time," Egil added as he stroked Camu's head lovingly. The creature seemed to be napping.

"The journey is long and hard," the Snow Witch said.

"Yes, but Camu is strong and always full of energy. I usually have to keep asking him to stay still," Lasgol said.

"He's not himself," Astrid added as she stroked his crested back.

"How long has this been going on?" Brenda asked.

"Ever since we arrived here," said Lasgol. "Perhaps he got sick on the ship and we're now witnessing the consequences.

"I see," Brenda nodded. "My knowledge of healing is that of a Snow Witch. I'm no healer and I don't have experience with Creatures of the Ice either."

"Any help is welcome," Lasgol told her.

"Very well. We'll see what I can do," The Witch searched in her traveling bag for several saucers with different engravings on them. She sat down with her legs crossed and started to prepare a potion on three of the saucers. She poured some liquid components she carried with her and mixed them with her bare fingers; the concoction turned greenish brown as a strong smell filled the tent.

"Can we help in any way?" Egil offered.

"Let's surround the saucers with our bodies—I need to create a small flame for the spell and it's better to avoid being seen," Brenda said, glancing at the tent and the darkness outside.

"That's true, let's not attract any unnecessary attention," said Astrid, watching what the Witch was doing very carefully.

Brenda lit a flame in one of her saucers, and as soon as it was strong enough she started conjuring with both her hands over the flame. She closed her eyes and her words became some sort of chant. The color of the Witch's fingers turned yellow as she cast her spell. She opened her eyes and slowly passed her fingers over Camu's body; first the head, then the back, and finally the tail, moving her hands and leaving ten yellow stripes on Camu's scales.

Astrid, Lasgol, and Egil watched, intrigued, trying to understand what she was doing. Brenda turned and placed both hands on

Camu's head, who seemed to be sleeping, oblivious to what was going on. The Witch went on with the ritual and the spell seemed to take shape: the stripes she had painted on Camu's body began to glimmer.

Suddenly the glimmer of the yellow lines seemed to come alive and went from Camu's body to the Witch's hands and from there to Brenda's head, which she threw back. She entered a trance and shut her eyes. The yellow stripes shone and the light they gave ran through Camu's body to the Snow Witch's head.

"It... doesn't appear..." Brenda started to say without opening her eyes.

Astrid, Lasgol, and Egil were hanging from her every word.

"Yes?" Lasgol said.

"To be any... illness..."

"There isn't?" he asked, puzzled.

"Or... poison..." continued Brenda.

"That's weird..." said Egil.

The Snow Witch went on for another moment, letting the flashes of the stripes reach her. Then she opened her eyes and with a word of power stopped the ritual. The yellow stripes stopped shining and the flame went out in its saucer.

"I can't find anything wrong in this creature. What's happening isn't physical, at least as far as I can see. This is the first time I've done this ritual on such a special creature, so I can't guarantee I can see everything that goes on with him. If it were directed at either of you, this ritual would find the illness you had if you did."

"Maybe it's something related to his magic," Astrid ventured.

"That could be, but I'm not trained in this type of mystery."

"We understand. Thank you for trying," Lasgol said.

"Has he eaten anything?" Brenda asked.

"Very little, based on what he's used to," Egil replied.

"I'm going to prepare a vegetable soup with various additional ingredients for him which will give him energy."

"Thank you, Brenda," Lasgol said, grateful. He had no idea what might be wrong with Camu, but he was beginning to think it was something to be concerned about. That night he could not rest thinking about his friend. Astrid tried to comfort him with sweet words and caresses, but the worry he felt for Camu would not go away and he could not sleep.

Chapter 35

At dawn they took down the tents and started moving. It was a crisp morning, so they hastened their departure to keep themselves warm. There was nothing worse than staying still when the temperature dropped or the icy winds hit them like a whip. Lasgol made sure Camu ate some of the soup Brenda prepared for his breakfast.

Can you go on? He transmitted, troubled.

I can.

Are you saying this because you can really go on or out of stubbornness?

Yes, I go on.

Lasgol was not sure that was the right answer, but since the group was starting out and they could not stay in the middle of the tundra, he had to take it as it was.

They continued in a northeastern direction. The huge blue glacier was becoming a giant presence in the horizon; with every step they took in its direction, the more its majestic presence loomed. They knew they had to approach fast and stealthily, and so they did. Whoever had created the colossal storm that hung over Norghania was at the foot of the glacier—that was what the Tracker marked. The Royal Eagles wanted to arrive and end the threat as Thoran had ordered.

They arrived at the glacier. It was colossal, a giant structure of ice and snow, distilling blue beauty. As they were reaching its southern face, they began to hear a sound. First it sounded muffled by distance and the cutting winds, but it gradually became more audible. An indeterminate number of voices were reciting some kind of litany in a language they did not recognize.

"Beware!" Ingrid warned from her forward position.

"That sounds like a spell," Nilsa said in a tone of protest and disgust.

"A spell that many are chanting," Viggo said.

"How much is many?" Gerd asked as he caught up with them, Brenda on his back.

"I'd say more than a hundred voices," Egil calculated as he

cocked his head, trying to guess what was being said and the number of voices.

"We'll soon know," Astrid said, pointing at a small hill that obscured the ritual chanting's origin.

The group reached the top of the hill of ice and snow, where Ingrid halted them.

"Everyone, lie low!"

The group did so at once, dropping onto the snow and ice. They were in front of the southern face of the glacier. They saw that between their high position and the glacier, there lay a frozen valley.

They poked their heads over the rim to see what was going on and were struck dumb.

They saw over a hundred Wild Ones of the Ice, with the same number of Tundra Dwellers and Arcanes of the Glaciers, in the middle of some kind of evil ritual. Lasgol watched with a lump in his throat. Egil, beside him, looked very troubled.

The Wild Ones of the Snow, along with the Tundra Dwellers and the Arcanes of the Glaciers were forming a large circle while they sang and moved to the rhythm of a ritual dance, brandishing their weapons and moving their arms up and down. It certainly did not bode well.

But this was not the most surprising thing. In the middle of the circle, they could see a remarkable white monolith. It looked snow-white and polished, about twelve feet tall. Lasgol recognized the monolith—he had seen it or one like it before, when his mother had united the leaders of the West with the leaders of the Peoples of the Frozen Continent to reach an agreement against Uthar. It was a sacred monolith these Peoples worshipped.

Lasgol recalled that his mother had managed to make them all swear on the monolith in a ritual in a secret cavern. She had managed an alliance that would have granted them victory had she not been betrayed. He also remembered that Shaman Azur, then leader of the Arcanes of the Glaciers, had warned them once he had performed the ritual that "the oath made before the Ice Gods cannot be broken. Whoever does not fulfill his oath will suffer a terrible death and will call a curse of death upon his own people."

A deep sigh of sorrow escaped from Lasgol's chest. Everything had gone wrong after that oath, when they had victory at the tip of their fingers. Azur, Darthor, Asrael, Austin, Arnold, and many others who had been in favor of the treaty and had sworn in blood upon the monolith had died… many betrayed by the same people who had also sworn in blood to respect the treaty. Betrayed by Jurn, Sarn and Asuris… the accursed Asuris…

He snorted. If it were in his hands, he would finish them all, not only out of revenge but for justice—what the good leaders who had died trying to end the war and achieve peace between the Norghanians and the Peoples of the Frozen Continent deserved. A peace that seemed very distant. The ambition of the new leaders had no end, and they had even tried to conquer Norghana using a Frozen Specter. Lasgol was happy they had been able to destroy the Specter and thereby force the forces of the Frozen Continent to retreat. But it had served as clear proof that the leaders of the Peoples of the Frozen Continent would never stop until they had conquered Norghana.

He felt once again that life was not fair… it did not always smile on the noble of heart, the honorable and respectful, on the good people with good intentions. Sometimes the miserable; those who had no guts; the twisted; evil and treacherous; the venomous snakes of life were victorious again and brought death, destruction, and great pain to many good people. Everything would have been different if the perpetrators of the betrayal had respected their oath. His mother would be alive, Azur and Asrael would still be leading the Arcanes of the Glaciers, and there would be peace in the north. Instead, greed had overpowered Asuris, Jurn, and Sarn, leading them to betray their own people and allies. Lasgol relived again the betrayal scene in the throne hall in his mind. He saw Azur die, and then his mother… he saw Asrael fall… the pain returned to his heart and his eyes moistened, as they did every time he remembered the event. The tragedy and the trauma did not fade, no matter how much time went by.

"Look, two figures are approaching the monolith," Ingrid warned in a whisper.

"Watch out," said Astrid squinting.

"D'you think they're having a party? Will they have *firewater*, you think? Maybe we should go down and join them," said Viggo.

Ingrid threw a handful of snow to his face.

"Don't be an idiot, the situation is very serious."

"That's why I'm being an idiot, we seem to be at a funeral."

"If you don't stay focused this very well might turn into a funeral, ours!" Ingrid snapped.

"What little sense of humor... really... look how funny the Arcanes of the Glaciers are, dancing so rhythmically."

Now it was Nilsa who threw snow at him.

"Don't be so foolish. Pay attention to the fact that there's a whole army down there."

Viggo grinned and nodded.

Lasgol did not want to miss a detail, so he called upon his *Hawk's Sight* and *Owl Hearing* skills. Two silhouettes, who seemed to be responsible for the arcane ritual, came to stand before the sacred monolith. One of them Lasgol recognized at once; he had seen him in the visions of his mother's medallion the Experience Marker. It was none other than the bearish erudite Hotz of the Arcanes of the Glaciers. Lasgol recognized his weary walk, his hunched form, how he leaned on what looked like a staff made of ice. The old man, who seemed to have lived more than all the other Arcanes of the Glaciers, had a face marked by deep creases and looked drowsy. He recognized the surly look of Hotz's small gray eyes which did not appear interested in anything.

He recalled what Hotz had explained to his mother and the Council of Shamans around the Eternal Flame. He had insisted that the only important thing was the study of what the ice hid, the power it had buried in it, and the power the ice was protecting. Once they found and studied a creature of great power trapped in the ice, they would be able to get rid of the Norghanians and any other enemy. Lasgol also remembered that Hotz had called Mayra, Azur, Asrael, and the rest of the council useless for not agreeing with his idea of searching in the ice instead of fighting. He had told them that one day most of those present would not be there because of the erroneous decision they had made. A shiver crept down Lasgol's spine; that was the case. His macabre premonition had come true, as if it had been a curse from heaven. He remembered Hotz saying that he would keep searching for the treasure in the skies and that, when he found it,, it would mean the end of all the enemies of the Peoples of the Frozen Continent. Also that they would not see it because they would all be dead by the time this day arrived.

Had this day arrived? Had Hotz discovered the treasure in the ice he yearned for?

Lasgol also recognized the second silhouette at once and started to think the worst. It was the strange creature the shaman had dug out of the ice and which Lasgol had also seen in another of the visions from his mother's pendant. It had a reptilian body but it stood erect on two legs and a long tail. The upper limbs were also reptilian, like an enormous crocodile, only the head was like a snake's, with reptilian yellow eyes and a forked tongue. It was a mixture between a crocodile and a snake and remained erect like a man, which left Lasgol nonplussed. Another thing that struck him was that the creature was twice the size it had been when they had taken it out of the glacier ice. It seemed to have grown quickly upon coming to life again. It was now four times the size of a man.

"That semi-giant with the face of a snake and a crocodile's body looks most charming," Viggo commented. "Don't you feel like going down there and greeting it with a hug?"

"That's an abomination," Nilsa said with loathing.

"It's enormous and looks strong," Ingrid said, wrinkling her nose.

"It looks to me like a dangerous monster," said Gerd.

"You shouldn't judge it just by its looks, I bet it's most charming and pleasant," Viggo said, smiling.

At that moment, the great reptile opened its mouth, revealing two huge fangs. It hissed so loud toward the sky that they had to cover their ears, even though they were quite a distance away.

"You were saying?" Astrid said to Viggo.

"Nothing, I sometimes talk too much," he replied with mock horror.

"This thing is going to present a serious problem," Ingrid said.

"More than that, because if I'm not mistaken that's a Magical Creature," Egil said, looking at Brenda who was down beside him.

"It is," the Witch said as she lay there with her eyes closed, murmuring words of power. "It's a creature of great power. An ancient power. I can feel it from here."

"Wow… that's all we needed," Nilsa moaned.

"As if we didn't already have enough with all those chanters…" Gerd said, nodding toward the Wild Ones, the Dwellers, and the Arcanes, who went on singing and moving strangely in the midst of the ritual they were performing.

Lasgol did not miss a detail, trying to stay calm before what he was witnessing.

Camu, do you feel this creature's magic?

Camu opened his eyes slightly to look at Lasgol.

Not feel. Magic not good.

Don't you worry, you'll be better soon, Lasgol transmitted to him, although he didn't know how he was going to heal his friend.

He remembered that Camu had told him that this reptilian creature was a relative, which had left Lasgol quite stunned, even more so now that he saw how big and powerful it had become.

Hotz huddled in his seal skin coat and opened his arms before the monolith. He closed his eyes, said some arcane words, and joined the ritual chanting with the rest of his people. The great reptile stood beside him.

"The show begins," said Viggo, who was already guessing that Hotz had begun to cast a spell.

"I'm not going to like this at all," Gerd commented.

"Me neither," Nilsa joined.

"I don't understand why, this is most interesting," said Egil as he watched, fascinated.

Hotz raised his arms, and in his hands, there appeared what looked like bear claws, only they were bluish, clearly magic. He went on casting his spell while he moved his arms and looked up at the overcast sky. All of a sudden, the great white monolith flashed with an intense mother-of-pearl gleam.

"Wow, he's activating the power of the monolith," Brenda said.

"That's not good for us, is it?" Viggo asked.

"It's an Object of Power, a natural one. It has its own magic and you can use its power to amplify other spells," Brenda explained.

"That old geezer of the Glaciers is using the monolith to make his spell more powerful," Viggo reasoned.

"Something like that, yes," Brenda replied.

"It's fantastic," Egil said under his breath.

Lasgol did not think it was fantastic at all—quite the opposite. He preferred not to see it, or, better still, that it did not happen.

Hotz kept casting his spell and a blue fog covered part of the monolith, enveloping it. They could only see the top of it. Lasgol was looking at Hotz's spell with growing concern. He knew this was going to get ugly, and quickly.

"Beware," Brenda warned them. "I can feel powerful magic taking place."

"This is turning ugly," Ingrid said, narrowing her eyes.

Chapter 36

All of a sudden and to everyone's surprise, the great reptile opened its mouth and began sending a stream of pure energy toward Hotz, a jet of power that went straight to the ancient Arcane of the Glaciers. Hotz deflected it toward the monolith with his bear-claw gloves.

"This is getting fun, that giant lizard-snake seems to have a powerful breath," Viggo said ironically.

Then suddenly Hotz started casting another spell. With one hand he deflected the creature's breath of pure energy to the monolith, while with the other he worked a spell so it would go up from the monolith to the sky. A great bluish-white beam shot up to the clouds from the monument.

"That explains how they manage to send the magic…" Brenda mused.

"I don't understand anything," Viggo said.

"How odd. Shut up and listen to Brenda," Ingrid snapped.

"He's sending the energy that the winter storm consumes in Norghania," Brenda explained.

"Is that what they're doing?" Nilsa asked, upset.

"Yes. The core of the storm needs energy to keep it active. What we're witnessing is how they send that energy to the storm so it goes on punishing the city without being consumed," the Snow Witch explained.

"Wow, that's simply fascinating!" Egil said.

"And he's sending it there from here?" Gerd asked, looking baffled.

"That's right."

"Wow, that ancient Arcane *is* powerful," Astrid said.

"He's powerful, but really he's only doing the job of channeling the creature's power. That's the really powerful one," the Witch explained.

"How much more powerful?" Astrid asked.

"A lot more. The Arcane can barely control the amount of energy the creature's sending him, and he himself is quite powerful."

"So, what's the monolith got to do with all of this?" Viggo wanted to know.

"The monolith works as a dispenser. It sends all the power where the ancient Arcane indicates through the spell."

"I don't get it," Gerd said.

"To use a simile, the monolith is the bow, the creature's energy is the arrow, and the Arcane of the Glaciers is the archer."

"Ahhh… okay, now I get it," Gerd nodded repeatedly.

"I understood it the first time," Viggo lied through his teeth.

"Yeah, sure," Nilsa said, shaking her head.

"It's simply fantastic and fascinating," Egil stated excitedly.

"That creature's magic is impressively powerful. That of the Arcane too—more than any mage I have ever met," Brenda said. "I can detect the power of that spell. It's colossal."

"The old Arcane, Hotz, who's casting the spell is the most powerful among all the Arcanes of the Glaciers," Lasgol told his friends, remembering that Asrael had told his mother so.

"Great, we ought to go and greet him," Viggo said, showing his knives.

"Greet him very carefully," Astrid warned him.

"He goes around seeking creatures sleeping the Ice Sleep, the creatures that lie frozen in the ice in a never ending sleep," Lasgol explained.

"Well, he seems to have found one…" Ingrid said, "and he's woken it up!"

"That creature's going to give us a lot of trouble. I can practically see it already," Gerd said ominously.

Lasgol watched the reptilian creature as it went on sending its powerful breath as if it could go on forever. At that moment, Lasgol knew that Hotz had found what he had been searching for and that with the creature's power he would destroy the Norghanians and any other people he might encounter.

The spell continued for quite a while. A large amount of energy was sent to the sky and driven to Norghania to feed the killer storm. Finally, the creature stopped sending its breath of power. Hotz stopped the spell and lowered his arms. The mist enveloping the monolith faded until it was completely gone. The bear claws also vanished.

And if what Lasgol had witnessed had troubled him, what came next turned his stomach and soul. He had not been expecting that. Part of the ritual circle opened and three figures walked up to Hotz and the reptilian creature in the center by the monolith.

Lasgol recognized the first one: Jurn, the semi-giant, leader of the Wild Ones of the ice. He was unmistakable, tall as three men and wide as three more. His skin was blue and similar to that of the Wild Ones of the Ice, but it was covered with white diagonal streaks. His hair and beard were long and white as snow and the single eye in the middle of his forehead with a completely blue iris struck fear into whoever looked at it. He was said to be very intelligent. Upon seeing him Lasgol was reminded of the great betrayal, and he wished he could gouge out that hateful eye.

Beside Jurn there was Sarn, leader of the Tundra Dwellers. His skin was crystal white, reflecting the light of day. His snow-white hair shone equally intensely, as if it had turned into frozen snow. His eyes were a deep gray. His athletic, slim body was not very muscular, but he was as tall as a Wild One of the Ice. Lasgol had heard he was slippery—he recognized his face and remembered the throne hall, when Sarn hurled his spear at Austin's back during the betrayal.

And the third figure was Asuris, with his odd violet eyes that still shone with a life he did not deserve to live. Lasgol nearly retched. Asuris was the Arcane of the Glaciers who had betrayed his leaders and stabbed his mother Mayra through the back in cold blood when he was her bodyguard.

The three traitors of the throne room were there. Alive.

Lasgol's stomach burned and the flames climbed up his chest, scorching his throat and reaching his head. He wanted to get up and shoot at them, but they were too far away for Lasgol to hit them. Egil's hand held him down and stopped him from standing. Lasgol looked at his friend.

"I know what you're feeling and what you want to do, but now's not the time," Egil said, shaking his head.

"It's them. They're all there and still alive," Lasgol said furiously.

"I recognized them too. I also feel rage and frustration. Jurn gave my brother a deadly wound, through the back, treacherously."

"Then you want the same thing I do."

"Yes. But we won't get it if we attack now."

"There might never be another occasion, and they're right there."

"If they see you, we'll be risking everyone here," Egil told him as he nodded at their friends around them.

Lasgol was about to ignore his friend's words. He wanted to kill all three. This was the moment. Rage blinded him. But Egil's words reached his subconscious and he had to admit he was right. He could not endanger the group no matter how much he wanted revenge. He thought again and calmed down. He lay down on the ground again.

"You're right," he told Egil.

"We'll have our day of justice," Egil promised.

Lasgol doubted they would, seeing how powerful the three traitors were with all those warriors under their command. He turned to his comrades lying beside him.

"Those three are Asuris, Jurn, and Sarn. They're the traitors of the throne hall," he told the others.

"You're kidding!" Viggo said. "Is it really them?"

"It is them," Lasgol said heavily.

"I thought they'd have died already," Nilsa said. "Well, I wished they had."

"They seem to be still leading their Peoples," Ingrid said.

"Unfortunately…" Gerd said.

"We have to kill the three of them for what they did," Astrid said, as if determined to do so herself.

"Take it easy all of you, let's not lose our heads," Egil told them. "It's madness to attack them, and even if we did it would mean our end."

"Can't the Snow Witch cast a spell or curse on them?" Viggo asked.

Brenda sighed. "I could, but considering that this Arcane has a creature of such great power with him, I'm afraid I'd be counterattacked and his attacking spells would be more powerful than mine."

"You don't have powerful attacking spells?" Gerd asked.

"I'm afraid not. I'm a Snow Witch. A healer, a seer. I don't have much attacking power…"

"Well, that's neat," Viggo protested. "That's just our luck,"

"In any case, we're not going to attack," Ingrid said. "It would be suicide, with or without magic. Down below there's a whole lot of Arcanes besides Asuris and Hotz. Too many. Even for an army."

"Well, there should be a way to finish these traitors," Astrid insisted, looking at Lasgol and seeing the pain in his eyes.

Ingrid nodded. They were all aware of who they were facing, what they had done, and what justice required. Unfortunately, often life and justice did not go hand in hand but were on opposing sides. Everyone knew this and had to put up with it.

Asuris, Jurn, and Sarn reached Hotz. Lasgol listened carefully to their words. He craned his neck to try and pick them up, even if the distance was so great. He remembered that to be able to understand what they said he needed to activate the ring his mother had given him: the Ring of the Frozen Languages. He activated it and   listened in the direction of the conversation.

"…. Managed to reinforce… storm?" Asuris' voice reached him haltingly and far away. Lasgol could barely hear it. He gestured to his comrades to be quiet to make it easier for him to understand. They were all still and silent.

"… the strengthened core… days…" Hotz's voice reached him.

"… death to the Norghanians…." Now it was Jurn speaking.

"… recover our lands…" he heard Sarn speak.

"… conquer Norghana… all the north… ours …" he heard Asuris.

"… repeat… one week…" Hotz said.

"… create… another… killer storm…" Jurn said.

"… creature… rest… another storm… later on…" Hotz told them.

"… attack… kill them…" Jurn insisted.

"No… only with creature… definite… victory…" Hotz said, adamant.

"Come back… one week…" Asuris said.

The four leaders went on speaking a while longer, but unfortunately the wind changed direction and the sound did not reach Lasgol anymore.

"Now I can't hear what they're saying," he told his friends.

"Could you find out what they were talking about?" Egil asked, intrigued.

Lasgol nodded. "I couldn't understand it all, it reached me haltingly, but I got part of it."

"Well, what did they say?"

"They're the ones attacking Norghania. Hotz has created the storm with the creature's help."

"Yeah, that's what it looked like," Egil said.

286

"Brenda was right," Lasgol went on, "they're using the ritual and the magical creature to send power to the storm, to strengthen its core."

Brenda nodded.

"Jurn and Sarn seem to want a direct attack on Norghania. Hotz refuses. I think he wants to go on attacking with the power of the creature."

Ingrid looked worried.

"They're going to create another storm… I think. I'm not sure. But what I did seem to understand is that they'll meet here in a week."

"Interesting…" said Egil.

Ona growled—it was a warning.

Lasgol turned to look at her.

What's up, Ona?

She growled again and all the hair on her back and tail stood on end.

"Watch out, something's up," Lasgol told his comrades, who turned round. From behind some frozen rocks about twenty paces away there appeared a patrol of a dozen Tundra Dwellers.

"Enemies!" Ingrid alerted.

An instant later Ingrid and Nilsa released. The Dwellers hurled their javelins and two of them put their horns to their mouths. Astrid and Viggo were already zigzagging toward them, sliding down the frozen surface.

Lasgol and Egil released. Ingrid's and Nilsa's arrows hit target; they nocked again and hit their target once more. Lasgol also took down two Dwellers. Egil missed, but Gerd finished the one Egil had been aiming for.

The horns of the patrol echoed the alarm. Everyone in the valley below heard them. They looked up where they were fighting. Before they finished with the last Dweller with a horn, the leaders of the ritual were sending warriors to finish them.

"They've discovered us! We have to get out of here!" Ingrid shouted.

Lasgol looked to the valley and saw the Tundra Dwellers and the Wild Ones of the Ice run in their direction.

"Where are we going to go?" Nilsa asked.

Ingrid was scanning the land around them.

"To the glacier by the sea!" Egil cried.

"Are you sure? That's to the north!" Ingrid said, looking at the plain to the south.

"We won't manage to shake them off now that they've seen us and we've shed blood. The Wild Ones might not but the Dwellers will catch us. They're faster than us on the tundra."

"That's true," Egil told her.

"We have to hide, and the only place to do so is the glacier," Egil pointed north.

"Okay! Let's get to the glacier!"

"Brenda, up you go," Gerd said, bending his knees so the Witch could climb onto his back.

"I'll clear the way!" Nilsa cried as she ran off.

Come on, Camu, we have to flee!

Camu opened his eyes. *I flee.*

Ona, look after your brother and make sure he keeps running.

Ona chirped and gave a little shove to Camu so he would get up. Then she sprang off and Camu ran after her.

Lasgol ran after them and Egil joined him. Astrid and Ingrid lagged behind, watching the enemy come at a run. The Dwellers were fast, very fast.

"Another short race to exercise the legs will be good for us," Viggo joked to ease the tension of the flight. He was running alongside Gerd, who eyed him wearily.

They could hear the shouts of the Tundra Dwellers and the Wild Ones in pursuit.

They arrived at the immense glacier, which really looked like several glaciers melted into one another based on the different ice hues they could see. They had some advantage over their pursuers, although not much. They began to go around the colossal structure and glimpsed the sea at the far end. The sight of the sea cheered them. It was a dark blue, beautiful but frozen. They could see isles of ice along the frozen coastline that seemed to crash against the sea. Several huge icebergs rose like mountains of ice in the middle of this sea, not far from the coast.

"Hurry up, they're gaining on us!" Ingrid warned them as she released to cover their flight a little behind.

"We have to go faster!" Astrid shouted.

The Dwellers were already on top of them. They started hurling their javelins at the Rangers. Astrid and Ingrid had to dodge them and sprint off so as not to fall captive or be pierced by an enemy spear, and they were massive weapons.

They arrived at the northern corner of the great glacier and Nilsa stopped to look back. She saw her friends arriving with the Dwellers almost on top of them. They were not leaving them behind.

"What are we going to do?" she asked, nocking another arrow.

"I think we'll have to fight," Viggo said, readying his weapons.

"There are too many, they'll slaughter us," Gerd said, looking back.

Lasgol, Egil, Camu, and Ona arrived at the corner in that moment, and Ingrid and Astrid ran with the Dwellers at their heels.

Suddenly, a figure appeared behind them. He had been hiding at the beginning of the glacier wall on the northern side. He was wearing a mask made with the head of a bear which covered his face and head and was dressed in a bear skin as well, as if he wanted to look like one. They had the impression that he had killed a bear and made his clothes with the head and fur of the great predator. He wore a bone necklace around his neck. He was not armed, but in one hand he carried a staff made of animal bones and decorated with different runes. It looked primitive.

"Follow me if you want to live," he said and pointed at the glacier wall.

Ingrid arrived running and saw him. She hesitated—they could not trust a stranger in the Frozen Continent, least of all one who looked that odd. She poked her head around the corner of the glacier and saw their pursuers running toward them, close behind. There were at least a hundred Tundra Dwellers, followed at a distance by as many Wild Ones of the Ice. She looked at the long wall of the glacier on her right and the sea on her left. There was nowhere to hide. They would not escape. They would have to risk it.

"What do we do?" Viggo asked Ingrid.

"Follow me if you want to live. Now!" the stranger insisted in an urgent tone.

"We follow him," Ingrid said.

Lasgol and Egil nodded repeatedly.

"Come, quick! Don't let them see you!" he urged them eagerly.

Chapter 37

The strange masked man led them along the glacier wall until they reached a steep ramp that went up the wall, disappearing in the heights. It was as if a God had chiseled a ramp in the vertical wall of the glacier. On the right side was a tremendously high wall of blue ice and on the left a drop that was gaining in height with every step they took.

"We'll go up here. Cling to the wall. Careful with the floor, it's slippery," the stranger said as he went up, surefooted with long, slow strides.

"Really? We're going up here? To a glacier?" Viggo protested in disbelief.

"Tread very carefully," Ingrid warned them as she followed the stranger.

Viggo and Nilsa followed her. Gerd, Brenda, and Egil were in the middle, and Lasgol called upon his *Hawk's Sight* skill to try to glimpse where the steep ice ramp ended. He noticed he could see another glacier behind the one they were climbing. He looked back and saw Camu and Ona following him without any trouble—the slippery, cold terrain was no problem for those two. Right in front of him was Astrid, who did not seem to have any trouble either. He, on the other hand, had already slipped a couple of times and was treading with extreme care. He called upon his *Improved Agility* skill just in case. He did not feel at all safe on that frozen ramp.

Viggo took out his knives and proceeded to plunge them in the wall of ice with dull blows to have a better hold in case he slipped. The others advanced cautiously. Brenda has also slipped a couple of times and Gerd had grabbed her arm so she would not fall. They continued climbing, every step increasing the distance between their pursuers and the ground below. They were going slowly and their pursuers would not take long to appear. Once they turned the corner of the huge glacier, they would see them climbing. Defending themselves on that slippery, frozen ramp was going to be very complicated.

"Keep going up, don't stop," the stranger told them. He did not seem to be having any trouble moving along the slippery surface.

"Come on, let's move!" Ingrid cheered them, looking back, fearing that at any moment a Dweller would turn the corner of the glacier.

They kept going up and up the ramp, all too aware that the enemy was about to catch them. With extreme effort and care they reached the top of the glacier.

Viggo snorted and threw himself on the ground as soon as he got to the top.

"Wow, it's high!" Nilsa said, looking down from the edge.

Ingrid turned to help her comrades. Brenda managed to reach the top with Gerd's and Egil's help and Ingrid pulled her up the last couple of paces. The Witch collapsed from exhaustion and tension.

"I need... a moment... to recover," she told them.

Lasgol arrived last with Ona and Camu and Astrid gave him a hand to finish.

Lasgol thanked her and looked down. Their pursuers had not reached the corner of the glacier yet.

"Move away from the ice ramp," the stranger ordered.

The Panthers looked at Ingrid, who nodded.

The strange masked man moved his staff over his head and began to cast a spell. The Panthers reached for their weapons.

"Wait! Let him cast the spell!" Brenda cried from the ground.

"Are you sure?" Ingrid asked, unconvinced.

Astrid and Viggo had their knives ready and were standing in position ready to attack the sorcerer and cut his tongue out.

"Yes, let him conjure. It's not offensive magic, it's an illusion spell," Brenda assured them.

The stranger finished his spell and the ramp on the vertical wall of the glacier seemed to blend in with the wall itself, vanishing.

"Wow! I like that!" Viggo cried.

The pursuers arrived at the spot where they had started going up the ramp and found that the trail did not go on and there was no trace of the group. They looked in every direction, but since the ramp had vanished and the Rangers were nowhere to be seen, it looked as if the tundra had swallowed them. Totally nonplussed, the Wild Ones of the Ice and the Tundra Dwellers began to argue amongst themselves about which direction to take to continue the search

From above, lying on the top of the glacier, the group waited. Ingrid and Viggo watched without being seen while the others remained silent.

The Tundra Dwellers continued the chase following the glacier wall, moving fast. The Wild Ones of the Ice decided to turn back and continue the chase the other way. Soon they were all gone.

"Great trick!" Viggo said to the stranger.

"Thank you, I have a better one still," he replied and went over to the ice wall of the adjacent glacier which was a more intense blue. He began to move his staff and cast another spell.

Ingrid and the group looked at Brenda, who had closed her eyes as if she were picking up what kind of magic the stranger was using.

"There's no danger," she promised.

All of a sudden, a silver rune appeared on the glacier wall in front of the stranger. It flashed several times and a round door appeared below the rune. The door opened at a movement of the stranger's staff, revealing a huge hole in the ice wall.

"Let's go inside," the stranger told them and, without waiting for a reply, he went into the glacier.

Lasgol and Egil looked at one another in astonishment.

"This trick is also quite good," Viggo said humorously as he went over to inspect the opening.

"What do you think, Brenda?" Ingrid asked her.

"I pick up magic, but it doesn't seem dangerous."

"I don't think we should stay here," Nilsa said. "There's no way to go down or up," she said, scanning the wall of the glacier before them.

"The ramp has to be there, even if we don't see it," said Gerd.

"But if we go back down, we might encounter the Wild Ones or the Dwellers," Astrid replied.

"We'd better go in," said Egil. "Let's see what we find inside, and we'll also be hidden."

Lasgol agreed.

"Fine, we'll go in," Ingrid said, helping Brenda to her feet.

They went into the glacier and found an enormous cave of blue ice walls. At the far end the stranger was waiting for them. They all stepped in and then the stranger moved his staff. The door shut behind them without a sound. They all stiffened and reached for their weapons.

Ingrid aimed her bow at the stranger, as did Nilsa and Gerd.

"Take it easy. Lower your bows, I assure you they're not necessary."

"If you say so…" Viggo said, showing him his knives and staring into the stranger's eyes, clearly not trusting him.

"You're safe here," the stranger assured them.

"And who says so?" Ingrid asked, frowning and staring at the solitary figure at the far end of the ice cave.

"I see you don't recognize an old friend," the stranger said, removing the mask that covered his head and face. Before them an old man was revealed, with bluish skin and areas on his neck and arms that were crystal white as if snow had crystallized on his skin. The face was very human, with intelligent, deep-blue eyes. He wore his head shaved and on it could be seen a white tattoo, a strange rune that covered most of his head.

"Asrael!" Lasgol cried, astonished. "You're alive!"

"It can't be!" Egil said, also shocked.

"But didn't you die?" Viggo asked, raising an eyebrow.

"It seems I'm still alive," he smiled, opening his arms.

"But I saw Asuris hurl one of his ice daggers at you and hit you," Lasgol said, unable to believe the old Shaman chief was still alive.

"He hit me, yes, and he nearly killed me," he said, touching his right shoulder with his hand. "But I managed to survive."

"That's fantastic!" Egil cried as he stepped forward to hug him. "I also saw you fall. I thought you had left us to join the Ice Gods in their realm."

"Some old men like me are like the vegetation of the tundra: hard to kill."

"I'm so glad to see you alive!" Lasgol said, hugging him tight.

"I'm also happy to see you again," Asrael said with a big smile.

The rest of the group greeted Asrael with smiling faces. The old shaman hugged them all, pleased to see them again.

"This is Brenda, a Norghanian Snow Witch," Lasgol said, introducing her.

The Witch nodded briefly. "A pleasure," she said.

"This is Asrael, an Ice Shaman, Chief of the Arcanes of the Glaciers," Lasgol said.

"Not anymore, I'm afraid" he waved his arms.

"What happened?" Egil wanted to know.

"I've fallen into disgrace. After the great betrayal at the throne hall in Norghania, Asuris grabbed the power. He is in charge now over all the Peoples of the Frozen Continent."

Lasgol swallowed hard, hoping his face would not show the pain his soul felt at the simple mention of the ill-fated incident.

"I'm so glad you survived," he told Asrael.

"And I'm terribly sorry to have failed your mother…"

"Thank you, Asrael." Lasgol's eyes moistened.

Asrael nodded. "All the older leaders were a hindrance to Asuris. He leads the Arcanes of the Glaciers. Together with Jurn, leader of the Wild Ones of the Ice, and Sarn, leader of the Tundra Dwellers, they control the fate of the Frozen Continent and its peoples. I, and others like me who opposed them, have been forced to hide to avoid being killed. Hence my strange clothes and mask."

"I'm sorry…" Lasgol said.

"And I'm sorry more than anything else in all the years I've lived for your mother's death. I'm sorry from the deepest of my heart. She was an exceptional woman in every aspect. Hers was an irreparable loss that broke my heart," Asrael said, very moved. "I'm so sorry. My heart bleeds for her."

"Thank you, your words mean a lot to me," Lasgol said, feeling his eyes moisten and a sharp pain in his chest.

"What happened in the throne hall of Norghania's Royal Castle haunts my nightmares every night. It won't leave my exhausted mind. I never imagined Asuris' betrayal. I didn't see it coming, and neither did Azur the leader of the Arcanes, or your mother Mayra, our glorious leader Darthor… I can't forgive myself for having failed her. With her, under her leadership, we would have achieved peace and prosperity for our people. I failed her. I didn't protect her."

"It wasn't your fault, Asrael. You were always a loyal friend of my mother's and she really appreciated you," Lasgol said with a lump in his throat.

"Thank you. It doesn't assuage the pain because I know that in the end, I failed her."

"No one could've imagined the betrayal that took place," Egil said. "I lost my brother that evening and I never imagined that something like that might happen either. Nor did my brother. It wasn't your fault. Sometimes fate deals us bad cards."

"You can't stand up to the freezing northern winds. Sometimes you must seek shelter and wait for them to pass," Asrael said with a shrug and a resigned face.

"We witnessed the ritual," Lasgol said.

"Asuris is obsessed with conquering Norghana. He'll try anything, no matter how outrageous. He tried with the Frozen Specter and he's now trying with the Killer Storms."

"Was it him that sent the Frozen Specter?" Egil wanted to know.

Asrael nodded heavily. "He, with Hotz's help. That old hermit has been finding and digging out the secrets of the ice. Asuris uses the discoveries of that surly hermit to attack Norghana. He did it with the Specter and now he's doing it with the storms that are generated thanks to the great power of the Draconian."

"Draconian? What's this about the Draconian?" Viggo asked, making a face.

"They're creatures with magic power and are members of the Dragon family," Asrael explained

"You mean that this thing is the cousin of a bloody dragon?" Viggo said, waving his hands.

"It's a simplistic way of seeing it, but yes, it's distantly related to a dragon."

"But it didn't have wings," Gerd said.

"Not all Draconians have wings. They're reptilian, large in size mostly, with great Magic, Power and intelligence," Asrael explained. "Several have been found in the Frozen Continent along the years."

"Like Misha?" Lasgol asked.

"Yes, like her."

"How is she? I hope she's doing well." Lasgol remembered Asrael's familiar fondly.

"My dear companion is perfectly well. We had to move due to the circumstances... but she's all right."

"It seems we always meet in complicated situations," Egil said to Asrael with a big smile.

"Our paths seem fated to cross on the slippery ice of the present we're moving in," Asrael smiled.

"Slippery, and with abysses on both sides," said Lasgol.

"Camu, you've grown so much, aren't you going to greet an old friend?" Asrael said, opening his arms to the creature.

Camu was lying on the ground beside Ona with his eyes closed. He did not move. He did not even open his eyes to glance at Asrael.

Camu, it's Asrael, don't you remember him?

Camu opened his eyes and looked at Asrael. He got up and took a step toward the shaman. Then he stopped, lay down, and shut his eyes.

Very tired, he transmitted to Lasgol, and he fell asleep.

"Isn't he feeling well?" Asrael asked, noticing that something was not right with him.

"We don't know what's wrong with him. He's been exhausted since we landed here," Lasgol told him. We think he might have fallen ill during the journey, but we don't know how to diagnose what's the matter with him."

"Dear me... I'm so sorry."

"Perhaps you can help us," Egil said. "Our knowledge about Magical Creatures is practically nonexistent."

"Let me examine him and I'll be able to tell you something," Asrael said as he came over to Camu.

"He can't manage to use his Magic," Lasgol told him.

"That's weird. It's one thing if he's physically ill and that's why he's so tired, and a very different thing if he can't use his Magic. That's a lot more significant."

"What we've been able to ascertain are his physical and mental exhaustion and his inability to use Magic," Egil said.

"I see." Asrael crouched beside the creature and lay his hands on Camu's head and back. He closed his eyes and began to chant something unintelligible. A blue energy came out of Asrael's hands and entered Camu's body. Only Lasgol and Brenda were able to see it, since the others did not have the Gift.

"He's using some kind of Healing Magic," Brenda said.

Asrael examined Camu for a good while. At last he took his hands away from the creature's body.

"There really is something wrong with him, but it's not an illness."

"It isn't? What is it then?" Lasgol asked, sick with worry.

"I'm afraid it's something more complicated and for which I don't have the necessary knowledge."

"But if it isn't an illness then what's wrong with him?"

"I believe he's entered some stage of hibernation. His organism is shutting down. The first thing that goes out in beings with power is their magic, then the rest of the body. But something's not right. The process isn't going as it should, and Camu is shutting down completely."

"You mean he's dying?" Lasgol asked him, overwhelmed by concern and feeling anguish coming up his chest.

"If he continues like this, I'm afraid he could die."

"We must avoid that any way we can! What can we do? How do we help him?" Lasgol was beside him with worry.

"I don't have those answers."

"And who does?"

"Someone must know what to do with the magic creatures of this continent in these cases," Egil said.

"There aren't many who study the creatures or who have the necessary knowledge," said Asrael. "But, there is one person I believe might help you with Camu."

"Take us to this person, please," Lasgol said. "We have to help him."

"Very well. I'll take you. But I don't know whether you'll be welcome."

"Why? Because we're Norghanian?"

"Because of that and many other reasons which are none of my business," Asrael said. "I'll try to get you acceptance. I'll do what I can."

"Thank you so much, Asrael."

"Not at all, he's a wonderful creature. It's my duty to help him."

"Take us to this person before it's too late," Lasgol urged him.

"Follow me. We'll take a shortcut through the glaciers," Asrael said and waved his staff for them to follow him into the glacier.

They went with uncertainty in their hearts, desperately hoping to save Camu.

Chapter 38

Asrael led the group through enormous caverns that looked as if they had been carved out inside the colossal glacier they were in. The cold increased as the Shaman led them further in. Lasgol and Egil were carrying Camu between them.

Their friend seemed to be feeling worse and he could barely stay awake for even a few moments. Lasgol was really scared; he was afraid Camu would fall asleep and never wake up again. Just thinking about the possibility made his stomach lurch. Astrid walked beside them, helping them carry the body, making sure it did not touch the ground as she glanced at Lasgol encouragingly. Ona was beside her brother, moaning constantly, very troubled. She sensed something wrong with Camu and she was in a state of distress. The other Panthers were also worried. Gerd's face looked most grim.

They all followed Asrael silently, in a state of wonder from what they were seeing as they went further into this world of crystal ice, mixed with concern for Camu. He led them through natural tunnels; the glacier was an amazing beauty of blue ice walls which, depending on the area and how much light they got, shone with a glimmer of light hues. It was an underground world of frost and ice where everything shone with icy brightness.

Ingrid and Nilsa took over Lasgol and Egil in carrying Camu when they began to show signs of exhaustion. Asrael went on, crossing the beautiful icy world without a word. At a certain point, they seemed to cross into another glacier somewhat darker, where bluish walls became violet-hued ones.

Lasgol and Egil moved closer to Asrael. "Are we going to go through all the glaciers?"

"It's the safest route," the Shaman explained.

"This world is an infinite labyrinth, how can it be safer?" Gerd asked, looking around. "There are infinite passages, forks, crystal grottoes... you could get lost here at a moment's notice."

"And would freeze to death without finding the way out," Viggo added.

"Very true, my dear friends; luckily I know the glaciers well, and I can move through them without getting lost."

"Is this how you usually travel?" Egil asked him, curious.

"That's right. I've been doing so my whole life. Most of the Arcanes do it like this. The Wild Ones and the Dwellers prefer the surface; they don't like to feel enclosed by the ice. I find it comforting, and it also protects you from the storms outside."

"I thought the Wild Ones and the Dwellers lived underground, isn't it so?" Lasgol asked.

"They live underground in large communal caves," Asrael explained. "It's their way of protecting themselves from the low temperatures and the storms. But whenever they can they come up to the surface. They don't like enclosed spaces like this at all. And you'll rarely see a Semi-giant inside a glacier."

"That's curious," Egil said.

"We all find ourselves forced to seek refuge underground in this continent to shelter from the weather. But that doesn't mean everyone likes it. I'd say that only the Arcanes of the Glaciers do."

"And the Ice Creatures?" Lasgol asked.

"They, just like the Arcanes, prefer to shelter in caverns and glaciers. They don't usually go out to the surface. That's why they're such a mystery for many people."

"Fascinating," Egil said, delighted with the conversation and the knowledge he was acquiring.

Ona moved to the Arcane's side and he stroked her, smiling.

"This is a beautiful snow panther," Asrael commented. "What's her name?" He asked Lasgol.

"She's Ona, my familiar."

"Ona, don't worry, we'll save Camu," Asrael told her.

"We will, won't we?" Lasgol asked the Shaman, his throat tight with emotion.

"The paths of the ice are many. If you choose carefully, you will reach your goal," the Shaman replied with a mystical air. "We will," he added to ease Lasgol.

Ona chirped once.

They continued their way for several days without ever leaving the inside of the glaciers or underground passages that led to caverns that then led them through tunnels to other glaciers. It was like traveling through a world of ice. They could barely sleep, it was so cold and damp in this environment. Exhaustion began to set in among the group, mostly in Brenda, whom Gerd and Astrid were looking after.

At last, they came to a long tunnel. At the end they found a cavern. Asrael told the group they were getting closer.

"Thank goodness, because with this cold and dampness even my hair is freezing."

Gerd looked at Viggo with incredulity and choked in the middle of a guffaw.

Nilsa laughed so hard that for a moment they feared she would bring down one the stalactites from the cavern's ceiling.

Ingrid rolled her eyes and muttered curses under her breath about Viggo's mental capacity.

Egil and Lasgol looked at one another and chuckled.

"You're one of a kind," Astrid told Viggo as she slapped his back.

They arrived at a blue wall of pure ice at the end of the cavern.

"We can't go on this way, It's the end of the passage," Nilsa said.

Asrael used his staff and began to cast a spell under his breath with his eyes closed. Nilsa stepped back at once, glaring at the Shaman out of the corner of her eye. Then suddenly, a blue rune appeared on the wall, shining bright. A beam of bluish light issued from the rune and hit Asrael.

"Beware!" Lasgol warned him, but the Arcane went on casting his spell as if he had not heard the warning.

"It's Magic… I'd say not the harmful kind… it's a recognizer…" Brenda said to Lasgol.

The beam of blue light bathed Asrael completely. After a moment, a circle the size of two men appeared on the wall of ice. They stared at it intrigued. There was a sound like ice breaking. The circle of ice on the wall slid inwards.

"Wow… a door…" Gerd said, staring at the opening blankly.

"Only I have permission to enter," he told them. "I'll be back presently. Wait here."

"We'll wait for you," Lasgol told him.

For a long time, they waited for Asrael to come back. It was frigid in there. They all tried to keep warm by pacing around in circles and patting their sides and shoulders.

At last Asrael returned. He had not taken that long but the wait had seemed never-ending to them.

"Lasgol, Camu, you may come in. The rest will have to wait here."

"No way!" Astrid cried. "If he goes I go too."

"And so do we!" Ingrid said.

"I'm afraid it's not possible," Asrael told them. "The person we're going to see is very special and doesn't grant audiences to many people. Only these two will be received."

"And if we go anyway?" Viggo threatened.

"Then there'll be no audience and I'm afraid we won't be able to help Camu," Asrael said gently.

"Why doesn't this person want us to accompany Lasgol? For fear?" Ingrid asked.

"Wouldn't you be afraid if the situation were reversed?"

"Well, to be honest, yes…" she admitted.

Asrael waved his hand, implying it was natural to fear a group like theirs.

"You must let me go alone. It's the only way to help Camu," Lasgol pleaded, looking directly at Astrid.

"I can promise that nothing will happen to him," Asrael pledged.

"It's not that we don't trust you, but we don't like situations that aren't crystal clear," Nilsa said, "least of all those that come wrapped in magic."

"Totally understandable," Asrael agreed. "I swear on my life that nothing bad will happen to him."

"Well, it's your life," Astrid said, taking the oath seriously. "You'll die if anything happens to him."

"Astrid... Asrael's a friend—" Lasgol started to say.

"Whom we haven't seen in a long time," she cut in.

"Unfortunately, loyalties tend to change. We've suffered that in our own flesh," Ingrid said.

"I find it fair," Asrael said. "Lasgol's life and mine are linked as of this moment. If anything happens to him, let it happen to me as well."

"Very well, then everything's tied up." Viggo said. "Now go, have done with this audience or whatever fast, we're freezing."

"I can help with the waiting," Brenda said and took out one of her bowls with runes. She began to cast a spell and poured two different liquids, putting several strange leaves she took out of her traveling bag into it. A moment later an intense fire started in the bowl. An unnatural flame over three feet tall seemed to burn the air of the cave.

Gerd gasped in surprise.

"It will hold for a while and will warm us well," the Snow Witch said as she stretched her arms, her palms up seeking the warmth. I call it a purifying flame. It's used for purification spells but I think it will be good to warm up a little."

"Oh yeah, I like this flame of yours," Viggo winked at her.

"I can imagine. You have a lot to purify," Brenda replied with a half-smile full of irony.

"That's very true," Ingrid laughed.

They all huddled close to the flame to get warm amid smiles and laughter.

Camu, you're coming with us.

Okay, he transmitted back, along with a feeling of great weakness.

Can you walk a little? It's not very far.

I can, Camu assured.

Lasgol sighed; he hoped he could but he had his doubts.

Ona, you stay here.

The good panther chirped twice, unhappy.

Sorry, Ona, but you have to stay. We'll be back soon.

Ona did not agree and chirped twice again.

It's for Camu, so he gets well. Do it for him.

Ona looked at her brother, who was so weak, and gave a long moan.

Thank you, beautiful. You're the best, Lasgol said, stroking her head.

Asrael, Lasgol, and Camu went into the tunnel behind the ice wall. The passage walls were blue ice. They walked a while longer, taking several forks. Lasgol was alert to Camu, who seemed weaker by the moment. It was cold, and although this did not affect Camu, it did affect him. Asrael did not seem very affected either.

They finally came out into a giant cavern. It was rectangular with bluish-white walls of ice. From the ceiling hung blue stalactites of pure ice. The floor of the cavern was not rock; it looked like a blue-white frozen lake, very smooth. In the middle of this lake waited a solitary figure sitting in what looked like a throne made of ice.

"Who is it?" Lasgol asked Asrael.

"One of the most powerful beings of this continent."

Lasgol shivered.

"I hope it'll be willing to help us."

"Come, we're expected," Asrael said as he kept walking.

They walked on the lake to the figure. Asrael knelt before the frozen throne. Lasgol did the same and gazed at the person they had come to see. Right away Lasgol realized this was no person but the being he had seen in one of the visions of his mother's pendant. Her skin was bluish, like the peoples of the Frozen Continent. She was tall and slim and looked human and fragile. Her face was covered in white dots, like frozen droplets on her blue skin. She had no eyelashes, and her eyes were huge and completely round. The irises were silver and shone with an intense brightness. It gave the impression that instead of eyes she had two diamonds, shining brightly. The timeless beauty of this amazing, singular, crystal face captivated Lasgol.

She had serrated crests of icy white on her head, arms, and legs that came down her whole body in several strings. She was dressed in polar bear skins. In one hand she carried a staff of blue ice on whose tip shone a large white sphere. Lasgol was aware of the power this being possessed. Her Gift was so powerful it made Lasgol shiver simply from being in her presence. He also felt something else. Not only the hall but the body of this singular woman radiated cold. It was as if her mere presence made the temperature go down.

"Thank you for seeing us, my lady," Asrael greeted her respectfully.

"The Shaman of the Ice is a friend and is always welcome in my realm," she said in an icy voice.

"It's an honor to count on your friendship, my Lady of the Glaciers," Asrael replied, honored.

"Call me Izotza, we've known one another for a long time," she said with a smile.

"My lady Izotza, this is Lasgol Eklund, who has asked to see you and is the reason for disturbing you today."

"You never disturb me, Asrael. May I see your face, young Norghanian? Your eyes tell me much, but I wish to see your face," Izotza said.

Lasgol pushed back his hood and removed the Ranger's scarf so Izotza could see him properly.

"A face and eyes I recognize indeed," she said. "You are Mayra's son."

"I am, Ma'am," he replied, noticing that she was scrutinizing him thoroughly.

"Asrael had told me already. I have granted this meeting, even though I no longer grant audience to anyone, because you are Mayra's son, a great woman I respected."

"She was a great woman," Lasgol said.

"There are not many people I esteem. Take it as a compliment to your mother."

Lasgol bowed his head respectfully.

"Please, rise," Izotza told them. "I do not like to see people kneeling before anyone."

Thank you, my lady," Asrael said, and they both rose.

"You are welcome to my home," she said, and although her looks and voice were icy, Lasgol felt she meant it with certain warmth.

"I thought that, being who he is, you'd want to see him," Asrael said, looking at Lasgol.

"And you were right, as usual. Mayra tried to help my people, and whoever helps us has my favor. I watch over the wellbeing of all who live in the glaciers. This is my goal and vocation."

"She was betrayed by those same people." Lasgol replied, unable to hold back his resentment.

"Well... I see the young Norghanian has fire in his veins like his mother. I like that. Do you also have the Gift and the power she had?"

"I... I have the Gift, yes... but it's not as powerful as my mother's."

"Is it not? Curious.... from one generation to the next the power of the inherited Gift does not usually decrease, and your mother was very powerful."

"The truth is... that well... it seems that... I have trouble accessing my power... so I really don't know how much power I have. And what I can use isn't much."

"Interesting," Izotza said, staring at Lasgol intensely. "This is a conversation we should have another time, when there is more trust between us."

"I'd like that... that there would be more trust... and of course, to continue this conversation."

Izotza nodded and closed and opened her large eyes, which shone as if they were real diamonds.

"It is only fair that your mother's death should generate these feelings against my people in your heart. Let me tell you that it was not my people who betrayed her but some traitors to my people who I hate just as you do."

Lasgol was surprised to hear her say that. That the Lady of the Glaciers was against the present leaders of the Peoples of the Frozen Continent sounded shocking to him.

"Our Lady is the guardian of the Peoples of the Frozen Continent and of the creatures of the Glaciers. She looks after them and protects them," Asrael said respectfully.

"I have always tried to protect them, since long ago when really powerful creatures ruled the glaciers."

"If she tries to protect them…" Lasgol said and looked at Asrael and then at Izotza. "Couldn't the Lady use her great power to finish the traitors? They represent a danger not only for the Norghanians but for the whole Frozen Continent."

Izotza smiled and the specks of crystal on her face shone like tiny diamonds.

"I see you are brave and determined, like your father."

"I'm not sure I'm that much like him…"

"Although I would like to make them pay for their betrayal—and believe me when I say I would like that very much—I cannot use my power directly against them," Izotza admitted. "Unfortunately, I cannot leave this cave, my realm. My power is great still, but I cannot leave this glacier. This is the place I created to stay alive," she said, pointing at the floor, the ceiling, and the walls. "And now, it has become my eternal prison. I have lived a very long life, too long. Here I can go on existing. If I should leave my realm and go outside, I would turn into drops of ice that the icy wind of the north would drag away. Time does not forgive, not even the most powerful of beings. It is always your enemy, remember that."

"Oh… I see… I'll remember."

"You might be powerful today, but tomorrow… tomorrow you may not be so much. And one day you will stop being powerful and death will catch you since he comes after us all, even if we hide inside a glacier to try and freeze the passing of time."

"Wise words," Asrael said.

"Are you here because of them? The traitors?" Izotza asked Lasgol.

"We came here to stop the attack on Norghania. I did not know the traitors were also involved."

"They are. Asuris is now the leader of my beloved people; a terrible leader with a sadistic obsession to conquer Norghana and destroy all the Norghanians, an obsession that will lead our people down a frozen gorge toward a freezing death."

"We'll stop the attacks," Lasgol said. "We managed to destroy the

Frozen Specter, and we'll destroy Hotz's storms."

"That old erudite… I do not know what has happened to him. Before he was only interested in the secrets the Ice held, the power the Ice hides. I never thought he would join Asuris… I thought he would have more common sense."

"Asuris gives him what he needs for his studies. Besides, Asuris supports him in his way of understanding how to defeat the enemy, Norghanian or of any other region of Tremia," Asrael explained.

"Those two are a bad combination," Izotza said ruefully.

"And they also count on the support of Sarn and Jurn," Asrael added.

"I know they are looking for you to kill you. You must be careful," Izotza told Asrael.

"I am, don't worry, my lady. I can still defend myself."

"Camu…" Lasgol started to say, seeing that his friend had lain down and was breathing heavily as if every breath was an effort.

"This creature is the reason for your visit, is it not?" Izotza guessed.

"It is. He's not well and we fear for his life," Asrael said with a worried look on his face.

"He's… dying… and we don't know what to do," Lasgol said anxiously.

"I recognize this creature. It's the one I granted to your mother, at her request, so she could give him to you."

"Yes, he's the one."

"It's a very special creature, magic, of the glaciers. There are not many like him. Do you know why your mother gave him to you?" Izotza asked, staring at him with her large round eyes.

"Because my mother wanted to protect me…"

"Exactly. This creature is your guardian," Izotza said, pointing at Camu.

"Guardian? I don't understand…." Lasgol looked at poor Camu and found it impossible to see him as his guardian.

"This creature will keep you from harm. He's extremely powerful," the Lady of the Glaciers explained.

"Camu?" Lasgol watched him lying on the floor, weakened, dying, and could not agree with Izotza's words. Not even when he was healthy had he had that feeling, rather the contrary. Lasgol had always felt like an older brother to Camu, whom he had to look after, not the other way around. He shook his head in confusion.

"I see you're finding it hard to believe. Do not worry, it is not the time. One day you will see and understand everything. But let me assure you that this is one of the most powerful creatures to have ever existed on Tremia."

"No… I… we must help him," Lasgol muttered.

"I feel he is having trouble. Let me examine him," Izotza asked.

Lasgol stepped back at once.

Izotza rose from her throne of ice and came over to Camu gracefully. She walked past Lasgol and seeing her so closely he realized that her timeless face seemed frozen in time. As if her face were not real but one frozen a long time ago which she still used. As she walked, an icy white mist froze everything at her passing. Asrael signaled to Lasgol to move back and not let her touch him.

Izotza knelt beside Camu and left her staff on the floor. She lay her hands on Camu's head and heart and closed her eyes. From Izotza's lips an icy breath came out which enveloped Camu's whole body. The hands of the Lady of the Glaciers began to shine with thousands of tiny flashes.

Lasgol and Asrael watched in fascination. They did not know what Izotza's powerful Magic was doing, but it was hypnotizing to watch.

The flashes went from Izotza's hands to Camu's body like thousands of tiny diamonds that ran along his skin from his crested head to the tip of his long crested tail. The flashes looked alive and moved along his body as if they had a life of their own.

Izotza opened her eyes, said something unintelligible in an archaic language, and the vapor that enveloped Camu turned blue. She let the Magic act on Camu for a long while. Finally, with a word of power, the vapor vanished, and with it the thousands of tiny flashes that covered Camu's body. Izotza stood up.

"How is he? Have you healed him?" Lasgol asked, eagerly hoping she had performed the miracle of restoring him to his usual self.

Izotza heaved a deep sigh.

"I cannot heal him because he really is not ill."

"But then, what's the matter with him?"

"He is about to hibernate."

"Hibernate? How?" Lasgol asked blankly.

"This is a creature that needs to hibernate at certain times."

"We didn't know that… then he's all right?"

Izotza shook her head.

"I am afraid he is not. The hibernation is not going as it should."

"Isn't it? Why? What's the matter?"

"This creature has a birth defect. His organism is faulty, so he cannot hibernate as he should. And if he does not hibernate, he will die since he will be unable to develop."

"He'll die? Oh no! What can we do?" Lasgol was desperate.

"We will help him hibernate as he should."

"But how?"

"I have made him stable and also slowed down the hibernation process so that you have time to reach the Serenity Valley. That is a place where many Creatures of the Ice—the Magical Creatures of this continent—hibernate. It is a special place because of the conditions of temperature and magic, favorable for the hibernation of these wonderful beings. Take him there. If you manage to get there in time, he will be saved."

"Then we'll go right away!" Lasgol cried.

"I will be their guide," Asrael told Izotza.

"Go now," she warned them.

"Let's go, now!" Lasgol said urgently.

"Once you have saved the creature, come back to see me. I will help you with something else. For your mother and for my people," Izotza said to Lasgol in a mysterious tone.

Lasgol nodded, "I will come back as soon as we have saved Camu."

"Go, now, Lasgol. Hurry and save him," she said.

Chapter 39

They left the Cavern of the Lady of the Glaciers and went back to their comrades who were waiting for them intrigued, and, thanks to Brenda and her purifying flame, not as frozen by the cold inside the glacier.

"We must get going!" Lasgol told them as they arrived at a run, with Camu a few steps behind.

"What's the matter?" Astrid asked him, concerned with his urgent tone.

"We have to take Camu to the Serenity Valley as soon as possible or he'll die," Lasgol explained.

"Where?" Viggo asked, raising his eyebrows.

"Right away?" Gerd asked blankly.

"I'll explain more on the way, but we must leave now. His time is limited."

"Let's go then," Astrid said, recognizing in Lasgol the seriousness of the matter.

Ingrid nodded, realizing this was a matter of life or death.

"Follow me this way," Asrael said, leading the way.

The group went after him as he led them though the glacier into another adjacent one and deep into the ice core.

How are you doing? Lasgol asked Camu.

Very tired but better.

Will you be able to keep up?

Izotza magic good. Help.

I'm so glad. I hope it will help you get where we're going.

Yes, I get there, Camu assured him. Of all the times Lasgol had been sure Camu was exaggerating, this one was without a doubt the clearest. He was putting on a brave face, as usual, but Lasgol seriously doubted he could make it.

As Asrael led them through ice passages and frozen caverns, Lasgol told them what had gone on and what the Lady of the Glaciers had explained to them.

"This doesn't bode well, poor Camu," Gerd said, shaking his head with moist eyes.

"The bug isn't exactly a charmer, but I don't want anything bad to happen to it," Viggo said. "We have to save him."

"Yes, we must," Nilsa said, watching Camu walk a little behind.

"Of course we're going to save him!" Ingrid replied. "We never let anything bad happen to one of ours."

Ona moaned sadly.

Astrid stroked her head as she walked beside her.

"He'll be all right, you'll see. Don't you worry," she said to the good panther.

Egil was also watching Camu as he walked and stroked his head.

"Nothing's going to happen to you. We won't allow it. We'll take care of you and you'll come out of this strong and healthy and better than ever," Egil said confidently.

All you very good. I happy, he transmitted to Lasgol, along with a feeling of gratitude and happiness to be with his friends.

"Camu wants to thank you all for your good wishes," Lasgol told the others.

They reached the end of the glacier they were crossing and Asrael stopped before going out to the tundra.

"What is it?" Lasgol asked him.

"There are several tribes in this part of the continent. We must be wary so they don't discover us."

"I'll take charge of our trail," Lasgol said. "I'll erase it so they can't find it and follow us."

"But even so, they can see us in the distance," Ingrid said with a look of disgust.

"If we all stay close together, I can deal with that," said Asrael.

"Can you really?" Egil asked, interest piqued.

Asrael nodded. He stepped out on the snow outside the glacier and made a sign for them to crowd around him. The Panthers surrounded the Shaman of the Ice.

"Get down, please," he told them.

He began to cast a spell with his staff. There was a blue flash. He circled the staff over the heads of the group as they remained at a crouch with Ona and Camu lying low. All of a sudden, the ice and snow on the floor started to rise as if floating around them. The old Shaman used more of his magic to create a thick blizzard of ice and snow that surrounded them.

"This is fantastic," Egil commented, thrilled. He was looking around and reaching to touch the blizzard that swirled around them.

"He's creating a small snow storm to cover us," Lasgol said.

"That's right. Let's go. I'll keep it up as long as I can. In the distance it will look like a regular winter blizzard in motion," Asrael told them. "Something common here—it won't raise suspicions."

The trick worked well, even better than the Panthers might have imagined. During their journey they crossed with several groups of Wild Ones of the Ice and Tundra Dwellers, and even a group of Arcanes of the Glaciers. Luckily, and thanks to keeping a safe distance and the fact that they were all dressed in snow-white, they were not discovered inside the blizzard.

They reached a new glacier, far north. This one had extremely tall walls of ice so transparent it shone like crystal. Asrael led them to the western side. Halfway there he stopped. There was a gigantic entrance that looked like the mouth of a terrible creature with enormous crystal teeth.

"We have to go through here," Asrael told them. "Out of precaution, only I and Lasgol, with Camu, will go on from here."

"We're separating again?" Astrid protested, not liking the idea at all.

"This cave is the entrance to a realm where only Creatures of the Ice have permission to enter. Humans are not welcome."

"The more reason to go with you," Ingrid, who had been expecting this, said.

"Nobody tells me which cave I can go into or not," Viggo said, puffing his chest and wrinkling his nose.

All of a sudden the ground started to shake. They all looked at one another, trying not to fall from the quaking under their feet.

"What's the matter?" Lasgol asked Asrael.

The Shaman looked into the cave.

"Move back!" he shouted and ran to get out of the way.

They all did the same and cleared the entrance of the great cave.

A huge horn emerged out of the cave. It was followed by a creature that struck them all dumb. It was colossal, over fifteen feet tall and thirty feet long. It moved on four strong, stubby legs. With a short neck and long tail, it had a huge reptilian body. It looked heavy and robust at the same time. The head was enormous, somewhat rectangular with the great horn above its nose. The whole creature was covered in brown and white scales, which gave it a strange appearance. It looked strong and the horn looked like a dangerous weapon, particularly considering the size of its owner.

They all watched it come out and flattened themselves against the wall to avoid being seen and trampled. The creature did not pay any attention to them, so they did not know whether it even saw them. It went off, treading hard and making the earth shudder under its feet.

"Well... perhaps I spoke hastily..." Viggo said with a horrified face.

"The Creatures of the Ice are powerful," Asrael said.

"And how will you go in if access to humans is forbidden?" Ingrid asked.

Asrael smiled. "I've asked for help. It will soon be here."

The group waited at the entrance of the cave for the arrival of the help Asrael had promised. Viggo glanced into the cave several times, but he did not dare set a foot inside, just in case.

Lasgol sat beside Camu to make sure he was doing fine. Astrid sat down beside them and stroked and patted them both. Concern was clearly visible in her face.

Help did not take long in appearing, and it surprised everyone.

A colossal creature that looked like a white dragon without wings out of a Norghanian mythological tale appeared, coming toward them with powerful strides. The shape of its body and head, which were covered with crystal scales, looked like a dragon's. It moved on four sturdy legs that ended in strong, whitish claws. The head was that of a gigantic reptile, with large reptilian, golden eyes. A high crystal crest started on the top of the head and went down the neck and back to the tip of the tail. It was so white and crystalline that it seemed to be made of pure ice. The same was true of the scales. It shook its long tail and opened its mouth to show two rows of huge teeth. It was a creature as majestic and enormous as it was unbelievable.

And it was no other than Misha, the Creature of Ice, Asrael's familiar.

"Misha, thank you for answering my call," Asrael said.

Misha lowered her head and raised it again in greeting.

I always come to the call of a good friend, she projected her thought.

Lasgol remembered that the Creatures of the Ice could not speak but were capable of projecting their thoughts to someone with the Gift, so that Asrael, Brenda, Camu, and himself were able to hear her.

310

The rest could not.

"The Creature of the Ice speaks in my mind, it's amazing," Brenda said, surprised and delighted.

It is the way we have to communicate with humans, Misha projected to her.

Lasgol realized that, although it was not the same Magic he used for his *Animal Communication* skill, it did work similarly.

"Thank you for coming," Asrael repeated.

"We're very happy to see you," Lasgol said, and the rest of the group joined in greeting the impressive creature. Misha greeted them one by one, lifting and bowing her head.

"I'm glad to see you again and that you are well," Egil told her.

The great creature nodded at him.

Then she saw Camu, and she must have noticed something was not right because she gave a sort of long moan.

Camu, my little creature, what is the matter with you? Misha asked, concerned.

She came to Camu and licked his head and whole body with a long blue tongue, just as she had done on their first meeting. Lasgol once again had the feeling they were like a mother and her pup. Asrael had told him that, although they were both Creatures of the Ice, they really belonged to two different species.

He's very weak, Lasgol transmitted.

I asked you to look after the creature well, human, Misha said, unmistakably reproachful.

I've done the best I could.

He is a very special creature.

He is, Lasgol nodded.

Misha let out a freezing breath from her mouth and surrounded Camu with it.

"She seems to be treating him," Lasgol said to Asrael.

"She's trying to help him, like Izotza did," the Shaman of the Ice replied.

Misha good, help, Camu transmitted to Lasgol, along with a happy feeling at seeing the great creature.

She'll help you, she's good, Lasgol assured him.

Of course I will help a poor Creature of the Ice in need, human. I always have and always will.

Thank you for helping him, Lasgol said, overwhelmed with gratitude.

Misha looked at him and nodded.

It is my duty. I am a Matriarch, I look after all the Creatures of the Ice.

"Izotza told us we need to take him to the Serenity Valley," Asrael told Misha. "Can you help us?"

The Lady of the Glaciers is wise and intelligent. Yes, that is where we must take the little creature.

Let's go then, Lasgol urged.

Misha picked up Camu in her mouth carefully and delicately put him on her colossal scaled back. Camu used his paws to cling to her. Ona wanted to go with him, but Misha was so tall that she looked at her pleadingly.

Misha understood what the panther wanted but shook her head.

The panther cannot come with us, human, she told Lasgol.

You can't come, Ona, Lasgol transmitted to her.

Ona moaned.

I okay, not worry, Ona, Camu assured her.

Misha moved her tail and pointed at the entrance to the cave.

"Let's go," Asrael told Lasgol.

"Will we be allowed in?" he asked.

"Misha is a Matriarch of the Creatures of the ice," Asrael explained. Lasgol remembered that indeed Asrael had introduced her as such to the group when they had first met, but he had never known what the title meant. "She protects the Creatures of the Ice and is respected by them," Asrael went on. "Her decisions are accepted, if she allows us in, the other creatures will respect that."

"Well, then, let's get going." Lasgol replied.

"Be careful," Ingrid told them.

"If you need us let us know," Astrid said, looking worried at Lasgol.

"We'll be fine," he said confidently.

They went into the great cavern, leaving behind their comrades, who watched them disappear into the blackness of the cave with great concern.

Chapter 40

Lasgol and Asrael walked beside the immense presence of Misha, who turned her head every few steps to see how Camu was doing on her back. As they went into the giant glacier, Lasgol began to feel that this place was not like the other glaciers and ice caves they had been through. All the hair at the back of his neck was standing on end, and it was not because of Misha, but because of the place they were entering.

The first caverns they went through were dark and gave the impression they were heading to a hostile and inhospitable place. But then, suddenly, in the midst of that freezing darkness they saw two reptilian golden eyes on one of the walls. Misha stopped and so did Lasgol and Asrael, waiting to see what would happen next.

The eyes that were staring right at them shone with silver flashes. The flashes were followed by a hiss so loud it made Lasgol and Asrael cover their ears. Another colossal creature, like a giant snake and completely white, revealed itself. It must have been over sixty feet long and three feet wide. It looked archaic, as if it did not belong to this time but to one long past, about a thousand years past. The body of this being was partly round and partly square. The head was square and long. It rose about a third of its full length and glared at them with those threatening eyes. It opened its enormous mouth and instead of two giant fangs there were two rows of sharp, large teeth.

"It's a warning," Asrael explained to Lasgol, trying to keep him from entering a state of utter panic.

Lasgol observed the creature, which looked like something out of a horrible nightmare.

"Let's hope so…" he replied.

Who dares approach the Serenity Valley in search of entry? The snake projected into their minds. Its voice sounded deep and hissing.

Misha stretched her neck and straightened. She opened her mouth and gave out a deafening roar which hit the walls of the cave, making it echo with even more strength. Then, in a show of power, she let out of her mouth a breath of freezing air which she kept projecting before her like an enormous jet of liquid ice. She did not direct it at the white snake but to her right, as if she were responding to the warning by showing her power and who she was.

Misha, Matriarch of the Creatures of the Ice, is here, she projected.

I recognize Matriarch Misha. Does she seek entrance? The giant polar reptile asked.

I seek entrance with the right that is mine,
Does the Matriarch vouch for the humans that accompany her?

She does, Misha projected with great confidence.

Lasgol was watching the exchange nonplussed. Both powerful and ancestral Creatures of the Ice were exchanging mental messages. It was incredible, not only because such majestic and impressive beings existed, but because they were beings with intellect—rational, intelligent creatures, which was something absolutely marvelous and amazing, at least for Lasgol. Probably not for all "humans," as the Creatures referred to them.

The eyes of the giant snake seemed to blink and flashed again with a silver gleam. Misha replied by flashing silver in turn and partially illuminating the dark cavern.

Entrance is granted to the Matriarch Misha and her companions. The snake withdrew and vanished in the dark.

"It's a guard. It's letting us through," Asrael whispered to Lasgol,

"A terrifying, wonderful creature," Lasgol replied in another whisper as he shook off a shiver.

Asrael nodded. "There are creatures in this place that defy our comprehension," the ancient Shaman warned him.

"I'll try to keep an open mind," Lasgol said with a light grin.

Misha urged them to keep moving and led them through another series of caverns to one at the end where they could already glimpse light coming in. Lasgol felt his spirits rising—this must be the place they were heading for.

They were nearing an exit when suddenly a creature as chilling as the snake appeared before them, preventing their entrance to the valley beyond the cavern. Lasgol looked at it in wonder and horror. He stood before some kind of giant tarantula. Only it was a lot hairier and all white. A dozen round yellow eyes seemed to be studying them. Lasgol felt like a dwarf beside the colossal spider, whose legs must have been over fifteen feet tall as well as the body.

Halt! Entrance to the Serenity Valley is forbidden, it projected with such power that Lasgol felt a hard mental blow. He put his hand to his forehead.

"It's another guard," Asrael whispered again.

Misha stepped up and, as she had done before, introduced herself, letting the guard see the extent of her power and who she was.

We have been granted access. I am Misha, the Matriarch of the Creatures of the Ice.

At once the colossal snow-white tarantula gave a tremendous leap and climbed up the wall to their right.

The Matriarch and her guests may come in. Welcome, it projected to them from the wall.

"These guards are terrifying, and the fact that they can communicate and have an intellect is absolutely awesome," Lasgol commented to Asrael, and he knew he would have nightmares in which these two guards would appear chasing after him to eat him. For some reason he knew he would not be able to fool them.

"As you can see, we needed Misha's help. They don't like humans. They can smell us from a league away."

"Yeah, I can see that, and the Creatures of the Ice?"

"They are allowed in. Here they can always rest in peace whenever they want. It's a place to recover," Asrael explained. "Just like as they can smell us, they can recognize creatures like them."

"That have Magic you mean?"

"That's right."

"Then that snake and tarantula have Magic?"

"Indeed, here there are only Creatures with Power."

"Phew… I don't even want to imagine what kind of Magic they have or how they use it."

Asrael smiled lightly. "Not pretty, indeed."

The Power of the Creatures of the Ice is diverse, ancient and fearsome, Misha projected to them.

I have no doubt, Lasgol said, not wanting to imagine what they might do.

Misha entered the valley.

We are here, she announced and looked at Camu with hopeful eyes.

It was a giant valley, covered in ice and frost which seemed to run through the whole glacier from one end to the other. It was vast, and to Lasgol's surprise it let in a lot of light, since the whole upper part of the glacier consisted of transparent crystal ice. It looked as if the whole valley had been frozen inside what, with the passing of time, would become a glacier.

"Welcome to the Serenity Valley," Asrael said to Lasgol.

The first thing Lasgol felt was all the hair on his body standing on end, caused by a wave of strong magic that bathed him from head to toe. This was a special place where Magic was intense and powerful.

"It's as if… the valley had been frozen inside a giant die of ice walls," he said, noting how strange this place was.

"That's right. The valley froze thousands of years ago with several wondrous creatures inside. With the passing of time and the terrible temperature of this part of the world, a gigantic glacier was formed, which swallowed the valley. Now it looks like a world within four great walls of ice."

Lasgol realized it was so. The floor, the ceiling, and the walls were of ice. A cool breeze caressed his face, and Lasgol wondered where it might come from. There was life here so the air moved around. It most likely came in through the caverns. Lasgol saw many at different heights—some high, over a hundred and twenty feet tall.

Out of one flew a creature that was a mix between a reptile and a great white bird. Lasgol glimpsed the colossal beak and noticed it had teeth, which left him stunned. The snowy wings of the creature were strange, similar to those of a giant bat.

"There really seem to be some remarkable creatures in here," Lasgol said, nodding.

"Don't be afraid, within the valley we're safe," Asrael assured him.

This is a place of rest, meditation and tranquility. No one will disturb you, Misha projected.

She led the way. Lasgol was worried about how quiet Camu was. He had not said anything since the beginning of the journey and this meant he was very low on energy. Lasgol could see that Camu's eyes were open and he was looking around from the back of the majestic, beautiful Misha.

They passed by a cave, and there appeared the head and half the body of an enormous reptile. The scales were white and it barely had a neck, but the head was long. The body was long and heavy—it barely lifted off the floor on four short legs. They could see the tail inside the cavern. It opened its mouth and Lasgol saw rows of large teeth. It almost looked like a giant albino crocodile.

Misha gave what sounded like a greeting in the form of a deafening roar, and the great reptile bowed its head respectfully to the Matriarch.

A little further ahead they passed another cave, and as if the creature inside could feel it was Misha passing by, it came out to greet her. The Matriarch roared loud and a reptilian head, equally enormous, appeared in the shadows. It bowed its head and backed up into its cave. This time Lasgol could only glimpse a pair of huge reptile eyes.

"What are they doing in those caves? Do they live in there?" Lasgol asked in awe of the strange creatures he was seeing.

"No, they don't live in them. This is a place for withdrawal, to regenerate. It's temporary."

As they went on, Lasgol saw a creature that resembled the ancestor of an Ogre of the Snow. It looked even more terrifying and was a lot bigger than the Ogres he knew. He did not want to imagine the kind of Power that creature might have. He also saw what looked like a giant woolly elephant, totally white and with two long, curved silver tusks. He knew at once that its power would have to do with its incredible tusks.

Then all of a sudden Lasgol glimpsed something he recognized. In the middle of the great valley, upon a small hill of ice and rock, stood a White Pearl. It was identical to the one in the Shelter above the Lair. The only difference was that this Pearl was about ten times bigger than the one at the Shelter.

"That White Pearl…" Lasgol started to say.

"Yes?" Asrael said.

"There's one just like it in Norghana,"

"That object is one of great power," the Shaman said. "There are several of different sizes scattered all over Tremia."

"Are there?" Lasgol was taken aback.

"So I understand, although I have only seen two in my whole life."

"I thought our Pearl was unique…"

"Life is full of surprises and mysteries," Asrael smiled.

"And that power it emanates… do you know what it is? Or what it's for?"

Asrael shrugged. "It's an enigma for me. The only thing I can tell you is that the creatures here worship it."

It is a very powerful object. Only certain powerful creatures can use it, Misha projected to them.

"Can you?"

Misha let out a sound that sounded like a guffaw.

No, human, not even I can use it.

Wow…

Keep moving, we are close.

They went on. Lasgol found this world fascinating. He was sorry Egil could not be there with them to experience it. He would have to tell him all about it afterwards and Egil would ask for thousands of details which Lasgol was now memorizing. Finally, after covering half of that amazing valley frozen in time, Misha stopped before a cavern and roared as if calling out the creature that occupied it.

The creature that came out of the cave left Lasgol frozen to the spot.

It was the spitting image of Camu but of a gigantic size!

It came out walking on its four strong legs and its enormous bulging eyes checked him from head to toe. They were reptilian yellow eyes with blue irises like slits. The enormous head, flat and oval, was crowned by a rectangular crest. Two others went down the back and ran all along the tail. The whole body was covered in blue scales specked with silver which looked like an impenetrable steel armor. It did not have claws on its paws, but some sort of wide rounded fingers or toes. Camu's famous everlasting smile was also present in this unbelievable majestic creature, only slightly less ostensible.

Lasgol noted the colossal size of this being and how powerful it looked. It must have been over a hundred and eighty feet long by forty-five feet wide. It was as gigantic as it was majestic.

Lasgol's jaw dropped as he tried to take in the incredibly powerful creature.

Family… Camu transmitted to Lasgol, who was still numb from the impression.

I recognize Misha, the Matriarch of the Creatures of the Ice. I welcome her and greet her with respect, the enormous creature projected, and its power was so great that both Lasgol and Asrael put their heads in their hands. The mental blow of the splendid creature's thought almost flattened them both.

I recognize Drokose, Great Leader of the Higher Drakonians, Misha replied with great respect.

"This is Drokose Ilargigorri, at a time Azur's familiar—the past leader of the Arcanes of the Ice. When our leader died, betrayed by Asuris, Drokose decided to retire to the Serenity Valley to rest and recover to be able to continue with his extended existence," Asrael explained to Lasgol, who was beginning to react.

"He's... he's like Camu..." he muttered, still shocked by what all this meant and how unexpected it was.

"He is. Remember, you asked me whether I knew what kind of creature Camu was and I said no, but that he reminded me of Azur's familiar... whom I had only glimpsed once and at a distance..." Asrael apologized.

"I remember, and now I understand why."

This little creature you carry on your back is one of mine, Drokose recognized, and his projection was filled with surprise. It almost flattened Lasgol and Asrael with its power.

He is. I have brought him to you for help, as leader of your own.

Little one, what is your name? Drokose asked.

I Camu.

I am Drokose, a leader of your species.

We family?

That is right, little one, we are family.

You dragon? We dragons? Camu asked, very excited.

Drokose laughed with deep heartfelt guffaws.

No, we are not dragons,

Oh... I want... Camu was disappointed.

Lasgol felt sorry for poor Camu, who was convinced he was a dragon—or rather wanted to be one.

Drokose laughed again, and his guffaws were like hurricanes coming out of his mouth. Lasgol had to hold Asrael up as he stumbled.

And why would you want to be a small dragon, little one, when you are much more powerful than any of them?

Lasgol was puzzled. More powerful than a dragon? Was he being serious? Was there a more dangerous creature than a dragon? Of course, Camu did not seem to be that.

I more powerful than dragon? Camu asked, unable to keep his eyes open.

You are, little one. You always will be.

Oh... fantastic... Camu's eyes shone with excitement, but a moment later they closed.

Misha picked him off her back delicately in her mouth and left him before Drokose, who looked at him with great attention. The gigantic creature breathed out a silver vapor which enveloped Camu. A moment later he inhaled the vapor, making it vanish,

Humans, I must take the little one into my dwelling with me in order to help him.

Can we go with him? Lasgol asked at once.

No, human, this place is only for those of our species.

Lasgol heaved a deep sigh. *What will happen to him? Will he heal?* He asked anxiously, thinking he might lose him.

The little one needs to hibernate. Something is stopping him. I am going to use my power to help him.

Will you save him?

If he manages to hibernate he will live. Now go. I must look after him. There is not much time and I cannot waste it.

Let us leave, Misha insisted, as if she knew it was better not to upset Drokose.

When will I see him again? Lasgol asked.

Drokose, who was already carrying Camu into his cave, replied without looking back.

This first hibernation will be short because it is the first. It is more a rehearsal of his organism than a real hibernation. The next one will be longer. The following ones will take even longer. The colossal creature disappeared inside the cave, which released a cold that nearly froze their souls.

Lasgol wanted Camu to heal more than anything. He was aware that, unfortunately, he could do nothing more for him. Against his heart's wishes, he had to turn around and leave Camu with the great creature.

Chapter 41

Misha led Lasgol and Asrael back to their comrades, who were waiting, impatiently, outside the Serenity Valley. Lasgol could not stop thinking about poor Camu, and he hoped with all his heart that he would be able to hibernate and get well. He told himself that with Drokose's help Camu would. He had to.

"You're back! We were getting worried." Astrid welcomed them with a big smile at seeing them alive.

"Where's Camu?" Egil asked with a look of deep concern.

Lasgol explained everything that had happened inside the valley with as much detail as he could.

"Poor Camu…" Gerd said sadly.

"But he'll be all right if he's with a leader of his species," Ingrid said.

"Yes, he'll take good care of him. Particularly if he's as powerful as you say," Nilsa reasoned. "Besides, in any case he should be with his family, right?"

"He should be with us because we love him and he loves us," Egil said. "We are like his family. Blood isn't the only thing that makes someone family—the heart does too."

"Well said," Lasgol agreed. "We're Camu's family."

"Everything you've told us is amazing," Brenda said. "It must have been a wonderful experience."

"And I've missed it all," Egil sighed disappointedly, shaking his head. "I'm devastated. It would've been fantastic."

"Next time," Lasgol said with a wink.

"So, what do we do now? We still have our mission to accomplish and we're nowhere near doing so," Nilsa said.

"True. We have to stop Hotz and the creature he dug out of the ice," said Ingrid.

The creature's name is Suge Edur, Misha projected to them.

Lasgol stared at her. "Do you know it?"

No, but I know what creature it is. Other Creatures of the Ice are speaking of its return. It has been frozen for thousands of years. It is powerful.

"Do you know how we can stop it?" Astrid asked. "If its power is so great, it's going to be very complicated."

The creature is helping Hotz out of gratitude. The old Arcane of the Glaciers has rescued it from the ice and now the creature is helping him as a debt of honor.

"The Creatures of the Ice, like many animals, are loyal and faithful if they are well looked after and helped," Brenda said.

"What's going on? We're not getting any of this," Viggo protested, realizing they were speaking to Misha.

Lasgol related the conversation.

"I think it's best to slit both their throats," Viggo said, as sharp and sure of himself as usual.

This Viggo still does not understand that a human being will never be able to destroy a powerful Creature of the Ice, Misha projected.

Asrael repeated it out loud so they would all hear.

"Nonsense. You'll see if I don't, both of them."

"It's a complicated task," Asrael warned him.

"I also think it's going to be difficult to finish them," said Egil, raising an eyebrow and looking thoughtful.

We know when they're going to do the ritual," Ingrid said. "That's an advantage."

"And where. It's an advantage that lets us surprise them," Astrid insisted as she gave Lasgol a confident look.

"True," Egil agreed. "But even with the surprise factor, we're at a clear disadvantage. They have numbers and power. We aren't remotely close to equaling them."

"Izotza told me to go back to see her once Camu settled down, that she could help me."

"With this little mess we're in?" Viggo asked.

"Maybe. I'm not sure. Seeing the situation, I don't think we lose anything if I speak to her and see whether she can offer any help."

"I think it's a good idea, any help she might give will be handy," Ingrid said.

"Yeah, I think we should do that," said Egil. "Besides, it gives me some time to plan the surprise."

"Yeah, you get your surprise ready," Gerd said, slapping his shoulder so hard that he stumbled.

"Fine. So it's decided then. We'll go and see Izotza, the Lady of the Glaciers," Lasgol said. "Asrael, if you'd be so kind to guide us…"

"Absolutely, it'll be my pleasure."

The journey back turned out to be complicated, but they managed to arrive without serious incidents. They had an encounter with a patrol of Wild Ones of the Ice who they escaped from at a run, and they also saw a group of Arcanes in the distance which made them take a detour, although not a long one. Unfortunately, they encountered a patrol of Tundra Dwellers and could not avoid combat. They appeared out of the blue from behind a glacier, and the fighting was inevitable. They finished with the patrol, but in doing so, they announced their presence in the area. They had to flee as fast as they could.

When they arrived at the cave of the Lady of the Glaciers, Asrael opened the door using his magic and invited Lasgol to go inside.

"Aren't you coming with me?" Lasgol asked, surprised.

"The Lady of the Glaciers invited you to come back. There's no need for me to go with you, you're welcome."

"Oh... thank you, Asrael."

The old Shaman nodded.

Lasgol went to meet Izotza. He entered her frozen lair and found her sitting on her throne of ice.

"Welcome, Lasgol," she greeted him with a friendly smile.

"Thank you for receiving me, Lady of the Glaciers," he said with a bow.

"I will always receive whoever wants to help my people."

Lasgol nodded. "If I can, of course I will," he assured her respectfully.

"I see you are wearing the gifts I gave to your mother," Izotza said, indicating Lasgol's hand and neck.

"Yes Ma'am, the Ring of the Frozen Languages is very useful to understand the peoples of this continent."

"And to obtain valuable intelligence from them," Izotza insinuated.

Lasgol nodded. "It has helped me, yes."

"And you're also wearing the Experience Marker. Have you been able to witness the experiences your parents marked for you to relive?"

"Not really... I've only been able to relive some and I can't use it as I'd wish. I'm not able to control when or what visions I can see."

"That is strange. You are of their blood so you ought to be able to use the medallion without any trouble."

"It's a complete mystery to me the way the medallion works, and I certainly can't make it obey my wishes."

"The mysteries of life and magic are many. I have spent over a millennium in this world and I have still merely begun to understand many of them."

"The Lady of the Glaciers will live for another millennium and will unravel them," Lasgol said wistfully.

Izotza smiled and shook her head. "The time of the final sleep is near, and I feel it nearer every day."

"Oh… I'm sorry…"

"Do not worry. I accept what I am, what I have lived and the legacy I leave behind me. I chose your mother as a worthy successor to look after my people. She would have done it well."

"She would have done it very well, I know," Lasgol said, convinced.

"Unfortunately, not all plans and dreams come true," Izotza replied with sorrow in her voice.

Lasgol nodded heavily.

"You say you are unable to reach your inner energy, that you have trouble visualizing it and using it."

"That's right. Edwina, the Healer at the Camp, noticed that my pool of inner energy had grown, but for some reason I can't see it or access that additional energy."

"Something is blocking it," Izotza guessed.

"That's what I believe, but I really don't know."

"I can help you with that," the Lady offered.

"I would really appreciate it."

"But I want something in exchange," she said in a dry tone.

Lasgol looked at her, worried. "What does the Lady want of me?" he asked, wondering what it might be.

"I want something which you want too and I will help you get it."

Lasgol was intrigued now. What was this thing they both wanted?

"All right, I'll listen to my Lady Izotza's proposition."

She nodded. "I want my people to stop suffering. For that we need a change in leadership. I want you to finish off the traitors, and I will help you do it."

Lasgol was stunned—he had not been expecting this.

"The traitors? All three?"

"That is correct," she confirmed, and her eyes shone like diamonds in the sunlight.

"That isn't our mission. Our mission is to finish whoever is creating the storms, and that's Hotz."

"Hotz is carrying out Asuris' orders—the one you are really after and the one to eliminate is Asuris."

Lasgol sighed deeply. This was a very interesting proposition, one he longed for as much as or more than Izotza, but there was a problem: it would endanger his comrades.

"The proposition is tempting, but I can't accept it without first speaking to my comrades, since they would be involved and be in danger."

"True. If you go against Asuris, they will be in danger. But, you have a unique opportunity."

"The ritual…" Lasgol said.

"Exactly. It is a moment when the three traitors will be together at the same place. It is a unique moment we must take advantage of."

"It's true that Asuris, Jurn, Sarn, and Hotz will be there, but that creature Suge Edur will be there too, as well as several hundred Wild Ones, Dwellers, and Arcanes."

"Very true," she nodded. "That is why I am offering my help, so that it is not a suicide mission but one with a possibility of success."

"And how remote is that possibility of success?"

"I will not say it is going to be easy, because it is not, but with my help you will have a good chance; albeit only one."

"I'll have to talk to my friends."

Izotza made a face and then smiled.

"I see you are a fair and honorable person. Someone else would have accepted the proposition seeking his own personal gain."

"I can't seek my own gain when I'm risking my friends' lives," Lasgol said, shaking his head.

"You are a worthy son of your mother and because of this and in her memory, I will help you whether you decide to go after the traitors or not."

The change in the deal puzzled Lasgol. Had she been testing him? Probably. After all, this woman, this ice being, was over a thousand years old. She was a powerful, wise woman, and she had lived longer than nearly all the beings of Tremia.

"The Lady of the Glaciers will help me?"

Izotza rose from her ice throne and approached Lasgol.

"I helped your mother. I do not see why I should not help you," she smiled. She raised both her arms, and from the ice floor there emerged two crystal pedestals on which rested two objects that captivated Lasgol. They were two fifteen-point stars that looked made completely of ice with a blue gem in their center.

"What are they?" Lasgol asked, staring at them as if spellbound, since they shone as if the ice were diamond.

"They are Stars of Glacial Energy, one of the things that time and knowledge have helped me create."

"They're not natural, are they?"

"No, they are from my hands. I created them a long time ago with the Power, the Gift and the energy that fortunate beings like you and I possess. Today they will help us understand what is wrong with you and the reason why. I must warn you that its touch is very cold for someone like you. It will burn a little. You will have to bear the freezing contact of the star surface. I think it will be worthwhile."

Lasgol nodded. "Okay, go ahead. I'm ready."

"Very well. Let us begin then," Izotza said and picked the first star. She pressed the blue gem lightly and then placed it on Lasgol's chest, right where he felt his pool of energy. All at once an icy cold spread through his clothes to his flesh. The jewel started shining with a blue pulse.

"It's... very cold..." he muttered as he felt his flesh freezing and burning like when you put ice directly on your skin.

"Bear with it, young Ranger," she said as she activated the other star and placed it on her chest at the same level as that on Lasgol's.

"I'll bear with it..." Lasgol said clenching his jaw; his very soul seemed to be freezing.

Izotza began to cast a spell with her staff and some arcane words thousands of years old came out of her mouth. A moment later the blue gems of the stars joined together with a beam of blue light.

"I am going to examine you," she told him and continued her spell. The beam of blue light seemed to have joined the sources of power: Lasgol's and that of the Lady of the Glaciers.

"I can feel... the freezing energy..."

"Yes, do not resist. My power is freezing, I am simply analyzing you."

Lasgol felt as if an arcane, icy energy ran through his body from his head to his feet. Then it entered his mind and he felt it practically becoming ice.

"How curious… and interesting," Izotza said as if she were amused by what she was finding. "You are special, just like your mother."

"Special…?" Lasgol could barely think with his mind in such a frigid state.

"Your source of power is not finite, as in the majority of humans blessed with the Gift. You are one of those few whose power keeps growing with the passing of time."

"My mother too…?"

"Yes, her source of power was growing. That is why she had so much potential, just as you do, since we do not know how far it can grow along your life. This is something wonderful and you should be proud of it. It's also something you ought to work on and always take good care of."

"Work on…?"

"Yes, so that your Gift expands and becomes more powerful," she explained.

"I don't even feel it… I don't know why…"

"Do you always perceive your source of energy in the same finite and stable way?"

"Yeah… I don't see it grow…"

"Interesting. Let me examine that mind of yours."

"Oh!… Agh!…" Lasgol felt as if Izotza's icy fingers penetrated his mind, causing a burning sensation he found hard to bear. After a while of examining his mind, which for Lasgol felt like he had been thrown naked into a freezing lake, Izotza spoke.

"There is a rupture between your mind and your source of power."

"Edwina… said something… similar…" he managed to mutter. "She said… that if the rupture… were complete I would lose my connection to my magic… and wouldn't be able to use it."

"True, but do not worry, the rupture is only partial. You perceive part of your magic, but not the whole of it. Something in your past, some event, very traumatic for you probably, broke the link between your mind and your source of power."

"My parents's... death?" Lasgol ventured.

"It might well have been that," Izotza replied.

"Can you... help me?" it was almost a plea. The cold was burning his body and mind terribly. "Edwina said that the erudites don't know how to do it... that there's no way to restore the broken link..."

"Humans certainly cannot do it," the Lady of the Glaciers said.

"Oh..." Lasgol's hopes began to deflate.

"Luckily for you, I am not a human. I am a Creature of the Ice and I certainly can repair the broken link with my magic."

"Can you?" Lasgol was about to pass out, he could not bear the cold any longer.

Izotza cast a quick spell at once and a beam of energy as white as the snow issued from the star on her chest to enter Lasgol's through the star on his. Lasgol felt the surge of energy shooting from the star to his mind, and something strange happened. Suddenly he perceived his pool of power in his mind. Only it was frozen. It was not the quiet pool of blue water it had always been. The surface slowly froze, and as it did, he realized that the surface of the lake was really three times as big as it had been till then. Not only that, but the depth had changed too, and as it froze and formed what looked like an enormous iceberg, he realized it was also three times deeper.

"Do you see it now, young Ranger? Do you see the size of your power?"

"I see it..." Lasgol replied, and his mind froze completely. He fell to the floor unconscious.

Izotza looked at him and smiled.

"A worthy son of his parents. They would be proud of him, very proud."

Chapter 42

Lasgol woke up freezing, from his head to his toes. He was still before Izotza's throne of ice. The Lady of the Glaciers was watching him closely with her strange, enormous eyes. He tried to rise and noticed Asrael at his side, who helped him stand.

"Are you all right?" the old Shaman asked him.

"Yeah… somewhat like an icicle, but yeah, I think I'm all right."

"This will help," the Arcane of the Glaciers told him as he cast a spell over Lasgol. A blue flash issued from the Shaman's staff and a blue energy went up from Lasgol's feet to his head and at once the cold vanished from his body.

"Thank you, Asrael."

"You're welcome. For those of us from this continent, fighting the cold and its consequences is like doing archery for you."

Lasgol smiled, already feeling much better.

"I am glad you are feeling well," Izotza said. "Now that you are back to being yourself, check whether you can see and access your inner pool of energy. All of it, not just partially."

Lasgol nodded. He shut his eyes and concentrated. He sought his pool as he always did, in the middle of his chest, and found it. It was a lot bigger and deeper than he remembered.

"It's… a lot bigger…"

"Try to use it by calling up one of your skills," Izotza asked him to make sure.

Lasgol nodded again and called on his *Hawk's Sight* skill, and at once a green flash covered his head. He realized that, compared with other occasions, he had a lot more energy left after calling up the skill, as if he had spent less energy. But he noticed that was not what had really happened—he now had a lot more energy and so using one skill did not seem to consume so much. He looked around and discovered something else; he could see further away and more accurately. The cavern was huge, but he could see with perfect detail even the darkest corner.

"I can use my power. The lake is a lot bigger now and the power of the skill seems to be greater as well… as if both the capacity and the power of my Gift have increased."

"That is excellent news! I was sure the capacity would increase once the link was re-established, but I was not so sure about the power. I am glad it is so," she smiled at him. "In repairing the link, you have not only gained greater energy but the magic you generate is also more powerful now."

"Congratulations! This is something to be proud of," Asrael told him, pleased with the improvement achieved.

"I owe it all to the Lady of the Glaciers."

"It makes me happy to be able to help you. But, I must warn you about one thing. I have re-established the broken link, but I have done this using my magic. It will not last forever. Magic, as you well know, is not everlasting. With the passing of time, it will lose strength until it goes away for good. When this happens, you will lose the link again."

"Oh...." Lasgol was very disappointed.

"It is the limitation of Magic. It is not all powerful. The human spirit, though, comes close. You must continue trying to repair this link. You will be able to see how I have joined your mind and power through my Magic. You must try and replicate this: not with magic, but with your mind. It will be difficult. It is not an easy task, but if you make the effort every day, you will do it, I am sure of it."

"I see. I must replace the magic link for a real one of my own."

"That is exactly it. Try to see it inside you," Izotza told him.

Lasgol closed his eyes and concentrated. At first he was not able to distinguish Izotza's Magic in his mind. He remembered he had developed the skill *Ranger Healing* and thought it might help. He called upon it and at once he was able to see three auras: his mind, his body, and his power. His body's aura did not seem in any way altered. He went on to check his mind's aura and glimpsed something odd. It was green but he could see an entry of icy white. He examined it and saw it was not only an entry but it seemed to arch and go on. He followed what seemed to be a narrow frozen bridge from his mind to his pool of power. He discovered that indeed the bridge went from his mind to the pool of power and linked them. A frozen link, which Izotza had created.

"I see it," he told Izotza.

"How does your mind interpret it?"

"As a frozen bridge, pure white."

"How do you usually see your magic? What color?"

"The flashes are usually green."

"Very well. In that case you must work every day to turn this white bridge into a green one; one that is of your own mind. As you progress, the bridge will gradually change color."

"Understood. I'll do that. The bridge doesn't actually exist, does it?"

"Correct. It is the way your mind interprets the magic link I have created with my power."

"I'll work on making the link my own."

"Good! And now, one last test. Use your mother's pendant, the Experience Marker."

"I will… although it doesn't usually obey my wishes…"

"Try anyway," Izotza encouraged him.

Lasgol took out the medallion and as he always did put a finger to his eye to get some moisture to put on the jewel. He waited to see whether there was the blue flash but it did not come.

"It's not responding."

"Now ask. Ask it to show you the memory of the last time your mother was here with me. Use your power. Really will it."

Lasgol really wanted it to occur so that was not the issue. He concentrated on the medallion, on its jewel, and tried to will it to act through his Gift. He wished to witness the last time his mother had been here, where he was now.. He was not expecting to have any luck, since up till now it had always ignored him.

To his surprise, he was wrong. A blue flash came out of the jewel.

"Wow…" he muttered.

And all of a sudden, on the white floor of ice, the memory Lasgol had asked for began to manifest. He saw his mother as Darthor speaking with Izotza. He saw them speaking about the future of the Frozen Continent, about the peace with Norghana, of a prosperous future for both nations. Dreams they both had—Mayra of seeing Lasgol again, Izotza of seeing her people happy with no more bloodshed. Lasgol watched the scene, spellbound. There followed the plans for the campaign that would take place during the invasion of Norghana. The scene started to fade away until it vanished completely.

"I asked her to mark it," Izotza told him.

Lasgol nodded. He was happy to have been able to witness the scene, for seeing his mother once again. He wondered whether now the medallion would always answer his requests of he would continue having trouble with it.

"The medallion responded to my wish…"

"Your magic is more powerful now. The medallion had no choice but to obey that magic."

"How I regret that everything turned out so wrong…"

"Me too. For you, for your mother, for my people, and for the Norghanian people. They will suffer still, and a lot, if we do not continue protecting them."

"You want me to finish off the traitors."

The Lady of the Glaciers nodded.

Lasgol was thoughtful.

"Asrael has offered to help us. I asked him to bring me the Glacial Star." Izotza said.

"Here it is," Asrael showed it to him. The Object of Power was ancient and shaped like a star. It was larger than the palm of his hand and appeared to be made of ice. A blue light pulsed inside it.

"It is an object of great power. We only know of the existence of five, and they are found in the north of the continent. We have one," she said with a wave at Asrael. "With the Glacial Star and my help, we can defeat the traitors and free my people of this leadership which will only lead to more bloodshed, suffering, and death."

Lasgol took a deep breath.

"I have to speak with the others."

Izotza nodded. "Go and let them know. We will wait for your decision."

Lasgol left the dwelling of the Lady of the Glaciers and rejoined the Panthers, who were waiting expectantly. He explained everything that had gone on and Izotza's proposal in detail. He wanted them to have all the information before they made a decision, since the matter was important and they would be risking their lives.

"The first one to react, of course, was Viggo.

"I say let's kill them all!"

"Wait… don't jump into the void," Ingrid said. "I also want them all to pay, but the stakes are too high. We must think wisely."

"Now we can count on the help of the Lady of the Glaciers, who has great power, right?" Viggo said, looking at Lasgol,

"Yes, she's very powerful and she'll help us."

"Do we know how?" Nilsa asked. "Magic, I guess."

"I believe so. I don't know the details, but I'm guessing she's preparing some kind of spell. She's asked Asrael to bring her a Glacial Star."

"They have a Glacial Star?" Brenda asked excitedly. "That's an Object of Higher Power, it's almost impossible to find one," she told them.

"So, we have the Magic to counter that of the snake-crocodile and the crazy geezer of the glaciers," said Viggo.

"That evens things out, but we're still at a disadvantage. They will have a couple hundred men between Wild Ones, Dwellers, and Arcanes at the ritual," Gerd said.

"We have the advantage of surprise. We know when and where. It's a great advantage," Egil said. He had been turning the matter in his head for a while.

"Do you think it's doable?" Lasgol asked him.

"It could be done... if we plan it carefully... and if we're smart..."

"Which we are," said Astrid. "We have a unique opportunity to do justice for the great betrayal at the throne hall and to end the threat to the realm. We can even prevent future wars, if we make the leadership change in this continent. I say we should try this stunt."

"I'm with you in this, I see it like you," Ingrid said. "The truth is that we face a dangerous situation."

"It is. Nobody said it was easy," Astrid stated.

"And since when have we been afraid of a little risk?" Viggo said as if this were easier than pie.

"I'm a little scared..." Gerd admitted honestly.

"I'm not dancing with joy either," Nilsa said, "least of all because we'll be using magic. But it's a stunt that could determine the fate of this continent and of our realm, because you all know that Asuris and the others won't stop. They'll keep trying to conquer us."

"And that will bring death, suffering, and destruction," Astrid added.

"Then there's nothing left to say. We do away with them all and: situation solved," Viggo concluded.

Lasgol looked at his friends to gauge their reactions. Egil nodded and Nilsa did as well. Viggo had been very clear. Astrid agreed too. Ingrid did so reluctantly. Gerd was going to say no but seeing the rest were all for it, he nodded too.

"I'm not a Panther, but I will join you too in this stunt, because I believe that what we can achieve is something big," Brenda said.

"Then we're decided. We'll do it. I'll go and tell Izotza and Asrael and we'll prepare the ambush."

"Tell her to create a good spell," Viggo told him. "One of those that leave you with your jaw hanging open."

"I will." Lasgol went into the cavern and had the feeling that this mission was one they would remember for the rest of their lives.

Chapter 43

The time came for the stunt. One so risky that even Ingrid had doubts. The Panthers stood in their established positions around the valley where the ritual that would drive the storm to Norghania was about to begin. The Panthers had been preparing the ambush for two days and, as they had expected, the participants in the ritual had already begun to arrive.

First a hundred Wild Ones of the Ice appeared, joined shortly after by the same number of Tundra Dwellers. A little later a couple dozen of Arcanes of the Glaciers arrived. They stood around the white monolith in a circle and started with their ritual chants. As soon as they did, the Panthers started feeling the tension of what was about to come. The ritual had started, they were ready, and once they acted there would be no going back.

The temperature was good for the region. The snow was falling heavily in great snowflakes from a gray sky full of clouds. It impaired vision, which was not good for the archers. The chanting and dancing of the Wild Ones, Dwellers, and Arcanes foretold an ill-fated end for the day, one which the Panthers wanted to prevent at any cost.

Lasgol was watching from an elevated position south of the ritual. He would play an important role in the ambush they had prepared and he was nervous.

With him were Egil and Brenda. Egil had been studying the plan designed during the night and had barely slept. He had come up with a complex plan in four stages which they would have to execute without failure in order to be successful. From what he had told Lasgol, the odds that it would work, considering the great number of complications that might come up, were not good. This calculation had not eased Lasgol's mind at all. Added to it was the fact that they were not sure how well Izotza's help was going to work. But not all was bad news. Asrael had spoken to the members of the Council of the Wise of the Arcanes of the Glaciers, who had gone into hiding like him on account of being opposed to Asuris, and they had granted their support to Asrael. Four of them were there with them to help.

Viggo had commented, irony loaded, that he was delighted to count on the old geezers' support. Although as they could barely stand on their own two feet, he was not expecting them to be of much help. Asrael and Brenda, on the other hand, were glad to have them with them since, although it was true that the five old men were almost ancient and did not look too healthy, it was always good to count on powerful allies.

The guests of honor to the ritual finally appeared, and they all stiffened when they saw them. Hotz entered the ritual circle from the east. The old arcane erudite was followed by Suge Edur, the huge creature half-crocodile and half-snake, larger than a Semi-giant as he walked erect like a human.

Ignoring the others present at the ritual, Hotz bowed respectfully before the monolith in front of which he stopped. Suge Edur stopped beside him. At once Hotz began to conjure under his breath, as if enraged.

Lasgol called upon his usual skills to see and hear better, as well as to increase his agility and reflexes. With each skill he activated he realized that the effects were more pronounced than before, which delighted him. He also activated his mother's ring to understand the conversations in the Frozen Continent's languages.

Hotz was conjuring, waving his arms. In his hands appeared the arcane blue bear claws. He continued casting his spell. Snow was falling on his face but it did not seem to bother him. Suddenly, the great white monolith shone with a mother-of-pearl flash.

It was the moment they had been waiting for.

Egil's plan was getting under way.

The first stage began: eliminating the watchmen.

Egil had guessed that since they had been caught spying the last time, those responsible for the ritual would have sent groups of watchmen to sweep the upper areas of the valley. He was not mistaken. A group made up of a dozen Wild Ones of the Snow were combing the western side of the top of the valley. Three of them carried horns to sound the alarm if necessary. The Wild Ones went by a pile of snow when, suddenly, two figures emerged from underneath the pile and jumped on the first two. Astrid's knives plunged deep into the neck of the Wild One as she climbed onto his back. He tried to grab her, but as she was hanging from his back, he could not manage. He tried to turn round when he realized he could not breathe. He was dying; he coughed blood on the snow, put his hand to his neck, and found the knives buried in it. He collapsed dead with Astrid rolling off his back as he fell on his face. Viggo, with a similar move, slit the throat of his Wild One from ear to ear with his knives before his opponent could even realize Viggo had fallen on him. He tried to defend himself but Viggo was already jumping onto the next one, knowing the other would die in brief moments from his wounds.

The two Wild Ones at the rear reached for their horns to sound the alarm. From another pile of snow Nilsa and Gerd emerged with their bows ready. The Wild Ones put the horns to their mouth but two arrows hit each of them in the heart. Surprised, they looked at the archers instead of ringing their horns. They tried to correct their mistake but by then Nilsa and Gerd had released again. With two accurate shots the Wild Ones fell to the ground dead.

The third one carrying a horn tried to cover from the archers by hiding behind his comrades that were still alive fighting Astrid and Viggo. The two Assassins moved with awesome speed and agility. The enormous Wild Ones tried to hit them with their axes which were able to split a man in two effortlessly. The problem was that the two Assassins moved and attacked with such celerity that by the time the Wild Ones raised their axes to deliver the blow, they already had five wounds in their bodies, three of them deadly and two incapacitating. It was like watching an elephant trying to catch a mosquito with its trunk.

The one with the horn crouched and tried to sound the alarm, hiding behind one of his comrades. An arrow hit the horn, making it fly out of his hands. Ingrid had made the shot from a crossed position. The Wild One grunted in rage and ran to the horn on the ground, but Ingrid got him in the head twice as he bent to grab it and he keeled over, dead.

Nilsa, Gerd, and Ingrid released at the rest of the Wild Ones Astrid and Viggo had been fighting until there were none left standing. They hid the bodies and then hid themselves once again. From the east of the valley, taking a detour from the south, a patrol of Dwellers approached.

Meanwhile, Hotz went on casting his spell and enveloping the monolith in a blue mist. He only left the upper part clear. Suge Edur

337

opened its great snake's mouth and sent a stream of energy at Hotz, who deflected its course and sent it to the sacred monument.

Lasgol was watching and itching to act, to stop the strengthening of the storm in Norghania, or worse, to stop them from sending another to a second important city with the consequent loss of human lives it would entail. Yet, for Egil's plan to work they needed to wait—they could not afford to be hasty. The plan had four stages, and they were only on the first.

As they had already anticipated, Hotz started to deflect the energy to the monolith with one hand and with the other he cast a spell so the energy would rise from the monolith to the sky. A great surge of energy issued from the monument toward the clouds. He was sending power to the storm over Norghania.

The Dwellers arrived at the second spot where the eliminators waited in hiding. Ingrid, Nilsa, and Gerd came out of three piles of snow and released. The Dwellers, caught by surprise, did not have time to react. Three of them died instantly. The other dozen fought back; they threw their javelins at the archers, but the Rangers had already expected this and they threw themselves on the ground and crawled to find another position from which to release. This allowed Astrid and Viggo, who had been hiding behind the last Dwellers, to jump upon them before they even realized the attack. The last two were carrying the horns, but they died with their throats slit without even hearing the Assassins arrive. Then Viggo and Astrid lunged at the other two in front. With lightning speed and accurate slashes, they delivered death to the Dwellers in the blink of an eye. The last one standing tried to put a horn to his mouth to call the alarm but Ingrid put an arrow through his head with a master shot and he fell dead without even noticing.

Astrid, Viggo, Ingrid, Nilsa, and Gerd managed to finish with the whole patrol without them giving any warning of their presence.

Meanwhile, the ritual went on in the center of the valley around the sacred monolith. Hotz stopped the flow of energy and began to conjure again. As Lasgol had feared, it seemed he had recharged the storm over Norghania and was getting ready to create and send a second storm to some other city—the spell was a bit different. Not only that, but from his old coat he took out a map, as if he were deciding which other city in Norghana to send the storm to.

Lasgol wanted to stop him before he could create the new storm, but they could not act yet because the guests of honor to the ritual were still missing. And until they arrived, they could not move on to the next stage in Egil's plan in order to catch them all by surprise, which is what they were after. Acting now would endanger the whole plan, and with it the lives of everyone. Lasgol took comfort in thinking that if everything went as planned, they would defeat Hotz and the storm he had just created too. In such a short time, the new storm, no matter how strong, could not do as much damage as the one over the capital had. It would need days which the Panthers were going to make sure it did not have.

They watched with apprehension as Hotz sent the second storm, hoping it would not be another city but perhaps a military encampment, a big one which would be better suited to withstand the brunt of it. After a while the old erudite stopped conjuring. Both he and Suge Edur seemed to have consumed much, if not all their inner energy in conjuring the two storms.

At last, the three people they were waiting for made their appearance. Lasgol recognized Jurn, the Semi-giant, now leader of the Wild Ones of the Ice. Beside him marched Sarn, leader of the Tundra Dwellers. The third figure was Asuris, leader of the Arcanes of the Glaciers. The traitors were entering the ritual circle. At last.

Lasgol looked at Egil and he nodded. The moment had come to continue with the next stage of the plan:

The Grand Distraction.

At a signal from Asrael, the four Arcanes of the Glaciers who were with him began to cast their spell. They did it together, following the chant Asrael was intoning. They were creating a spell between the five and they were doing so from a hidden elevated position to the north. A cascade of mist fell to the ground and the mist started moving towards the ritual circle. The snow was falling more heavily now, and at contact with the snow, the mist turned whitish and reached no higher than two fingers.

"There goes the mist," Lasgol commented, since he could distinguish it perfectly although to the common eye it was invisible.

"Let's hope they don't notice it," said Egil. "This stage is essential for the plan and one of the riskiest. I feel like holding my breath until it's done."

"With the snow falling this heavily they shouldn't notice it," Lasgol said, letting the huge snowflakes land on his hand. It was wishful thinking though.

"The Magic of the Arcanes is powerful and subtle," Brenda said as with her eyes shut and moving her strange staff, she picked up the essence of the Magic.

"Besides they're keeping up their singing and dancing," Lasgol said, watching the Wild Ones, Dwellers, and Arcanes continuing with the ritual. They were very busy.

The mist reached the northern part of the circle and started weaving in and out of the participants of the ritual, who did not notice, what with the falling snow and how deeply entranced they were in the songs and dance of the ritual.

"They are now directing the mist," Brenda told them.

As if it were a living entity, the mist went on moving throughout the outside of the ritual circle, moving only where there were Wild Ones, Dwellers, and Arcanes. It did not enter the circle itself—Asrael and his Shamans were directing the mist deliberately so as not to be discovered.

In the center of the circle the three traitors were talking with Hotz. Lasgol was listening, thanks to his ring and his *Owl Hearing* skill. To his surprise he could now hear them a lot better than the last time he tried to spy on them.

"Have you created the second storm?" Asuris asked Hotz.

"I have just created it. Right now it is punishing the Norghanian fortress."

"The Fortress of Skol, like I told you, right? Where that swine of Orten and his troops are sheltering?"

"Yes, just as you wished."

"That will make them run away, the cowards, with their tail between their legs," Asuris laughed.

"It is likely that Orten and his forces were no longer there," Jurn said.

"It does not matter, it shows them our power and humiliates them," Asuris said.

"That's true," Sarn agreed, "it will make them react."

"Do you think they will dare to come here?" Jurn asked, doubt in his voice.

"That is what I want," Asuris said. "To make them come. If we press them enough, Thoran the idiot will organize an invasion to destroy us all. But this time we will be waiting, well prepared, and they will all die before they know what hit them. The last thing those Norghanian swine will see is the white of our beloved tundra."

"I like that plan," Jurn said.

Sarn was not as optimistic.

"If you don't need the services of this old erudite, I'll withdraw…" Hotz said, intending to leave.

"You will leave when I tell you to, if you want to stay alive," Asuris threatened him.

"Of course, I follow our leader," Hotz said, bowing deeply.

"Remember that however powerful you are and though you have this pet from the past," Asuris said and then jabbed his finger at Jurn and Sarn, "I have these two, and all those as well," he added with a wave at the crowd participating in the ritual.

"Yes, I will remember that. I am your ally, not your enemy."

"I will be the judge of that. You would not want to end up like the mighty Darthor and those who supported him, would you?"

"No, of course not… I have no ambitions. I owe myself to the secrets of the ice, to their study, and I use what I discover to punish the enemies of my people."

"So, keep doing what I tell you and everything will be all right," Asuris told him, making it clear who the boss was and reminding Hotz of it.

The old erudite bowed his head again, nodding repeatedly.

"Continue sending energy to the two storms. I want those Norghanian swine to know our power!"

"We barely have any energy left…" Hotz started to say.

Asuris' eyes shone with a deadly violet glare.

"Use the last drop of energy you both have!" he ordered.

"We will," said Hotz, turning to Suge Edur. The Arcane and the Creature of the Ice communicated mentally, but Lasgol could not pick it up. Hotz began to cast again, and Suge Edur sent his energy to feed both storms.

The mist already formed a complete circle under the feet of everyone participating in the ritual. Asrael and the other Arcane Shamans changed the spell. The mist began to rise from the celebrants' feet, up their legs, and up to their heads. That was their goal. Asrael gave a command, and the mist turned blue and entered the minds of the celebrants.

All of a sudden, they stopped singing and dancing. They turned to one another and looked around them. They reached for their weapons and without a word began to attack one another as if they were all enemies.

"Wow, it's working!" Lasgol cried, delighted.

"Asrael's and his friends' power is impressive," Egil said.

Brenda agreed, nodding.

The leaders noticed what was going on and started shouting orders.

"Stop! What do you think you're doing?" Sarn and Jurn shouted incredulously.

"It's magic! Arcane Magic!" Asuris realized as he looked in every direction, searching for whoever was responsible for the spell.

Sarn and Jurn kept trying to bring their people back to their senses: "Stop! Don't fight your own! Don't kill one another!"

Hotz stopped the spell at the confusion and watched what was going on. Suge Edur was also looking around.

"Hotz, you must dissipate the spell, quick!" Asuris ordered him.

The old ice erudite understood what was happening. He nodded at Asuris and they both began to conjure. Meanwhile, the Wild Ones were attacking with their axes at their own comrades and anyone else they came across. The Arcanes of the Glaciers were casting spells at themselves and the others. Chaos took over the ritual circle.

"This is looking good," Lasgol said.

Ona growled, lying low beside him.

"They won't last long," Egil predicted. "They'll soon react."

"They're already conjuring," Brenda warned.

Asuris' spell was powerful. He sent a strong icy hurricane that pushed back the mist, freeing a quarter of the circle from Asrael's group's spell. Hotz created another icy wind that managed to disperse the mist round another quarter. They had cleaned the northern half of the circle, and those who were no longer under the effect of the mist were staring at one another in total confusion. There were dead and wounded all around.

"It's time for stage three," Egil said, looking at Lasgol.

"My turn. I'm ready."

Stage three was beginning: The Setting.

Chapter 44

Lasgol grabbed the white satchel where he carried the two objects he needed: one was shaped like a star and the other one was a pearl the size of a man's head.

"Brenda, if you please," Egil asked.

Brenda got on her knees, took out her strange staff with amulets, and started casting a spell over Lasgol. He, in turn, activated all the skills that might help him in that situation, one by one. The green flashes came with more intensity than before; he had more power and he could feel it, both in the skills and in his own mind.

A thick white mist enveloped Lasgol, clinging to his skin, and suddenly it was as though he had been covered with warm snow, although it really was not. Lying on the tundra ground with real snow falling from the sky ceaselessly, he looked like a swirl dragged by the wind.

"I can't use more Magic, or else Asuris and Hotz will recognize it."

"I think it'll be enough," Egil said, looking at Lasgol as he was kneeling. "The snow you've created looks real, and that, together with the winter clothes he's wearing, hides his presence well," he congratulated the Witch.

"Not for nothing am I a Snow Witch," she smiled.

"If they look at you, stay still," Egil advised him.

"The snow won't come off your body for a good while."

"I can't even see your eyes," Egil said excitedly.

"Okay, I'm leaving, wish me luck!"

You won't need it, you'll be great," Egil said confidently.

Lasgol snorted: he was not so sure.

Stay here and wait for my return, he told Ona.

The good panther moaned in protest, but she obeyed.

Lasgol left his position and ran at a crouch toward the Wild Ones at the southern part of the circle, those who were still fighting among themselves in the midst of terrible chaos. He found a passage made of dead Wild Ones and Dwellers on the snow and carefully crossed it, bent double. As Egil had predicted, those still affected by Asrael's and his friends' spell did not notice him, since the spell made them fight anyone near them and armed. But they did not even bother when a strange swirl of snow moved past them too fast.

He saw Hotz and Asuris, who had their backs to him; Sarn and Jurn sideways; and Suge Edur all looking up at the sky. They had not seen him, so he ran to the center, passing by where they were standing. This was the riskiest part of the plan. Astrid had been opposed to Lasgol carrying it out and had volunteered to do it in his place. But there was only one problem—it had to be someone with the Gift. Asrael or Brenda might have tried, but they were too old for an incursion mission like this one and would not have made it.

He kept going. He was already halfway from the center of the circle.

Suddenly, Hotz and Asuris turned south.

Lasgol threw himself on the ground and stayed still like a pile of snow would. Beside him was the white satchel also covered by Brenda's spell.

Hotz and Asuris resumed chanting with all their power to create spells as powerful as possible to free the rest of those affected who were still killing one another, ignoring the deafening shouts of Sarn and Jurn to stop the madness.

The two Shamans were conjuring with their eyes shut, intensely focused. And Lasgol knew that his moment had come. He slithered like a snake, dragging his satchel along until he was dangerously close to Asuris and Hotz.

Jurn and Sarn had managed to make about twenty of their people come back to their senses.

Lasgol took the Glacial Star out of the satchel and put it on the snow. A faint blue light began pulsating inside it, as if it were alive. Quickly he took out the second object: the Ice Pearl. Izotza had created it for this occasion and the Lady of the Glaciers had imbued it with incredible power. It shone with iridescent flashes. Aware that he was running out of time, Lasgol placed the Pearl on top of the Star.

Asuris and Hotz opened their eyes. They had freed the other half of their men, those still alive, and they noticed something odd in front of them.

"What's that?" Asuris asked, pointing at Lasgol, who was kneeling.

"It looks like a pile of snow…"

Suge Edur hissed, long and shrill.

"What's the creature saying?" Asuris asked.

"It says there's power here. Lots of power."

Lasgol was covering the two Objects of Power with his own body, hoping he would not be discovered, but he knew his time was up.

"Sarn, Jurn, check that pile of snow," Asuris ordered.

The moment had arrived.

Stage four was beginning: Activation.

Lasgol concentrated and put his hands on the Glacial Star. He focused his Gift and tried to activate it. Izotza and Asrael had sworn he would be able to but he was not as confident. He focused on sending part of his energy to the Star to activate it as Izotza and Asrael had explained to him. He tried, but the Star did not activate.

Jurn was striding over to where he was, carrying a monstrous two-headed axe of blue ice. Sarn, right behind him, carried a long javelin, the tip made of ice. They could pierce any armor with those and Lasgol was not even wearing chainmail.

He concentrated again and managed to send a large amount of his power to the Star—not only more energy but also more powerful magic, and this time the Object reacted. The Glacial Star began to sparkle with strong blue flashes.

Out of the corner of his eye, Lasgol saw he already had Jurn on top of him, that he was going to discover him. Lasgol sent another charge of energy and power to the Pearl this time, which activated at once.

He had done it. Now he only had to get out of there alive, although it did not look very viable.

He ran off to the south just when Jurn reached his position.

"It's a Norghanian!" Jurn shouted, seeing him.

"Sarn, run him down!" Asuris cried.

The leader of the Tundra Dwellers raised his javelin to throw it a Lasgol through the back.

At that moment they saw the Glacial Star and the Ice Pearl flashing, the former with blue sparks and the latter with mother-of-pearl ones.

"Beware!" Asuris warned them.

"There's a great concentration of power!" Hotz said.

Suge Edur hissed loud in alarm—it could also feel it.

The flashes from both Objects increased in frequency and rhythm.

"It's going to burst!" Asuris warned.

"Take cover!" Hotz said.

The Ice Pearl rose above the Glacial Star to above mid-height.

Lasgol looked back and saw the javelin leave Sarn's hand straight for his back. Making use of his *Cat-like Reflexes* and *Improved Agility* skills, he threw himself forward with Ona's grace when she leapt onto a quarry. The javelin brushed his back but did not even graze it.

"Lie low!" Asuris yelled as he covered himself with an anti-magic protective sphere.

Hotz also raised a protective sphere and warned Suge Edur, whose scales covered its whole body with protective energy.

The Ice Pearl exploded.

There was an enormous wave of colossal power which, starting at the Pearl at the height of half a body, spread throughout the whole valley, freezing everything it found in its way.

Jurn, Sarn, and Lasgol had lunged at the ground, and the wave passed over their heads without touching them.

Asuris, Hotz, and Suge Edur were hit by the powerful wave, and although their protections saved them, they were thrown backward several paces and hit the ground hard.

The Wild Ones of the Ice, Tundra Dwellers, and Arcanes of the Glaciers in the ritual circle who were still alive were caught by surprise and were hit by the wave. Because they were standing, upon contact with it, they were frozen alive, a thick layer of ice covering them from head to toe. Their bodies froze in an instant.

And then came the moment they were all waiting for: the end of the traitors.

Lasgol looked at the Glacial Star, which no longer emitted pulsating flashes, and the Ice Pearl, which had been destroyed. Then he looked around and saw everyone frozen alive. The plan had worked. They only had to finish the mission.

He stood up slowly and looked south. Six people in white were coming toward him at a run. He waited for them while Jurn, Sarn,

Asuris, Hotz, and Suge Edur got to their feet.

Astrid, Ingrid, Nilsa, Gerd, Egil, and Viggo reached him. Astrid threw him his bow, which Lasgol caught in midair. He swiftly nocked an arrow.

"If you surrender you'll be judged in Norghana for the crimes committed," Ingrid said. "If you resist, you'll die here and now. Your choice."

"Bloody vain Norghanians!" Asuris was furious, his violet eyes glaring with hatred. "You'll pay for this intrusion!"

"No Norghanian is going to judge me," Jurn said, and the impressive Semi-giant rose and passed his huge double axe from one hand to the other.

"We're giving you the chance not to die now. You should take it," Ingrid told them.

"Don't make us laugh. You're the ones who aren't getting away today." Sarn reached for two other javelins he carried on his back and held one in each hand.

"Well, I say we kill them and that's that. We've been courteous enough and we've offered them a way out and blahblahblah…" Viggo said, toying with his knives and looking bored.

"Asuris, do you know who I am?" Lasgol asked. He pushed back his hood and removed the scarf from his face so he could see him well.

Asuris looked into his eyes fixedly.

"You are the flimsy son of that Norghanian sorcerer who believed she could fool us and rule over our people."

"I am Lasgol Eklund, son of Mayra and Dakon, and I'm here to do justice."

Asuris laughed out loud.

"Very funny. You're going to die just like your foolish mother, and with you the poor wretches who have followed you. I rule over this continent, and I decide who lives and dies. Soon I will also rule over Norghana."

"Can we kill them already?" Viggo asked, rolling his eyes.

Ingrid looked at Lasgol, awaiting the order.

"Let's finish them up," he confirmed.

In an instant everything happened in a blur. Asuris raised a protective sphere against physical attacks with staggering speed; it was blue-brown and covered his body. Sarn grabbed his javelins and stood to throw them. Jurn stepped forward to deliver a blow with his massive axe.

Ingrid released against Jurn and hit him in the heart, but the Semi-giant's skin was so thick that the arrow did not go in deep enough to really hurt him.

Gerd and Nilsa released against Hotz. Their arrow hit the protective sphere. Small fragments sprung off, but the sphere held and the arrows did not penetrate it.

Lasgol released against Asuris and the arrows hit the protective barrier, barely denting it. Asuris laughed and sent more energy to strengthen the sphere. His violet eyes shone with the gleam of one sure he would defeat his enemy.

Egil released against Sarn right when he was going to throw his javelins. His arrow hit the Dweller in his right cheek. It did not kill him but it made him miss his target, the javelins brushing past Lasgol and Ingrid. Sarn roared in rage and cursed Egil.

"Today I will have justice for my brother Austin," he told Sarn, whose expression changed. He seemed to have finally recognized Egil.

Viggo and Astrid hurled themselves at Suge Edur. In a tremendous leap, Viggo plunged his two knives in the torso of the beast, where a human's heart would be.

"Die, vermin!" he yelled. With horror he found that his knives had not penetrated the great reptile's scales.

Astrid attacked the creature's legs with swift slashes, seeking to maim it. Just like Viggo, her attacks did not penetrate the scales of the giant reptile.

"They're tougher than steel armor!" she cried.

A few paces away, Jurn tried to split Ingrid in two with his enormous axe, but she stepped aside enough to avoid the blow and released at the Semi-giant, catching him again in the heart area but without penetrating enough.

"You won't be able to kill me with your small bow!" Jurn laughed and delivered another blow with all his enormous strength.

"We'll see about that," Ingrid said, stepping away swiftly and avoiding the blow. She released again at the torso of the Semi-Giant, at the heart.

Not far away, Sarn was threatening Egil.

"Today you'll die by my hand like your brother did," he told him in passable Norghanian.

"You plunged a javelin in my brother's back. You have me right in front of you."

"From the back or the front is the same, Norghanian. You'll die with one of these in you," he said and took out another javelin from the quiver on his back.

"Today I'll have justice for my brother," Egil promised him and released again.

Sarn moved to one side and Egil's arrow hit him in the right arm.

"Bastard!" he yelled and threw his javelin at him.

Egil threw himself to one side and, to his surprise, his body reacted with strength and speed. He rolled over his shoulder and stood, ready to release again. The Improved Training was working, and his body was reacting like that of a fit Specialist.

A little to the right, Asuris began to cast a spell on Lasgol, who recognized what was happening and thought of how to avoid being hit by the spell. Camu could have canceled the magic of the Arcane but he was not there with him, and he could not count on Asrael or the other Shamans, since they were going to use their remaining energy on the confusing spell for the remaining ritual members. The Panthers would have to fend for themselves, and against magic they were at a clear disadvantage.

Gerd and Nilsa were releasing against Hotz again as he conjured under his sphere's protection. And they could not get through the protection. They did weaken it though and shards came off it. Hotz looked at Suge Edur and gave him a mental order they could not understand. The creature opened its mouth and sent its energy to Hotz, ignoring Astrid's and Viggo's attacks which could not manage to penetrate the scaly armor of the huge reptile.

The Arcane gathered all the energy with his bear-claw gloves and began to create a black cloud above his head. All the energy Suge Edur sent his way gathered in the cloud, making it grow in size and blackness.

"He's conjuring something terrible!" Gerd cried.

"Release! Don't stop!" Nilsa told Gerd, knowing that the only chance they had was to destroy the Arcane's protective barrier and bring him down.

Lasgol released repeatedly at Asuris' sphere but could not destroy it. He had managed to chip several fragments off at face level, but nothing more. Asuris was smiling as he cast his spell; a violet flash issued from his staff and Lasgol knew he was in serious trouble. The spell hit him in the head—he felt it at once, as if some strange energy had penetrated his mind. And suddenly, without wanting to, he stopped releasing and lowered his bow.

"Prepare to die, Norghanian scum," Asuris said. Lasgol's ring translated the words, and he knew he had to do something.

But against his will he dropped his bow on the ground. What was this? He did not want to do that. He tried to pick it up, but his muscles would not respond. He could not control his body. He saw Asuris grin and mutter something under his breath. Lasgol reached for his Ranger's knife. But it wasn't himself, it was Asuris controlling him. His hand turned toward his own stomach, and Lasgol understood at once what Asuris was trying to do. He was going to make him plunge his knife into his own stomach and be responsible for his own death. He tried with all his might to stop his right arm by using his left and finally managed to.

"Arghhhh!" he grunted as he tried to keep the deadly stroke at bay.

"You won't stop it. You'll die at your own hand. Don't you find it poetic? To come for revenge and end up dying like your mother? I find it extremely rewarding," Asuris said sarcastically.

Lasgol knew he was not going to be able to hold his arm away forever—the spell was too strong for him. Asuris was going to kill him in a horrible way. He looked at his friends, but they were all fighting for their lives. If he was going to survive this situation, it would have to be by himself.

Asuris strengthened the spell so that as soon as Lasgol's left hand failed, and it would, he would die. Besides, the spell was affecting his mind as well. But Lasgol suddenly realized that, although Asuris had control of his body and part of his mind, he still did not control his magic. So he called upon his *Aura Presence* skill while he pulled back with his left hand on his right arm. As he had hoped, Asuris was not aware of his Gift. Lasgol activated the skill and was able to see the auras of his mind, body, and magic. His body and mind were completely overtaken by a violet energy he could clearly see. He concentrated as far as he was able and directed his *Ranger Healing* skill to fight the contaminating energy and saw his green power struggling against the violet one. The tip of the knife was already piercing his flesh.

"You… won't… kill me…" he grunted under his breath.

"Oh, of course I will, you and all those with you. None of you will leave here alive." Asuris laughed, sure of his victory.

Lasgol sent more healing energy into his body while he struggled not to kill himself, falling to his knees from the effort.

"No…"

"Oh I like it that you die on your knees, Norghanian swine," Asuris said.

Lasgol made one last effort and sent even more energy from his pool, and to his surprise, not only was the pool larger, but his power was much stronger—it destroyed the invading spell, his mind and body auras shining again in their natural colors. Having eliminated the contaminating spell, Lasgol pulled the knife away from his stomach and got to his feet.

"I'm not going to die. It's you who'll die here today," he said, pointing his knife at Asuris.

"It can't be! How did you manage to free yourself from my spell?"

Lasgol sheathed his knife and picked up his bow from the ground. Asuris was about to cast a new spell when a shout of warning reached Lasgol.

"Winter storm!" Gerd cried.

With the last ounce of energy left in Suge Edur, Hotz had created a storm above them. The temperature dropped at once.

Asuris and Hotz changed their spells for protective ones and raised their magic spheres.

"Beware!" Ingrid cried as she released at Jurn.

"We're going to freeze!" Astrid cried as she changed her target and hurled herself at Hotz. She reached him and with her knives delivered blow after blow on his sphere.

Icy winds lashed at them and Lasgol felt his body begin to freeze, his arms and legs cramping with the drop in the temperature. Nilsa keeled over from an icy gust. Gerd tried to help her to her feet but their bodies were freezing. Their cloaks frosted all over.

"We're going to freeze alive!" Viggo cried as he kept attacking the Creature of Ice unsuccessfully. His movements were slowing down.

Egil released against Sarn, but his arms were freezing and he missed.

Sarn laughed. "It appears the Norghanians can't cope with a little cold, huh?"

"They will die from the cold of our land," Jurn said, also laughing. The two leaders of the Frozen Continent could cope with the low temperatures and the Panthers could not. They watched as they all fell shivering, slowly dying.

They all lay on the battlefield, covered in frost. Jurn and Sarn stepped back to get away from the effect of the storm, because they could not withstand the spell either.

At last the storm died out. Suge Edur and Hotz had run out of energy.

"Kill them off. I don't want them getting up again," Asuris told Sarn and Jurn.

"They're dead all right, nobody could bear this storm," they said, looking at the bodies lying on the tundra completely covered in frost.

"Only an idiot doesn't make sure his enemies are dead. Do as I say!" Asuris ordered.

Jurn and Sarn exchanged looks and reluctantly went over to check the Panther's bodies.

Lasgol moved a leg, Viggo an arm, Ingrid her head, and Astrid turned over in the snow.

"What's this! It can't be! They have to be dead!" Asuris cried, unable to believe what he was witnessing.

Sarn and Jurn stopped in their tracks and looked at them blankly.

Lasgol got to his feet and picked up his bow.

"You see, Asuris, you're not the only one who has Magic," he explained nonchalantly. "These cloaks have been charmed by an Enchanter friend of ours so we can bear the lowest temperatures. Surprise!" he said, releasing at the leader's sphere.

"No! Kill them!" Asuris cried, beside himself.

Nilsa sprung up and grabbed her bow. Gerd rose like a large bear waking up after hibernating. Astrid and Viggo had already jumped to their feet and were ready to attack.

"Death to the Norghanians!" Sarn yelled and reached back to his quiver for another javelin.

Egil saw it and released at him with his half-frozen arms. He hit Sarn in the forehead in a shot as accurate as it was unlikely. Sarn howled in pain and surprise and Egil released three more arrows that hit his torso.

Nilsa and Gerd were releasing together against Hotz, who was retreating with a look of horror on his face. He no longer had any energy left. He called Suge Edur for help, but the creature had also run out of energy and did not seem at all interested in continuing the fight. It moved away and headed to the great white monolith where it stood with a lost gaze.

Ingrid was releasing against Jurn who, was attacking enraged, delivering tremendous axe blows. Viggo lunged to help her while Astrid ran to help Lasgol.

Egil finally brought Sarn down, wounded by the many arrows buried in his body. Egil stepped up to the leader of the Dwellers and took out a Ranger's Knife.

"I told you you'd die today. This is for the Olafstones," he said and plunged the knife deep into his heart.

Sarn died as Egil had told him he would.

Gerd's and Nilsa's arrows managed at last to destroy Hotz's sphere and he received two final shots to the heart. The old erudite fell to the ground with a grimace of pain on his face. He looked at Suge Edur beside the monolith. The creature seemed lost. The old man exhaled and died.

Jurn's axe hit the ground so hard a large piece of rock and ice flew off against Ingrid's head, who had just dodged the blow. She was hit squarely and was stunned, barely keeping her balance.

"Gotcha!" Jurn yelled euphorically and gave his deadly blow.

The axe came down over Ingrid's head, who was very dizzy and could not move. She was going to be split in half.

Viggo came like lightning and dragged Ingrid away at the last moment, just when the axe hit the spot where she had been. She was saved by a hair's breadth.

"If you mess with my girl, you mess with me, you bloody giant!" Viggo growled, threatening him with his knives.

"Hah! And what's a fly like you going to do against me?" Jurn said vainly.

"This!" Viggo sprinted toward him. Jurn's axe tried to catch him but Viggo was too nimble, even with the after-effects of freezing. He dodged it and with a prodigious leap stepped onto the giant's thigh to leap onto his head.

"What? Get off!" Jurn cried.

Viggo had climbed onto the back of his head, and although Jurn tried to hit him with his axe, he could not because of Viggo's position. Viggo grasped his two knives and plunged them deep in the one eye of the Semi-giant.

Jurn cried out in pain. Vigo plunged his knives repeatedly into the wound and amid screams of pain the Semi-giant fell down with Viggo jumping off him as he fell. Once on the ground Viggo went on attacking until he was dead, and when he was sure Jurn was really dead he went over to Ingrid, who was still half dizzy, and kissed her passionately.

"The Semi-giant's weak spot was the one eye, not his heart," he told her. "Oh, and you're welcome," he said with a smile.

Ingrid wanted to say something, but she could not and so put her hands to her head.

The only remaining threat was Asuris. Lasgol was releasing against him when he saw Astrid come to his aid. Asuris saw her too and swiftly cast a spell against her. Astrid suddenly stopped, frozen in mid-race.

"I can't move!" she cried.

"It's a spell! He's manipulating your mind!" Lasgol warned her.

"And now I'll finish you once and for all!" Asuris told Lasgol, who knew he was lost unless he managed to penetrate the defensive barrier. The sphere was indeed damaged at face level but it still held.

Asuris began to cast another spell on Lasgol, who wished with all his heart to be able to pierce the protective sphere, but in order to do that he would need three successive shots. Something similar to the *Fast Shot* skill he had been trying to develop unsuccessfully for quite a while.

Asuris' spell was almost complete.

Lasgol tried to call upon the *Fast Shot* skill. He had never managed to before but, if he had ever needed it, it was now. But one thing had changed—he now had more power.

There was a green flash, and in the blink of an eye three arrows flew one after the other out of Lasgol's bow. The first one hit the weak spot, making a shard fly off. The second one finally made a hole in the sphere, and the third one flew in through that hole and buried itself in Asuris' forehead as he finished his spell.

Asuris fell over dead, his violet eyes wide open in surprise.

Lasgol realized he had just developed the *Fast Shot* skill he had been seeking for so long. He went over to Asuris' body.

"Justice has been served. For you, Mother."

Chapter 45

After the battle the Panthers tended to their wounds with Brenda's priceless help. The Snow Witch had brought out her saucers and conjured up several concoctions with her staff. According to her, they would help with their wounds and replenish their energy spent in the battle. They were all very grateful as they sat on the ground in the middle of what had been the ritual circle before the monolith, recovering from the hard struggle.

The scene was most unusual. Beside the monolith, a few paces away, the traitors and Hotz lay dead. All around were several hundred Wild Ones of the Ice, Tundra Dwellers, and Arcanes of the Glaciers who were frozen alive from the effects of Izotza's Ice Pearl's explosion.

Lasgol felt weird. He had obtained justice for his mother after wanting it for so long, and yet he did not feel the peace he thought he would deep down in his soul once he had avenged her. He still felt the void and the pain of her loss in his chest. Even so, the circle was closed. His mother and those who had supported her and had died at the betrayal could now rest in peace. Those who had betrayed them had not reached their final goal and lay dead before him, by his hand or that of his comrades. He could turn the page in that particular chapter of his life and consider it closed.

Lasgol snorted.

"Are you all right?" Astrid asked him, noticing that he was looking at the dead with a lost gaze.

Lasgol looked at her and smiled, nodding.

"I'm okay."

She kissed him. "I'm glad."

"The nightmare's over," he said.

"Let's build dreams and forget nightmares." She kissed him again.

"Yeah, let's do that," he replied.

A few paces away Viggo was sharpening his knives.

"I'd say it's been a most entertaining mission and quite simple," he said, making light of everything they had gone through.

"Oh yes, very simple," Nilsa said, making a face.

"It's been horrendous…" Gerd said, looking with horror at their enemies frozen in life.

"What matters is that we did it and we're all still well," Ingrid said, going to each one of them, checking that they were all right.

"Egil's plan—once again he made it. What a sublime strategy," Lasgol said gratefully to his friend as he petted Ona, who was sitting on the cold ground.

"The merit is all yours. The plan alone is no good at all. You're the ones who carried it out, and very well," Egil said.

"I was spectacular, as usual," Viggo said, wiping imaginary dust off his shoulders.

"You've been as vain and unbearable as always," Ingrid said, "Although you haven't done so badly," the blonde admitted. Viggo was left in the middle of a retort with his mouth wide open, since he had not been expecting a compliment. Ingrid went over to him and kissed him passionately.

"Wow… I… certainly wasn't… expecting… this," he muttered when Ingrid finished.

"Don't get used to it," she replied with a smile.

"See? Told you we were together," Viggo said to the rest of the group as they watched the scene, smiling broadly.

"Keep dreaming," Ingrid said. "You still have a lot of work ahead of you before we're together.

Viggo beamed from ear to ear.

"But we will be," he said confidently, looking roguish.

They saw a group of Shamans and Arcanes of the Glaciers approach and they stiffened.

"It's us," Asrael greeted them, waving his staff to ease them.

The Panthers relaxed, recognizing their ally.

The group reached them at a slow pace.

"You've managed something unthinkable," Asrael said, looking at the dead bodies of Asuris, Jurn, Sarn, and Hotz. "You'll always have our gratitude," he added, pointing at himself and at the other Shamans of the Council.

"Will you be able to rule the Peoples of the Frozen Continent now that the traitors are no longer alive?" Egil asked.

Asrael looked at his companions.

"We will create the Council of Shamans again and will speak to the new leaders of each of the Peoples. I hope we'll be able to reach an understanding."

"And if they don't understand, we'll make sure they do," Viggo said, brandishing his knives.

"That's not the best way... I hope the new leaders will be wiser than those who have lost their lives. They should be! We'll guide them and decide the future of our Peoples. Seeing how these leaders have met their ends, I hope and pray the next will have more common sense."

"They will," one of the Shamans said. "We must watch who rises to power now and make sure they're the right ones for our people."

"If there's need to 'deal' with any who doesn't conform to expectations, you just let us know, Asrael. I'll deal with them personally," Viggo said, passing his thumb along his throat.

"Your offer is appreciated and will be taken into consideration. But we hope it won't be necessary," Asrael replied with a chuckle.

"Let's hope so," Ingrid said; she had not liked Viggo's offering in the least.

They saw Misha arriving. The enormous creature joined the group with powerful strides. Asrael had called her so she might help with the strange Creature of the Ice. Suge Edur was still standing beside the monolith and did not seem intent on moving. It looked lost, confused.

I am taking the Creature with me. There is much to talk about, Misha projected.

"Thank you for looking after it, it needs help," Asrael said gratefully.

It is a Creature of the Ice, archaic, but of our own. I am a Matriarch. It is my duty to look after all creatures like it.

"Even so, thank you," Lasgol said.

There is no need to be thankful, I do it with pleasure.

"Where are you taking it?" Asrael asked.

I think I will take it to my cavern; there I will instruct it. Once it is ready, I will take it to the Serenity Valley. It needs to rest and recover.

Asrael nodded, "Good idea."

"I hope everything turns out well," Lasgol said.

It should. It is not an evil creature, just simply lost. It has awakened in a world it does not recognize with beings it does not understand.

"With your help and some time, it'll understand the new world it has woken up into," Asrael said.

That is my wish.

"If you see Camu when you go to the Serenity Valley… tell him we love him and are waiting for him…" Lasgol said.

I will, rest assured. Camu is fine, he only needs to rest. He will soon be with you, when he recovers.

"We'll be waiting with open arms," Lasgol said.

Misha bowed and raised her head.

I will leave now and take Suge Edur. You have my friendship, forever.

"Thank you very much, Misha. You have ours," Lasgol said.

Misha and Suge Edur left in the direction of the northern glaciers. They all watched the two majestic Creatures of the Ice go.

"What will happen to them?" Lasgol asked with a wave at the hundreds of frozen figures that surrounded them.

Asrael exchanged a few words with the Shamans.

"The spell should lose strength and fade with time. They'll return to the world of the living when that happens."

"How long do you think they'll remain frozen?" Egil asked, interest shining in his eyes.

Asrael shrugged.

"Maybe a week, maybe a century. In any case, it'll be a warning to all who believed in the wrong leaders."

"I like that they stay there like ice statues as a warning," Viggo smiled.

"It's a little heartless but effective I guess," said Gerd.

"So, what now?" Nilsa asked.

"Time to go back to Norghana. We've finished the mission," Ingrid said.

"D'you think Captain Tomason'll still be waiting?" Gerd asked.

"Hopefully. If not, we'll have to send a message so they come to pick us up," Ingrid said.

"I can get you a vessel if necessary," said Asrael.

Ingrid nodded gratefully.

"I don't want to leave…" Lasgol admitted. "I feel as if I were abandoning Camu."

"He'll be all right, he's with his kind," Astrid said, putting a hand on his shoulder.

"I agree with you too," Egil said. "But, we don't know how much longer it will take Camu to hibernate and we can't stay here waiting. The most sensible thing to do is to get back to Norghana and wait there for news of his recovery. I'm sure our friends will let us know as soon as they know something," Egil said, looking at Asrael and the other Shamans.

"Absolutely," Asrael promised. "As soon as the creature comes out of hibernation and leaves the Serenity Valley, I'll let you know."

Lasgol was very reluctant to leave Camu there, but he could not stay there indefinitely waiting for his hibernation to end. Besides, he must let Camu decide what he wanted to do once he was recovered. He had now found his home in the Frozen Continent and some relatives. He might prefer to stay with Drokose instead of coming back to him. Lasgol heaved a deep sigh. He would not make Camu come back if he was not willing.

"Okay..." he said. "Let's get back to Norghana and inform King Thoran that we've eliminated the threat."

"The Council of Shamans will always be grateful to you," Asrael said, on behalf of himself and of the other Shamans." You'll always be welcome in this land."

The Panthers bowed, honored. "Thank you," said Lasgol.

"I'll come with you to the coast to make sure you leave without any trouble," Asrael offered.

"They all thanked him."

The Panthers took their leave of the Shamans and headed to the coast. It took them several days to reach the beach where the Captain had left them and where the ship should wait to carry them back. As they had already guessed from the time passed, the Captain had returned to Norghana, considering them dead.

"How nice, our Captain," Viggo protested. "When we meet again, I'm going to tell him a couple of things..."

"He did as he had been ordered to, so no couple of things..." Ingrid warned him, wagging her finger at him.

"Yeah, but he's left us in the lurch," Nilsa complained.

"Don't worry, I'll take care of this," Asrael said.

The Shaman got them a small boat, which they could man themselves, with supplies to go back to Norghana. It was a small, rustic but robust boat, the kind used by the Wild Ones to cross to the Frozen Territories on the north of Norghana.

The Panthers embarked and said goodbye to Asrael. They set course for Norghana with Ingrid acting as captain and the rest at the oars. They found no dangerous storms and, without forcing the navigation, reached Norghanian land in little over a week.

Chapter 46

It took them another week to reach the capital once they landed, and to their great joy they found it free of storms. The city was slowly recovering and there were only a few parts that were still frozen in the big rocky metropolis. Those that had still not thawed were all in the north of the city and access to them was forbidden. But otherwise, the citizens were back in their homes and had resumed their lives. Thoran and the Court had also returned, as well as the army, which was now sheltered in the big city.

At their arrival they were informed that the second storm, the one that had attacked the Fortress of Skol, had also vanished and that the damage done had not been much or cost much to repair.

During the next two weeks, the Panthers spent hour after hour giving detailed explanations to King Thoran and Gondabar. Once everything had been told and they were duly congratulated by both leaders, they were allowed to return to the Shelter and continue their special training.

They were quite taken aback to be congratulated by the King himself, as well as being proud themselves, of the good work they had done. Thoran was particularly happy with the fact that not only had they eliminated the creator of the storms, but all the leaders of the Frozen Continent as well. This was good news for him—three enemy leaders dead and without having gone to war was something to celebrate. Of course, the Panthers kept to themselves what had happened to them. There were things the King did not need to know, from their friendship with Asrael and Misha to the Serenity Valley.

Gondabar congratulated them effusively before they left. He told them he was proud of what they had achieved and greatly appreciated their good work for the Norghanian people. He even became emotional, which the Panthers really enjoyed.

Viggo was about to ask for an increase in pay and longer vacations, but Ingrid put her hand on his mouth before he opened it.

They left for the Shelter once everything was cleared and they received permission to go.

They rode fast, and in a few days made the journey from the

Capital. It was midnight by the time the group arrived at the Lair. They were returning to their new home to continue their training. Some, like Egil, were thrilled, while others like Viggo were less enthusiastic. He spent most of the way protesting.

Above the White Pearl, on top of the Lair, they saw something strange—some intermittent silver flashes. Since it was quite dark, they could not see more. They thought it was probably Sigrid or Enduald doing some experiment or rehearsal, because they did not sense any danger.

They stopped and watched from a distance though.

"We'd better go over and see what it is," Ingrid said.

"Nothing like arriving home and already having to look into weird stuff..." Viggo said ironically.

"Surely it'll be nothing," said Gerd,

"Yeah, but just in case..." said Lasgol.

Astrid nodded.

They reached the White Pearl and were met with a tremendous surprise.

A creature appeared on top of the Pearl.

It was Camu!

"Camu! You're here!" Lasgol cried, overjoyed. He could not believe his eyes.

"The bug? What's he doing here?" Viggo asked, surprised.

"How is it possible?" Ingrid said.

"This is a fantastic appearance!" Egil said with a big smile.

"But is it really him? he looks odd," Nilsa said.

Be me, Camu transmitted to Lasgol and Ona.

The panther moaned happily.

It was indeed Camu, but he was different, changed. He had grown in size, but it was not only that, his scales had changed. They were also bigger and brighter. They looked new, as if he had just gotten them.

I happy, Camu transmitted and he started doing his happy dance, flexing all four legs and wagging his tail.

"It's the bug all right," Viggo said.

"You look wonderful!" said Astrid

"You're bigger and stronger!" Gerd had been staring at him with wide eyes.

"It must be the hibernation, it's transformed him," said Egil, studying him with avid eyes and smiling broadly, happy to see him back. "It's fantastic!"

"How did you get here?" Lasgol asked him, still astonished.

By pearl.

I don't understand, what do you mean by pearl? Lasgol asked him, puzzled.

Pearl be portal for dragons.

You mean to say this pearl is a portal of some kind?

Yes, portal.

Portal in the sense that it takes you from one place to another?

Yes, portal. Travel.

You've traveled from the Serenity Valley to here?

Yes, I travel.

Are you sure? Lasgol could not fathom what Camu was telling him.

Yes, I come by portal.

But… how?

Using power pearl.

You can interact with the power of the pearl?

I can. Drokose show.

But isn't it a portal for dragons?

I more than dragon.

Lasgol sighed heavily.

I have my doubts about that.

Drokose say.

You can't believe everything you're told.

Drokose family.

Yeah, but even with family you can't believe everything they tell you.

I know.

"He says he got here by using the power of the Pearl. That it's a portal for dragons."

"Oh, that's great, more magic!" Nilsa protested.

"This is fascinating!" Egil said, thrilled. "Then… he's used the great pearl you told me you saw in the Serenity Valley?" Egil said to Lasgol.

"I think so," Lasgol nodded.

"Amazing!" Egil was very excited. "You have to tell me everything," he told Camu.

I tell, Camu replied.

"Wow… the surprises keep coming…" Ingrid said, looking at the

Pearl with her hands on her hips.

"We've always known it had Power," Lasgol said. "What we didn't know was what that Magic was for."

"So, mystery solved," said Astrid. "It's a portal to another Pearl. I wonder whether there are more in Tremia."

"Most likely. If there's one in Norghana and another in the Frozen Continent it's very likely there are others in other regions," Egil reasoned. "What we don't know is where. Finding them and mapping their locations could be a great adventure!"

"Leave great adventures alone, we've barely finished this one," Viggo said.

"You look fantastic, Camu," Astrid said, looking at him fascinated and lovingly.

"Yeah, the bug has grown," Viggo nodded, "These new scales look good on you, they make you more attractive," he said, smiling at him.

I more handsome.

"Don't encourage him… it'll go to his head," Lasgol told Viggo.

"It's going to be difficult to hide him now," Nilsa said. "He's the size of a Norghanian War Horse!"

"Yeah, or a Rogdonian war Thoroughbred," said Ingrid, "and he shines. Why does your whole body shine?"

Hibernate. Bigger. Change skin.

"He says that in hibernating he's grown and he's changed his skin, his scales."

"That's something truly fantastic. He's changed his skin as he's grown, like reptiles," Egil said, fascinated. "You must tell me everything in detail. I want to know everything you went through during the hibernation."

I bigger, stronger, more powerful.

Lasgol told them what Camu had transmitted.

"I don't know… I have the impression that the bug has put on weight from sleeping so much and has polished his scales, that's all," Viggo said, teasing him.

I show, Camu transmitted, offended by Viggo's comment.

Lasgol felt Camu activating his Magic and suddenly a silver aura surrounded Camu's body. It was a very powerful aura and it glimmered. Lasgol wondered whether his friends could see it.

"Do you see Camu's aura?" he asked.

"Do we see it? That luminous thing around him can be seen from a league away?" Viggo said.

"It's fully visible, yes," Ingrid confirmed.

"And of a very bright silver hue," Astrid added.

"Is he using magic?" Nilsa frowned.

"He is. It's fantastic and fascinating," Egil said excitedly and smiling.

Lasgol was wondering what type of Power Camu was invoking. Would it have to do with his skill to camouflage and vanish? With his skill to cancel magic in others? Was he going to camouflage them all at once? What was he going to do?

Not even in his wildest dreams had Lasgol imagined what happened next.

On Camu's sides there appeared two enormous wings.

They all stared open-mouthed. They were not physical wings, but created by Camu's Magic, and they shone intense silver.

By the Ice Gods! The bug has wings!" Viggo cried incredulously.

"Wings… they're wings…" Gerd muttered, unable to believe it.

"Magic wings. Those aren't real," Nilsa said, shaking her head.

"They're huge…" Ingrid whispered.

"They're beautiful," Astrid stated.

"Amazing, fabulous!" Egil said, clapping his hands with glee.

Lasgol's mouth was hanging open as he tried to take in what he was witnessing. Camu had a new power that allowed him to spring wings.

"They must be decorative, I doubt the bug can fly," Viggo said with a wave of his hand, not believing that Camu could use his new wings.

Camu spread his great wings in all their magnificent span and shook them hard. They looked like real wings, dragon wings. With a little hop Camu beat his wings hard, and began to rise vertically above the Pearl. He rose about fifteen feet and hovered there in the air, flapping his wings.

I fly.

Ona chirped excitedly and leapt, imitating her brother.

The Panthers could not believe their eyes.

Camu could fly!

I more than dragon.

Lasgol knew that a new stage was beginning for Camu and for the

Panthers. A new stage full of adventures.

"This is going to be fantastic!" Egil cried.

The end Book 11

The adventure continues:

While you wait for the next installment of the Path of the Ranger, I invite you to explore my other series that have different protagonists, but are related:

THE SECRET OF THE GOLDEN GODS

This series takes place three thousand years before the Path of the Ranger Series

Different protagonists, same world, one destiny.

Click the image or link.

The Ilenian Enigma

This series takes place several years after the Path of the Ranger
Series. It has different protagonists. Lasgol joins the adventure in the
second book of the series. He is a secondary character in this one,
but he plays an important role, and he is alone…

Click the image or link.

Acknowledgements

I'm lucky enough to have very good friends and a wonderful family, and it's thanks to them that this book is now a reality. I can't express the incredible help they have given me during this epic journey.

I wish to thank my great friend Guiller C. for all his support, tireless encouragement and invaluable advice. This saga, not just this book, would never have come to exist without him.

Mon, master-strategist and exceptional plot-twister. Apart from acting as editor and always having a whip ready for deadlines to be met. A million thanks.

To Luis R. for helping me with the re-writes and for all the hours we spent talking about the books and how to make them more enjoyable for the readers.

Roser M., for all the readings, comments, criticisms, for what she has taught me and all her help in a thousand and one ways. And in addition, for being delightful.

The Bro, who as he always does, has supported me and helped me in his very own way.

Guiller B, for all your great advice, ideas, help and, above all, support.

My parents, who are the best in the world and have helped and supported me unbelievably in this, as in all my projects.

Olaya Martínez, for being an exceptional editor, a tireless worker, a great professional and above all for her encouragement and hope. And for everything she has taught me along the way.

Sarima, for being an artist with exquisite taste, and for drawing like an angel.

Special thanks to my wonderful collaborators: Christy Cox, Mallory Brandon Bingham and Peter Gauld for caring so much about my books and for always going above and beyond. Thank you so very much.

And finally: thank you very much, reader, for supporting this author. I hope you've enjoyed it; if so I'd appreciate it if you could write a comment and recommend it to your family and friends.

Thank you very much, and with warmest regards.

Pedro

Author

Pedro Urvi

I would love to hear from you.

You can find me at:

Mail: pedrourvi@hotmail.com

Twitter: https://twitter.com/PedroUrvi

Facebook: https://www.facebook.com/PedroUrviAuthor/

My Website: http://pedrourvi.com

Join my mailing list to receive the latest news about my books:

http://pedrourvi.com/mailing-list/

Thank you for reading my books!

Note from the author:

I really hope you enjoyed my book. If you did, I would appreciate it if you could write a quick review. It helps me tremendously as it is one of the main factors readers consider when buying a book. As an Indie author I really need of your support.

Just go to Amazon and enter a review.

Thank you so very much.

Pedro.

See you in:

PEDRO URVI

DRAGON
SPIRIT

PATH OF THE RANGER   BOOK 12

Made in United States
Troutdale, OR
02/26/2024